WRETCHED LOVE

THE SONS OF TEMPLAR MC - NEW MEXICO

ANNE MALCOM

Cover: TRC Designs
Editing: Kim BookJunkie
Proofreading: All Encompassing Books

For my husband. Always.

CHAPTER ONE

I WAS PUTTING on mascara when he came in.

I met my husband's blue eyes in the mirror. Those eyes ran over me with hunger. Appreciation.

My skin tingled.

I wasn't wearing anything particularly revealing. A tailored dress, white with little flowers all over it. It showed off my figure, trim because my husband liked me that way. I was religious about my diet, about my morning Pilates class. The same with my Botox appointments, expensive facials and a standing appointment with my hair stylist to add honey highlights and keep my naturally midnight black hair a softer chocolatey color so I never had roots.

We had an image to maintain after all.

Preston swept my hair aside and kissed my neck. "You look good enough to eat, babe."

My stomach clenched as his hands went down to my hips, his

front pressing into my back, his intention clear. My heartbeat thrummed as my body responded to his, attuned after all these years.

"I'm already late," I sighed.

Preston's hand at my hip tightened, and he whirled me around.

His fist plowed into my stomach in one smooth move.

I doubled over, wheezing as my breath was sucked out of me.

"Manage your time better," he said coldly. "And don't ever refuse me again."

His shoes echoed on our heated bathroom tiles.

I stared at the pattern, frowning at a speck I must've missed when I was cleaning the floors earlier this morning.

Once the pain subsided, I straightened, stared at myself in the mirror for a second, then resumed putting on my mascara.

———

"I fantasize about cheating on my husband with the neighbor when I'm masturbating," Luanne said.

The women laughed, and I merely smiled tightly.

"I don't come to the thought of cheating," she continued with a sly grin. "It's the thought of the pillow talk after, being able to complain about my idiot husband that sends me over the edge."

More shrieks of laughter.

I sipped my iced tea.

Luanne drained her rosé. It was her second, and she lifted her hand to the waiter in a way that was patronizing and dismissive, signaling another.

Her eyes zeroed in on me. Luanne didn't like me. Of course, she never came right out and said it. No one in this little group of wives were *honest* about how they felt—beyond their fantasies about the neighbor. It was just pointed comments, backhanded compliments, whispers behind each other's backs.

She didn't like me. For many reasons. Mostly because I was younger than her, and she was threatened by that. And also because she wanted my husband. She didn't try to hide it. Not even a little. She was always stroking his arm when we had parties, standing a little too close, laughing at his jokes, rubbing her fake tits on his arms.

If only she knew what being married to Preston was like, she wouldn't be so eager to rub up against him.

"What about you, Kate?" she asked, narrowing her eyes. "We've all shared. Who do you fantasize about when you use your battery-operated friend? Even though your husband is a man made of fantasy."

I smiled tightly at her. "He defies fantasy," I said smoothly.

They all waited with bated breath. All the ladies who lunched. The group of women Preston had urged me to befriend once Violet went to school and I had 'nothing' to do with my time.

Despite the fact that I cleaned our entire house daily because he could see any speck of dirt. That I made everything in our home from scratch because he didn't want processed food. That I took his shirts and suits to the drycleaners, also daily because he wanted everything 'fresh.' That I spent hours on dinner because he expected me to serve him gourmet meals.

Then there were our gardens that he needed to be impeccable. He didn't hire anyone. Except to do the grass and the pool, but they came on an exact day at an exact time. Otherwise, he didn't want strangers in our home. Didn't want them snooping. Seeing things they shouldn't.

We'd bought a much larger house when Violet started high school and Preston took over for his father as president of the bank. Our mansion was only minutes away from his parents which meant his mother could and often did stop by. Her home was always immaculate, and Preston would not hear of me embarrassing us both by having the house 'out of order.'

So it was a full-time job to keep everything how he wanted. To avoid punishment, even though he often found something wrong, something out of place.

These women, with husbands and grown children, had full-time help. They wouldn't dream of scrubbing a toilet. They had endless time to day drink and talk about their trainers, their current diet, how their husbands didn't satisfy them. Whatever it was that they considered 'problems.'

I did not have that time.

But these were the women to be seen with in our small town. These were the circles to run in. To keep up appearances.

"Come on, Kate," Karen urged. "Your secret's safe with us."

I pursed my lips. My secrets were most definitely not safe with them. The first time I had lunch, I'd had a particularly bad day, so I'd had two glasses of wine with lunch. One was normally my limit, and even that was rare. Preston didn't want a 'drunk' for a wife. It was unseemly.

But I'd been excited. Rarely had I been given leave to go out and have lunch with other women. Preston was on a business trip too. All the way across the country. I felt freedom I'd not experienced... ever.

And I'd gotten tipsy.

The women were complaining about their husbands and had looked at me expectantly.

Even in my wine daze, I'd known not to say something scathing about Preston. Certainly not the ugly truth. But I'd wanted to belong to this club. The women who laughed like they didn't have a care in the world. Who were buffed, tanned and plucked within an inch of their lives, with big hair and even bigger bank accounts.

Yes, it felt carefree and foreign.

Belonging to something, even if it wasn't who I wanted to be.

So I'd blurted out something about Preston leaving his socks right beside the hamper instead of putting them in.

It was nothing compared to what the other women said. Nothing.

Yet somehow, it had gotten back to him. He'd flown into a rage as soon as he got home, dragging me into our bedroom by the hair. Violet was at a friend's place for dinner. It happened rather last minute, and it was later I'd realize it was by design. So Preston could punish me properly. For embarrassing him, making his friends think he was a "fucking slob."

So yes, I knew not to say a word about Preston or our life together at these lunches. And I never touched a drop of wine, no matter how much the women urged.

They thought I was boring.

Which was fine.

Safe.

"If she doesn't want to share, she doesn't have to," Nicole put in, defending me.

Nicole was a relatively new addition to the group. Only a few years older than me with a boy a little younger than Violet.

I liked Nicole. She was... nice. She didn't have hair 'out to there,' her forehead moved when she made expressions and her life didn't seem shiny and perfect.

She seemed beautifully flawed and didn't fit into this group one bit.

But her husband had taken over the development for some big set of apartment buildings coming into town, and he went to the club with our husbands. He was important. So she joined the lunches. Those were the rules.

Luanne sighed dramatically. "You don't have to be such a prude, Kate," she said. "We're all friends here."

"I know, Luanne," I said with a false smile on my face. "I just have nothing to tell."

Which was the truth.

I did not own a vibrator. If I did, Preston would find it and punish me thoroughly. My body was his. And if he decided I deserved pleasure, he would give it out.

He knew all the ways he could hurt me and not leave a mark. He also knew all the ways to make me come loud enough to scream.

It was my curse.

He was.

I was owned by him.

Therefore I was not entitled to any agency over my own body.

I wouldn't tell these vultures that.

Luanne was still staring at me in challenge. She was on her third wine. They could make her nasty, more direct.

I could see it in her eyes. She wanted to push me. Taunt me a little. She saw me as meek, weak. And deep down, beneath all the makeup and filler, she was a bully. I was an expert at recognizing one now. After all, I'd been married to one for almost eighteen years.

All the years we'd been 'friends,' she'd made an art of bringing me down, making me feel small.

The other women saw it, of course, but they ignored it. Luanne was the unofficial leader of this group. Her husband was the mayor. He owned half the town. She was the queen of this town. She could ruin someone, even me, if she so wished. So I did my duty, kissed the ring, made sure to never stand up for myself.

I wouldn't know how to do that anyway.

Nicole also saw Luanne readying herself to lay into me. Nicole didn't know the rules. Nicole was a nice person.

So she stepped in.

"Kate," she said, bringing my attention to her. "Isn't Violet studying abroad now?"

I blinked at her change in subject, the pointed look she gave Luanne before focusing on me.

"Yes, she is," I said. "Um, Paris. She's always loved the city. And her French is wonderful. She left two days ago."

I missed her like a limb. More than a limb. There was an ocean between me and my baby. I'd never been this far away from her in my life. It hurt merely thinking of it. Of how empty the house was without her.

She was all I had.

Preston and I had tried for another for years. Or so he thought. It was the one single thing I hid from him. The thing he very well might kill me for if he ever found my secret stash of birth control pills. It was the one risk I took. The one act of rebellion I took against him.

I would not bring another child into our home. I got lucky with Violet. She was sweet. Caring. Not a mean bone in her body. I couldn't risk it with another. I was terrified if I had a boy, what his father might turn him into.

In this one singular way, the universe looked after me. He had never found the pills.

"You're an empty nester now," Karen grinned. "Welcome to the club."

Most of the women I lunched with had children in college or

beyond and were older than me by ten years. I'd had Violet young, and Luanne never failed to bring that up.

"Well, she doesn't have to be," the woman in question said. "You're what..." she trailed off, eyes inspecting me as if I were a strange specimen, not someone she had lunch with twice a week for the past six years. "Thirty-eight now? That's not too late."

"Thirty-six," I corrected, which she well knew. I also looked a lot younger than that, thanks to a religious skincare routine and the only good thing my mother gave me: her genes.

Luanne acted as if I never spoke. "Preston tells Tom all the time how he's planning on another one with you. He wants a boy this time." Her face softened into faux pity. "I know you two have had some trouble conceiving, but I told Tom to give him the name of the best IVF doctor in the state. Preston was going to surprise you with the appointment." She smiled like an alligator, presenting personal information at a table of ravenous women in a feeding frenzy. "He knows how much you want another, and I expect all he wants to do is to make you happy."

My smile was frozen on my face.

There it was. My one victory over Preston. The one thing I could hold on to. The last shred of control I had, gone.

There was no way I could get out of the appointment. I wasn't sure what kind of tests the doctor would do, if they would be able to tell I was on hormonal birth control. Even if they couldn't, they'd likely be able to tell Preston there was nothing wrong with me. No explanation as to why we weren't getting pregnant. He'd argue, of course. He was good at that. He'd order them to go ahead with IVF, make sure I got pregnant.

And that was best case.

Worst case was he somehow found out about the birth control. Violet was not home anymore. She wasn't due to come home for another six months. He wouldn't hold back.

My hands went clammy.

Nicole's covered mine. "Sweetie?" she asked in real concern.

I blinked the table back into focus. The women were all staring at me.

"Oh, dear. I really did ruin the surprise," Luanne said with a smile. "I hope you're happy about this? I could tell Tom to talk to Preston, give you some time."

"No!" I yelled, just the thought of what would come of that conversation sending bile up my throat.

Even Luanne looked shocked at my outburst. I did not yell. I spoke in soft tones, barely audible, really.

I scrambled for my purse. "I just, um, I forgot about... dry cleaning," I spluttered, standing from the table. I was the meek little mouse who only squeaked, never roared.

I spilled my iced tea once I got my purse, my throat closing up. "I'm sorry," I apologized, mopping it with my napkin.

My skin was hot. Too tight. I needed to escape. "I'm... um. I've got to go." I smiled tightly at the women who were watching me carefully. "I forgot about a waxing appointment." The lie didn't come out smoothly or convincing, but it didn't matter at that point.

"We'll do lunch next week, you can tell us all about the doctor appointment," Luanne said, stretching her lips wide. Her husband would be hearing about this 'outburst' the second he got home.

I nodded tightly. "Of course."

Then I turned on my heel and calmly walked out of there, got into my car and didn't stop driving.

⊏⊐

I was in Manchester.

Three hours away from the small, wealthy town of Carver Springs, New Hampshire, where I'd lived all my life. I'd never, not once, been this far away without Preston. We traveled, sure. Trips for the summer. Italy. Spain. France. Always with a group, either his parents or his business buddies.

But I never went anywhere alone. He kept my passport locked in his safe.

It was in Manchester that I realized what I was doing. That it had been three hours since lunch. Preston would be home in another hour. Maybe two if he was having drinks at the club as he did more and more often these days.

Not enough time to make it home without him knowing. And there was no lie I could conjure that would explain where I had been. Did he have some kind of tracker on my phone? It made sense if he did. He needed to know where I was at all times and likely checked against what I'd told him to see if he could catch me in a lie. He never did because I never lied. I behaved exactly as he expected me to. I was trained well. I never broke the rules.

Until now.

My heart was pounding as this set in.

I was screwed.

I could still go back. Try to lie and take the punishment if he didn't believe me. He wouldn't leave marks. We had that doctor's appointment. And he was serious about another baby. He wouldn't risk genuinely hurting me.

Eighteen years. Another *eighteen years* with him.

My blood thrummed with fear and dread as I even considered it.

I couldn't do it.

Wouldn't do it.

Although I'd never dreamed I would or could do this, I was running.

And I had nothing with me but the clothes on my back.

The credit card in my purse would alert Preston when and where I made a transaction. I was lucky the car was fully gassed.

The car.

The hideously ostentatious and expensive car. We traded up every two years. I was not the legal owner of the god-awful thing. And when he found out I was gone, he'd be able to track it. Track me.

I pulled into a parking lot as true panic set in. My breathing turned rapid, and stars danced in my vision.

"Get it together, Kate," I whispered, gripping the staring wheel.

The glint on my finger caught my eye. My wedding ring and band. Both hideously ostentatious too. Preston had upgraded three times in our eighteen-year marriage, each time at huge anniversary parties his parents threw for us yearly. Like the car, the house, the lunches, it was all for show.

This ring was worth a lot of fucking money.

Preston made sure I didn't have the tools to escape. Made sure I didn't have access to large sums of cash, couldn't book anything out of the country, had all of my important identification. But his ego had given me my ticket out of his life.

Same with the earrings at my ears. The watch I wore. The purse.

All of it was bought as gifts. Not for me. For himself, so the town would see how much he spoiled his beautiful wife.

I grinned as I drove out of the parking lot thinking of what the town would say when it became clear that his spoiled, beautiful wife had left him.

Three hours later, I was driving out of the city in an old Toyota. It was bright red, smelled faintly of cigarette smoke and had only cost me a couple of thousand dollars.

I had much more cash tucked into my cheap Walmart backpack. A lot more. I hadn't sold everything. Not at once. It would be dangerous, a woman on the road alone, carrying large amounts of cash.

No more dangerous than living in my McMansion in New Hampshire for nearly two decades, but I'd had my share of violence. I would be cautious but not afraid.

I was done being afraid.

It was just like that. A switch flipped. I wasn't sure how such a thing was possible. Weakness was a character trait at this point. I'd been so sure I didn't have a backbone, a personality of my own.

But whatever it was inside me that snapped, I grew from the cracks of that. Me.

There was a scene in *Gone Girl*—I'd watched the movie countless times and read the book twice as many—where Rosamund Pike was driving down the road in a piece of shit car, stuffing her face with food after framing her husband for her murder. She looked so utterly free in that scene. I'd watched it over and over with envy.

Not that Ben Affleck's character quite deserved to be framed for her murder—he was a cheater and kind of a selfish asshole, but he did not deserve that.

Preston, on the other hand, thoroughly deserved to be framed for my murder. Unfortunately, I was not as smart as Amy was in the book. I did not have the guts or the intelligence to fake my own murder and frame my husband, no matter how much I fantasized about it.

It was that car scene I fantasized about. Not my trainer or my neighbor or the hot guy at the coffee shop who always flirted with me. No, it was her in that scene, free for the first time in years, knowing that no one knew where she was, and no one knew *who* she was.

Unfortunately, I could not *Gone Girl* my husband, even if I'd had the smarts and the guts. Because of my daughter. The child I adored. The child who worshipped her father and knew nothing of what kind of monster he was.

I would and did endure years of torture for my perfect daughter. I would do anything to protect her from harm. And knowing the truth about her father would hurt her. Wound her. Call in to question the entire foundation of who she was. Would affect her future and every relationship she had with a man.

No, I could not and would not do that.

I couldn't just disappear, as much as I wanted to.

And I knew, if I did, Preston would find a way to play it to make him the hero. He'd report me missing. Fake something ridiculously elaborate. Whether it be my state of mind, some unseen enemy, I couldn't be sure. But I knew if I let him control the narrative, I'd be screwed. Eventually back under his thumb. And that couldn't happen. So I made a series of phone calls. To ensure that he couldn't orchestrate a narrative. That he couldn't warp it. Surely he'd try, I knew that. But I was fighting now. He wasn't used to that. It would unnerve him, to see his wife's backbone. I had the element of surprise and the upper hand.

So I made the calls.

Then, after copying down all the pertinent numbers, I smashed my phone and bought a cheap new one. Maybe it was overkill, but I wouldn't put it past Preston to be tracking my location.

After that was done, I pulled into the nearest drive thru, got myself a triple cheeseburger and got on the freeway.

I was gone, girl.

CHAPTER TWO

SWISS

THE NIGHTMARE CAME to me last night.

I hadn't had one in almost three years.

A record.

I'd been lulled into a false sense of security. I'd let myself believe that they no longer lived inside of me. That I'd banished all of those memories, scrubbed them clean with the actions of the past ... fuck, almost twenty years.

When I jerked awake, I was drenched in sweat, my heart jumping out of my fucking throat and my hand on my piece in an instant.

"Baby?" a voice croaked from beside me.

A red tipped nail trailed down my soaking chest.

Fuck, I'd untied her and forgotten to kick her the fuck out last night.

Had I been that wasted? That kind of oversight was not the norm for me. If bitches stayed over, they did it bound to the bed.

And that was usually because I was too drunk or tired to kick them out. Or because I liked the way they obeyed me and wanted to get one last fuck in the next morning before I never saw them again.

"Baby."

This time it was a purr, and it grated over my skin like sandpaper.

I didn't even look at her. She'd probably be a knockout. All women were... in their own way. I didn't give a shit about body type, race, religion, hair color. No, I did not discriminate when it came to women. I could spot them a mile away, the ones I wanted. Not that I'd spotted one I'd really wanted in a long fucking time.

"Get the fuck out," I snarled, still holding on to my piece with an iron grip. The bitch didn't hesitate, even seconds after waking with what was likely a killer hangover, her survival instincts kicked in.

Club girls were usually some of the hardest I'd met, but that didn't mean they didn't know when to run.

And everything about my energy was telling her to run. Not to mention my reputation that spoke for itself. Bitches wanted to fuck me because of that reputation. And the patch, of course. But they wanted to be the one to tame the beast. They wanted to prove that they could handle me.

No one could. Not really.

I glanced over at her ass, jiggling as she struggled to get into the jeans she wore last night.

"I tell you to fuck around and get dressed?" I snarled. "Out!" My arm, the one holding the gun, pointed to the door which led to the hallway.

The bitch jumped and scuttled out the door, scrap of fabric pressed against her bare tits.

Someone would probably be up in the club common room and see her exit. It wouldn't be the craziest thing they'd seen here.

Not by a long shot.

Fuck, we had a club party last night, so there were probably naked bitches covering the floor like rugs.

I didn't lie back down, didn't try to find sleep again. Not after that nightmare. I wouldn't sleep for the next two days at least. This was a cycle I knew well, one my body was prepared for. Already my blood was pumping, hot and urgent, a call for something.

Death.

I jumped out of bed and yanked on my clothes from the floor before shrugging on the cut.

Good thing I was patched into the Sons of Templar MC... Death was part of the fabric.

THREE WEEKS LATER

I was bored with the night before it even began.

Not a good sign.

There was a time when I lived for this shit. When I first patched into the Sons of Templar MC, when I was running from my demons, when I was a broken piece of shit, I couldn't believe the energy at the club parties. The energy was always wired but relaxed, a fight or two breaking out was expected. Nothing more than a couple of black eyes, maybe some cracked ribs or a minor stab wound. The violence solved beefs, and bloodstained handshakes often followed a brawl.

As much as I reveled in the blood and violence, it was the women that excited me. I felt like a fucking rock star.

I got off on that.

The power. The fact that bitches were worshipping at my fucking altar because of the patch I wore. That bitches were willing to get depraved, that they weren't scared. They knew that sleeping with a Son meant there were no fucking safewords. That they were fucking the Reaper. They knew that with me right off the bat.

And they fucking loved it.

I fucking loved it.

Or I had.

I wasn't sure when it had changed. When I stopped getting that same satisfaction out of it I used to. My blood didn't sing anymore, seeing them submit to me. My cock still worked, of fucking course, but my heart wasn't in it.

Then again, my heart had nothing to fucking do with it.

That fucker was black as night and cold as ice.

Things were quiet on the club front too, so I couldn't even find excitement in my other favorite pastime. We had no enemies to torture, to kill. Things were as peaceful as they were ever going to be with the Sons of Templar MC.

Which was good, I supposed, considering I had brothers who were wifed up with kids. They didn't want club shit blowing back on them, endangering them. The club, this charter in particular, had lost enough. Lost almost everything. A war would feed my beast, sure, but at what cost?

And I didn't want that either, as much as I craved to peel someone's skin from their bones.

Maybe I'd go on a trip somewhere. Do some outsourcing. Or go nomad again. This was the longest I'd been at a charter since I'd patched in. I'd heard that the Washington charter was having some issues with some Nazi fuckers trying to take over territory.

Yes, that might satisfy the hunger within me. Quiet the rattle in my bones.

"Picked tonight's victim yet?" Hansen, my president asked as he sidled up beside me, beer in his hand.

It was rare to see him at one of our Friday night gatherings. This late anyway. He showed his face early because he was the president, but once things got wild—which was always about an hour or two in to the night—he went home.

Fucker had a wife and kids now. He was all about monogamy, which in my opinion, went against everything our lifestyle stood for. But he was happy. So whatever the fuck. And when my eyes followed his, landing on his wife who was downing a beer of her own and laughing at something Freya was saying, I understood it.

Macy used to be a club girl. In another lifetime. Before someone took out almost the entire club, save Hansen and a couple of other brothers. She'd been with the club years. Everyone loved her.

It was impossible not to.

I felt a pang, watching him watch her. Something totally unfamiliar and something that pissed me right off.

I forced my eyes to scan over the women in the room. Most of them were familiar faces. We had a stable of club girls who hung around, fucking whoever wore a patch, hoping someone would put them on the back of their bike.

Macy and Hansen were their Cinderella story or some shit. They were holding out hope that might happen to them.

But it wouldn't.

None of those women were Macy. Or Scarlett, the one other 'club girl' who was now an Old Lady in the California charter.

It was a rare thing that anyone would want to make a club girl theirs.

That's not to say we didn't respect the women. We did. But most of us weren't looking for anything more than a warm body and a good fuck. We didn't put a patch on our backs because we wanted to live within the confines of society's rules.

I paused my gaze on... Sienna? Fiona? Crystal?

The knockout redhead was wearing a dress that showed off her perky tits, her pebbled nipples and barely covered her pussy.

I'd fucked her before. Had come to find out she was a natural redhead. And had a fucking great pain tolerance. The more I'd hurt her, the wetter she'd become. I'd been able to take her further than I'd taken a bitch in a long while.

I'd liked that part. I did not like the hungry look in her jade green eyes when we were done, though. The way she'd clung to me. The way she was looking at me right now. Like I was her next fucking meal.

I was the predator here.

"Nah," I replied to Hansen's question, looking my president in the eye before the redhead got any ideas. "Sure we don't have any weapons runs?"

He shook his head.

"Enemies who need to be eliminated?" I tried with false hope.

Another headshake, this time with a wry grin, the fucker. "All is quiet on the Western Front, brother," he replied, clapping me on the shoulder.

I sighed, downing my drink.

"Now if you'll excuse me, I'm going to go and make the most of my wife being shitfaced and our kids being with a babysitter," he said with a grin.

I watched him work his way through the crowd, not even glancing at the practically naked women he passed. It was pathetic, really, how fucking in love with his woman he was. It somehow wasn't a weakness, though. He'd rallied once the club had almost been wiped off the map, rebuilt it from the ground up and sought revenge on those responsible. Sure, he loved his wife and kids, but he was a ruthless motherfucker just like the rest of us.

Though I understood I was a little more fucked-up than the average outlaw. I got off on causing women pain. Of course, they got off on it too. I would never hurt a woman without her permission. That distinction was very important to me.

I also got off on causing people pain who deserved it. Who betrayed us. Loved watching them bleed. Writhe in agony. Fucking reveled in the light leaving their eyes.

So torture and killing was my number one hobby. Well, maybe tied with fucking.

And it had been a while since I made someone bleed. Since I ended someone. Almost a month ago, after the nightmare. Some fucker who was trying to snitch on us. I'd killed him too quickly, the high had long worn off. I was feeling itchy.

Almost desperate enough to go back to the redhead I knew would try to attach herself to me like a barnacle.

Almost.

Then my eye caught on something else.

Someone else.

The second I saw her, I fucking startled.

Like I was pissing on an electric fence.

The effect was that fucking violent. And I was not a fucker known to get dramatic about that shit. I was also a fucker who could be considered immune to women's beauty.

I'd seen everything and anything the fairer sex had to offer. Sampled it all. Fuck, did I appreciate beauty in all shapes and sizes, but it wasn't something that drove me. I would not be led around by my dick.

But *her*...

I knew she didn't belong in here the second I laid eyes on her. There was an unease. A fear about her that turned me rock solid.

A voice somewhere deep inside told me that she was it.

She was mine.

KATE

I had no idea how I ended up in a biker compound.

Okay, I kind of did.

I had taken my *Gone Girl* thing a smidge too far.

It had gotten off to a bit of a rocky start. Freedom, as it happened, was complicated. Very freaking complicated. I had not made a decision for myself in years. Almost two *decades*.

Preston chose my clothes, my hairstyle. His mother was the one who helped me when it was time to redecorate. Preston approved weekly menus at the house. He chose where we vacationed. He made detailed lists for the grocery store down to the brand of milk he liked.

I didn't make any choices for myself.

So that first day, when I started to get tired and it came time for me to stop at a motel, I had a panic attack. Which one did I choose? What exit did I get off at? Did I go for a mainstream chain or a bed and breakfast situation?

I'd pulled up to a Hilton on instinct.

Whenever we traveled, it was the best hotels. The luxury of it all had impressed and delighted me at first, but I was immune to it. Disgusted by it, almost. If we were traveling, Preston would turn his nose up at a Hilton, but given the options in the middle of nowhere, it would be his only acceptable choice.

It hit me that I was deferring to him even now. I was making a decision based on what *he* would want.

That realization, and the realization that I couldn't do something as simple as chose a hotel for the night, had me crying for five minutes in the parking lot.

Then I got my shit together.

A bed and breakfast, I decided, would be nice. But people who owned bed and breakfasts liked to talk. To get to know their guests. Ask what they were doing, where they were going.

No, I did not need any of those kinds of questions.

I needed somewhere that would take cash, that was clean and reasonably safe. I found it in a mid-range, roadside motel off the interstate. The clerk was a bored teenager scrolling through her phone. She'd barely glanced at me.

I'd been so wrapped up in my world, thinking I was the center of everything, that I forgot that people existed outside of my little universe. That there were people living their own lives who didn't give a shit about me. Who didn't notice me. Who would forget me in a moment.

It was liberating.

I'd lain in bed the entire next day, watching movies that I'd never got to watch, eating food that Preston never would've let into the house, and feeling relaxed in a way I never had before.

The sheets were scratchy. The walls were thin. The shower water was either scalding hot or ice cold. But it was paradise to me.

I stayed for two nights, reveling in my newfound freedom, not thinking of the future, of a plan. I worried that if I did, it might ruin everything. I'd made a promise to myself on the first night there, giving myself a deadline. Three months. I could have three months of exploring the country, eating what I wanted, sleeping when and where I wanted, without pressure. Without acknowl-edging the realities that lay ahead.

After that three months was done, that's when I'd make the scary decisions. That's when I'd research divorce lawyers, figure out what exactly I'd tell my daughter when she got home, and make a plan for my future.

But if I lived smart, I had more than enough money for three months in mid-range hotels, eating food from chain restaurants. I might even find somewhere I wanted to settle. Somewhere small, somewhere far away from Carver Springs. Somewhere without McMansions and manicured lawns and yoga studios. Somewhere with a soul. But I had no destination, no itinerary, nothing.

Which was how I found myself in Garnett, New Mexico. Even though it was spelled with an extra 'T', I couldn't help but feel like it being named after my birthstone meant something.

I loved it the second I set foot in it. The sweltering heat, thick and unyielding. The vast desert, mountains in the distance. The town itself was small, houses varying in size, but almost all of them were well maintained, had personality to them. The main street was littered with homey mom-and-pop stores. Of course, there were still big-box stores—there was nowhere you could escape a Walmart or a Target—but it felt like it had a personality I was looking for. Appealing to the eye without being pretentious. Small but not so small that I'd stick out as a stranger in town.

Safe.

I was only beginning to understand what that word meant, what that feeling was. Although I'd felt freer than I had in years, there was an edge to there too. An undercurrent of panic, unease, inevitability. That there was a time limit on this, that eventually he'd find me, drag me back, and I'd once again be trapped in that life.

It was that edge that had me turning up to a biker compound for a party.

It was pure chance that even had me knowing about it. I'd been at the gas station picking up some snacks and a six pack of beer—I'd acquired quite a taste for it—when a man in a leather vest had approached me.

He was quite possibly the most attractive man I'd seen in my life. He was younger than me, maybe. It was hard to tell. There was a... *man-ness* about him that seemed utterly timeless. A dark, heavy brow, a slightly crooked nose and riveting gray eyes. His beard was chocolate brown, just like the shoulder length hair on his head, and it only accentuated his ruggedness.

Then there were the muscles.

Holy hell.

They damn near ripped apart the fabric of the black tee he was wearing underneath the leather vest. His chest was broad, pecs defined underneath the fabric. The skin that was exposed was covered in tattoos. Absolutely covered. Right to his fingers.

He was imposing. With his muscles, his stature, the beard and the vest, I knew that signified him belonging to some kind of motorcycle gang. Given my history, I should've turned around and ran when such a man approached me in a quiet gas station.

But if there was anything I'd learned, it was the look of cruelty in a man's eyes. The absence of something.

This man's eyes were warm, melty. They made my stomach flip in a way that I hadn't thought was possible, reminded me that I was a woman. One with independent desires and needs.

"Hey, darlin', haven't seen you around before," he drawled, his voice deep and throaty.

I had to blink and glance behind me to ensure it was me who this muscled bad boy was addressing.

There was no one behind me.

He grinned and sauntered closer. Not close enough to be threatening or make me uncomfortable, but to show he was addressing me. That he was interested in me.

"I'd remember if I'd seen you before," he continued, eyes running up and down my body slowly.

Again, this somehow managed to not be leery or sleazy. As

absurd as it sounded, he was checking me out... *respectfully?* In a way that seemed like a compliment.

I had not gotten dressed this morning with any kind of male gaze in mind. Getting dressed had started out to be quite a challenge at first, especially since I'd thrown out the outfit I'd left in.

The outfit I'd *escaped* in.

I'd started with cheap sweats from Walmart. Shapeless. I had wanted to hide, wanted to be swallowed by cheap polyester, wanted to look as different from myself as I possibly could. I wanted to melt into the background so people didn't look at me twice.

It took me two weeks to discard those thoughts and the sweats. To remember that I had loved clothes. That I liked showing off my body in the days that came before Preston.

God, it felt like I imagined those days when I thought on it. I could barely remember a life when I wasn't under Preston's thumb. Mostly because when I wasn't under his thumb, I was under my mother's. And I couldn't inspect my childhood too closely. Not now, while I was hanging on by a thread.

But what I did remember was flipping through Cosmos, creeping into my mom's closet when she wasn't home. I hadn't had the means or time to explore my style in my teens. I'd had to wear whatever I could afford with my part-time job, then when I started dating Preston, he'd mentioned that he liked me in dresses. Quickly, I started dressing like his mother, going shopping with her, adopting their taste.

The mere thought that I hadn't really had the opportunity to truly dress myself my entire life was utterly horrifying. At first, a hot wave of shame had overcome me, and I found it hard to breathe, to stand up.

But then I'd taken a breath. Cleared my mind—those yoga classes had worked for something at least—and told myself that I couldn't change the past. But I had a modest amount of money and the opportunity to start to explore who I was. What kind of style I liked.

By the time I found myself in Garnett, New Mexico, I had gained ten pounds—I was still unlearning a lot of behaviors from my former life and the beauty standards thrust upon me, but I was pretty sure I could do with gaining at least ten more.

My body's natural curves were coming back, my hips becoming fuller, my thighs more shapely. My breasts were still full and high because Preston had arranged for me to get them 'fixed' after I stopped breastfeeding Violet. He'd been disgusted at the way they'd sagged and emptied. He'd also been disgusted at the stretch marks which served as evidence I'd brought our daughter into the world, but thankfully, there was no type of surgery for that. Unfortunately, I didn't get many, and he wasn't disgusted enough to stop touching me.

I suited the extra pounds, I discovered. My face was fuller, cheeks rosier. I didn't look so gaunt and hopeless.

I also found I liked dressing for this figure. Tight jeans, strappy tanks, Converse. Cowboy boots. Nothing with a heel too high. I'd worn enough pairs of grossly overpriced footwear for three lifetimes.

But I liked feeling sexy. Slutty and trashy, Preston likely would've called it.

I'd dyed my hair midnight black, its natural color without all of the highlights. I didn't have the confidence or inclination to get it cut or styled. I wanted to grow it long, well past the middle of my back.

At the gas station, I was wearing ripped jeans. I felt a little too old for them, since my daughter wore a pair extremely similar, but I'd loved the way they'd fit my body like a glove, and they were comfortable as hell. I'd slipped on some flat sandals and a tank top sans bra in order to go and grab my beers.

My hair was in curls touching my shoulders, and I had on makeup because I couldn't unlearn almost a whole lifetime of behavior. I'd never left the house without makeup in the time before. Not to go to Pilates, not even when I'd forgotten milk for a cake I was baking. I'd had an appearance to uphold.

But me wearing it now wasn't about that. I liked wearing it. Liked feeling pretty in my own way. And the look I was wearing was completely different than the expensive, subtle and feminine makeup I'd perfected over the years.

I'd discovered I loved a 'smoky eye' with dark liner smudged around my eyes. It made me look younger, a little edgier than I really was.

Which, along with my lack of bra—and the air conditioning inside the gas station—was likely why the biker approached me.

It had occurred to me I still hadn't said a word to him, and for the life of me, I had no idea what to say.

He didn't seem bothered by my stunned silence, his grin only widened, showing straight, white teeth.

"We're having a party," he said, nodding outward.

My eyes followed the jerk of his head. There were three other men sitting on Harleys by the gas pumps. All were wearing the same leather vests, all were muscled, menacing and devastatingly handsome.

My gaze stuttered on the one in the middle. His arms were exposed, muscles rippling in the sunlight, his ebony skin flawless and glistening in the sun. I stared at the column of his neck, the way he held himself on the bike. He had a bald head, only serving to make his masculine features all the more striking, even from this distance.

"Our clubhouse is about two miles away," the man continued.

I jerked my head back, the back of my neck suddenly hot.

"Follow the main road out of town, you can't miss it," he explained.

I blinked rapidly, digesting all of this.

"Pretty lady like you shouldn't be drinkin' alone," he said, nodding to my beers.

I narrowed my eyes. "How do you know I'm drinking alone?" I asked, finally finding my voice and a bite to my tone I didn't know I was capable of.

His grin didn't falter a bit at my tone. "Lucky guess," he replied, voice deep and teasing. "I can promise you a good time and a night you'll never forget."

My stomach dipped at his words, at the pure sex in them.

"Hope to see you there," he winked, then he turned on his motorcycle boot and walked out.

I stood there staring as he mounted his bike and all of them turned on with a roar that vibrated in my bones.

My eyes found the man in the middle once more, then the patch on the back.

The Sons of Templar MC.

A motorcycle gang.

Yeah, that was the last thing I needed to get wrapped up in.

I'd done the sensible thing, paid for my beer, got in my car and drove back to the quiet, cheap and clean pay-by-the-week motel I'd found.

But once I'd let myself in my room, opened a beer and sat on the bed, that was when the loneliness set in.

The quiet.

I hadn't noticed it until that very moment. Before then, I'd been moving. Busy. Discovering things about myself. Which side of the bed I liked to sleep on—the middle. What TV shows I liked —I tended toward anything magical or anything with a woman getting revenge. What kind of food I enjoyed—the junk food was short lived, and I longed for a kitchen to cook my own food once more.

Shoot, I had only just figured out the way I liked to do my makeup. I was relearning everything about being an adult woman. It was a full-time job. Beyond that, I'd been in fight-or-flight mode at every new motel I landed in. Looking over my shoulder, half expecting Preston to find me and drag me back by my hair.

But something had changed here, in this town.

I wasn't an overly spiritual person—because Preston's family were good Christians who went to church every Sunday and shunned away anything alternative to that—but I felt like something had pulled me here. I felt as if I was meant to be here. Something in my soul relaxed here.

But with that relaxation came the quiet. Came the realization that I had no one. Absolutely no one.

No friends.

No family.

No one to help me.

And that reality was an unbearable roar in the quiet room.

So I'd downed my beer, thankful for the way it lightened things ever so slightly. And with that buzz came the wild hair that had me pulling on a pair of heeled wedges, spritzing some perfume, swiping on some light pink lipstick, and getting in my car in search of the Sons of Templar MC 'clubhouse.'

CHAPTER THREE

KATE

I NEARLY TURNED the car around once I found the outlaw clubhouse.

It was on a rather desolate industrial road on the outskirts of town. All of the businesses were long closed, the only lights on coming from outdoor security or overhead signs.

The club was like a blazing oasis in the desert, the entire thing fenced in. With serious fricking fences, barbed wire on the top and everything. The gates were closed, and there was a little camera and speaker, almost like what you'd see at a drive-thru except a lot more... high tech. These guys had money, and they apparently needed more security than a U.S. Embassy.

Yeah, I definitely should've turned my car around.

But I did not. I stayed inside it, staring from the gates to the camera, wondering if there was some kind of codeword I missed when I was drooling at the biker in the gas station.

I jumped as the gates opened, and a man in a black vest sauntered toward me. My headlights illuminated him, and he looked much younger than the ones I'd seen earlier. Twenties, maybe.

But he was covered in tattoos like the man at the gas station, from his neck to his fingertips—which grasped the door of my car because I was stupid enough to have my window all the way down. He could reach in here, take out my keys, and I'd be trapped in the middle of nowhere with men I was pretty sure were criminals. That thought solidified when I saw the gun tucked into a holster underneath his vest.

My heart thundered as I stared at the young man who could not be much older than my daughter. His eyes were strikingly blue, his features rather boyish compared to all the tattoos, biker attire, and weapon strapped to his swimmer's body.

Those eyes flickered over me. "You here for the party?" he asked.

Here it was. I could say I was lost, and I thought this was my Airbnb. Or say something a little more convincing. The main thing was, this was my escape hatch.

"Yes," I said instead of constructing some lie.

What in the heck was I doing?

The boy stared at me a beat longer, and I thought maybe he'd save me from myself and declare I was much too old and not at all edgy enough to be let into this party. I could go back to my small motel room and learn to accept the quiet loneliness.

Instead of this, he winked at me.

Winked.

Sexually.

I didn't even know someone could wink sexually, let alone someone that young, and armed. But apparently, it was a thing.

"Have fun," he drawled after the wink, stepping back from the car.

I idled for a little while longer before I slipped the car in gear and drove forward, parking in one of the open spots closer to the mechanic side of the place rather than the clubhouse with bikes lined in front of it.

The last thing I needed was to accidently back into one of them. I didn't know much about bikers, but I figured they considered damaging their ride a personal affront.

I hadn't even thought about the logistics of what I was doing.

I'd had three beers at the motel. I had a slight buzz on. All of Violet's teenage life, I'd drilled into her how terrible drunk driving was. How it could ruin and end lives.

Yet here I was, being a hypocrite. Although I wasn't exactly drunk; I was still in control of all of my faculties. I just had a strong enough buzz to think this decision was a good idea.

But to keep thinking this was a good idea, I'd likely have to have more drinks once inside the clubhouse. Many more.

Then I wouldn't be able to drive back to the motel. And I certainly wasn't staying here.

"You can still leave, Kate," I told myself.

That wasn't entirely correct. I was under no obligation. But a quick glance in the rearview mirror told me the gates were already closed. Instead of making me feel trapped and terrified, the closed gates filled me with... relief.

They were shutting out the world and everything I was running from. Surely a party at a biker compound was unpredictable at best and dangerous at worst, but it was no more dangerous than waking up in a mansion beside my husband for almost two decades.

Even if Preston was out looking for me, he could never find me here. Even if he had found his way to Garnett at that very moment, even if he'd found the little hotel room I was staying in—the one with the flimsy deadbolt lock and a bored teenager working checkout who would likely give him my information—he would never find me here. He wouldn't be let in here.

That thought alone had me turning off the car and opening the door.

And no one knew me here. Not a soul. There were no expectations of me. I was not required to act in a manner befitting the man I was married to.

The thump of the music got louder as I walked across the parking lot.

People were milling around close to the entrance of the clubhouse. There were picnic tables scattered around, smoke rising from fire pits, the smell of barbeque wafting through the air. Someone had threaded fairy lights on a patio area to the far left.

My stomach was twisting as I got closer, as people saw me. The men in vests varied in age, size and attractiveness. Some had women clinging to them in various stages of undress—also different ages. Some looked barely legal, others closer to my age. Their eyes shifted to me. Some of their gazes were curious. Others were warm. And a handful were hostile.

I didn't focus on the way the men were looking at me. I needed a drink for that.

Many drinks, I decided once I was inside.

The room itself was large, larger than it appeared on the outside. And more tastefully decorated than I would've thought. The sofas that were covered with people were in soft shades of brown, plush and clean looking. The coffee table was littered with beer bottles and glasses, but most of them had coasters. *Coasters.* I would not have expected that from a biker party.

The stripper pole in the corner with the naked girl on it— except for a G-string and nipple tassels—was more what I was imagining. Some men were gathered around, gripping beers, watching with appreciation and speaking to each other.

But plenty more were gathered in mini man huddles, and a good amount were making out with women. Some were playing pool. Most of the men had on the leather vests. Not all of them had the patches on the back, though. There were some which only had the word 'Prospect' right at the very bottom. Most of them were as young as the boy at the gate.

The music was louder here, but not too loud as to suppress conversation. All of the stimuli were overpowering, but I was just glad that there were so many people here that my entrance had gone unnoticed. Who would notice me and my decidedly modest outfit and subtle makeup with all the hot, young, scantily clad women around?

I found my way to the bar in the room, thankful for the bucket of beers on top of it that were unopened and twist top.

Another thing I'd drilled into my daughter, especially with her traveling to a country with a lower drinking age: never drink something a man gives you if it's open. Never leave your drink unattended. Even though Violet was smart and sensible, every moment of the day I was filled with an undercurrent of worry about her.

The beer was cold, and I gripped the cap in my left hand after I opened it.

I drank greedily from the bottle, both for the liquid courage and for something to do.

I'd never entered a party of any kind alone. Not once. Even as a teenager, I was always with Preston. As an accessory, as a trophy. I'd come to resent it wholeheartedly, but here, for a split second, I missed the structure of it. There was none of this nervousness or fear, of standing awkwardly with no one to talk to, with no role to play.

But then I remembered that there was fear with him. Fear that I'd say the wrong thing, look at the wrong person, smile at the wrong man and then pay for it later. Be called a dimwit, a slut or a bad wife.

No, there was nothing to miss about those days.

Plus, with half the beer drained, I was beginning to feel less self-conscious. I'd approached the bar at the very edge, most of the people congregated around it were bunched in the middle. I had my own little area where I could lean against the cool wood unnoticed, watching the party like I was at the zoo, and these were creatures I'd never seen before.

Which was truly the case.

All of the parties I'd been to were stuffy, fragranced, and pumped with fancy food and expensive champagne. There were flowers, classical music playing at a tasteful level. Expectations on how to act.

No one here seemed to be playing by any kinds of rules. Especially the women. I found myself enchanted with them.

All of them had *something* about them. A way they handled themselves, an energy that I could feel even from a brief glance. They were wholly their own. They were not trophies. They could dance with their heads thrown back in the air—like one woman in a pretty flowing dress was doing—or could be basically having sex with a man in the corner. They could slam shots—like the one at the end of the bar, shouting at a man with a goatee that he was a 'pussy who couldn't handle his booze.'

Laughter mingled with the rock music. I smiled to myself, content to be in this little corner. Maybe I'd finish this beer, watch for a while longer and leave. But even the thought of it had me uncomfortable.

Inexplicably, I felt safe here.

Because I'd been musing on that thought, I didn't see him approach. That he got close enough to me for his leather vest to brush the skin of my arm attested to just how deep in thought I'd been.

"You look lonely."

I blinked at the words, the rasp of the voice. Low and rumbly. The tenor of it brushed over the exposed skin of my arms.

My eyes found his, deep hazel, swirling with gold flecks.

The man. From the gas station. The one who had caught my eye for no apparent reason—well, other than being attractive beyond what I'd thought was actually real.

He was here. Right in front of me. Close enough to feel the warmth of his body. To inhale his scent... crisp, masculine, woodsy. My body reacted to that scent.

Well, and his overall hotness.

Up close, he was even more handsome. His skin was deep brown, lips full, jawbone strong and angled. His neck was the same, thick, smooth, inviting. I had an urge to lean forward and inhale his skin. But even if I did lean forward, I'd be face to face with a sculpted pec. He was that tall. And muscled.

The skin of his arms was exposed, the cords of his muscles looking like they were carved from freaking marble.

It was then I remembered he spoke.

"I look lonely?" I repeated, my voice scratchy. I cleared my throat and downed more of my beer to hopefully lubricate it.

Other parts of my body were already well lubricated in this man's presence.

His eyes were on my throat and had been since I swallowed. The gaze was unbridled and uncensored. There was need there. Want.

He wanted me.

Me.

Out of all of the attractive women in this room, one of the arguably most handsome and badass wanted me.

He nodded, watching me intently.

I waited for him to say something more.

He didn't.

He just stood there, much too close for a polite stranger to stand, staring at me with a gaze that burned off my clothes, my very skin. A gaze that set my panties on fire.

I was not aware that men could turn women on with a simple fricking look. It seemed I'd been missing out on a lot.

My hand shook as I took another sip of my beer.

"What about me looks lonely?" I asked in a husky voice that did not sound at all familiar.

He leaned forward even closer, and I held my breath, unsure of what I was supposed to do.

The wood bar pressed into my back.

Slowly, his eyes flit over me from top to bottom. It was pure torture. As if he were staring at me naked, uncovering every one of my secrets.

Unable to stand it, I let my breath out in a low puff.

His hazel irises locked with mine. They were hickory fire. He didn't speak for at least thirty seconds. It could've been a full minute. Could've been a lifetime. The music was no longer playing. There were no more people around us. The air stilled. We were the only people on this planet.

"Your eyes," he said finally, voice a rough whisper that cut through the silence we'd created.

The thump of the music returned. I heard laughter and cursing once more.

"You have lonely eyes," he continued. "Mesmerizing. The most mesmerizing eyes I've been lucky enough to look into." His hand lifted, and he brushed hair from my face, fingers skimming my cheek as he did.

If I'd heard this interaction anywhere else, from anyone else, it would've been cheesy. I would've rolled my eyes at such a line, designed to get into my pants.

While this man was making it clear he did want to get into my pants, there was nothing cheesy about his words. About the way he said them. There was an intimacy in his gaze that should've been impossible for someone I'd just met.

Not even technically met. He'd walked up to me and started speaking about my mesmerizing, lonely eyes.

All of this washed over me like a rogue wave, in addition to the buzz from the beer I'd drained in less than five minutes. Though I'd acquired a taste for beer, I had not acquired a tolerance.

So I think the beer was partly to blame for what I said next. The cocktail of emotions that I was feeling and the freedom that was wholly foreign to me also in play.

Oh, and because this man was hotter than Hades himself.

"I would like, very much," I said, my voice breathy. "If you would have sex with me."

I had not planned on those words coming out of my mouth. I did not know who was more shocked, me or the man in front of me. My face flamed with embarrassment and discomfort... for a hot second. Until the shock cleared from his face and his expression turned into pure lust.

My stomach dipped, and my skin burned with something other than embarrassment.

The man stepped forward so his body pressed into mine, hand moving to my chin to tilt it upward.

Desire pooled in my stomach at what I found in his eyes. No one had ever looked at me the way he was looking at me right now. Certainly not a man.

I didn't know men looked at women like that in real life.

It was him branding me with a mere look. It was a promise of something that I wasn't quite sure I was able to do.

"You came," a deep gravelly voice exclaimed.

I struggled to tear my eyes from the hazel gaze that was driving me crazy, but I managed. On reflex, I'd tried to step away from the man in front of me. He caught my hips in his large and strong hands, pulling me so I collided with his body, his arm moving to tuck me into his shoulder.

It was an intimate move that should've felt odd since I was tucked into the shoulder of a stranger. His body was warm, his muscles hard, but I somehow found something soft. Something that felt natural. I leaned into him because I liked that, but also because his hand told me he wasn't going to be letting me go any time soon.

I met gray eyes. Familiar gray eyes.

The man from the gas station, the man who had invited me here stood in front of us, casually holding a beer, eyes on me. Or more appropriately the hand on me.

"Swiss, I believe you need to get your hands off my date," he said, eyes finding mine but quite obviously addressing the man whose shoulder I was tucked into.

Swiss.

Obviously a nickname. An odd one for a biker. I'd imagined they were all called Striker or Snake or something menacing and badass. Not that Swiss wasn't badass. It was, just because it belonged to the dark, dark and impossibly handsome man beside me.

"Can't do that, brother," Swiss replied easily, holding me a little tighter. "Your own stupid fuckin' fault for lettin' her walk into this club alone. She's mine now."

My heart skipped a beat.

"She's mine now."

I should've found a lot of things wrong with their interaction. Two men talking about me as if I wasn't even here. As if I were an object.

But somehow, it didn't feel derogatory. I didn't feel objectified. I felt... incredibly turned on. The masculine energy underpinning both of their casual tones seemed to make the air vibrate.

Both of them wanted me. They were making that very fucking clear.

Out of all of the women in this club, the much younger, much more scantily clad women, the two sexiest men in the room—which was really saying something—were essentially fighting over me.

Me.

"She's mine now."

The sentence vibrated in my head.

Gray eyes focused on me. "Now, we're a little more progressive than all that," he drawled. "We don't declare ownership over women without them havin' a say in it."

"Speak for yourself, motherfucker," Swiss said, voice throatier than before. "And she had plenty of say in the matter." His head tilted downward, and my gaze drifted toward him like a magnet.

My entire body jolted when our eyes met.

"No, I don't keep women prisoner... unless they beg me," he murmured.

My mouth went dry, and my knees shook.

"Now I can either fight Cody for you... which I fuckin' will," he continued. "Or we can get the fuck out of here, and we can go and do the thing you just asked me to do. And I'll spend the entire night doin' it."

My heartbeat was a roar in my ears.

I was quite sure I'd lapsed into a dream or beer infused hallucination.

Both men were looking at me expectantly.

It was a weight, a physical weight, those stares. My knees struggled to hold me under them.

It was overwhelming, terrifying... exciting.

Not one month ago, I'd been sitting in some McMansion, eating Keto snacks while planning the towns' anniversary festival, debating over whether we wanted to serve vegan food alongside the BBQ and worrying about the color of the tablecloths 'sending the wrong message.' All the while, I was stressing about whether the drycleaners would have Preston's shirts ready on time because if they didn't, I'd have hell to pay.

Now I was in a biker compound with two men making it clear they wanted to have sex with me.

You could not make this shit up.

At that juncture, it would've been sensible to turn on my heel and walk out the door. I was a *mother*, for chrissakes. Beyond that, my life was enough of a mess as it was without getting myself tangled up—quite literally—with one of these outlaw bikers.

Instead of walking out, I looked up into the eyes of the man who was still holding me tight to his sculpted side.

"The second one," I whispered, barely audible above the thumping music.

The grin that stretched across his handsome face was something I felt carnally.

His eyes flickered to the original man, the one he had just addressed, but for the life of me, I could not remember the name of. "Tough cookies, brother," he winked. "Would advise you to never let one like this go, if you're lucky enough to find her."

Then, just like that, he turned us around and walked us out of the room.

Obviously, my feet must've contributed to our exit because

CHAPTER FOUR

KATE

I HAD no idea what I was thinking as I stepped into the room at the end of the long hall that led off the main living room. This clubhouse was much larger than it appeared at first and had somewhat of a dorm room setup. Each of the doors off the hall looked to be rooms for the various members of the club.

This room smelled pleasantly of a spicy aftershave. The same smell of the man behind me.

There was a large bed, made—which was interesting. I'd expected it to be messy, chaotic.

The covers were dark gray, pillows propped up neatly. I frowned at the two hooks on either side of the bed, wondering what they could be for.

But I didn't have long to wonder since my awareness was on the fact the door had closed and it was just the two of us. Alone.

The purpose of my presence here became stark.

I'd come into this room to have sex with this man. This

muscled, indescribably handsome, impossibly sexy man. One who was a member of an outlaw motorcycle club.

Who lived a life I couldn't even conceive of. And who, by the looks of the party, was used to young, sexy, slim women.

"I'm thirty-six," I blurted as he closed the door. My eyes homed in on the patch on his back—a skeleton riding a motorcycle with flames behind him—before he turned to face me.

"I know I'm probably not supposed to say such things," I continued before he could answer. "But I feel the need to make it clear since the women in there..." I pointed in the direction of the party where the low thump of music could still be heard, "are decidedly younger than me." I swallowed. "Despite my age, I have an inkling that they are decidedly more experienced in all of this," I waved my hand at his body, "than I am." I took a rapid breath, Swiss watching me with an amused glint to his eye, his large arms crossed over his impressive chest. "A long time ago, I had a husband," I said, even though it was a lie. It felt like the truth. It felt like it had been years since I was married to Preston.

I bit my lip, deciding not to explain that he was technically still my husband and that I ran away from him rather than left him.

"He is the only man I've ever been with... consensually," I babbled.

Swiss's eyes flared at this, no longer warm, sexy, amused. No, they burned with fire and brimstone.

Because I'd just casually mentioned that I had only had sex with one man consensually. Therefore insinuating that I had other, nonconsensual experiences. I was admitting this to a stranger. A sexy stranger. One I did want to have sex with. And these were not the kind of things you said to a man you wanted to have a one-night stand with.

I probably sounded certifiable. But I had committed to this, so I pressed on.

"I'm guessing that the women you're used to have been with more than one man," I continued. I wrung my hands. "Not to judge them or their lifestyle," I said quickly, eager to get away from any kind of conversation about nonconsensual experiences. "I'm... jealous of it. Up until recently, I had been with one man for eighteen years," I admitted, my face getting hot at the thought of Preston.

I quickly pushed him away. He didn't belong in this moment. This moment was mine.

"And I've had a child," I added.

Swiss's eyebrow raised slightly, and my breath lodged in my throat at the thought I'd well and truly scared him away.

"You would've found that out when you saw me naked," I told him, embarrassment washing over me. "But I feel it's my duty to tell you. So you know what you're getting into. So you can change your mind, go and find a woman without stretchmarks and a c-section scar and a heck of a lot more experience than eighteen years of the missionary position."

I'd just said all of that.

Talked about my stretchmarks and my c-section scar in front of the hottest man I'd seen in my life.

"In fact, hearing it all out loud makes me certain you'll want anyone else but me," I said quietly. "So I'm just going to..." I trailed off, intending to skirt around him, slink down the hallway, and quietly escape the biker compound.

A hand caught my upper arm. Firm but not painful.

The grip didn't trigger me like I thought it might. Didn't bring forth memories of trauma.

No, it excited me. Mostly because it was coupled with a gaze that set my limbs on fire.

"One thing I'm certain of, baby," he murmured, yanking my body to press against his. "Is that you're *exactly* the one I want."

Holy. Fuck.

I wasn't one to cuss, mainly because Preston abhorred women who cussed, but if there ever was a moment for a four-letter word, this was it.

"Need to inform you of the safeword before we go any further," he said against my mouth. Our lips brushed. Just barely. Electric shocks hurtled through my body from the singular touch.

"Safe-w-word?" I stuttered, amazed that my knees were still able to hold me up.

His eyes were burning as they met mine. "Yeah," he rasped. "By the sounds of it, you only know vanilla."

His finger trailed down my cheek. I shivered.

"And, baby, I'm everything but vanilla," he said.

My inner thighs tightened together in response to his words.

"I don't have limits when it comes to fucking," he told me, hand moving down my neck to massage it gently.

Like an expert, he found a spot to press his thumb into, and everything I had been carrying just fell away. There was nothing else in this world but this room.

There was nothing else but him.

"I'll take you to your limits, baby," he continued. "But I want to be sure I don't take you past them. And when I get in the zone, I tend to get... focused."

My heart was thundering in my chest. I was in over my head. Way over my head.

"So I need the word if any of this gets to be too much for you," he explained, voice throaty and so smooth, I wished there was a way to bottle it and drink it.

"This isn't going to be too much for me," I blurted. Somehow I was bold enough to maintain eye contact with him. "I have a feeling this is going to be just enough. That you're just enough." I said the last part on a whisper because something in Swiss's eyes changed. There was no longer just pure sexual hunger in there, a mahogany inferno. As I spoke, they softened.

"Fuck," he whispered, the cuss caressing my skin like poetry. He rested his forehead against mine in a gesture more intimate than what strangers should share. Then again, I was planning on having sex with him.

"I have a feeling you might be too fuckin' much," he breathed.

My insides melted.

Melted.

He didn't kiss me as I expected, as I craved. Didn't tear my clothes off like an animal, the way his hungry stare communicated. He didn't do anything. He just stared at me.

I could barely breathe. I swear, my heart paused beathing for the length of that stare. Could've sworn that stare lasted a lifetime.

"The safeword," I whispered.

He blinked, as if I had jerked him out of some kind of reverie. "What?"

"You told me there was a safeword, but you haven't said it," I replied. "And I'm really going to need you inside me in the next five minutes, so you better say it."

The inferno came back into Swiss's eyes.

"Coconut," he said. "That's the safeword. But you're not gonna use it." He lifted me up, and my legs instinctively went around his waist.

He was walking us toward the bed. Not that I cared. I was happy to stay wrapped around his waist for the rest of my life.

But then he threw me on the bed, and I stared at him standing there in his leather vest with his rippling muscles, the structure of his jaw, and I decided that lying on this bed looking up at him was pretty darn wonderful too.

"Fair warnin', baby. I'm not gonna be inside you for a long time yet," he said, his voice thick. "I plan on you coming at least three times before my dick enters you."

If humans could spontaneously combust, I was pretty sure that I would've done so at that very moment.

As it was, I stayed intact, though impossibly hot.

I moved to take my shirt off because I guessed that was what I was supposed to do in that situation, and because even the cheap, thin fabric was too heavy on my skin.

"Don't fucking move," Swiss ordered.

His voice was low, guttural, commanding.

I blinked, my hand pausing midair. The amusement that I'd witnessed earlier was nowhere to be seen. His expression was completely different. Darker. Sinister.

My heart was beating so loud I could barely hear around the roar.

"From now until when I decide, anything you do in this room, you wait until I give you permission to do it. You don't move an arm, you don't take off an item of clothing, and you don't come unless I approve it." He arched a brow. "You understand me?"

My body thrummed with need. And a little fear. That should've been the moment when my past trauma surfaced, when a panic attack started to take control of my body.

But I did not have control of my body.

Swiss did.

And despite my past—or maybe even because of it—I liked that. Loved that. He was a stranger. He could hurt me, yes. But I'd been hurt by a man before. That I could handle. I hadn't experienced the feeling of excitement and arousal in my blood before. Not once.

And Swiss hadn't even touched me. Hadn't even kissed me.

"Do you understand me?" he repeated.

I nodded. "Yes," I said, my voice husky.

His eyes flickered over me, slowly. "Good," he murmured.

Then he knelt at my feet.

Knelt at my feet.

Slowly, he pulled off my shoes. His fingers were cool and firm as they rubbed the soles of my feet.

My eyes rolled to the back of my head as he found some kind of pressure point that I didn't know existed.

With devastating slowness and reverence, Swiss's hands rubbed upward, underneath my jeans to my calves.

Then he stood, towering over me as he unbuttoned my jeans. My body was vibrating with need, my blood pumping through my veins white hot.

"Lift your hips for me, baby," Swiss said softly.

I instantly obeyed, even though my limbs felt like lead.

He rolled my jeans off me, discarding them on the floor before hovering above me, staring at me in my underwear.

The panties weren't bad. I'd changed into a nice pair when I'd made the decision to come here. Not because I'd expected anyone to see them, but because I always made sure to wear nice underwear.

Nice was relative considering what I used to wear cost hundreds of dollars.

These were cheap red lace panties from Target. But I'd never worn red panties. Was never allowed.

So the act of wearing them was rebellion.

And I was very glad I chose this particular pair for this particular night, despite feeling self-conscious. I resisted the urge to cover the sliver of my belly that he'd exposed when taking off my jeans.

Swiss's hands trailed over the faint stretch marks on my stomach, light and barely there. They traveled downward to the small scar where they pulled my daughter out.

He was exploring the history on my skin with a gentleness that I hadn't thought him capable of, certainly not after the warning he gave when we came in here.

His finger slipped under the lace panty, and I lost my breath. But it didn't go downward. Instead, his head lowered, and he kissed me gently, there, through the fabric.

I writhed on the bed, pleasure shooting from the core of me to my fingertips, which were clutching his comforter.

Swiss looked up, wicked hunger in his eyes, his fingers pushed my panties to the side, and my eyes squeezed shut in pleasure as they entered me.

"Open your eyes, and look at me," he commanded, voice a velvet blade.

My eyes opened without hesitation.

He was still watching me.

His fingers moved lazily but expertly inside me, as if he were trained in how to erotically torture women. My pussy pulsated as he made a 'come hither' gesture, black spots dancing in my vision as my climax approached.

As if he sensed it, Swiss stopped, fingers exiting me with that same torturous slowness that they entered.

Eyes never leaving mine, he put his two fingers into his mouth, sucking off every trace of me.

I was unable to look away. Unable to breathe.

Swiss grasped the bottom of my tank, peeling it off with that devastating slowness that was killing me.

Once it was off, he hovered over me, his body pressed into mine, mouth inches away.

We still hadn't kissed yet.

He'd tasted me, but his lips had not met mine.

I stared into the captivating abyss of his eyes, hoping for him to cross the few inches left between us.

But he didn't give me what I wanted. Instead, he pulled me to stand on unsteady legs, turning me quickly and roughly so I was bent over the bed, bent almost halfway, my feet still on the floor. My hands landed on the mattress on instinct, my heart roaring.

His fingers trailed down my spine, sending shivers with them.

When he unclasped my bra, I was already shaking. My knees couldn't hold me much longer.

It got even harder to hold my own weight as Swiss maneuvered me out of my bra, me having to lift one of my hands at a time to stay in position. His fully clothed body pressed into my back and the telltale hardness against my ass took my breath away.

Neither of us had spoken. There was only our breathing, mine rapid and Swiss's measured and calm.

The air felt thicker. Charged. My hairs were standing on end. My pussy was still pulsating with the memory of his fingers being inside.

Once my bra was off, my hands found the mattress again, and Swiss stood back up, his fingertips finding my spine again, ghosting all the way down.

His palms rubbed my ass, first the cheek, then going under so he could cup my pussy.

I fisted the comforter tighter.

His fingers found my center then trailed back, teasing that intimate, forbidden part of me.

"I'm going to take that ass," he murmured, his voice strangled with desire.

My body froze. I'd never done that. And I wasn't frozen with fear, but with excitement.

"Not tonight," he said, hands moving up and out to the sides of my panties. "I need to own this cunt first."

I sucked in a fractured breath as my shaking legs stepped out of my panties.

"Don't move a muscle," Swiss ordered.

My body obeyed, even as I worried about my ability to stay in that position much longer. If he ordered it, I'd stay until my limbs gave out.

I was staring at the wall, not at him. But I heard a drawer opening, rifling sounds. Then the low thump of his boots against the carpet. He was still fully clothed, and I was bent over his bed. Completely naked. In one of the most vulnerable positions you could be in, even if you were with someone you were used to. Someone who wasn't a complete stranger.

Darkness entered the corner of my eye as Swiss bent over the bed. I heard a metallic click. My brain was screaming at me to look right, to see what he was doing, what I was in for. Instead, I continued staring at the wall.

His breath was hot on my neck when he made it back to me. My knees shook. "Do you trust me?" he asked me, his voice velvet against my skin.

Did I trust him? I didn't even know him. Didn't even know his last name. Or his first, for that matter. Did he even know mine?

"Yes," I answered reflexively, not thinking, only feeling.

His hands found my breasts, tweaking each nipple to the point of pain.

I let out a moan as my body responded to the pleasure of that pain.

"Want you to be louder," Swiss murmured, tweaking my nipple harder. "Want you to scream for me before the night is out."

I let out a louder moan in response. Not by his command, but because I couldn't not. Something inside of me was opening, waking up. Something I didn't recognize, but something that felt natural.

"You talked about being fucked in nothing but missionary," Swiss said, hands going to my hips so he could lift me and place me on the bed.

He lifted me up like I weighed nothing.

My knees found the mattress on instinct. I was on all fours, facing the headboard. Now I saw what Swiss had been doing. He had been attaching leather restraints to the hooks.

My stomach swirled, and my heartbeat quickened.

"I really do want to see your face when you come for the first time," Swiss said, boots thumping once more as he walked around the bed. He leaned over to grasp my arm, his other hand going to my hip to take my weight as he fastened the first of the restraints on.

When the leather fastened around my wrist, my body quivered, my pussy pulsating.

In short, it turned me on.

Way on.

"But I want to give you something else," he continued. "Want you to feel me in your fuckin' throat too."

Holy. Fucking. Crap.

Another pulse. My entire body was taut as he finished restraining me, my palms going flat on the headboard to keep me steady. The restraints themselves were attached to chains that clinked every time I moved even slightly, giving me some slack to work with so I could move without being totally restricted. But I was still chained to the bed, the leather secure and not something I could get out of. Only Swiss could unlock them.

It should've, at this point, scared the ever-loving crap out of me that I was restrained and naked with a stranger, the music so loud out in the common room that no one would be able to hear me scream for help if need be.

But that only added to the furious tempo of my arousal. I could scream as loud as I wanted, and only Swiss would hear me.

I had no idea what he planned to do with me. Because he hadn't said I couldn't move, my head went over my shoulder, tossing my hair as I did. Swiss was standing beside the bed, still fully clothed, staring at me.

No, it looked like he was devouring me with his gaze.

Again, my body pulsated with need from just a look.

He rubbed his hand over his mouth. "Fuck, this image, you chained to my bed like this, might just be the best thing I've seen in this life," he uttered.

My stomach did a backflip.

His eyes met mine. "You're gonna sit on my face now, baby," he said, rougher than before.

I blinked.

My skin was hot.

Nerves mixed with my arousal.

I had never done that. Never been in that position, had that kind of control, had such an intimate experience. It felt forbidden somehow. Wrong.

Because I'd been conditioned for it to be that.

Which was why the part of me that I was just discovering, fucking loved the idea of it.

But I couldn't quite think of how the logistics of it would work.

Swiss answered that for me by gently lifting my arm and leg so he could slip under me. The chain clinked as it went taut to accommodate him. He was on his back underneath me.

"Hold onto the headboard," he ordered.

I did as instructed, the chains clinking.

His hands went to my hips then yanked me forward so my knees were on the pillows, and I was hovering above him.

His breath kissed the apex of my thighs. I gripped the headboard harder.

"Ride my mouth," he commanded, voice near inhuman.

I couldn't do anything but comply.

I cried out the second his mouth met my pussy. I moved on instinct as his hands clenched on my ass, moving in rhythm with me. His mouth moved expertly, and my orgasm flew over me in an instant, tearing me apart. But I didn't stop. Or at least, he didn't let me stop. He kept me rocking on him as I battled with the aftershocks, went to war with the way my body split completely apart.

And that's when it started building again. Something larger than the climax from before. Something that caused me to leave my body. Everything went soft. Faraway.

Swiss let out a growl into my pussy, the vibration setting me off again, riding waves of pleasure I didn't think my body was capable of feeling.

I'd never felt so powerful. Like I was dominating a man, even though I was the one in chains. Even though I was the one naked. It was the power, the agency I had in direct dichotomy with the situation that annihilated me apart for the third time.

The world went blurry, nothing existing except the pain from Swiss's hands biting into my flesh.

My body twitched as I came down, Swiss no longer moving me. If my fingers could've ripped apart the wooden headboard, I was pretty sure they would've, I was clutching onto it that hard.

A burst of pain exploded in my inner thigh. I looked down to where Swiss had turned his head, lifting me so he could sink his teeth into me. Blood trickled from where he broke the skin.

"Taste of your pussy and your blood are the sweetest things on this earth," he growled.

My thigh throbbed, and my skin sang with his words.

"I need you to fuck me," I rasped, my voice unrecognizable.

I'd never uttered anything like that in my life. I was pretty sure it was against whatever Dom rules Swiss had—he was in charge, wasn't he?

But instead of chastising me for my words, his eyes flared with hunger.

"Oh, I'm gonna fuck you, baby," he responded. My blood painted his lips.

In one smooth move, Swiss lifted me in order to get up from beneath me. The bed creaked slightly as he yanked me back to all fours. He shifted his weight so he was on his knees, spreading my legs.

I sucked in an unsteady breath, my limbs shaking, still gripping the headboard for dear life.

A crinkle of foil punctured my reverie, the clink of a belt, of Swiss freeing himself.

The hand on my hip to steady me was the only warning I got before he surged inside of me. I screamed as he seated himself in me fully, as he bunched my hair and yanked hard as he started thrusting.

My body was tender, sensitive and ravenous. Pain exploded in my scalp, only making the pleasure from his thrusts more intense.

My throat burned from the way I screamed.

Time ceased to have meaning. The thumping music melted away. We were the only two people on this earth. I was sure of it.

Swiss was unyielding, without mercy as he fucked me. Like an animal.

As my own feral climax approached, his hand left my hip, and the pressure at my scalp was gone. Both of his hands had fastened around my neck before I could comprehend what was happening.

He squeezed to the point where I struggled to get air. He did not stop moving inside of me. My orgasm didn't pause the harder he squeezed. It only intensified as my lungs burned, as my body scrambled for oxygen.

The second it seemed like I might black out, Swiss let out a growl, and I broke apart, clenching around him as my orgasm shattered everything left inside me.

The room came in and out of focus as I gasped for breath. In that moment, I surrendered completely to Swiss.

I was his.

That much was crystal clear to me.

I was staring at the ceiling. My chest was rising and falling rapidly. My arms were still in chains above my head, the sockets of my shoulders burning ever so slightly in protest at being in such an unnatural position.

At some point, Swiss had adjusted my position. He wanted to be face-to-face. It was an entirely different experience, having him on top of me and staring at me as he slowly fucked me.

Swiss stretched above me, and a metallic click echoed in my ears as my hands fell down.

He caught my wrist in his hands, slowly massaging the feeling back into each one.

"I feel like I exist on this planet purely to experience that," I murmured, suddenly exhausted. It was like I'd flown upward, out of the atmosphere and was hurtling back to Earth.

My body was spent. Utterly. There was nothing left inside me. He'd taken everything out.

I didn't miss the way Swiss's eyes flared as I spoke, though.

He kissed my nose gently, and the gesture sent warmth seeping into my bones. "I feel like I was made to do that to you," he murmured.

Sleep was claiming me quickly. Darkness pulled me down. There was no way I could stay conscious after everything we'd done. Impossible.

"I feel like I was made to be yours," I whispered, or maybe I thought it. I couldn't be sure because I slipped off to sleep quickly after that.

SWISS

"I feel like I was made to be yours."

Those words kept me up for hours, long after she had drifted off to sleep. Or lapsed into unconsciousness. I'd drained her fucking dry. I'd been unable to stop, even seeing that she was on the edge, seeing that her muscles could barely hold her up anymore. But the second I tasted her, tasted her fucking blood, heard her ask me to fuck her in a tone that suggested she never asked a man that in her life, all of my control evaporated.

And she'd fucking loved it. Every second. If I'd taken it further, she would've gone until she collapsed. She never would've uttered the safeword I'd never given anyone but her.

No, I knew that.

She might have been new to this kind of shit, but she was

made to fuck like this.

She was made for *me*.

Not just because she was the hottest fuck I'd ever had, not just because she was fucking drop dead gorgeous—which she was. But because she asked me to fuck her before she gave me her name.

Kate Edwards.

That was her name. I'd gone into her purse and checked out her driver's license after she'd drifted off.

Kate Edwards from New Hampshire.

A housewife who'd left her husband. Who had somehow found herself out of her element at a club party half a country away from her listed address. Who had found herself standing next to the most dangerous man in the room in a room full of ruthless motherfuckers. Well, maybe Hades and I were tied for most dangerous man in the room.

She couldn't have known that implicitly, but she'd sensed it. There was something about me that awakened ancient survival instincts. I knew that. I also knew that people reacted one of three ways. One, they wanted to get the fuck away from me as quickly as possible. Two, if they were men, they wanted to challenge me in order to establish dominance—those men were not long for this world. Three, if they were women—or a man who went that way—they wanted to fuck me because they wanted to be close to death. Wanted to test their limits.

Everyone I fucked had a death wish.

Except Kate.

No, the thing about her that grabbed me by the balls was that she was wishing for something else.

Life.

And fuck did she awaken something in me. *Resurrected* something in me.

Those thoughts were not what kept me awake, though. I was nowhere near scared about feeling these things. Being with her felt fucking natural. As easy as goddamn breathing.

What was keeping me up was one comment.

One line.

"He is the only man I've ever been with... consensually."

There was someone out there, living, breathing who had touched her without her consent. The mere thought had lava in my throat, red film covering my eyes with one need.

To kill.

To kill whoever had done that to her.

But I needed to tread carefully. This might have been the first night I'd met her, but I saw that she was running from a lot. I had no idea what the fuck was going on with her past, but I could get the idea.

Husband who treated her like shit, didn't understand what he had in his home. Living for a kid. Playing some kind of role that did not match up with who she was inside.

You could fucking see it. Across the room tonight, I could see it. She was brand-new to this town, to this life. And she was terrified. Fear I knew. I specialized in it.

So yeah, I had to tread carefully.

But as I settled in bed, yanking her to me, I understood what was happening. She was fucking mine.

KATE

I woke slowly. Groggily. Which in and of itself was unusual.

For over a decade, I'd jerked awake at five every morning, my fight or flight instinct waking with me. Oversleeping was not an option. It would result in punishment. Beyond that, the quicker I got out of bed, the less likely Preston would be to decide he wanted to have sex first thing in the morning.

Which was why it was also essential for me to perfect the art of untangling myself from a sleeping man without waking him.

Though I was a lot less anxious to be out of this man's arms than Preston's. And despite the dull throb between my legs, I would've been very happy if Swiss woke and decided he wanted morning sex.

He held me considerably tighter than Preston ever had. The grip was warm, comforting. Safe.

I did not relish the thought of getting out of it.

I was not quite sure of the etiquette of a one-night stand. Though I could guess. Swiss was an alpha, badass biker. I didn't expect he was one for brunch dates. He'd got what he wanted from me.

Sex.

The best sex I'd had in my life.

I'd argue the best sex *anyone* had had in their lives, but that was neither here nor there.

Not that I knew anything about this man—apart from his ability in the bedroom—but I was taking an educated guess in what he wanted from me. And that was nothing now.

I had no idea how to act around him in the daylight. I had no idea how I'd look in the harsh light of day... not good, most likely. I'd slept in my makeup, a cardinal sin. So I most certainly looked like a mess.

The sun creeping through the blinds did wonderful things for Swiss, however. His ebony skin was smooth, flawless, save for some scars littering the skin of his muscled arms, his torso and a large one on his inner thigh that went all the way up.

His lips were full, luscious, and his closed lids hid warm,

coffee-colored eyes. Though he was pure, rugged masculinity, there was something softer about him as he slept.

When his brow twitched and he moved his head ever so slightly, I held my breath, realizing that I had been watching him sleep like some kind of psycho for five minutes.

Luckily, he settled back into a deep sleep and did not wake up to my panda eyes peering at him.

I took him in for a second more before I slowly, carefully climbed out of bed. My clothes were strewn over the floor, and I quickly and quietly dressed, half expecting Swiss to jerk awake. He was some kind of badass, wasn't he? Weren't outlaw badasses meant to sleep with one eye open, ready for conflict?

Half of me hoped he'd wake up, yank me back into bed, declare his love for me and... and what? Live happily ever after?

No.

I wasn't a romantic in any sense of the word, so that wish came out of nowhere. I quickly shook myself out of it as I slipped on my shoes.

Though I wanted to, I badly wanted to, I did not look at Swiss one last time before I snuck out of the room. It wouldn't do any good.

Instead, I walked out and closed the door quietly.

The common room of the club was as silent as a tomb even though there were people scattered on every surface, including the pool table. All of them were in various stages of undress. The room smelled of sex, booze and a scented candle burning on a side table.

I leaned down to blow it out as I walked out. The last thing I wanted was this place to burn down. There was something about it... as rugged, and messy and potentially dangerous as it was. Sure, it had a lot to do with the man who was naked and asleep in a room down the hall.

But it represented a part of me that I didn't know existed until last night.

I squinted against the morning sun as I exited the clubhouse. My head thumped vaguely, and I held my hand up to block out the sun, wishing for some dark sunglasses. But I didn't bring sunglasses last night because I hadn't been intending on leaving in the sunlight.

My footfalls echoed on the concrete, and I squinted to see movement in the garage. I guessed the bikers doubled as mechanics. Although I tried to dart my eyes away, a man in coveralls raised his hand at me. I smiled tightly and raised my hand back, hastening my gait as I made it to my car.

The interior still smelled faintly of smoke despite the air freshener that was meant to replicate pine trees. Although all scents paled in comparison to Swiss's unique and intoxicating fragrance.

Though I couldn't think about that. Or him. Instead, I turned the car on and pulled out of the lot. Luckily, the gates were open, and there was no one waiting there. In the bright light of day, the clubhouse looked a lot more... ordinary. Apart from the barbed wires fences, security cameras, club insignia and lineup of Harleys in the parking lot.

I took one last look at the clubhouse, feeling a pang of... something for leaving it behind. For leaving *him* behind.

But I forced myself to ignore that.

No good would come of that. Of me even entertaining the thought that I belonged in a place like that.

I didn't belong anywhere.

So I pulled out of the lot. I didn't let myself look in the rearview mirror.

I was standing in line at a very airy and trendy looking café. It was hip without being pretentious, cozy without being dated, and the smell of beans permeated the air. Coffee was essential after the night I had last night.

My head ached mildly from the beer, lack of sleep and probably some dehydration. I should've drank more water. Then there were the muscles. They were throbbing, like I'd had an intense workout.

Which I guessed I had.

My wrists still held faint red marks from the binds he'd used on me. My inner thigh burned with beautiful pain, where Swiss had sunk his teeth into the skin. Where he'd drawn my blood.

A blush crept up my neck from the very memory, and my legs quivered with need.

Despite the aches and the lack of sleep, I'd never felt more alive in my life. The world seemed brighter, sharper somehow. Like I'd had a film over my eyes for the past eighteen years—for my entire life, actually—and this was the first time I was seeing clearly.

However, a man could not be credited with this.

Though he played a huge part.

It was the decisions I'd made last night. The decisions I'd been making for the past three weeks. All of them my own. All of them outside of the person I'd been pretending to be all these years.

This, today, felt like the first day of my life.

"I'm warnin' yah now, there's gonna be like a quarter of an hour wait on the coffee," an accented voice informed me.

I blinked at the man in front of me, his brows pinched together with stress and his eyes slightly wild.

"My barista just quit," he informed me, speaking close to a shout over the screech of steaming milk. "And it took me years to train her because Yanks have no idea how to make good bloody coffee," he continued. "I'm usually the main chef here too, but because I am the only one within a hundred-mile radius who can make proper coffee, it's on me to do this." He nodded down to the machine, still yelling even though he'd stopped steaming milk.

"And because of that, word gets around so bloody everyone comes from three towns over to get my coffee," he grimaced, pouring milk expertly into a takeaway cup.

He fastened the lid on and yelled, "Flat white for Hannah!"

I winced at the sound and moved aside for a pretty young woman with a baby on her hip to take the coffee.

Indeed, the café was full, all of the tables occupied and many people standing around, obviously waiting for takeout. I'd been too deep in my head to notice all of this.

The man behind the counter looked very stressed, his hair was mussed, cheeks ruddy and red. He was short, in his mid to late forties, trim and muscular.

"I know how to use that," I blurted, nodding to the machine.

His eyes widened at me in disbelief. "I highly fuckin' doubt that," he scoffed.

Being cussed at in his accent didn't have the same effect as it might've if he was an American.

In fact, it was cute and endearing.

"I don't mean to be rude, darlin', but I'm just speaking from experience. Most of you Americans call dirty water coffee and consider a Keurig an 'espresso machine.'" He scrunched his nose in distaste.

I grinned at him. "I consider Keurigs a crime," I told him. "We have a very fancy espresso machine at home..." I trailed off.

Home.

I'd said the word without thinking, and it went rotten on my tongue.

The place with the espresso machine, chef's kitchen and expensive furniture was *not* home.

My only true home was a daughter on another continent.

The stressed man with the accent I was pegging to be Australian was staring at me, assessing me dubiously. I understood that. He was obviously passionate about coffee and naturally distrusting of a nation that had bastardized the name of coffee—one of the few things I was grateful to Preston for, introducing me to real espresso.

"You really know how to make it? Properly?" the man asked.

I nodded once. "Yes, I can make a flat white perfect as if my life depended on it," I joked, even though it wasn't far from the truth.

I had learned to use our intimidating, fancy machine because the consequences of fucking up were swift.

The man in front of me was still not entirely convinced.

"Or I can just leave you to deal with all of this on your own," I offered, waving my hands at the door where more people were entering.

"Fine," he said finally. "But you make me one first before I serve it to anyone. I have a reputation to uphold."

"Deal," I nodded, walking around the counter to situate myself at the machine. He handed me an apron I took gratefully.

And then, for the first time in years, I worked.

Six hours later, I was exhausted yet wired.

Julian—the owner of the coffee shop and the stressed man from earlier—flipped the 'closed' sign and locked the door.

"You saved my ass today," he informed me, handing me a beer he'd retrieved from a fridge under the counter I hadn't noticed.

Not that I had much time to notice the layout of this place beyond the coffee machine. For a small town, people really took their coffee seriously. It felt like every resident had come in twice for a cup of java. Well, everyone except the patched members of my favorite local biker gang.

My arm and shoulder burned from tamping the coffee—thirty pounds of pressure was what I'd come to learn created the perfect cup—and my legs ached from standing all day—I wasn't wearing the right shoes since I hadn't entered expecting to work at a coffee machine for hours.

My hair stuck to my dewy face, the air thick and humid even with the laboring air conditioning unit that was situated in the corner.

I sipped the beer, grateful for the cold, bubbling liquid sliding down my throat.

"I had fun," I told Julian honestly.

He raised a bushy brow. "*Fun?*" he repeated. "You won't think that by the end of the week."

It was my turn to raise my brow.

He took a sip of his beer. "You're the only person other than me who can make coffee correctly in this town, maybe this state. I'm not letting you go without a fight," he snickered. "I can pay you well above minimum wage. Business is good, and I over-charge for the coffee because everyone else does." He grinned. "You're in town for a while, aren't ya?"

I thought about that while I took another long sip. The plan had been to hop from town to town so I was harder to trace. The thought of leaving Garnett made me feel vaguely sick, though. I hadn't encountered anything like this place. Hadn't felt a sense of belonging like this... ever.

Then there was Swiss.

The biker who had rocked my world last night.

No, he blew me right off of my world. I'd landed somewhere else completely foreign and alien, and I liked it.

Choosing to stay here because of a man was dangerous. Reckless.

But leaving somehow felt fatal.

"Yeah," I agreed. "I'm in town for a while."

SWISS

She had a kid.

A *grown* kid.

One thing she'd said last night that I'd been marinating on. Well, one of the many things she'd said from last night I was marinating on. Among the many other things that I was marinating on including her managing to leave without me waking up.

I was in a shitty mood in general, but the kid thing was what I was ruminating on.

It pissed me off.

Not because it turned me off her. Not because I didn't want to have to deal with another man's child. No.

It was because the likelihood of her wanting to do it all over again was pretty damn slim considering she'd spent eighteen years being a mother.

The thought hit me square in the ribs.

I wanted kids.

Wanted another chance.

I'd vowed to myself not to think of that weight I carried around. The one that never left even after they took our dead daughter out of my arms. Every single thing I'd done after that moment was in pursuit of something to distract me from that weight. To erase the image of that.

Which was why I never repeated fucks. Never gave women

the wrong idea. I was on the hunt. For the woman who would submit to me, fuck dirty, accept every inch of my depravity yet be Old Lady material. I did it because I knew I'd never find it. Never have that chance again.

I'd found that in Kate. The second my eyes found her. It was an ancient instinct, I supposed. Or something not of this world. I didn't give a fuck about the why of it all, just knew she was mine from the moment I saw her.

Knew it from the first moment my cock landed inside her.

I knew I'd have to go slow because it would scare her. Terrify her. I sensed something in her, a skittishness. She wasn't completely sure of herself. Of her place in the world. It made sense, considering what she told me about her life before.

I needed to go slow with her. As much as I was fucking aching to claim her in every way I could, have my name on her body, put my kid inside her, I knew there was a risk she might go running.

Although she wouldn't make it far.

I'd chase her to the ends of the earth.

But I had time.

"Brother?"

I jerked up to see Hansen staring at me. Something in his gaze told me this wasn't the first time he'd tried to address me. I was sitting at the bar nursing a beer.

"We got a job," he told me. "Or we've got some payback to deal to a bunch of low level gang bangers trying to fuck us over on a gun deal," he expanded. "Figured you'd want to be in on this one."

He would've figured right in any other scenario. It was either me or Hades the club went to when there were people to be punished. Sure, any brother would deal out vengeance in an instant, but it was Hades and I who truly enjoyed it. Who made a fucking *art* out of it.

If I hadn't met her last night, I would've been chomping at the bit for this.

"Nah," I said, abandoning the half full beer. "I've got something to do."

The shock on Hansen's face was amusing, but I was too far gone to appreciate it.

I was going to get my woman.

CHAPTER FIVE

KATE

"MOM?"

I jostled the phone in the crook of my ear as I took the turn toward my motel.

"Violet!" I cried out. One could almost call it a yell. "We had an agreement. Three phone calls a week... minimum. I haven't heard from you in almost a week."

If I was honest, no matter how much I missed my girl, it was convenient that she wasn't calling because I had to lie to her less. She thought I was in California taking care of a great aunt who she'd never met.

Violet sighed over the phone. I could imagine the slight roll of her eyes, and I missed her so intensely I could barely breathe.

"Well I figured you'd be busy," she started. "And I texted you," she countered. "And sent you voice messages. Plus like sixteen videos of everything I ate this week."

"You did," I agreed, pulling the sun visor down. "And in all of your videos I saw the same masculine looking hand."

I hadn't mentioned the hand in my reply texts because it was not a conversation I wanted to have over text—I didn't like having any conversations with my daughter over text unless it was about picking up something from the store or what time she was going to be home—since it would be much easier for her to avoid the questions.

"His name is Jacques, and he's amazing, Mom," Violet gushed. "I met him on the way to one of my classes. Well, actually, I was lost, and he showed me where I was going. He was so polite. And he understood my terrible French, and Mom, he's *so* handsome."

Violet spoke quickly, her excitement making all of her words run together like when she was a little girl.

I smiled despite the worry that had spiked within me since I saw the edge of that masculine hand. Violet had brought a total of two boys home before. Both of whom she didn't seem overly interested in, both of whom she'd dated because she thought her father would approve of them. They were football players, from good—read rich—families, handsome, polite. Always shaking Preston's hand, looking him in the eye and calling me ma'am despite my repeated insistence that they call me by my first name.

Preston wouldn't have liked that anyway.

Violet had lost her virginity to one of those boys. James. Quarterback. Sweet. Square jawed. Adored Violet—as did most of the boys in her high school. She told me about it the day after it happened. I'd tried my hardest to make sex an open and healthy topic between the two of us. I wanted her to feel comfortable with her sexuality. I didn't want her having the issues with sex that I did.

So when she told me it hurt, it was quick and James had no

idea what he was doing, I was able to tell her that most boys didn't. Then she promptly told me she was done sleeping with boys.

That had scared the crap out of me. But luckily, she didn't bring home or sleep with any middle-aged men.

"And Jacques is a student too?" I asked, a pit in my stomach.

Her pause told me all I needed to know.

"He's *technically* a teaching assistant," she said, already defensive. An argument that she'd no doubt rehearsed in her head. "He graduated early... He's a genius, by the way, Mom. He speaks four languages."

"He's a European," I muttered. "That's not that impressive."

"Mom." The single world was a long-suffering scolding that had luckily occurred only sporadically in her life. The word 'mom' could be a signifier of many things. Could communicate hundreds of ailments, needs, moods and wants.

It was the only title that I was proud of my whole life. Mother.

She was my one accomplishment. My kind, well-adjusted, smart, caring and fearless daughter. One who was traveling another continent, falling in love, needing me less.

"How old is he?" I asked with a sigh. My eyes were blurry with tears. Tears due to missing her, grieving for her childhood.

"He's twenty-six," she said. "Like a *young* twenty-six. But also an old soul. Like me."

I smiled as a tear streamed down my face.

A rabbit scurried across the road, and I swerved to miss it. You weren't supposed to swerve for animals, but I couldn't help it. My phone fell from the crook of my ear and down into my lap.

"Crap!" I called out, struggling to catch my phone before it fell down the dreaded crack between the seats. The car swerved ever so slightly, but I didn't crash into anything.

"Mom?" The word was stated with concern now.

"I'm fine," I yelled, fumbling for the phone with one hand, steering with the other, and doing my best to peer at the road while bent down.

My hand found the phone, and I managed to straighten myself without causing an accident.

"What was that?" Violet asked, anxiety coloring her words.

"I just dropped the phone," I told her.

"Mom." The word was chastising that time. "I told you how many accidents are caused by talking on the phone while driving. Why aren't you using your Bluetooth? Did the car disconnect it again? I can talk you through how to connect it again."

I smiled at my daughter's concern, at her tone, how grown up it sounded. My goal had been to keep her a child for as long as possible, shield her from everything happening in the house, and protect her against anything that could make her grow up too fast.

I did my best to act strong and independent around her so she didn't feel like she had to be the grown-up despite how young I had her.

But when it came to technology, Violet was definitely the grown-up.

My blood turned cold at her mention of Bluetooth. Of course, our top of the line SUV had Bluetooth. Reversing camera. Park assist. A middle panel that looked like a spaceship and made it impossible to find a way to turn on the radio.

The old Toyota I was driving still had a slot for a CD player. There was no reversing camera, and the air conditioning rattled. It was easy to tune the radio. The seats smelled faintly of smoke. There was certainly no Bluetooth.

As far as Violet knew, I was driving my car while in California, taking care of the aunt she'd never heard of or met. As far as Violet knew, her father and I were still together, and my trip was temporary. As far as Violet knew, she was coming home from her trip to her two parents who loved her, living in the same house, seemingly happy.

The reality of my deception was a pit in my stomach. My tongue stuck to the roof of my mouth as I tried to figure out what to say to Violet which wouldn't catch me further in a lie. As I was figuring that out, I pulled into the parking lot of my motel. And what I saw there had all of those—very legitimate—worries melt away.

"Sweetie pie, I've got to go," I said, trying my best to keep my voice even. "Be careful with Jacques, please. I want you to live your life to the fullest extent, but also remember not all men have your best interests at heart."

I could picture her rolling her eyes as soon as I said this. My girl was intelligent, shrewd and dauntless.

But she was still a teenage girl. And for better or for worse, teenage girls believed in love and gave with their whole hearts because they hadn't learned quite yet what men could do with them.

Even with what was happening in the parking lot, I hoped with my entire heart that my little girl would get the fairy tale. That her precious heart would stay intact. That she would escape that unique and soul crushing kind of hurt.

"Yes, Mom," she replied dutifully.

"And call me more," I demanded.

"I'll try my very best. Oh, Jacques is here, and we're going to meet some friends," she said, already sounding very distracted. "I love you."

"Be careful, I love you too," I called, but she'd already hung up.

I might've stewed on that for longer if it weren't for what was waiting for me in the parking lot.

Swiss.

He was here.

I could feel his eyes on me.

My first reaction to seeing him leaning against his bike was excitement. Second was desire. Third, nerves. Fourth, fear.

My legs burned as I walked up to him, hating the coldness at the base of my spine.

Heat quickly replaced that as he took off his black sunglasses and tucked them into the front of his gray tee. The gray tee that molded against the eight pack I knew was underneath.

His espresso gaze went down my body slowly, appreciatively —even though I was a sweaty mess with coffee stains on my shirt —and then back up to my eyes.

"Hey, baby," he drawled.

My stomach skipped at both the gaze and the casual greeting. As if he leaned on motorcycles in the parking lot of my motel every day. As if that were a thing. As if *we* were a thing.

I stopped a few feet away from him, making a statement with the distance. The easy expression on his face faltered ever so slightly.

I crossed my arms across my chest. His eyes flickered downward to where I'd unintentionally pushed my boobs together.

"How did you find out where I'm staying?" I demanded, my voice sharp but not as strong as I wanted it to be. There was a thinness to it... fear.

This man had figured out where I was staying in less than twelve hours. How easily could Preston find me? I'd covered my tracks well. Or at least, as well as someone like me could. I wasn't freaking James Bond. But I'd felt comfortable here.

Safe.

A safety that shattered with Swiss's arrival.

Not that I was scared of him exactly.

"We run this town, darlin'." His eyes flickered up and down my body once more. Cue all the melty feelings. "And someone like you does not go unnoticed."

The words warmed me and chilled me simultaneously.

Yes, it felt very good for him to find me attractive in the light of day, especially considering the state of me. But even my vanity couldn't ignore the 'we run this town' comment, nor the mention of someone like me not going unnoticed.

How many other places had my presence been noted? Stored away for someone to give the information to Preston—or whoever he hired to find me—leaving a trail of breadcrumbs to this very motel.

My palms went clammy.

I had to leave.

It was that simple.

I had to leave here. I had to be smarter. I had to make decisions that did not involve sleeping with outlaw bikers.

"Why are you here?" I demanded. My voice was even weaker now that fear and reality had set in.

Swiss's eyes narrowed, and all lightness and teasing left his eyes. "Why am I here?" he repeated quietly. Dangerously.

My skin prickled with unease and also desire.

Before I had the chance to inspect why I felt turned on and afraid at the same time—why the fear turned me on even further —Swiss had crossed the distance between us.

His hands were tight at my hips, making it clear that I couldn't escape. He was much, much larger than me. Definitely stronger. I couldn't fight my way out of this.

My past hurtled toward my present, memories of moments like this—when I was weak and helpless—clouding my mind, making everything blurry and sharp at the same time.

"Why am I here?" he said again, puncturing my thoughts.

I swallowed roughly, staring into the chasm of his eyes, desperate to escape but willing to do anything to stay in his gaze, in his arms. Despite everything, it felt safe. He felt safe.

"Were you present last night?" he asked. "I mean, I *know* you were present because I've got the scratches on my back to prove it."

Images flashed through my brain. At some point last night, when he was changing my restraints, I had scratched his back, hadn't I? Been desperate to make some kind of mark. I'd forgotten until now.

Lust smoldered in his eyes, and his words went right between my legs, caressing the places that were delightfully tender from him. His mouth. His cock.

Holy. *Fuck.*

Swiss's expression turned wicked, as if he could read my mind, as if he could feel what he was doing to me. "Since you were present last night, you should know that that's not something I'm gonna let happen only once." He brushed the hair from my face. "I'm planning on getting to know every inch of you, fucking you in ways you couldn't even imagine."

Holy. *Fuck.*

My mind went cloudy for a second. Okay, longer than a second. I let myself savor in the feeling of his hands on my body, his promises. The way every single nerve, every single fricking cell came alive in his presence.

It was tempting to give in to that again. To him. To let him take control, to forget about everything else.

But everything else was my survival. It was my daughter. It was my future. And I could not let that be dictated by a man. Even one as hot as Swiss. Especially one as hot as Swiss.

"You can't just turn up at my motel," I told him, a bite in my voice.

"Why not?" he asked, folding his arms across his chest casually.

I tried and failed not to look at the way his muscles bulged when he did that.

"Because..." I said, trying to find the reason why he could not just turn up at my motel.

"Didn't have your number," he said, filling my pause. "And you snuck out before I woke up." His eyes narrowed at me. "Which I'm not happy about, by the way. So I was left with no other choice but to turn up at your motel."

"Why would you be unhappy about me leaving?" I asked with real confusion. "Isn't that what you wanted?"

"What I wanted?" he repeated. "Fuck no, sweetheart. What I wanted was to wake up and taste your pussy first thing in the mornin'."

My face flamed. "You can't speak like that," I hissed, looking around.

The motel parking lot was absolutely deserted, the only person around being a woman lounging by the pool with headphones on.

Swiss was grinning now. "Why can't I?"

My eyes zoomed back to him. "Because it's crass," I answered lamely, sounding everything like the uppity suburban housewife I was.

Rather than being offended by my judgment, Swiss's grin widened. "By the way, your nipples are getting hard in that shirt. You like my being crass," he shot back.

Crap.

He was right.

I moved my arms to cover the aforementioned nipples, but the damage was already done. "We were just a one-night stand," I hissed. "There is no need for you to come here. In fact, it was a wasted trip. I'm leaving town. Tonight."

This decision was made on the fly, made out of fear, and it immediately felt wrong. Where else did I have to go? Another small town, most likely without the kickass coffee shop and offer of a job, with a roadside motel that wasn't as clean, comfortable or as affordable as this.

Swiss was no longer smiling.

"You're comin' to the club with me," he declared.

I tilted my head. "Didn't you hear me?" I asked. "I'm leaving town."

"Heard you well and good, Countess," he replied.

"Countess?" I repeated, momentarily distracted.

His eyes were twinkling again. "Even in jeans, baby, you make it clear you come from money. You got manners, the way you carry yourself, the way you speak..." he trailed off, brushing my bottom lip with his thumb.

My breathing was so shallow it was almost non-existent. He was wrong. I did not come from money. I came from lower-middle class with a gold digger for a mother. My husband came from money, and I was just well trained.

I didn't say any of this. I didn't speak at all, actually.

"You're fancy, Kate," he murmured. "And it was my great fucking pleasure to fuck all that fancy outta you. Not that I want it gone completely. It's sexy as fuck." His hand flexed at my hip.

"So you're gonna get on the back of my bike, we're gonna go to the clubhouse, and I'm gonna spend some time fuckin' the fancy right out of you again," he said.

I blinked at him, digesting all of the words. They went down smooth. Like chocolate. Like an aged whisky.

What else could a girl do?

I got on the back of his bike.

I had never ridden on the back of a motorcycle. There was never really the opportunity for me to do such things.

Our high school did not even have the quintessential bad boy who smoked, skipped class, and ruined the names of the good, quiet girls.

Our town was too fancy for that.

The bad boys were all shipped out to the next town over, where the 'riffraff' culminated.

Had I lived out the trajectory that my life should've gone in—the alternate universe where I never met or got impregnated by Preston because I myself was shipped to the next town over—there was a high likelihood I would've found myself on the back of a motorcycle at some point. There was also a high likelihood I would've got addicted to drugs and chained to some loser with a drinking problem who lived in a beat-up trailer.

I'd put a lot of thought into that alternate reality over the years. Sometimes I'd wished to be sitting in a beaten down trailer, next to my overweight, overserved, douchebag husband. It would've been a lot more honest than the glossy nightmare I'd been living in.

But then I never would've had Violet. And my daughter was worth every second of that hellish landscape I'd lived in. I would never, could never, wish her away.

I thought of her while riding on that motorcycle with Swiss. Pressed up against his warm and muscled back, my hands around his middle, holding him tightly.

The wind was cool against my skin, a welcome respite since I'd spent the day feeling damp and overheated.

It was like a form of meditation, what I'd pretended to do

after the hot yoga classes I went to. My mind could never be that still, that calm, that safe for such things.

Riding on the back of a motorcycle with a man I'd just met—and slept with—the night before wasn't exactly safe either.

But it was the closest thing to meditation I'd ever come to.

———

Swiss's eyes were glowing as we got off the bike, staring at me with satisfaction.

"You've never been on the back of a bike before, have you, Countess?" he asked, warmth in his voice.

I didn't trust myself to speak. Instead, I just shook my head slowly.

He stepped forward to grasp my hips, yanking our bodies flush. His hand framed my face, skimming around my neck to yank me forward.

Our mouths met easily. Hungrily.

I was surprised I was still standing when he ended the kiss. I *hated* that he ended it. But if he kept it going any longer, we would've been having sex right there in the parking lot.

His mouth hovered inches from mine. "Popped your cherry," he observed, voice lower and throatier now.

I didn't say anything. In fact, I let out a weird and horrendously embarrassing little moan that was mixed with a ... squeak? Did I just moan-squeak in one of the hottest moments of my life?

Yes, yes I did.

"Let's get you inside," he said, voice still thick with sex, obviously—and thankfully—not turned off by my moan-squeak.

He slung his arm around my shoulders, pulling me close to him and walking toward the club.

I'd never had someone show me affection the way he was.

Not in the eighteen years of marriage with Preston had I experienced such a natural, confident and authentic form of affection such as walking together like this.

Then again, Preston's form of affection was physical abuse.

There were good times, plenty of them, it wasn't all terror and misery. Even I wasn't so spineless as to stay with a man who constantly tortured and abused me. But even when things were good, they weren't easy like this. Preston, I was discovering, was not a confident man. He played one very well, but everything he did, down to his facial expressions and the way he touched me in public, was carefully thought through, dissected. He had no idea who he truly was.

Swiss knew exactly who he was and what he wanted.

At that very moment, it was me. He wanted me, and he had no qualms about making that known. There were no games, no playing hard to get as I had seen on sitcoms as the classic way dating was performed these days.

None of that.

Just him waiting outside my motel and spiriting back to his biker clubhouse.

He even opened the door for me.

The club was much quieter than it had been last night.

It was almost deserted.

And the common room was impeccably clean. As if it hadn't been littered with bottles and naked bodies when I left this morning.

There was an expensive scented candle burning on top of the coffee table. The coffee table with coasters, books and flowers neatly arranged on top of it.

Freaking *flowers*.

Every stereotype that I'd prepared for this club—for the man behind me—kept getting shattered, so I told myself to stop expecting things and just start experiencing them.

"Want a drink or anything?" Swiss asked from beside me, nodding to the fully stocked bar.

I shook my head. "I just want you."

The words were out of my mouth before I could think too much about them. I was surprised at myself for being so brazen, for saying something like that out loud—while stone cold sober nonetheless, not counting the beer I had with Julian.

There was a small pause after I spoke, and I suddenly felt self-conscious. Did people really say that in real life? Did it sound pathetic and desperate?

Swiss answered both of those questions when he pulled me in for another kiss, again stopping it before it could be considered R-rated.

"Jesus," he muttered. "It's like I dreamed you up." I smiled lazily. His fingers brushed my lips. "Yeah, I need to fuck you in the next five minutes, or I might go insane."

Holy crap.

He walked us back down a familiar hallway, and my blood pumped hot through my body. I was tense as we walked past the other doors, nervous about encountering someone. I was barely just handling one outlaw biker, and I was completely out of my element. I wasn't ready to socialize with anyone.

Beyond that, there was no thumping music like there was last night, nothing to mask the unmistakable sounds of sex. To mask the sounds that I couldn't help but make. There would be no way I'd be comfortable having sex in such close quarters if we did see someone else.

Luckily, we encountered no one on the short trip to Swiss's room. Without the haze of alcohol and the overstimulation from the night before, I caught myself thinking about the logistics of this situation. Did Swiss live here full-time? Did they all live here? Or was this some kind of crash pad scenario? Where they could bring women they wanted to have sex with without having to take them home?

Those questions, though important, did not stay in my mind for long because we entered Swiss's room, and he closed the door behind us.

Everything looked the same as it did last night except it was daylight now.

I stared at the messy bed, frowning ever so slightly.

Swiss caught my frown.

His hand caught my chin, moving it upward so his eyes found mine.

"You frownin', looking at the bed I plan on fuckin' you in isn't giving me warm fuzzies," he told me, his voice rough.

My stomach clenched at his words, desire spreading through my blood.

"You didn't make your bed," I said, realizing how utterly stupid commenting on that was.

His eyes twinkled ever so slightly. "I did not," he agreed.

I pursed my lips at his response. "It was made last night," I commented.

His eye twinkled more. "It was."

I narrowed my eyes at him. "Well, making your bed every morning is an important ritual to incorporate into your daily life," I told him, mortified once I heard the words out loud. I sounded uptight, like a mother scolding her child.

But I couldn't suck them back in. It was too late for that.

"An important ritual, huh?" Swiss asked, teasing in his tone.

I pursed my lips tighter. "Yes," I replied, a snap to my tone. "It sets you up for the entire day."

Swiss's hands settled on my hips now, pulling me so our

bodies were pressed together, and I could feel that this conversation was not turning him off in the slightest.

My blood turned hotter with need.

"Eating your pussy this morning would've set me up for the entire day," he rasped, mouth inches from mine.

"In addition to that, seeing those sheets all tangled from you." One of his hands moved from my hip, upward, underneath the fabric of my tank.

I let out a rough gasp at his callused hand running over my bare skin and inside the fabric of my bra.

He tweaked my nipple with the perfect amount of pressure.

"Seein' those sheets all tangled from you," he repeated, gaze hungrier now. "Knowin' that I was going to be putting you right back in that bed at the end of the day... What was the point in makin' it?"

I pursed my lips. I couldn't really argue with that logic.

"Let me ask you a question, Countess." He was shrugging off his vest—no it was called a *cut,* thanks to my googling—then placed it on the back of a chair. Placed it carefully. With reverence. I took note of that, storing it away with all of my other little tidbits about this man. Maybe because I knew that I had to leave him, and I wanted to visit these memories, savor them, long after I was gone.

He turned to face me, his expression wicked. Wicked in a way that made my stomach flip.

"Do you like to be punished?" he purred.

For a split second, my mind hurtled away from this room, all the way back to the home I'd escaped. The life I'd escaped.

"You like laughing at other men's jokes?" Preston asked quietly.

He was advancing on me, and I knew better than to retreat despite all of my instincts screaming at me to do so.

"I was being polite," I said on a whimper.

I knew the blow was coming before his backhand made contact.

My head whipped to the side, and my cheek burned. It was not enough force to push me to the ground. A blow of that magnitude would leave a mark on my face. Preston was very precise with his hits.

He grasped on to my chin so he could force my head back around, so I could make contact with his ice blue eyes.

"You were being a thirsty little slut," he murmured. "And for that, you need to be punished."

A hand on my chin pulled me back into the present. I was met with espresso-colored eyes. They were still full of sex, but there was an edge of concern there.

"Kate?" Swiss murmured.

I pushed away all of those terrible memories, pushed away the part of myself that was controlled by them, instead focusing on Swiss's hand on my chin.

"Do I like to be punished?" I repeated, my voice a purr of its own.

His eyes flared, and my body responded instinctively.

"Why yes, I love to be punished," I whispered.

That coldness overtook his face, the same from last night. But it was not cruel, divest of feeling, as I had the proof of. It was something else. He was someone else when he got into this room, this zone. There were no smiles, no easy jokes.

No, this was utterly serious. And somehow, that turned me on. I responded to the structure of it. Of him. Knowing that in this room, it was only him and me. Nothing else existed. No one knew I was here. It was... liberating.

"You left this morning," he said quietly. "When I was

nowhere near done with you." His hands went to the bottom of my shirt, peeling it off.

I shivered in delight as he did the same with my bra, his fingers brushing against my skin.

My nipples pebbled as he exposed them.

But he didn't look there. His gaze had not left my face.

"You're gonna bend over the bed," he told me, unbuttoning my jeans.

My heart thundered as I did what he said.

In what felt like seconds, my jeans were rolled down to my ankles, and I stepped out of them. Swiss gently kicked at my legs, widening my stance.

I sucked in a breath as his hand caressed me there, for just a moment, then it was gone.

My breathing was rapid and shallow as Swiss walked around the room, the rattle of a drawer opening causing my stomach to clench in anticipation.

Something cold and foreign ran over my ass as I fisted the sheets.

"I'm not gonna ease you into this, Countess," Swiss informed me, his voice ice. "You're gonna take what I give. You're gonna hurt. And you're gonna fucking love it."

Then, that cold and foreign thing made contact with my ass.

I let out a hiss. It did hurt. The sting radiated through my skin. And I didn't have time to breathe through it because another blow landed in the exact same spot. My teeth sank into my lips, and I tasted blood.

Swiss's hand rubbed the skin that was burning, that I knew was an angry red. Then he slipped his finger forward, to where I needed him most.

"Soaking fuckin' wet," he rasped, coating his fingers with me.

My body coiled up from that touch, already ready to explode.

He was right... I did love the pain.

There was no chance to explore how screwed up that was because his fingers were no longer there, and the cane came down again.

Instantly, I was wetter, more tense, every nerve ending on fire.

Swiss was merciless. He did not give me respite. He was not going easy on me. But I knew that if I made a sound, if I whined, if I gave any inclination that I wasn't liking this, he would stop. The intensity that he looked at me with told me he was cataloguing every inch of me, paying attention, noting things.

But I didn't move my palms from the bed. Didn't say a word. Not even as my skin burned, and I wondered whether I could take any more.

Not just because of the pain, but because I was right on the edge of climax. Without him touching me. With him *hurting* me.

Just as I was tensing for the next blow, nothing came.

Something fell to the floor. Swiss's belt clinked. Foil crinkled.

There were hands at my hips, and then he surged into me.

I came immediately.

"Yeah," he grunted as I exploded around him. "You were fuckin' made for me, Countess. And I'm far from fuckin' done with you."

Then he spent a long time proving that.

CHAPTER SIX

Kate

"I need sustenance," I declared, my voice breathless and ragged.

Which made sense since I hadn't exactly been using it for conversation these past hours.

Hours.

My limbs burned from exertion. My skin was electrified. My ass still stung. My mind light and heavy at the same time. I'd never felt so exhausted, so satisfied, so *starving* in my entire life.

The arms around me flexed, and I was moved so I was no longer splayed on top of his muscled torso, moving me *underneath* that muscled torso.

Swiss braced himself on his elbows, not giving me his full weight. His eyes danced as he caught my gaze, not looking at all tired after everything we'd done together.

The stamina of this man was beyond impressive.

"You need sustenance?" he repeated playfully.

A blush bloomed in my cheeks. I had no idea why his lighthearted tone caused me to blush considering what he just did to me.

I nodded instead of replying.

"Is that your fancy ass way of sayin' you're hungry?" he teased.

I bit my lip. "I don't consider it overly fancy," I said, a grin teasing the edges of my mouth. "But yes, a more common expression would be to say I am hungry."

Swiss's eyes danced with amusement. And something warm. Something that made me feel like someone.

Made me feel worth something.

And that there was the difference. That *he* was why I could let him hurt me without my trauma triggering me, without having a mental breakdown. It was almost... liberating to take ownership of myself in that way. To redefine the experiences, the horrible ways in which Preston had hurt and controlled me. Because even though Swiss was the one holding the strap, tying me up, marking my body, I felt powerful. In control the entire time.

A therapist would likely have a lot to say about so quickly trying to erase old memories with new ones. And none of those things would be positive. Maybe I was screwing myself up even more.

But I wasn't going to overthink it. At least, I was going to try my best not to overthink it. I was just going to... be. Follow my instincts.

Swiss sat up in bed, taking me with him and somehow setting me down on unsteady feet. Even though I still needed to gain a few pounds, I was not exactly light, so him lifting me from a horizontal position was pretty darn impressive.

"Let's go get you some food then," he declared, kissing my forehead then walking over to retrieve his clothes.

I stood exactly where he put me, watching, rapt as he pulled on his jeans—commando—and slung a tee over his head.

Swiss's eyes found me. "You keep lookin' at me like that, standing there naked, food is gonna be a distant memory, darlin'."

I swallowed roughly, my body needful, despite the—three?—orgasms I'd had not minutes ago. My stomach protested at the pause I made, and I realized I hadn't eaten but a few bites of a muffin today, and had done more physical work than ever.

I quickly moved to retrieve my clothes, but Swiss stopped me.

"Nah," he said, circling my wrist that was holding my tank. "Want you in my tee."

I dropped my tank and straightened, taking the clothing from his hands. Before I put it on, I lifted it and inhaled, smiling at the mix of fragrances that were unique to him.

Then I realized that I'd just smelled an item of his clothing right in front of him, and that probably made me seem like a serial killer or something. I quickly shoved the shirt over my head, my face hot with embarrassment. The shirt was soft. Softer than French silk. It had been washed so many times it was thin, cozy. Though I had curves, I was a good deal shorter than Swiss which meant the shirt was more like a dress on me.

Once I was brave enough to swallow most of my embarrassment, I looked back up at him.

His expression was a punch in the stomach. There was heat in his eyes, yes, but not the same kind of inferno from earlier. Not a desperate, carnal hunger. No. This was something else. Tender. Reverent.

Pure.

"Like you in my tee, baby," he said softly.

I didn't reply. I couldn't.

We lingered in the moment longer than we should've. Something passed between us. Something that shouldn't have existed after only two nights together. Between two practical strangers with lives, personalities, secrets outside of what we'd shown each other, outside of this room.

But it existed nonetheless.

"Food," I broke the silence on a hoarse whisper.

He jerked. "Food," he agreed.

He walked toward the door, opening it for me.

I hesitated for a second before crossing the threshold. This room was small. It smelled like sex, like Swiss. This was our own little universe. Though it was the middle of the night and there wasn't likely to be anyone roaming the halls—the lack of music thumping from the common area told me there was no wild party going on—I still couldn't shake the feeling that stepping out of this room was dangerous. Fear was a state of mind for me, and I'd pushed my limits enough these past few days.

But I also had to eat.

I was debating how much of a coward/bitch I'd sound like if I asked Swiss to retrieve food for me while I curled back into bed when he spoke.

"Scared, Countess?" Swiss's breath was hot against my neck, and shivers went down my spine as his front pressed into my back.

"No," I hiccupped.

"I can promise you, anything out there isn't gonna bite half as hard as I do," he rasped, nuzzling my neck.

Another shiver. This one a whole-body shiver.

"I can promise you the fridge is well stocked too, and clean," he added. "If that's what you're afraid of. We keep a clean house. And we shop at Whole Foods."

I choked out a laugh.

Swiss kissed my neck and then gave me a gentle nudge out

the door. As stupid as it sounded, I wasn't afraid of anything as long as he was beside me.

———

Though it was close to two in the morning and the clubhouse was quiet, it did not mean it was deserted.

I found that out when we made it to the kitchen. The extremely impressive kitchen.

I wasn't expecting a whole lot since we were in a biker clubhouse. But thinking about the scented candles, the pillows on the sofa, the understated style of the whole place, I shouldn't have been that surprised.

The kitchen was large. Like a kitchen in a fancy frat house or restaurant kitchen, complete with a restaurant quality stove and gigantic refrigerator. There was a gleaming kitchen island, neatly arranged olive oil and vinegar cruets, even fricking *cookbooks*.

It almost looked like I'd wandered into a Nancy Myers movie.

Except for the three men standing in the kitchen drinking beers, passing around a bag of chips, wearing cuts, and all of whom stared at me the second I walked in.

One of them I recognized. The one from the gas station. The one who had almost had a fight with Swiss.

Over me.

The other two, I didn't. One was older, maybe my age. He was tall, muscled—that must've been a signing requirement or something—with a dark beard streaked with gray. His eyes were an unnerving shade of blue.

The third man was leaner than the rest. And had a completely different look. The first two really embodied the traditional 'biker' aesthetic. Beard, tattoos, overall aura of baddassery.

Not that the third didn't look like a badass. He did. But not a biker. He looked more like a... hipster. I only knew that term because of Violet, who was my tutor on all things popular culture.

His long hair was pulled into a man bun, and he was wearing thick rimmed, black glasses. He was covered in tattoos, his lean forearms showing that from the dress shirt he was wearing with the sleeves rolled up, buttoned all the way to the top. And he had on skintight black jeans tucked into worn Doc Martens.

They were an interesting threesome. A hot as balls threesome.

And all of their eyes were on me.

Standing in Swiss's tee and nothing else. My hair likely mussed from the bed and my cheeks probably still flushed from all of the sex and the embarrassment that I was standing in front of these men wearing nothing but a t-shirt. No bra. No panties. My ass bright red and covered with welts from where Swiss had spanked me with a cane.

"I know you," the one from the gas station drawled, grinning.

"Um, hello," I greeted with a lame little wave. "I'm Kate. I don't think we've had the opportunity to exactly exchange names, but it's, ah, a pleasure to meet you," I stuttered, wanting to turn and run, but the manners that were beat into me stopped me.

"Cody," he said, pointing to his muscled chest. "Elden," he nodded to the man directly beside him.

"Lucas," the hipster one offered.

I smiled at them all, my body burning with discomfort, and at a loss of what to do, I did a little curtsy thing.

A curtsy.

I just curtsied to three outlaw bikers while clad in another man's t-shirt.

Oh my god, was this my first day on Earth?

It kind of was, since this was definitely a whole different world than the one I was used to.

All three men were grinning at me now.

Well, except Elden, the older one in the middle. He had a little upward tilt to his mouth which was what I guessed was his version of a smile.

Now that I'd adequately humiliated myself, it was time to run.

"If you'll excuse me," I said quietly, mortified. I whirled on my heel, intent on escape of any kind.

It was then I was faced with Swiss, who had been silent during the entire interaction and hadn't jumped in to save me from myself. Then again, he wasn't someone who professed to be a hero of any kind.

He was leaning against the doorjamb, grinning from ear to ear, obviously having seen the entire ridiculous exchange.

I did not find anything about this funny, and all my fond feelings for this man dissipated immediately. My bare feet stomped in solidarity with that feeling, but his body blocked me when it became clear that I was heading for the door.

I stopped inches from him, careful not to get too close, and restraining the urge to use both hands to push him out of the way. Violence was never the answer. Plus, there was no way in heck I was going to be able to move him even an inch.

"Where you goin'?" he asked.

I stared up at him. Which was a decent way since I was barefoot, and he was much taller than me. "I'm going to find some pants," I stage whispered.

He frowned. "Why do you need pants?"

My eyes widened. "Um, I don't know, since there are a bunch of other people here, and I don't want to show my ass to all of your friends?"

Swiss grinned. "Coupla things... First off, that shirt damn near goes down to your knees," he said. "So unless you plan on doin' some acrobatics that I don't know you're capable of, then you're good. Second, these are my brothers. You are wearin' my shirt. Means you are mine. So if by some accident your ass is exposed and their eyes wander anywhere near that direction, they'll be answerin' to me."

Though there was a hint of violence in his tone, it didn't scare me like it should've. It warmed me.

"Not that they are that stupid," he added, his eyes flickering behind me before meeting my gaze once more. "Though I know they don't exactly look it, these are respectful men. Well, maybe not. They're fuckin' scoundrels, honestly. But one thing we all do in this club is respect women. They aren't lookin' anywhere but at that gorgeous face, sweetheart. And if they look at it in a way I don't like, then God have mercy on their souls."

I was blinking rapidly, trying to process everything he just said.

But he wasn't done...

His hand stroked my face gently, tucking some rogue strands of hair behind my ear. "But if you don't feel comfortable wearin' my shirt, then you go change. Just know you're safe here. Safe with me."

Though I had years of experience—actually a lifetime—proven to me that men couldn't be trusted, and I certainly was not safe with them, I believed Swiss. Down to my soul.

I stared at him a long time, forgetting all about the people around us. "Okay, I'll wear your shirt," I whispered quietly, my voice thick with emotion.

Swiss nodded sharply then bent to kiss me gently on the mouth. "Good," he murmured.

His eyes went behind me. "What are you fuckers doin' here?" he asked.

Cody popped a grape into his mouth. "Just got back from a run."

I had no idea what a 'run' was, but I guessed it was some biker task that required the cover of darkness.

"Well, don't think you're gonna get a bite of what I make," Swiss told the men. "I'm cookin' for my woman and my woman only."

My woman.

He just said that.

To his badass biker buddies.

I gazed up at him. "You're going to cook for me?" I asked quietly.

He looked down. "Well, of course. I'm not going to expect you to be barefoot in the kitchen, I'm a feminist."

Cue stomach jump.

"He's also a terrible fuckin' cook," Cody put in, breaking the gaze between us.

"Him serving you food could actually be legally considered as attempted murder," Lucas added with a grin.

Swiss glowered at them. "Fuck off," he growled.

I smiled and patted Swiss's chest. "I appreciate how progressive you are," I told him sincerely. "But I've cooked for a lot of people and haven't poisoned one yet. Beyond that, I'm very excited about the stove and would revel in the opportunity to utilize it."

Swiss blinked at me. "You're excited about the *stove*?"

I nodded. "It's chef's quality. High-end kitchens use this stove."

His eyes danced. "Do they now?" he asked in a tone that raised gooseflesh on my skin.

I nodded hesitantly and then looked to the men who were watching us. "If y'all are hungry, I'd be happy to make extra," I offered.

"Fuck yeah," Cody said at the same time Swiss grumbled, "Hell fuckin' no."

I smirked once more before going up on my tiptoes to kiss Swiss's nose. A gesture that I didn't think about, one that was much too intimate, but it was too late to take it back.

"I don't mind," I told him, blushing and moving away quickly before I could see his expression.

I figured that badass bikers didn't like women kissing them on the nose in front of their buddies.

But Swiss proved me wrong by catching hold of my wrist and yanking me back to him. Then he kissed me.

Not on the nose.

On the mouth.

With tongue.

In front of his buddies.

"Appreciate you, baby," he murmured against my mouth.

Then he let me go. As if he expected me to walk around on two feet after that.

I managed.

Barely.

And I was uber aware of four sets of male eyes on me as I walked around the kitchen island toward the fridge. They might've spoken, to each other or to me, but I couldn't hear anything beyond the low ringing in my ears and...

"Appreciate you, baby."

Not once, not once in eighteen years of marriage had Preston told me he appreciated me. Nor had he thanked me for keeping the house clean, for hosting his business dinners, for surviving the terrible wives, for serving him all of his food and cleaning every single one of his dishes.

For hiding my bruises under makeup and lying about the wince that my mother-in-law caught while I was reaching for a salad plate.

Not once.

But Swiss said it. Easily. After two nights together. Like it was natural. Like it was as easy as breathing.

Luckily, I was distracted enough by opening the fridge and marveling at all of the ingredients in it, giving me something to focus on.

Swiss hadn't been kidding. They were fully stocked up. With fresh, organic ingredients.

Grass fed butter, fresh herbs, every kind of meat imaginable. Fricking oat milk.

It was a total dream.

I stood in front of the fridge for a good five minutes, cataloguing everything and figuring out what would be the tastiest and quickest.

Once I decided on penne alla vodka, I closed the fridge with my arms full of the classic ingredients and some things I added to make it 'mine.'

Warmth appeared at my hip. Warmth attached to a tall, muscled, impossibly sexy man. Then the clink of a glass sounded on the stone kitchen counter.

"Figured you for a red wine drinker, Countess," he said, kissing the side of my neck before walking back to the man huddle at the kitchen island.

He didn't wait for me to thank him, to shower him with praise for performing the simple, thoughtful act.

My hand was shaking as I took the wine glass and took a long and grateful sip. Then I focused on chopping, thankful I could use the onions as an excuse for the moisture in my eyes.

"Holy fuck!" Cody exclaimed.

Or more like shouted.

"I have never eaten anything this good in my fucking life," he continued around a mouthful of pasta.

"If I had a child, I would sell that child for one more bite of this," Lucas added, running bread along his plate to catch the last traces of sauce.

"You can stay," was all Elden said, which I'm pretty sure was his stamp of approval.

My own plate was clean because I had not realized just how starving I was. When it came time to serve everything up, Swiss had helped me put everyone's plates on the dining table—with cloth napkins and everything, *cloth napkins...* What universe had I entered into? —and he'd looked at the portions I'd served up. Obviously the men had gotten large portions because they were, well, large.

My own was modestly small. Tiny, really. I'd done that out of instinct, ignoring my gnawing hunger that had only grown more intense as the fragrance wafted up from the plates.

For years, I'd honed what portion to give myself based on Preston's expectations, based on what would maintain my weight. Overeating and gluttony were unattractive to Preston.

Swiss hadn't said a word as he switched our plates. His was the largest. I'd opened my mouth to argue.

"Don't say a fuckin' word, Countess," he grumbled, picking up his fork. "Eat."

Because I was so shocked, and because muscle memory set in, I did as he commanded.

There was conversation during the meal but not much. Mostly just the clang of forks against plates.

Swiss's hand was on my bare thigh the entire meal.

I'd only been able to function because I was so starving and had eaten every single bite.

Which brought us to now, when I was getting showered with praise and didn't quite know what to do with it.

"It's just pasta," I said quietly.

"Just pasta?" Cody repeated. He shook his head. "No. That is not just pasta. That is fucking sorcery."

Heat crept up my neck. "It's a simple recipe. And I didn't simmer it for as long—"

"Nope," Swiss interrupted. "I can tell you're going to try and criticize either yourself or that meal, and I'm not fuckin' havin' it." He squeezed my thigh and looked to the other men at the table. "I trust you fuckers can clean up all of this since my woman was generous enough to cook you an incredible meal. Now, if you'll excuse us..." He pushed up from his chair, lifted me from mine, threw me over his shoulder, and carried me out of the room.

Carried me out of the room.

And somehow, he managed to expertly move so none of my private parts flashed the men at the table as he did so.

And that concluded one of the best nights of my life.

Well, there was still a little bit to go.

"I was serious, you know," I whispered into the darkness. I couldn't be sure that Swiss was even still awake, but his breathing had a cadence that hinted to him being alert.

"About what?" he asked, voice low and thick.

"About leaving," I said.

His arms tightened around me, and he didn't respond for the longest time. "Why?"

His voice was quieter now. Softer. Curious. But with an edge.

I sighed. Why was such a simple question. With such a messy, complicated answer.

The truth hovered on my tongue. I could tell Swiss everything. All of it.

There was something inside of me that told me he could fix things somehow. Get me out of this situation. Hadn't I seen the news stories about biker gangs helping battered women get their things out of their houses when they left their husbands?

Battered women.

That's what I was. *A battered wife.*

And a sixth sense told me that somehow, this man whose arms were around me, would fix it.

But that would turn me into a battered woman to him. Nothing else. I would cease to be Kate, the woman who was traveling around the country after her divorce, Kate who was brazen enough to go to a biker party all on her own and proposition the first man she saw.

It would make everything real. There would be an urgency to fix it all, to stray from this fantasy.

I was not ready to do that yet. I was comfortable in my denial.

"Because leaving is the... sensible thing to do," I answered, hating myself.

"The sensible thing," Swiss repeated after a long moment.

I didn't reply because I couldn't force any lies out of my

mouth. Lying by omission was still lying, something I'd drilled into Violet when she was entering her teen years.

Swiss pulled me suddenly so I was straddling him. My hands landed on his pecs for balance. They were warm, hard. His hands went to either side of my hips, grinding me against him.

I let out a hiss as my sensitive flesh rubbed against his hard cock.

"Countess, I've got a feeling that you've spent your life doing the 'sensible thing,'" he murmured.

I struggled to maintain a coherent thought, my body yearning for him despite all the sex we'd had in the past twelve hours.

"I may or may not have," I told him, deciding not to dive into the intricacies about whether staying with an abusive husband could be defined as 'sensible.' "But walking into this club was the least sensible thing I've done in my entire existence."

Swiss's fingers pressed into my hips. "No, baby, walking into this bedroom was the least sensible thing you've done in your life," he countered. "And I'm fuckin' thankful for that. I'm not here to make sure you do what's most sensible."

He continued to grind me against him, my breath becoming shallower and shallower.

"In fact," he murmured. "My job is to make sure you don't do anything sensible like leave."

He lifted me up so he could lower me onto him. So he could plunge into me.

My body accommodated his length... just barely. It was as if he were made for me. Or I was made for him. Pleasure shot through me to my fingertips.

Swiss's hands landed back on my hips to hold me stationary. I tried to fight against him, needing movement and friction, but he was much too strong for that.

"My job," Swiss ground out, his voice thick with pleasure. "Is to keep you here, with me."

His hands stopped restraining me and helped move me in the way I needed.

My breath quickened as I rocked in rhythm with him, my body coiling up in preparation for release.

"Fair warnin', Countess," Swiss grunted. "I'm going to do everything in my considerable power to ensure that you stay here. With me."

His words sank into my skin, wrapping me up in him. In us.

My skin heated up, my very insides starting to turn to flames.

One of Swiss's hands stayed at my hip while the other went to the back of my neck to pull me down, closer to him.

The grip bordered on painful, and my body responded to that pain with immediate pleasure, my climax hurtling toward me.

"Tell me," he demanded, voice hoarse.

My breathing was too rapid to get any words out.

"Tell me," he growled, tightening his grip. "Tell me that you're not going to leave me, Kate."

My blood thrummed, sang for him. "I'm not going to leave you," I vowed.

And that's what it felt like. A vow.

One I surely couldn't keep. But one I made nonetheless.

CHAPTER SEVEN

KATE

I DID NOT SNEAK out the next morning.

Swiss woke up before me.

And he woke me up with his mouth.

Then his dick.

Suffice it to say, it was almost noon before we got out of bed.

I had never stayed in bed 'til noon.

Ever.

Even when I was sick with a horrendous flu and had a temperature of over one hundred, I was up making Preston's egg white omelet at six in the morning. Even without my expectant, abusive husband, there was Violet. She loved to sleep. Ever since she was a baby. It was quite concerning at first. And once she started school, I had to physically pull her out of bed.

She was a dreamer, my girl.

Then there were her lunches I had to make, no processed

food or sugar, everything fresh, homemade. There was inevitably some kind of event or bake sale I had to contribute to.

Moms didn't get to sleep in.

Even during this whole... road trip? Psychotic break? I'd kept my regular hours, both out of routine and fear. I hadn't been sleeping well at all. Nightmares.

Except for the two nights I'd had with Swiss when I'd slept like the dead.

After we woke up the most hedonistic way a person could wake up, we took a shower together.

I was delighted that Swiss's small but cozy room also had an attached bathroom. I'd feared some kind of communal scenario before I'd seen it. It was a decent size too. And clean. There were a few products littering the vanity, products that were now arranged neatly.

Swiss stared at them. "Countess, did you organize my toiletries?" he asked slowly, sounding like he was choking back a laugh.

I bit my lip. "I couldn't help myself," I blurted. "I was in here, you know, using the facilities." My face flamed with the realization that I was talking to Swiss about *peeing*. "And after washing my hands, I just... straightened things up." I threw my hands up in the air in surrender. "Mom habit." I looked down then back up at him. "Do you think I'm terribly lame?"

His eyes were soft, dancing with amusement. "No, baby, I think you're the cutest and sexiest woman I've ever had the honor to know."

Holy. Crap.

I hadn't had a moment to process that because at that moment, he grabbed on to me and hauled me into the shower where he fucked me again.

Because of my post orgasm haze, it was only when he was

about halfway through cleaning me that I realized what he was cleaning me with.

"Is that two-in-one?" I asked, blinking to try to focus on the red bottle in his hand.

To be fair, being in the shower with Swiss, there were a lot of other, more important things to focus on rather than a red bottle of shampoo.

"What?" he asked, his fingers working my scalp as he massaged the shampoo into my hair.

With lead arms, I managed to snatch the bottle from him. "Oh my god," I whispered. "This is three-in-one."

"What the fuck does that mean?" he asked, moving his hands to shield my head so the shampoo did not roll down into my eyes.

"It means that this should be burned in a fire," I said, holding up the bottle. "This says it works as shampoo, conditioner and body wash. I yanked it closer to my face, squinting. "And face wash! It's *a four-in-one*. Criminal. Absolutely criminal."

"It's soap, baby," was Swiss's response, laughter in his tone.

I tried to look up at him, but he pulled my head gently backward to wash the offending 'soap' from my hair. "It is not soap," I argued. "This is not something any individual should own. It's especially criminal that your skin looks how it does, and all you've been using is this!" I held up the bottle for emphasis.

"How does my skin look?" he teased.

"Perfect!" I cried. "Which makes no sense."

He laughed. It was low and throaty and like butter.

He pulled me to his wet, naked body—how was I talking about soap right now?—tilting my head upward now that my hair had been rinsed out. "Countess, my genetic makeup means I'm blessed with pretty good fuckin' skin regardless of what kind of shit I put on it."

I pouted since it was true.

"Though we'll make a run to Walgreens or your motel to get toiletries that don't horrify you so much," he added.

As the words sank in, I realized what they meant. They meant that he thought I was going to be here long enough to put shampoo and conditioner in his shower.

My mind wandered to his words from last night. The promise I'd made.

Swiss didn't notice me ruminating on that for the rest of the shower, or after when I'd gone through the motions of getting out with him and taking the towel he handed me.

I mean, I wasn't that gone to not notice Swiss drying himself, seeing the way his muscles ripped, how the water trickled down his back.

The back that did indeed have scratches from my nails. But it also had something else.

A tattoo.

Swiss did not have any other tattoos like most of the men in the club. His skin was smooth, unmarred, except for the scars on his body. But this tattoo was a replica of the patch on the back of his cut. A skeleton riding a motorcycle, flames behind him.

'The Sons of Templar MC' at the bottom.

Though I was still learning about what life was like in a motorcycle club, I got the idea that membership was for life. Swiss was serious enough about it to have it inked on his skin.

I watched that ink as he kissed my head, slung the towel around his waist, and walked out of the bathroom.

Then I focused on the task of getting ready for the day... though I had no idea what this day would entail.

Once toweled off, I looked at my naked body in the mirror. It was covered in marks, faint discolorations from the pads of Swiss's fingers. Redness at my wrists and ankles from the bindings he'd used on me. I turned to see raised welts on my ass from his cane. The skin around my neck was slightly red from his hands gripping me there as he came.

This was not the first time I'd catalogued injuries in the mirror given to me by a man. However, it was the first time I'd had marks put on me that I'd chosen. That I'd enjoyed. There was a huge sense of power in that.

Ownership.

Somehow it felt like I was taking my body back, as utterly screwed up as that sounded.

"Like seein' that sexy body with my marks on it," he drawled.

Swiss was standing by the door, watching me.

Naked.

There were plenty of marks on his body from me too. From where my nails had sunk into his skin, clawing at him, desperate to feel his blood on me. Desperate to make a mark, as proof that I existed. Proof that this time with him existed.

"Want to brand you one day too," he added, walking forward.

My eyes widened, and my skin prickled with fear.

And excitement.

"Brand m-me?" I stuttered.

He nodded, grasping my hips, rubbing the area underneath my c-section scar with his thumb.

"Yeah," he said, looking down at it. "In the future, the near future to be sure. I want my name on you. Want my scar on you."

I was utterly and genuinely blown away. For a variety of reasons. Granted I had been out of the game for a long time—technically forever if you looked at my history—but I wasn't aware that branding people was something romantic partners did with one another.

Then again, people lied about what romance was every damn day. Books, movies, people who we had dinners with. If you asked any of them, they'd say mine and Preston's relationship was the most enviable of them all. Was the most 'normal.'

Who was I to think branding someone was outside the realm of possibility? To think it was screwed up?

Except I didn't think it was screwed up. Which made it all the more confusing. I *liked* the idea of it.

What was confusing was that Swiss had known me for such a short time. Unless this too was a common occurrence.

"Is that..." I trailed off, my throat dry. I swallowed and tried again. "Is that something you do with a lot of women?"

I could not suddenly assume that I was special. How narcissistic of me. I'd seen the lifestyle of these men, seen all the women hanging off them at the club party. They were sexually free and open—as they had the right to be, as long as everyone was consenting. Just because I'd lived some square life with good Christian ideals drilled into me did not make me any kind of authority on how many sexual partners one should have, and if one should or should not brand those sexual partners.

Again, as long as everyone was consenting.

Heck, there was probably a whole gaggle of women out there bearing Swiss's brand.

His eyes were stormy as I came out of my head. "No, Kate," he ground out. "That is not something I do with a lot of women." His grip tightened at my hip. "That is not something I've done with any woman."

I blinked at him, my body sagging with relief but my mind still reeling. "Why do you want to do it with me, then?" I whispered.

Swiss stared at me with raw male intensity.

A loud knock on the door made us both jump.

"Get the fuck up, lovebirds. We're having brunch!" a male voice yelled from beyond the door.

I stared at Swiss. "You guys do brunch?" I asked, flabbergasted.

He grinned, showing straight, white teeth. "Babe, our president, sergeant at arms, and second in command all have Old Ladies. Those Old Ladies are generally kick-ass bitches. They are also very intense bitches. Therefore, they are serious about things like scented fucking candles—which I don't hate—flowers—again, nice touch—and brunch."

He kissed me quick and close mouthed. "As much as it probably endangers my cock and balls to say this, I fuckin' love brunch."

I stared at Swiss for a hot second, waiting to see if there was a punchline. There was not one. He was dead serious.

Once I realized that, I threw my head back and laughed.

This biker. The one with the muscles, the air of badassery, the one who moments ago had been talking about *branding me,* loved brunch. And flowers. And scented candles.

Once I got hold of myself, Swiss came back into focus. He was staring at me with that soft, intense look on his face once more. "You're fuckin' stunning when you laugh, Kate," he murmured.

I blinked at him. It was such a simple compliment, but it made me want to burst into tears. I actually had to jab my nail into the inside of my palm in order to stop my eyes from welling up. I was well trained in hiding my emotions, in making sure that no one would glimpse a single trace of a tear in my eye.

Still, Swiss tilted his head ever so slightly and his lips flattened as if he could see the swirl of emotion behind my mask.

I stretched a false smile onto my face. "Shouldn't we get dressed?" I asked, moving out of his grip.

For a second, I worried that he wouldn't let me go, that he would call me out, demand to know what was behind my eyes.

But luckily, his hands only flexed for a moment before he released me. I busied myself with finding my clothes.

"Fair warnin', baby," Swiss said as we dressed. "There's probably gonna be a bunch of nosy fuckers out there," he nodded in the direction of the common room, "waiting to meet you."

"Me?" I repeated as I buttoned my jeans. I was wearing the same clothes as yesterday. Although Swiss had tried to insist I wear his tee again, I argued it wouldn't work as well in daylight. He did not agree, but he also didn't push the matter.

"Why would anyone want to meet me?" I asked, nerves building up.

His head drew back at my words, and he walked over to me, lifting his hands to smooth my wayward hair. "Why the fuck wouldn't anyone want to meet you?" he asked, kissing my forehead.

Although I was of the opinion that any kind of kiss from Swiss was absolute heaven, there was something about the forehead kiss that just... hit different, as Violet would say.

"Cody and Lucas have probably been gossiping like old ladies at a hair salon since the moment we left the room last night," he continued, still holding onto me, his hands now at the back of my neck. "Singing your praises," he clarified, as if he could sense the doubt and dread in my stomach.

Something in his expression changed, turning slightly uneasy. It was the first time I'd seen this man unsure of himself.

"On top of that," he said slowly. "I have somewhat of a... reputation around the club."

I looked at him more closely, as if I'd find an explanation. "A reputation?" I repeated, thinking the worst. Was he some kind of polygamist? Did he have four wives somewhere?

He nodded, watching me carefully. "I like to fuck," he shrugged. "Rough. I like kink."

Despite the situation, my stomach swirled, not unpleasantly, thinking of the rough kink that I had experienced with Swiss.

"That is not a secret," he continued.

I looked down at my nails, thinking about the tight living quarters and the way people were going at it at the party. It made sense... Sex should not be a secret, taboo, shameful thing. That's what I'd tried to teach Violet, at least.

Swiss's thumb went to the middle of my brow where I'd pinched my brows together in thought. He smoothed the wrinkle away.

"It also isn't a secret that I don't fuck the same bitch twice," he said quietly. "It's something I take very fuckin' seriously. And when we continue this, when we get deeper with each other, I'll tell you why. Needless to say, you bein' here with me, more than once, that means something."

Suddenly, it was more difficult to suck in a full breath of air.

Everything that had come out in the last... five minutes? Ten? Was more than a woman like me could handle.

Was it really only a month ago that I had a husband telling me how worthless I was because I forgot that we had a dinner with his golf buddies? How stupid I was because I didn't know the answer to some obscure question at trivia night?

I was not used to a man being open and free with affection, with purpose.

"When we get deeper with one another."

He said *when*. Like it was a forgone conclusion. Like he'd already decided I was worth it.

Although it was nice to hear, beyond nice, I felt uneasy. I didn't trust it. I was tense, waiting for the other shoe to drop.

Swiss was still watching me intently as I realized I had not spoken yet, and I probably had a look of shock and awe on my face. But I still didn't speak because I had no idea what to say and really hoped he was going to explain more.

He took a breath. "As much as I would like to keep us between us, that's not how it works here," he said. "We're a family. A fucked-up one to be sure, but a family. I'd like to say it's all on the Old Ladies, but some of the patched brothers are worse than fuckin' women."

He held his hand up in mock surrender. "Not that I'm making a generalization about your sex or implying there is anything wrong with being a woman. Men should be more like women. We're scumbags, all of us."

Despite the barrage of emotions running through me in that moment, I couldn't help but smile.

He shrugged on his cut. I wondered if he wore it every day. I liked him in it. Despite what I'd been conditioned into thinking it symbolized—criminals, violence, drugs, lawlessness.

I didn't know a whole bunch about the Sons of Templar or what they stood for, and I could've been completely wrong, but I got the feeling there was a whole lot more to his club than met the eye.

I already saw there was a whole lot more to this man than met the eye.

A gaggle of female laughter came from beyond the door, and it jerked me into action. I realized that there was a whole bunch of people out there, waiting to meet me. The woman Swiss was serious about.

Swiss. The sex god.

And I was wearing day old clothes that smelled of coffee, had on not a lick of makeup, and my hair was still wet from the shower.

"I can't meet your family like this," I exclaimed as I stared at myself in the mirror.

I was still learning to get used to my naked face. It was so rare that I saw it in the daylight. In the past, I was required to look my best at all times.

Preston had made it clear he didn't like the way I looked without makeup. And enough years had gone by that Preston's likes and dislikes had become my likes and dislikes. Out of need for survival, I supposed.

So I had some level of self-hatred, I guessed. Nonexistent confidence. My fight-or-flight mode that was almost always engaged.

In short, I was screwed up.

And I was diving into a completely crazy scenario with a crowd of people I'd never met.

Without hair or makeup, without the things that had served as my armor for so long.

Without it, I looked younger, my skin lineless, pale because my natural skin tone was alabaster. I blushed easily and bruised even easier, something that helped my face a lot these past years. My eyes were wide, lashes dark, framing the dark blue eyes that I thought were my best feature. My lips were pink, full—because of the injections that Preston insisted I get—and slightly too big for my face in my opinion. But they suited me more now that my face was getting rounder with the weight gain. My cheekbones weren't so high and gaunt anymore.

Swiss came up behind me in the mirror. "You're right," he agreed, eyes flickering over my bare face, my rosy cheeks, my wide and bright eyes.

My stomach dropped.

His arms slipped around my waist. "You look *too* fuckin' good," he murmured, nuzzling my neck. "Freshly fucked," he continued, speaking against my skin. Inhaling. "Glowing." His eyes met mine. "Not enough of my brothers are loved up. I'm definitely gonna have to shoot at least one of them for trying to steal you from me."

I rolled my eyes. "Be serious."

He thought on it. "Okay, you're right. Shooting might be too messy and loud. There will probably be children there. I'll stab them. Flesh wounds only."

I shot daggers at him with my eyes. "Seriously?" I cried. "I don't have any makeup with me. My hair is still wet!"

He stared right back at me. "Who gives a fuck? You look gorgeous."

"I don't need you to lie to me," I snapped.

Swiss frowned at me, then his hands ran up my belly to my breasts. "You're telling me you don't think you're fuckin' beautiful?" he asked quietly, massaging my breasts. "You don't think these tits, these nipples are the most magnificent things you've ever seen?" He yanked up my tank to expose my pebbled nipples.

My breathing was ragged as his other hand slipped into my jeans and panties, cupping my pussy before moving back around my hip.

"You don't think this is the juiciest, perkiest, most fuckable ass on the planet?" he asked.

I did not answer because I was pretty sure that his questions were rhetorical.

Also because I had quickly lost my ability to speak.

Swiss's eyes were scorching as his hands left the intimate parts of my body. I was both disappointed and relieved.

He righted my shirt and turned me to face him, clutching my neck. "I am not blowin' smoke up your ass, Kate," he said quietly. "Shitty thing to be honest about, but I feel this moment needs it because you are thinkin' bullshit things about yourself." His thumb moved up to brush my jaw. "Would not have walked up to you at the party if I didn't think you were the most beautiful woman in the room. The most beautiful woman I've ever seen. Men are wired like that. We're simple creatures, driven by our dicks. And the way you looked that night yanked at my dickstrings."

I blinked at him, and a bubble of hysterical laughter escaped from my throat. Only Swiss could say something serious at the same time as uttering the word 'dickstrings.'

He grinned in triumph before he continued.

"You had your hair done. Makeup on. The outfit. And you looked good," he said. "But not better than you do right now. Right now, with your face fresh, clean, glowing from the many times I made you cum."

Desire pulsed between my legs.

"Your eyes glowing in a way they weren't that night," he continued softly. His thumb found my bottom lip. "Smilin," he murmured. "A real smile," he corrected. "Now I don't consider myself to be an expert on women, but I know that you're thinkin' all sorts of shit because you know the Old Ladies are out there, and you want to look your best. And I also know that my opinion may not win against the shit swirlin' inside you, but for what it's worth, I think you look your absolute best in this moment."

My head thrummed with everything he'd said. And not in the past minute or so. This entire morning.

I felt like I was about to explode under the weight of the unequivocally wonderful things he was saying to me. The honesty in which he was saying them.

I didn't trust it. Instinctively.

I'd spent almost two decades being belittled, insulted, abused. As fucked-up as it was, that was my normal. There was a kind of... safety in that. I knew what to expect. Had conditioned myself how to respond to it.

This was all new. And unnerving. I felt like I was in freefall.

"On top of that," Swiss continued, obviously unaware of the turmoil inside my head. "These are not women who would ever judge you or treat you different because you didn't have lipstick on or whatever the fuck."

I stared at him, battling the ideas and routines that had been conditioned inside me for years.

It wasn't like I had a bunch of other options. Yes, I could hide in here the entire day, but I'd eventually have to leave. Swiss's window was large enough for me to crawl out of, but I wasn't quite desperate enough to crawl out a window.

Beyond that, I didn't want to leave Swiss. Not yet. An empty motel room waited for me. Decisions. Reality.

"Okay," I said. "Let's go."

He grinned and kissed me. "That's my girl," he rumbled against my lips.

CHAPTER EIGHT

KATE

I WAS IMMEDIATELY furious at Swiss when we walked out into the common room that had been transformed at some point during the morning. How I hadn't heard the people, the moving of furniture, the sound of the setup was beyond me.

Oh, right... Swiss and the orgasms probably.

There had been a pool table to the right of the sofas as you walked into the room, and that was nowhere to be seen. Instead, there was a long table full of food with flowers and places set. People were everywhere. Men wearing the leather Sons of Templar cut were plentiful, there were children and babies and women who I guessed were the 'Old Ladies.'

It was a completely different vibe than the first night I was here. The room smelled of French toast and scented candles.

The reason I was furious at Swiss was the women who were scattered around the room. There were only three that I could see, and boy did they stand out.

The first was wearing a long, flowing maxi dress with the back cut out. Her tanned skin was toned, and her arms were sculpted, wrists full of bracelets. Her hair was cut short, and with her delicate features, she looked like a pretty pixie or fairy or some magical creature. She was placing food on the table, laughing at something the bald man behind her was saying. The bald man was most definitely her man since he was checking out her ass as she bent over. There was an intense possessiveness that even I felt.

He was hot as balls, but was that a surprise?

The next woman I recognized.

Caroline Hargrave.

I didn't really like to watch the news... It made me nervous and terrified for the world that I was releasing my daughter out into. Preston needed to watch the news. Be informed. Be the most cultured man in the room, up to date on every tragedy, political scandal or market fluctuation.

He watched it, therefore I watched it.

He hated Caroline Hargrave. Hated that a woman was out there in warzones, reporting, doing a 'man's job', not giving him the angle that he wanted.

He'd been glad when she went off the air. Preston, I was coming to realize, did not like strong women. Women he wouldn't be able to control. It unnerved him. Angered him. Which was in direct conflict to how we'd raised our daughter. She was strong, outspoken, independent. He did not try to squash that in her... thank God. But I also knew he harbored the idea that she would meet a good old boy when she went to college and would promptly fall in love with him, pop out babies and find her 'place.' He'd said something to that effect at dinner with his parents once, and his mother and I had exchanged a knowing look.

Preston did not know his daughter very well or at all. Or at least he saw what he wanted to see in her.

Violet would be so jealous that I was having brunch with Caroline Hargrave. She was her hero.

And it seemed she'd swapped warzones for life with an outlaw motorcycle club. A man with a large scar across his face—that did not mar his handsomeness in the slightest—pulled her away from the child's face she was trying to wipe to kiss her full on the lips. With tongue.

She responded and laughed, wiping her trademark red lipstick off his lips when he released her.

The last woman was standing in the corner, next to one of the most intimidating men I'd ever seen. Dark hair, tall, menacing. Covered in tattoos. Absolutely covered. Even his face had some.

What stopped him from being completely menacing was the small infant that was strapped to his chest.

He was standing in the middle of a room full of tough guys, badasses and biker alphas yet still managed to look like the most dangerous man in the room with a baby strapped to his chest.

He also was looking at the woman beside him like she was responsible for the very air he breathed.

The woman looked vaguely familiar. Her long blonde hair was in loose waves around her face. Even from across the room, I could see her makeup was absolutely stunning, expertly applied. She had tattoos covering her arms, wearing a skintight dress that showed off every curve and high heeled boots. Because of the way the man was looking at her, I assumed it was her baby that was strapped to his chest and gave her a silent round of applause for looking like that months after having a child.

I looked like that months after having Violet only because I was a child myself, my metabolism was fast, and gravity hadn't yet got the memo.

"Finally!" someone yelled.

"I thought I was going to have to drag you out with my bare hands," Lucas yelled, teasing.

Swiss's arm was slung tightly around my shoulder, otherwise I might've taken off running with all of the attention focused on us.

"You did that, you would've lost both of those hands," Swiss replied easily, obviously not on the verge of a panic attack over all of the attention.

Then again, this was his family. He was comfortable around them. He knew all of them. And the bastard looked GQ ready just throwing on some clothes after using his four-in-one.

In quick succession, I was introduced to everyone. The bald man was the president, Hansen. He smiled softly and shook my hand. Macy, with the maxi dress, was his wife. She hugged me in greeting, squeezing my tightly. She smelled of patchouli and lavender. Jagger was the man with the scar, Caroline's husband. I tried my best to pretend I didn't know who she was when she also hugged me in greeting. Hades was the man with the baby strapped to him.

Hades.

That was his name.

He did not shake my hand or smile. He did a masculine chin lift thing. His wife was Freya who smiled easily, kissing me on both cheeks and squeezing my upper arms. Then we all quickly sat down to eat. I had lapsed into autopilot, used to being on a man's arm, introduced as his accessory. Not that that was how Swiss or anyone made me feel.

I made myself feel that because it was more comfortable. More plausible. So I smiled, I replied when spoken to. I did all the things expected of me in such a moment.

I remained close to Swiss's side the entire brunch, overwhelmed and overstimulated. People spoke to me. Freya, seated close to me, chatted easily but didn't ask a whole bunch of questions that required me to speak a whole lot. I got the feeling she sensed that I was quietly having a heart attack and made sure to smile warmly at me to make me feel welcome in a subtle way. All of the women did that. Most women, especially being in the circles I was forced to run with, had an ability to pick up and put off certain vibes around each other.

Violet would call it the 'you can't sit with us' vibe.

My previous group of 'friends' positively radiated that vibe. Each of them would've loved to kick me from the table if it weren't for Preston and his family's name. Each of them made points to subtly but brutally bully the other women in town that they judged to be 'below' them.

If somehow one of Preston's single or divorced friends had debuted a new woman at any kind of event, one who was dressed like I was without a lick of makeup, my group would've eaten her alive. She'd probably leave in tears, never to be seen again.

And I would've just sat by the wayside watching, not joining in, but not doing anything to help her either. Because I was a coward. Because if I made any kind of waves, Preston would hear about it, and I would pay.

This group, this family, was nothing like that. I could feel the warmth radiating off the women.

And off the men too. Sure, they were gruffer, more rugged and definitely more dangerous, but they weren't terrifying... well, except for Hades. And Elden, he had a silent menace radiating off him that kept me wary. The rest, though, made me feel almost comfortable. They weren't heathens and didn't act in whatever way I might've expected them to. They were fathers, husbands, friends. They smiled. Laughed. Teased each other.

Though I was coiled tight, I let a little of that warmth seep in.

Let myself pretend, at least for a while, that I could possibly be part of this.

There wasn't a moment during the entire brunch that Swiss did not have his hands on me. Whether it was his arm around my shoulder, him pausing his meal to kiss my cheek—which he did three times—or placing his hand on my thigh while eating with his other, he made sure to acknowledge me. To let me know that he was thinking about me. That he cared.

It was odd. Amazing. But too intimate, too casual for people who had been sleeping together for two days.

It felt natural to me too. I felt like I could get used to this.

Which was why by the end of the meal, I was completely overwhelmed and needed an out.

Luckily, I had the excuse to stand and start gathering plates, all but running to the kitchen once my hands were full.

There were men in there, which surprised me. I hadn't thought bikers were the dishwashing kind of guys. Though they were all very nice and welcoming, they had the vibes that they were 'men' and completely comfortable with conventional gender roles.

The men at the sink didn't have the patch on the back of their cuts, only the word 'Prospect.' I guessed it was like pledges for a fraternity, and this was their induction period.

"I'll take those," one of the men said to me, divesting me of the duty and the purpose that came with that duty.

My heart started beating rapidly with my empty hands and the thought of heading back into the common room and making conversation. Finding a place without a table and a plate of food in front of me was beyond daunting.

Macy appeared in the doorway I was dreading walking through, carrying two long stemmed glasses.

She handed me one of them. I took it thankfully.

"I figured you may need a break from the circus, and a mimosa," she said softly.

I smiled in thanks.

She nodded to the breakfast bar, and I perched on a barstool and she settled on another.

"I've been with the club for years, so I'm used to all of this." She waved her hand to the prospects then back toward the room where conversations and laughter could be heard. "But it's a lot, so I'm sorry your first introduction to all of this had to be so intense. We're really nice, I promise." She laid her hand on mine.

I was comforted by the gesture, despite Macy being younger than me—or having a very good dermatologist—and a stranger.

"Alcohol helps," she added, lifting her glass.

I laughed at that and took a sip of my own.

"You don't have to worry, we like you already," she said.

I almost choked on my mimosa.

"Also, we heard that you made some of the best pasta on planet Earth, so we're definitely going to have to taste that," Freya added.

I hadn't seen her walk in.

"Oh, definitely," Macy added.

"We'll have a dinner party," Freya decided.

"At our house," Caroline said.

I blinked at her, at how all of these women had noted my exit and took it upon themselves to come in to make me feel comfortable.

"I'll make brownies," Freya grinned.

I was going to try to argue. To tell them that I likely wasn't going to be around long enough to attend dinner parties, but I got the idea that that would go how it went when I told Swiss I was leaving. Well, kind of differently, but the same result.

So, kind of like how I did with Swiss, I submitted to these women. Let them welcome me in.

———

I hadn't realized it at the time, but the women had come into the kitchen to make me comfortable—and tipsy—enough to make it back into the large common room where everyone was hanging out.

Swiss found me the moment I walked back into the room, listening to Freya and Macy try to figure out the best day for the dinner party.

He walked over and kissed my head. "You okay, baby?" he asked, low enough for only me to hear.

I nodded once, not quite sure whether I was lying or not.

Somehow, he sensed that and walked us to the sofas where everyone settled next to their respective husbands and 'shot the shit.'

At some point, the men disappeared behind double doors with 'church' scrawled above it.

This had me perplexed for a second. I hadn't seen any religious paraphernalia anywhere—they had a wall of framed mugshots for goodness' sake, mugshots that also could've doubled as GQ covers—no one had said grace when we sat down to eat, and there was no sign of a god of any kind being a ruling force in this club.

"It's a place where they all meet, discuss club business," Macy offered, nodding to where I was staring, obviously seeing my confusion.

"Mandatory once a week," she continued. "After brunch."

"Something that we decided was also mandatory," Freya said, adjusting the baby at her hip.

I nodded, wondering what exactly constituted 'club business,' but I didn't think it was wise to ask. The fact that the men conducted such business from behind closed doors told me that it was private.

"So you've got to tell us about you and Swiss," Macy urged, patting the spot beside her on the sofa.

Her two boys were running around the room, screaming in glee at whatever game they were playing. Caroline and Jagger's toddler was chasing them, also screaming in glee.

I sat down on reflex more than anything else.

"Oh, yes," Freya agreed, somehow managing to top up my mimosa—it was basically just orange colored champagne at this point—without spilling a drop with the baby on her arm. "I am *dying* to know about how you two met."

Caroline sat down beside me. "We have been placing bets on who was going to be next," she offered.

"I won," Macy announced with a wide smile.

"I really thought you were bonkers for putting your money on Swiss of all people," Freya smirked, settling Eva down in the playpen they'd set up. She brushed her dark brown head tenderly before coming back to join us.

"I'm a romantic," Macy told her. "Plus, I had a feeling it was his time."

Caroline rolled her eyes at this. "We are not talking about *feelings*. In fact, we are not talking at all." She nodded to me. "We need to give Kate the chance to talk."

I took a large gulp of my drink with three sets of inquisitive female eyes on me. None of their gazes were hostile. Not in the slightest. They were kind, warm, curious.

"I, um, we've only known each other for a few days," I said.

Macy nodded.

"So, um... I don't know if there's anything to tell?"

All of the women gaped at me.

"Honey, two days in the alpha male world is like... *forever*," Freya offered. "These guys don't fuck around," she paused, looking toward the double doors. "Well, Hades fucked around, if you want to get specific. But that's only because he was trying to protect me from himself or whatever." She waved her hand. "He knew with me the second I picked him up off the parking lot ground after he was stabbed."

Now it was my turn to gape. "Stabbed?" I repeated.

Another dismissive hand wave. "Oh, ancient history. He was fine." She looked at Caroline. "And technically, with Jagger, she thought he was dead for like what, a decade? But that again was because he was trying to protect her from himself. And then he had to hold her captive for a little while because she was doing a story on the club."

I was not sure whether my mouth was just hanging open right now or not, but it sure did feel like it.

"Don't worry, our story has a happy ending," Caroline offered with a warm smile.

"Let's not scare Kate off now," Macy jumped in, patting Freya's thigh. She focused her green eyes on me. "What's she's saying, honey, is that these men are... different. The life they've chosen to lead makes them more in tune with their emotions than your garden variety man." She took a sip of her drink. "I'm not going to lie to you, this life can be dangerous."

Her eyes went faraway for a second before she refocused on me. "So the way the men in the club live their lives is like they are going to die tomorrow," she said. "And before they meet their woman, the way they do that is by screwing a lot of other women. They know immediately whether it's just fucking or if it's something more. And once they know, it's done. They're done. They don't question it. They commit."

My mimosa was gone by that point, and I didn't even remember drinking it.

"Commit?" I repeated. "You mean Swiss is committing to me for..."

"Ever," Freya finished for me happily.

All of the women were smiling at me. No, beaming at me. They were obviously happy for me. Happy for Swiss, as it was clear that they cared about him. Loved him.

And, if I was somehow a different person, without all of the baggage, without all of the lies, I'd be happy too. Ecstatic even.

But it was not that simple. It never was.

"Welcome to the family!" Macy cheered.

I smiled my best fake smile and gripped my wine glass, hoping it wouldn't break. Hoping I wouldn't break.

I didn't decide to get drunk.

First, I was caught up in the festivities of the morning. And then there were the women who were constantly refilling my glass. At some point, there were tequila shots.

I had never done a tequila shot in my life.

Once Freya had found that out, she began feeding them to me until her, Hades and the baby left. She informed me that since I wasn't breastfeeding that she had to live vicariously through me.

The other two women were not breastfeeding, and they had husbands who were staying sober. Husbands who, by the way, made it clear that they adored their women. They were always touching them, staring at them, kissing or yanking them away for a quickie down the hall somewhere.

That was Caroline and Jagger. She came back without her lipstick on, her hair mussed and eyes bright.

The entire situation was like nothing I'd ever experienced. It only amplified my feeling of unease, an imposter syndrome that I couldn't shake.

Well, I learned that I could shake it.

With tequila.

As the day turned into night, all of the women eventually left. They had small children, after all.

It made me miss Violet like a severed limb. Nostalgic for the time when she was small and chubby and would hold tightly onto my fingers.

It made me wish that I had the experience of a man carrying our sleeping baby while letting me drink mimosas, not at all bothered by any switch in gender stereotypes or concerned about image.

I was happy that these women had that. Even after only one afternoon with them, I knew that they deserved that.

But I was feeling weird. I was picturing Swiss with a baby strapped to his chest.

Our baby.

I was picturing our baby. After two days together.

While I was still technically married.

So yeah, I got drunk.

The night got decidedly blurrier and rowdier after the married couples left, and the single men remained. I understood that it was a completely different vibe... The scantily clad women from the party having returned. All of whom were perfectly nice to me. One even cried and told me how pretty I was while I was walking toward the bathroom.

I might've even cried too.

At some point during the night—after I had got up and

danced with the woman from the bathroom line—Swiss dragged me off to the bedroom. Or maybe I dragged him off.

I distinctly remember backing him up against a wall in the hallway—a very public hallway—and making out with him. Maybe even dry humping him. My hand definitely went underneath his tee.

We made it to his room, and that was where things took a turn.

For the better.

The clearest memory I had from the night was the door closing and me looking Swiss straight in the eye and asking, "Do you like to be punished?"

Swiss's eyes were an inferno. "Countess, you want to draw and quarter me, I'll give you the fucking knife," he'd bit out, voice coated in sex.

Then there were handcuffs. And they weren't used on me.

It turned out tequila shots and Swiss brought out a whole other side to me. One I didn't even know existed.

And I liked it.

CHAPTER NINE

KATE

A SHRILL RINGING jerked me awake.

And awake was not the best thing to be at that moment.

Awake was the most terrible thing to be.

My head pounded, and that ringing seemed to be coming from the depths of hell, rebounding off my skull which currently felt like it was made of very fragile glass. My throat burned with thirst, and the room was spinning.

"What is that?" I cried out.

The arms around me tightened. "Phone," a sleepy voice grunted. "Yours."

I reached blindly to the side table I very vaguely remembered placing my phone on last night.

Though I could've just let it ring, lapsing back into delightful unconsciousness, I had no option to do that—I was a mother with a daughter halfway across the world. I needed to be accessible at all times in case of emergency. Realization jerked me wide awake, and I launched up to grasp the phone before it stopped ringing.

"Hello?" I greeted urgently, my heart already thundering in fear.

"Where the bloody hell are you?" an accented voice asked over the phone.

I blinked, not completely calming down but feeling relieved it was not Violet or some French speaking official on the other end of the phone.

"Who is this?" I asked, falling back on the bed.

"It's bloody Julian!" the voice exclaimed. "And I'm at the café, battling the throngs of caffeine hungry people. I'm about to bloody throttle someone, so you better get your ass here soon."

I opened my mouth to tell him that I most certainly would not be there soon because I was currently dying of a hangover, but I got a dial tone on the other end of the phone.

"He hung up on me," I muttered, throwing the phone down on the bed.

Swiss's arms went around me to pull me back to my previous position, on my side with my back against his front.

His scent and warmth soothed me, though I was feeling incredibly unwell.

"Want me to kill him?" he offered.

"Not just yet," I sighed.

"Well I may just have to anyway," he grunted. "What fuckin' man is calling you first thing in the mornin'?"

My skin prickled with fear, though it was a lazy kind of fear, unable to wade through all of the fuzz of the hangover. "It's not first thing in the morning," I refuted, picking up my phone to glance at it. "It's almost ten."

"Which is first thing in the mornin', considering when we went to bed."

I did not remember what time it was when we made it to his room last night, but I knew we did not go to sleep when we did. A thrill ran through me at the blurry images of what we did in this room in the wee hours of the morning.

My body ached with the evidence of it.

"It's Julian," I answered his question.

"The guy from the coffee shop?"

"Uh huh," I groaned. "He wants me to go there. To make coffee."

I opened my mouth to explain how and why me making coffee at the café made sense, but the story seemed too long, and I didn't know whether I was capable of telling it without throwing up.

I had not been this hungover... ever.

"I do not feel good," I exclaimed, burying my head into the pillow.

A low, throaty chuckle was the first sound this morning not to pound against my head. It was somewhat of a salve. "I would imagine," Swiss muttered, voice still thick with sleep. "You were wasted last night, baby."

My stomach dropped. Not with nausea, though that was swirling in there too. Cold dread momentarily paralyzed me.

"I'm so sorry," I whispered.

Swiss's arms went tight around me before he moved me very gently to my back.

He propped himself up on his elbow. I squinted up at him because I was not brave enough to open my eyes all the way yet. I didn't trust the dim sunlight coming from the curtains not to burn my retinas out. I also did not want to see the expression on Swiss's face.

"Why the fuck are you apologizing, Countess?"

I slowly creaked my eyes open.

The light did in fact sear against my eyes, but I focused on Swiss. He did not look disgusted or furious with me. He did not look like he was planning on kicking me out of this bed or out of his life.

"Because I was drunk," I answered slowly.

"So was I," he shrugged. "So was everyone. It was a party. And you're sexy as fuck when you're drunk." His hand moved under the covers, down my bare stomach, in between my thighs.

I let out a gasp.

"And you fuck like a wildcat when you're drunk," he murmured. "We've established that I like control when I'm fuckin', but even I wasn't brave enough to go against you last night." He leaned down to kiss my neck.

My body forgot about how hungover it was.

"I was happy to submit to you," he said against my neck. "And I'm tempted to get you wasted more often to see what else you do."

My eyes rolled back in my head. "So I didn't... embarrass you?" I asked quietly.

The hand between my legs paused, and Swiss's head came up. "That's what you're thinkin'?" he asked. "That you embarrassed me?"

I nodded slowly, hot with shame.

Swiss grasped my chin. "Kate, I have no idea what kind of asshole your ex was, and by the sounds of it I really don't want to because then I'll be taking a trip to meet him." His eyes went dark. "And that would not go well for him."

My breath hitched.

"But," Swiss continued, "you are not with him anymore. You're with me." His eyes blazed, emphasizing his sincerity. "And you do not have to worry about fuckin' embarrassing me. Not ever. You party as much or as little as you like. You wear whatever the fuck you like, preferably without a bra."

His hand moved to tweak my nipple.

"I know you're new to the outlaw world, babe. But you'll learn that we live hard. That we party harder. We don't give a fuck about appearances."

I stared into his eyes, my head thumping and my heart fluttering.

"I don't know what shit you've had before, but you don't need to apologize to me about havin' a good time." His burnt coffee orbs sparkled as he brushed a strand of hair from my face. "And you certainly don't need to apologize for what you did last night. It was a first for me, which is sayin' a lot."

Blurry images ran through my mind as I remembered the power I felt last night, liberated by tequila. I immediately knew I wouldn't be able to replicate that night, that feeling again. But that's what made it so special.

And the only dread I had about last night completely dissipated. Despite how close to death I was feeling in that moment—soothed quite a bit by the look Swiss was giving me—I'd had fun. Beyond fun.

My phone buzzed. I groaned. "That's got to be Julian," I said, my voice ragged. "I only met the man once, but I know he's serious about coffee and have a feeling he's not going to stop calling until I arrive."

"I don't give a fuck," Swiss replied, yanking the covers back to expose my naked body. His hands went to my legs, spreading them so he could settle in between them. "I'm serious about eating my woman's pussy first thing in the morning."

And I could not formulate an argument to go against that.

Swiss gave me a ride to work.

On the back of his bike.

Well, first we stopped at the motel so I could change into different clothes and put on a little makeup. Swiss had lounged on the bed and watched me the entire time. He did not hurry me. To the contrary... He acted like he didn't have anywhere else to be but right there.

It was both comforting and unnerving. My nerves were frayed from these past few days, battling both of those feelings. Battling my fight-or-flight instinct. It was really only in moments of pause when such thoughts became overwhelming. When I had too much time to think about it all.

Which was why it was a good thing I quickly got ready and back on the bike to go to the coffee shop.

Aside from a vague throbbing of my head, my hangover was mostly gone. Sex must've been the ultimate cure for that. I had a feeling that sex with Swiss was a cure for almost everything.

Though it was still mid-morning, the air was warm and balmy, even on the bike. It was gearing up to be another hot New Mexico day. My skin soaked up the sun, already hungry for me. Although I didn't grow up in the dry, unyielding heat, I felt like I was made for it. Like my body was desperate for it.

The bike roared to a stop at the front of the café, which indeed did look busy.

Swiss surprised me by getting off the bike at the same time as me.

"You don't have to walk me in," I told him, running my hand through what was probably helmet hair.

"I sure as fuck do," he replied, pulling me to his side to kiss my head. He started walking us inside, opening the door for me. "Plus," he said, holding the door, "I need some java, and this shit is like crack." He winked.

I breathed in the smell of coffee grounds and food cooking in the kitchen, already feeling amped up for the day ahead. Though I already missed the man beside me.

"Good, you're here," Julian muttered, looking up, barely glancing at Swiss. He picked up a plate and shoved it in my direction. "Eat this."

I glanced down at the plate. It was what looked like a breakfast sandwich, and my mouth watered.

"Figured you'd need something greasy, by the way you sounded," he said as he looked at Swiss. "These bastards know how to party."

"And you know how to make good as fuck coffee," Swiss retorted, his arm still around me. "Which is the only reason I'm not taking you outside for callin' my woman and draggin' her out of bed in the morning."

I gaped up at him and at the threat he delivered that only slightly sounded like he was joking.

Julian, to his credit, didn't look surprised or intimidated. Not even a little bit.

"Well, your woman can give me a run for my money, so she's worth risking a tousle with you," he shot back, winking at me.

Swiss chuckled, shaking his head. "You're the only fucker who can get away with talking to me like that."

"It's the accent," he smirked. "I'm adorable." Julian looked at me. "Eat that." He pointed to the plate. "Say goodbye to your old man, make him a coffee to keep him happy, and then we've got work to do."

Julian did not wait for a response, he turned back to the coffee machine and barked at a customer to "Wait a bloody second."

The customer in question blinked in surprise but then stood quietly as ordered.

I grinned as I took my first bite of the sandwich.

Then I made a noise at the back of my throat. The bread was perfectly toasted, slathered in butter and soaking with bacon grease. Exactly what my body needed right then.

Swiss watched me eat. I normally would've been really self-conscious about him watching me eat in such a messy and unla-dylike way, but I was much too hungry and hungover to worry about that.

"You gonna share some of that with me?" he asked, teasing in his tone.

Wordlessly, I handed the plate to him. Swiss picked up the sandwich and took a large bite, looking at me while he did it before handing it back to me.

The act of sharing food was incredibly intimate, despite everything we'd done that could've been perceived as very fricking intimate too.

I took another bite then handed him the plate once more. We went back and forth until the sandwich was done, and my stomach no longer felt so unpredictable.

I wiped my face with a napkin, and Swiss leaned in to kiss the corner of my mouth.

"Gonna make me a coffee now, Countess?" he asked quietly.

I nodded once.

"Good," he winked. "Makes sense, you set me up for the day with your pussy then your coffee."

My cheeks burned, and Swiss grinned wickedly.

"I know me being crass is turnin' you on, but we're in a public place. Get a hold of yourself," he quipped, reaching back to squeeze my ass.

I grinned back at him, and as if I was floating on air, I walked to the coffee machine and proceeded to make my man a coffee.

Once I'd handed it to him, he yanked me in for a long kiss not suitable for public consumption.

"I'll pick you up later, baby," he murmured.

I nodded, breathless.

Then I watched him walk out.

I was not the only one.

"Stop pervin' at your man, and get me a latte," Julian barked.

I jumped to attention and did as he said. My mind was on Swiss and coffee for the rest of the day.

———

I didn't know when I started living at the clubhouse... It kind of just happened. Just like how I started working at the café.

Julian did not bat an eyelash at 'paying me under the table,' nor did he question why I couldn't provide things like a social security number or why my address on file was a motel.

The motel that served as a symbol more than anything else. Storage for my meager belongings and the place where I'd hidden the remaining items I was keeping in case of emergency.

A diamond tennis bracelet. My wedding and engagement rings. I should've pawned those first. The second I made the decision to leave. I wasn't sure why I was still holding on to them. They were a symbol of the pain I'd lived through, of the control Preston had had over me.

But I couldn't let go of them. Even though both of the rings were worth thousands. Tens of thousands. More than enough to set me up.

I'd need to pay for a lawyer eventually, though. A good one. And although I hadn't had much experience of the real world in my adult life, I understood that a good divorce lawyer was likely to cost more than the rings and bracelet were worth. Maybe ten times more.

That thought made me itchy and panicky, so I tried to avoid it and the motel. I only went there under the pretense that I had some kind of life outside of Swiss and the club.

Which I really, *really* didn't.

I slept at the club. Ate at the club. Cooked for the club. Shopped for the club. And if I wasn't eating there, I was eating at Hansen and Macy's, Hades and Freya's or Jagger and Caroline's place.

And when I was shopping, I was more often than not with one of them—the Old Ladies.

Old Lady... That's what I was. Biker slang for going steady. But a lot more serious than that.

I understood that everyone was surprised that Swiss had declared that he had a woman. I was not sure if people were surprised by who he chose. No one judged me. No one made me feel unwelcome or out of place. Even though I was. No, from the beginning, every single member of the club made me feel like family.

Which made my deception all the more horrendous.

I'd almost told Swiss a hundred times. The longer I went without telling him, the harder it was to tell the truth.

He knew about Violet. He knew that I was estranged from her father. But he thought that estrangement was a formal, legal arrangement. I'd never lied outright to him, but he'd assumed that. And I'd let him. Swiss didn't ask a whole lot about my past. He didn't seem to care about what got me there, just the fact I was there.

Though I was infinitely curious, I never asked about his either. I wanted to know him. Desperately. I wanted to know him deeply and intimately, more deeply than anyone ever had. There was a lot underneath the muscle, the charm, the cheeky humor, the smoldering, sexual intensity... the danger. There was something dark. Something painful. I sensed it the more time I spent with him.

As much as I ached to know about his pain, there was no way for me to ask him without offering the same in return. It was unethical to demand to know about his past when I was keeping so much from him.

So I was living in a biker clubhouse and deeply, deeply in denial.

I was also making coffee at the cafe' six days a week. And helping out in the kitchen. But as much as Julian seemed to be impressed by my cooking, he was very serious about who he let use the espresso machine. Him and me. That was it. No one else was 'approved.'

Making coffee was meditative for me, but my heart was in the kitchen. And although Swiss constantly told me I didn't have to cook for the club—which all of the members within hearing distance argued with, good naturedly, of course—I liked doing it. They appreciated everything I cooked for them. I was currently working through *The Joy of Cooking*. Kind of as an ode to Julia, and to my daughter who was currently sampling wonderful French food. And a French man I didn't entirely approve of. But she was happy. She sounded it when she called. She spoke fast, telling me everything she was doing, asking every now and again about my 'aunt.' Luckily, I managed to change the subject quickly.

When I was making coffee, I let myself dream. About cooking. About opening a quaint little restaurant here in Garnett. Finding a house in the desert, making it my own. Making it ours. Mine and Swiss's.

Although I knew that would only ever be just a dream.

I liked working.

Loved it, in fact.

I adored the bustle of the morning coffee rush. The quiet, first thing in the morning. The smell of freshly ground coffee. The weight of a tray of food as I took it from the kitchen to a table.

Loved speaking to people, smiling, laughing. I adored feeling tired at the end of the day, the ache of my feet. The sense of purpose.

I got lost in the rhythm of it all, my mind not straying to places I was avoiding—like the knowledge that Violet was due back in the country in a few months, and my three-month deadline was looming. That I'd have to leave this place. The mere thought of it had my stomach lurching, despite how much I missed my daughter and needed to see her. The logistics of seeing her and avoiding Preston were keeping me up at night, no matter how tired I was, no matter how tight Swiss's arms were around me.

The lies I was telling weighed heavily too. I was falling deeper for this man every day, forming relationships with everyone in the club. And I was deceiving them. The walls were closing in on me, and I had no clue what to do. I had no one to ask for advice, despite how close I had been to telling Swiss everything multiple times.

And Macy and Freya, who seemed kind, capable and without any kind of judgment.

But I'd held back. Because I didn't want them to think differently of me. Less of me. Didn't want them to think I was some weak, spineless housewife who had no idea how the real world worked. Who had no idea how to file a fucking tax return or do anything a grown adult should know how to do because her husband had made sure of that. I felt more seen and known than I ever had in my life in so many ways here, yet I also felt more of an imposter than ever before. Sure, I'd been playing a part of the 'perfect' wife and mother all of my adult life. But that role had been crafted out of necessity. For my survival. And I'd never been around people that cared about me like this. I'd never wanted to tell the truth as much as I did now. The fear stopped me, though.

Because the afternoon rush had slowed, I had an opportunity to ruminate on this, a pit forming in my stomach with the knowledge that there was no way that this could end well.

That was until the bell over the door tolled, and motorcycle boots thumped on the wooden floor.

My heart skipped as my eyes locked with Swiss's. All my troubles shrank, and my body sang with his presence.

His eyes slid up and down my body slowly. My knees shook under the weight of his stare.

The café was housed in one of the older buildings in town, and it had AC that was fine if you were sitting down enjoying a coffee and something to eat, but not so much if you were running around and in and out of a hot kitchen. Beyond that, it was New Mexico in the middle of summer. The heat was dry, unyielding, and seemed to seep through every crack of the building.

Not that I minded it. I adored the summer. I hated winter. Trudging through the snow, my fingers numb if I forgot gloves, the sensation of never being able to get warm.

I was in my element here. Especially since there was absolutely no dress code at the café and not an eyebrow was raised at the frayed denim skirt I was wearing paired with cowboy boots and a slouchy black top that exposed my left shoulder.

I didn't consider the outfit 'sexy' in any kind of way, but that all changed with Swiss's eyes on me.

The New Mexico summer had nothing on the heat he emitted.

My breath went shallow, and I opened my mouth to greet him, or to declare my undying fealty to him, but he spoke first.

"Kate's on break," Swiss barked at Julian.

I scowled at him, a simple expression that I was only just learning I was safe to have. Along with the pissed tone I spoke in next. "You are not the boss here," I hissed. "And you do not have the authority to tell the owner of this café when I can go on break."

While I was saying this, Swiss was untying my apron, and I was too dumbfounded to physically fight him.

I stood in horror as he tossed the apron on the counter.

"Swiss!" I scolded. "I've got work to do."

A chuckle sounded from behind us. "Sweetheart, don't think he's gonna take no for an answer, and I for one am not brave enough to fight him with that look in his eyes," Julian interjected. "Plus, you're due for a break."

I opened my mouth to argue with him, since there was still a long line of people waiting for coffee, but Swiss took that moment to drag me off.

Drag. Me. Off.

I didn't fight him at first because I was surprised, and because I didn't want to make a scene. Then I got a look at his face, the look in his eyes, and I was no longer thinking about fighting him.

I was thinking about something else entirely.

"Swiss, you can't just drag me out of work because you want to have sex with me," I protested as he pulled us off the sidewalk and down the alleyway that ran down the side of the building.

The alleyway itself was quiet. The building on the other side of it was a quaint antique store that was closed on weekends. I looked lovingly at the window displays of the store whenever I walked into work, imagining walking in there, buying the jade green lamp or the vintage oil painting of a cottage garden.

But I never went in.

Because I did not have a home to put a jade green lamp in or a wall to hang a painting on.

Right now, though, I was not thinking about lamps or paintings. I was thinking about Swiss taking me down an alley in broad daylight with a certain look in his eyes.

"Swiss!" I snapped when he didn't respond to me, yanking the arm he was dragging me with.

He stopped walking, but he did not turn to have a conversation with me. Instead, he pushed me against the brick wall and started kissing me.

I responded immediately, the reality that there was a sidewalk at the opening of the alley not far away disappearing from my mind. The brick was rough against my skin as Swiss pressed his body into mine, his hands shoving my skirt up to my waist.

I wasn't sure whether I was clawing at him, trying to tear his clothes off, or if I was just holding on for dear life. All I knew was that I met his desperate, carnal hunger with something animal of my own.

Maybe I blacked out, or maybe I was drowning in the clashing of our mouths, but at some point, he'd freed himself from his jeans, and my panties were pushed to the side. My leg went around his hip, then he plunged inside of me. I was already soaking wet for him, from the second he'd started to drag me from the café, despite my protests.

My head might've slammed back against the brick wall had his hand not protected it. One of them was half lifting me at the hip, the other was at the back of my head, making sure I didn't give myself a concussion.

His strangled grunts of pleasure echoed through my bones as his lips moved against mine.

Swiss fucked me with ferocious abandon, and I met him for every thrust, every cell in my body singing for him. My body was coiled tight, ready to explode.

Swiss's hand moved from behind my head to around my neck. The familiar pressure almost took me over the edge, the pain, the black spots in my vision beckoning me to the abyss.

"Look at me," Swiss snarled, barely sounding human.

My eyes found his immediately, drowning in the obsidian pools of his irises.

It was then, right then, that I exploded. That Swiss's grunts of pleasure harmonized with mine.

He emptied himself into me, each pulse of his cock causing aftershocks to ripple through me.

We'd had the conversation a week ago about me being on birth control, about me being comfortable with him not using a condom. He'd barely been able to keep his hands off me since then. And I was somewhat the same. To put it mildly.

Slowly, both of my feet settled on the ground, though I was not strong enough to hold my body weight quite yet. Swiss steadied me, keeping hold of my hips with one hand while righting my skirt with the other. He used a bandanna that was tucked into his back pocket to clean me and the cum trickling down the inside of my thigh.

I blinked the world back into focus, the light suddenly bright. Sounds of cars and people not that far away.

We just had sex in an alley in broad daylight. Essentially right outside my place of work.

And it did not bother me one bit.

It took a long time to compose myself, my breathing.

"You wear shit like that, Countess, I'm gonna drag you out of work and fuck you." When he spoke finally, his voice was thick and gravelly, causing my skin to prickle with gooseflesh.

"I'll make a note to buy three more of these skirts," I replied, my voice husky.

His eyes found mine, and they flared. "I'll buy you a whole fuckin' store of those boots too," he murmured.

I glanced down to the boots, grinning.

"We're heading off on a run," he said as he buttoned his jeans.

I glanced up at him. "A run?"

He nodded slowly.

"Am I supposed to know what that is?" I asked. The men had mentioned runs every now and then, but I was always busy doing something, and the alone time Swiss and I spent together was not used to talk about club slang and what it meant.

I didn't know what being a member of the Sons of Templar really entailed. Except for being criminally hot and wearing cool outfits, throwing great parties and living an overall awesome existence free of rules or social constraints.

Yes, I could hazard a guess as to what the club did.

Swiss wore a gun in a holster under his cut, and had a knife strapped to his belt. He would sometimes leave in the middle of the night and go straight to the shower instead of getting in bed with me when he came back.

I might've lived a sheltered life, but I wasn't a complete idiot. I understood it was highly likely that the Sons made their living off nefarious things. That Swiss broke the law.

He never pretended to be a saint. Though he didn't lay out the specifics of what he did, he didn't hide anything from me either. I had the feeling he would reply truthfully to whatever question I asked. That he would trust me with the truth. Heck, I had the feeling he was waiting for me to ask so we could cross over that imaginary barrier. So that I would settle into this place more permanently.

But I could not ask him to trust me, I could not seek that trust when I had not yet trusted him with my truth.

"Got a shipment comin' in," he explained, pulling me to his chest. "We're meeting some... business partners in Arizona." He looked at me expectantly, as if he were waiting for me to ask for more. To clarify his vague explanation as to what he was doing.

I supposed maybe that's what most women would do. We were innately curious. Especially about men we were sleeping with. Especially about men we were falling in love with.

And I was curious. Desperately so. More than anything, I was clutched with worry about Swiss. I could gather that his life-style was full of danger, both from him being hurt or locked up. The thought of either happening filled me with dread and panic.

"How long will you be gone?" I asked instead of the myriad of other questions I had on my mind.

Something flickered in Swiss's eyes, something that looked a lot like disappointment. But it was gone as soon as it appeared. And I could've imagined it.

"Two days," he replied, stroking my back. "Maybe three."

I nodded, feeling sick to my stomach. Two days. Maybe three. Not long. Not at all. Certainly not a stretch of time to have a panic attack about. But I was on the verge of one.

That was two, maybe three less days I had with Swiss. Violet would be home in a few months. I needed to be at the airport when she landed, regardless of what was going on with Preston.

I still hadn't contacted a lawyer. I'd gone as far as researching some of the best ones in our state. But I did not possess the courage or the capital to actually call the firms. So I was putting my head in the sand, pretending I didn't have a whole life to plan for, that I didn't have to face my abusive, estranged husband in the near future. That I had to leave the life I'd made here.

All of that was indescribably terrifying and not something I should've been able to ignore.

And I wouldn't be able to ignore it. Not without Swiss.

"I'll try my best to make it two," Swiss said, dropping a feather soft kiss against my lips. I stewed on that. "But we might have another... more legitimate, more fulfilling job to do, depending on how things shake out."

I tilted my head in question. The word 'legitimate' piqued my curiosity.

"One of the other charters started an organization," he elaborated, rubbing my arms now. "President of Oregon grew up seein' some tough shit, mother bein' smacked around by his dad... until he killed his father at sixteen. Got locked up for it. Patched the second he got out."

My heart thundered.

"Anyway, like most of us, he abhors men who are weak enough to lay hands on women," Swiss continued, obviously unaware of the rapid change in my body temperature.

It felt like I was being frozen to the spot.

"Have no fuckin' idea how it's structured, just know that we get a location, turn up and help a woman move out. Rough up the husband a little if he's stupid enough to be home." He grinned wickedly at me. "That's not a part that's advertised to the public, but it's a personal favorite of mine."

I smiled back at him. Or at least I was pretty sure that's what my face did.

There it was. Proof that Swiss and the club really could and would help me. They had a whole organization established to keep women safe from violent husbands. Well, at the very least, keep them safe while they left those violent husbands.

But I'd already left mine.

And getting their help would mean revealing a whole other part of me. One I was not willing to share with Swiss.

Not now.

Maybe not ever.

I took a deep breath and looked up at him, trying my best to hide the sorrow that was reaching my fingertips with the knowledge my time with this man was truly running out.

My eyes met his and I leaned into his touch. His smell. The safety of his presence.

There it was again. The truth. On the tip of my tongue. I could say it all now. We could figure this out together. He would not let me leave, once he knew the truth, I knew that. He would not let me face Preston alone. He would not let Preston hurt me.

I knew all of these things. Knew he cared about me.

No.

He cared about the Kate he'd met at the club. The Kate who drank beer and wore ripped jeans, who partied, who cooked, who worked in a coffee shop.

I wasn't at all sure how he'd feel about the other Kate. The one I was hiding.

"I'll miss you," I said quietly, opting for a much smaller, much simpler truth. "But you should stay longer to do that, help that woman," I added, thinking of what courage it must've taken for her to make the call to the club. Make the decision to leave. She deserved to have Swiss standing there, protecting her.

He searched my face. I worried about what he'd find there, even though I knew he couldn't possibly read my mind.

"I'll miss you too," he said, voice husky, forehead resting against mine. "Vision of me fuckin' my Countess against a brick wall in broad daylight is gonna have me rushin' home to you, though."

My body warmed at his throaty tone, at the reality of what he'd just said.

"Home to you."

Three small words that filled me up.

Even though they were based on a lie.

A lie that would keep me up later.

CHAPTER TEN

KATE

"DO YOU BELIEVE IN MAGIC?" I asked.

We were having a girls' night at Hades and Freya's house. Almost everyone's husband was away on this 'run,' which I figured meant it was important.

I'd tried to decline the invitation, deciding that now was the time I needed to distance myself from these women, to make it easier for me to leave. But they wouldn't hear of it. And I wasn't strong enough to argue with them. I was slowly finding my voice with Swiss, I was brave enough to disagree with him on occasion, but that was rare and when I acted on instinct. I couldn't unlearn a lifetime of behavior in a handful of weeks.

Weeks. That's what it had been. Almost a month. How could it have been such a small stretch of time?

I was mulling over that when I drove out into the desert to Freya's place.

Freya had greeted me at the door with champagne.

Her house was utterly beautiful, utterly her. A mix of bohemian and glam. Her friend Marilyn had been there most of the night and was an absolute delight. She was one of the most attractive women I'd ever seen, and she worked at the strip club Freya worked at before she had Eva.

That's where I knew Freya from. She had a wildly popular YouTube channel that Violet had loved, speaking about being a stripper, beauty routines and tricks of the trade.

It was wild that my daughter idolized two women I had fallen into hanging out with.

Marilyn had left earlier because her and her husband were getting ready for a baby of their own they were having via surrogate.

She'd invited me to the baby shower. In three months.

I'd accepted the invitation, knowing I'd never attend.

Now we were sitting outside, in the glow of the outdoor fire-place with the desert yawning around us and the stars twinkling above us.

It was total bliss.

I was thinking about everything that had happened in the past month, which had prompted me to ask the question about magic.

"Of course," Macy responded immediately.

"Oh, no. Don't get her started," Caroline rolled her eyes. But in a way a sister might, with softness, with good natured teasing, with love.

"Oh, stop," Macy shot back. "You loved *Lord of the Rings*."

"We did," Freya agreed, sipping her drink.

"The first time you made us watch it," Caroline added.

"Not the thirty times after that," Freya finished.

I smiled, watching them. There was an ease there that I

hadn't seen before. That I didn't know existed. I was instantly envious of them for what they had, desperate to belong.

"It was not thirty times," Macy snapped, unaware of how I was coveting her friendships. How I was coveting their lives, except with my own biker, with my own version of a happily ever after. Not the rapidly dwindling amount of time I had left with them all.

"More like forty," Caroline muttered under her breath.

Freya grinned into her drink.

"Like there is a limit to the amount of times anyone could watch that movie," Macy scoffed. She focused on me. "Don't listen to them. They believe in magic all right."

I smiled at her. "I think it was magic that brought me here," I said shyly. "I have no other explanation for it." I looked out toward the desert, promising myself I would one day have a place like this.

Even if it wouldn't be filled with the man I'd come to love. The women I'd come to love.

"I was driving, looking for... something. I don't know what. But I knew I was lost," I whispered. "And I found myself here. With Swiss." I glanced at the women who were all watching me intently. "With all of you. And I guess I just want to thank you." My words rushed out at the end as I was embarrassed at how candid I was being.

"You don't need to thank us, honey," Macy said gently. "The club is family. Which, if I could be so bold as to say—apart from your daughter, who we can't wait to meet, by the way—is something that you were sorely lacking." She reached across to squeeze my hand. "And that is the club's special kind of magic. Finding people who need us most. Bringing us all together. And, girlfriend, settle in. Because it's a forever kind of thing." She winked at me as I fought back tears.

"That calls for a toast," Freya declared, standing. She raised her glass. "To this forever kind of thing."

I stood on unsteady legs and raised my own glass.

"To the forever kind of thing," I repeated. I forced confidence into my voice. Even though I knew it was fraudulent. Even though I knew this wasn't a forever kind of this.

The clinking of our glasses echoed out into the desert. And I sent out a wish. That there was some way, somehow, I could find a way to stay here. With these people.

But even as I wished it, I knew in my bones it wouldn't come true.

I was not a runner.

Pilates. Hot yoga... Those were the two things I did to stay in shape, in addition to starving myself. Because that's what the women in my group did, and those were activities approved by Preston.

He didn't want me running on the streets. He certainly didn't want me in a gym where men could speak to me, hit on me. Nor would he want to run the risk of me getting strong enough to hit him back if I chose to.

Not that the strength to fight back came from lifting weights. It came from a place inside a person. One that did not exist inside of me. Otherwise, it would've awoken that very first day he hit me.

Those were the thoughts that had me putting on the cheap tennis shoes I'd worn the first two weeks and getting up to go for a run at two in the morning.

I couldn't be alone in this motel room, with only my thoughts and the crushing weight of the future threatening to ground me to dust.

Last night had been perfect. I was distracted enough with the company of the women. Then the booze and copious amounts of food had made it so that I was unconscious the second my head hit the lumpy motel pillow.

This was the first night I was truly alone with myself. All of the women had offered to do something with me, have me over, but I knew the invitations came out of knowledge that I would be sitting alone in a depressing motel room.

Swiss had tried to get me to stay at his room at the club while he was gone. While it was tempting, I didn't feel comfortable with that. Being there, existing there while he wasn't there. Sure, there had been nights when I'd fallen asleep without him, nights when he was out doing things I still didn't know about. But he always crawled into bed with me after. We always made the trip to the kitchen for breakfast together.

Even if I was there, cooking dinner for everyone while he was away doing something I didn't know about, there was comfort in the knowledge that he was coming back. He was my anchor to the club. Without him, I felt like some lonely, out of place house-wife pretending to be something she wasn't.

The motel was safer.

Or so I thought.

Until it became apparent I couldn't be alone with my own thoughts. Couldn't stand the scratchy sheets, cleaned with a detergent that didn't smell like Swiss. Like sex. I couldn't stand the thin walls that broadcasted whatever my neighbor was watching on TV. The sleepy street with the odd car driving by.

I had tried to watch TV shows that Freya had urged me to binge, had drank a couple of beers while doing it, but I couldn't relax. And I knew the only way to escape that feeling was to down a lot more beers.

Getting drunk on my own in a motel room was not a low that I was willing to sink to.

So I'd tried to concentrate on the shows. Then, I'd tried to concentrate on going to sleep. For hours.

Until it became clear I was not going to sleep, and I was very close to a complete breakdown.

I was desperate, shaking, scared of my own thoughts, and I was working on instinct more than anything else. So I'd shoved a hoodie on over the jersey sleep shorts I was wearing, put on the worn shoes and left.

I'd bought some cheap headphones—the ones that still had cords—at one of my stops. The only way I could sleep the first few nights was with music blasting in my ears. Putting those in to drown out the intrusive thoughts.

I had no idea where I was going as I pounded the pavement, running down a deserted main street. There was not a soul around. No one pouring out of bars—the only place open was the strip club where Freya used to work, and that was on the other side of town. Sure, Garnett wasn't perfect, but it was a pretty, sleepy and safe town, all things considered.

I didn't even see a car until I left the main street behind and worked my way toward the desert road leading out of town. The stars yawned above me, the ceiling of the night hanging low and heavy. My breaths were labored, and my limbs burned with exertion, a thin layer of sweat covering my entire body. I'd been going for at least thirty minutes, if not more, and I was getting well and truly out into the desert. Though this town may not be dangerous in terms of people, I was sure there were plenty of animals I could encounter that would see me as easy prey.

Prey.

That's what I was, still. An easy target with a will like tissue paper. Something you could tear through without effort.

As I spent time with Swiss, with the women from the club, I'd come to think that I'd managed to grow, strengthen.

That I was made of something thicker than that.

But I couldn't even handle a motel room without Swiss.

And very soon, I'd have to handle forever. A divorce. A new start. A real one. With my social security card, my nonexistent credit and a divorce that would likely leave me with nothing.

If Preston somehow agreed to divorce. If I somehow managed to keep out of his clutches for as long as the divorce proceedings lasted.

I forced my limbs harder, intent on pushing myself so hard that those thoughts would burn out of me.

I didn't even register the single headlight that roared past me as I ran; I was focusing on the burn of lactic acid in my lungs. So I didn't process it turning around on the road behind me. Nor did I hear the roar of the motorcycle. I didn't notice it until it slowed, pulling off to the shoulder in front of me, blocking my way, turning so the headlight illuminated me. I squinted against the light, lifting my hand to help with the glare.

My gait slowed, and my heart beat painfully against my chest as I watched a dark figure dismount the bike and block out the light with his body.

I immediately knew it was Swiss.

My body relaxed at his presence, at his strong and purposeful gait, though when I saw the expression on his face, I tensed up all over again.

He was pissed. That much was clear. His mouth moved rapidly as he approached me, and I rolled back on my heels just a little.

He stopped right in front of me, putting a very purposeful

distance between us, his mouth moving rapidly, hands fisted at his sides.

"What?" I asked, still squinting, music blasting in my ears. I didn't think to take the buds out of my ears, I was still disorientated and winded from the run. I was struggling to comprehend that Swiss was standing in front of me on the side of the road in the middle of the night.

"What the fuck are you doing running on your own, with headphones on at two in the fucking morning?" Swiss demanded after leaning forward and yanking the earbuds from my ears.

I didn't flinch back from his angry tone nor his hand flying so close to my face. I knew better than that.

"I'm sorry," I said immediately.

Fury flickered on his face, giving way to confusion. "Don't need you to apologize to me, Countess," he responded tentatively. "Need you to tell me what the fuck you're doing out here."

I stared at him, taking in a deep breath. Then another. I was gauging his face. His energy. Gauging my safety in that scenario. Once I was a little more grounded and working off my current knowledge, not off old memories that belonged to a different man, I realized I was safe. I was always safe with Swiss.

With myself, not so much.

"I couldn't sleep," I admitted meekly, my tone submissive.

"You couldn't sleep?" Swiss repeated.

I shook my head slowly.

"You can't sleep, Kate, you pop a pill." He pinched the bridge of his nose. "You take a tequila shot. Or two. You put on trash TV. Most importantly, you call me. You tell me that you've got shit swirling in your head so intensely that you're taking yourself out running in the middle of the night like you're fleein' from a fuckin' murderer."

He was no longer speaking softly.

"Why in the fuck didn't you call me?" he demanded.

I frowned at him. Why didn't I call him? Aside from not wanting to sound pathetic and clingy, I hadn't even considered it. Of course, I wanted to hear his voice, wanted to know what he was doing, who he was with, if he missed me. But I had no idea of the protocol for such things.

"I didn't want to bother you," I said quietly.

"You didn't want to bother me?" he repeated.

I shook my head.

"Kate, you're my fuckin' woman," he clipped. "Besides the fact that I was thinking of you the entire fuckin' time I was gone and hearing your voice would've been welcome at any point, you find yourself in a situation like this," he waved his arm at me, "then you call me. That is not a bother. You are not a bother. Me driving up on this, seeing this... *That*'s a fuckin' bother. Now get on the back of my fuckin' bike."

I stared at him. The last part was a command, no doubt about it. But I just couldn't bring myself to obey it. Not when the sweat from the run had dried on my skin, the breeze was picking up and my insides had turned to ice.

Swiss was staring at me harshly, but I stayed rooted in place. Finally, his jaw softened, his stance changing into something less hostile.

"Baby," he murmured, as if he were talking to an animal that might spook. Which, incidentally, was what I felt like right now. "I'm pissed at you. But only because it gave me the shock of my life seein' you out here, my mind running through the things that could've happened." He stepped forward, slowly, watching me.

Whatever he saw in my face had him crossing the distance between us quickly and pulling me into his arms.

I immediately melted into his chest, clinging to the sides of his cut, inhaling the smell of leather and the scent that was uniquely him.

Swiss kissed the top of my head. "I was scared," he murmured, pulling me back so we could make eye contact. "It terrifies me, the thought of something happenin' to you. And I'm a guy who functions off the belief that he's a badass in control of everything. Which means I don't do well with fear. And I'm sorry."

I blinked at him. He was apologizing. To me. Immediately after doing the thing that he was sorry for. As soon as he saw the effect his anger had on me.

There were a lot of things I could've—should've—said then, looking into the endless eyes of the man I loved. And I did love Swiss. In addition to my very real and scary problems, that was the main thing that had me out running.

Something I quite obviously could not tell him.

"You may have to carry me to the bike," I chuckled softly. "Because I haven't run in my life, and I fear I may have lost the use of my legs."

Swiss stared at me for a beat and then burst out laughing.

It was not a joke. Now that the fear and adrenaline had worn off, my muscles were locking up, and my knees were shaking under the stress of keeping my body upright.

Swiss gathered me into his arms once he'd finished laughing. "You gonna be able to fuck when we get home?" he asked, walking us to the bike. "Because I'm definitely gonna need to get inside you."

My body flushed. "As long as you do all the work," I told him.

A throaty chuckle. "I think I can do that."

And just like that, a biker on a Harley saved me in the middle of the night. From myself.

For the time being, at least.

True to his word, Swiss did all the work when we got back to the club. First, in the shower. Then in the bed, with me tied up.

He had just let me out of the restraints and pulled me onto his chest.

We didn't do much talking when we got in. It was all about our bodies, desperate for each other, rediscovering each other after only a day and a half apart.

But there were going to be words now. Swiss wasn't one to let something go. And me running down a deserted road in the middle of the night was pretty fricking weird and needed a little more explanation than what I gave.

"I'm... not ready to talk about it," I announced before Swiss could ask the question I knew was on the tip of his tongue. I could tell by his intake of breath, the energy in the air. And I was not someone to believe in 'energies,' but there was no other way to explain it.

Swiss rubbed my back. "I get it," he said. "I understand there's shit both of us are holding back because it's intense. 'Cause it's fucked-up. 'Cause it'll tear apart the awesome fuckin' thing we've created." His eyes narrowed. "Not break it or make it, so that I don't want you. Fair warning... When you are ready to tell me your shit, there's nothing that you can say that'll make me let you go."

Wrong.

Totally wrong.

But I didn't say that out loud, of course. I was too busy reveling in what he was saying. The emotion in his words.

"I'm just very aware that things have been good between us," he continued. "Really fuckin' good. And I know that you, arriving here with a duffel full of shit, stayin' at a weekly motel, a nice one to be sure, nothing to be ashamed of, but I'm pretty sure your life before was all about designer suitcases and fancy ass hotels."

I pursed my lips at how accurate his assessment was.

"I'm aware that the shit you left behind, the life you left behind was rough on you. Very fuckin' aware that you're emerging from a chrysalis, that I was lucky enough to see you come out a butterfly. And fuck if I'm gonna be the one to bruise those exquisite, brand-new wings. Not yet. You deserve this."

He sighed loudly.

"Fuck, I know I do. So I'm bein' a little selfish on my behalf. But, baby, you want to dive in right now, tomorrow, next week... I'm ready to go deeper with you. Fuckin' achin' to get to the core of you."

Tears filled my eyes. I was not aware that men were able to see things so clearly. Feel so deeply. String words together like Swiss just had. They wrapped around my heart like barbed wire, cutting me with every beat. He was doing everything right. Saying wonderful things. And the weight of it was foreign, uncomfortable after years of abuse.

"But we can wait." His fingers rubbed my tender wrists, the stiffness from the restraints dissipating with each stroke. "As long as you promise not to go runnin' anywhere in the middle of the night."

"I promise," I replied immediately. I hated myself for making a promise like that. One I knew I was going to eventually break.

The next morning I emerged from the bathroom early. The telltale twinge in my stomach had woken me.

Swiss was squinting at me. "Get back in this bed," he ordered. "Wanna fuck you," he added sleepily.

Despite what was going on with my ovaries, my body responded, seeming to have a mind of its own. I very much wanted him to do that.

"We, uh, we can't have sex," I said tentatively.

"Why the fuck not?" Swiss demanded, sitting up in bed now, obviously a lot more awake.

"I'm, um, on my period," I told him very quietly. I was thoroughly disgusted at the shame in my voice and coursing through my body. I'd made sure that Violet was never ashamed of what her body did. Made sure it was not a dirty, secret thing like it was when I was growing up. It was a part of being a woman. A part that wasn't always great but something to be proud of.

Violet, to her credit, was not embarrassed in the slightest. And I was proud of myself for not letting all my crap leech into her.

And to Preston's credit, he never shamed our daughter when she talked openly about her bodily functions. In fact, he'd celebrated her. Prided himself on being the father who would go in and buy her tampons, and then the Diva Cup that was *so much* better for her and the environment.

I loved that Preston was like that with our daughter, and to a point, with me. He never really wanted to know too much about it, but he would run me a bath. He'd get a heating pad for me if cramps were bad. Of course, only after I'd given him the obligatory blow job that he was entitled to when I was menstruating.

He certainly wouldn't touch me in any other way. He thought it was 'foul.' Because I didn't have anyone else to compare my situation to, I assumed that most men—certainly most men in my generation—were of the same opinion. It only served to shame me further when some of the times I was the most turned on were during the week that Preston refused to touch me.

That, of course, was coupled with the ever-present shame from still being turned on by the husband who beat me.

"You're on your period?" Swiss repeated, bringing me back into the small room that was once his that had become ours.

My clothes—a collection growing steadily, thanks to Macy, Freya and Caroline—were in the compact closet, and I had two drawers of my very own in the dresser. I had bought a scented candle to put on that dresser. Swiss liked that and bought more, discovering all of the things we could do with the hot wax.

A couple of pieces of cheap jewelry were arranged in a little bowl on the dresser. The bathroom was changed the most, with proper and separate shampoos, body wash and body scrubs in the shower, assorted skin care and makeup arranged beside the sink.

Now a little box of tampons stashed in the bathroom cabinet.

Swiss pulled back the covers, got out of bed—naked—and walked to where I was standing by the bathroom door. He didn't stop until he made it to me, one hand going to my hip, the other brushing hair from my face. I was only wearing his tee... most of the time I slept naked, and when I didn't, I was wearing something of his.

"You want to fuck?" he asked, his pillowy lips tilted up.

My skin flamed. "I can't," I murmured.

His finger went to my chin, lifting it up so I couldn't avoid his eyes. "I don't believe that was the question. Now, if you're hurtin', I'm totally down to go on a junk food run, tuck you up in bed and cuddle and watch whatever show or movie you want." His hand stroked my hip. "But if you want my cock, I'm more than happy to give that to you, Countess."

My eyes widened at him. "Don't you think it's, uh... gross?"

He frowned at me. "Not one single thing about the female body, yours in particular, that I think is gross, Kate." His hand skimmed across my stomach then up to my breasts, which were slightly swollen and tender.

I sucked in an unsteady breath.

"I happen to think the female body is fuckin' glorious," he murmured. "At any time of the month." He gently tweaked my nipple. "And in case you haven't noticed, baby, I'm more than a little fucked-up. I like to see a woman bleed." His finger brushed the swell of my breast where he'd ran a knife along it two nights before, licking the blood from the blade as he fucked me.

"To be able to fuck you, cover myself in the beauty of your body while going through its cycle," he rasped against my mouth. His lips found mine. "Fuckin' delicious. But something I'm discovering with you is that I get a different kind of pleasure just being with you. Whether or not my dick is inside you. So you want to wait, we'll wait." His hand skimmed down my stomach, and he watched me from inches away.

His fingers slipped into my waistband. "But I know you, know your body very well," he continued. "So I can see you want this. The only thing holdin' you back is whatever shit has been drilled into you in the past."

His fingers parted me, finding my clit and rubbing it gently. When I let out a little moan. He grinned wickedly. "Yeah, my woman wants me to fuck her." His finger found the string of my tampon and tugged gently. Not enough to pull it out but enough pressure to make his intentions known.

My body flushed with arousal and need.

It felt wrong, forbidden and exciting.

Swiss kissed my neck. "We're gonna go and take this out," he tugged the string a little harder this time. "Then we're going to fuck in the bed."

And we did just that.

The sheets were stained with my blood afterward.

And I wasn't ashamed. I loved it.

CHAPTER ELEVEN

KATE

ONE WEEK LATER

"WHY DON'T you have your own place?" I blurted.

I'd just got back from work at the coffee shop. Swiss had picked me up as he always did. We were lying on top of his bed, both drinking a beer. It was unusual for us to be sitting fully clothed on top of the bed after not seeing each other for a few hours.

Most of the time, we could barely get the door closed before we started tearing at each other's clothes. My appetite for him had not been sated. Not in the least. If anything, it had become more ravenous. And Swiss hadn't seemed to tire of me either. He was more needful, urgent, intense, violent and tender all at the same time.

But today we both seemed content enjoying each other's

company, the warm breeze blowing in from the open window, music playing from the common room where everyone was gearing up for the weekly party.

"I'm sorry," I apologized, embarrassed. "That's totally rude and intrusive of me to ask."

"Countess, you can ask me whatever the fuck you want," he told me. "Quite happy for you to intrude into every corner of my life," he added with a grin. After he took a long pull of his beer, he looked more serious.

"Came to the club a long time ago when I was very fucked-up," he told me. "A story for another day."

The way his eyes went faraway, shrouded with a pain I hadn't seen in him, told me that story would shatter my heart. I ached to scoop him into my arms. To protect him somehow.

But you couldn't protect someone from the past.

"Once I got my patch, I jumped around different clubs... was a nomad."

I frowned at this and Swiss caught my confusion.

"Patched members usually have a home club," he explained. "Either in their hometown or a place they adopted as theirs. I didn't have a home club. Liked being able to move on. To not put down roots. The patch, that was my only home."

My eyes flickered to the leather he was always wearing. Every day, I learned how important, how integral it was to his identity.

"Came here to help rebuild the club after it was almost wiped out on Christmas, few years ago."

I stared at him. "Wiped out?"

"A massacre," he nodded, his face grim. "Almost every patched member. Every club girl. Everyone except for Macy, Hansen, Jagger and Scarlett."

The words sunk in. Scarlett I'd heard about in passing. She

lived in California with her husband who was patched into the club there. But Macy, Hansen and Jagger I'd come to know very well. They were good people. The absolute best. And I'd seen what they thought of the club, how they considered it their family.

Swiss wiped a tear that had escaped from my eye. "Still bleeds, that wound," he shook his head. "Some cuts sink so deep they never even scab over."

My mind went to the past, all the way back to my childhood. To my own seeping, oozing wound. The one I ignored.

"I had intended to stay for as long as they needed me," Swiss continued. "But I found I liked it here. Liked my brothers." He took another long pull. "Lost another one, Claw, a while ago. Almost made me leave again." His eyes seared into mine. "But that would've been doing what I'd done my whole life... runnin'. Runnin' the second a place started to feel like home. So I stayed." He brushed my jaw. "Glad I did, 'cause I was here when you walked into the club."

My heart skipped.

"As you pointed out in my bathroom, I'm a low maintenance man. A bed. A bathroom. Place to put my shit. Screws in the walls." He shrugged. "It's all a man like me needs." He cupped my chin. "Until recently."

My entire body quivered. "Know that you're happy here, with me... for the time being. But I also know that you deserve a home. A place with a kick-ass kitchen. Where you can make it yours. Don't think I don't know that. Don't think I'm not making plans for that."

Panic spread across my skin at his words.

Plans. He was making plans.

For a home.

For us.

That thing I'd been dreaming about while I was making coffee. He was actually taking steps to make it a reality. Because, as far as he knew, I was starting fresh. As far as he knew, I could put down roots here with him.

It hit me then, square in the chest, the magnitude of what I was doing. How tangled I was with him. I was going to draw both of our blood when I extricated myself. If I didn't find the courage to tell him the truth.

While I was thinking all of this, Swiss was running his hands lazily up and down my hip, brushing my shirt up to expose the skin of my torso. At some point, his hands had roamed downward, going to my calves.

"Don't!" I cried out, scuttling away from him.

Swiss stared at me in horror as I tried to escape his grasp. Such a thing was not possible, of course. Swiss was much, *much* stronger than me. And he never used that strength against me. At least, not without my permission and always for my pleasure.

"Let me go," I demanded, wishing I was capable of sounding stronger.

"No fuckin' way," he shot back, not loosening his grip even a little. His eye contact was so intense and unyielding, I ached to look away but couldn't do it. "You're gonna tell me what the fuck that was."

He was speaking softly. In a tone I recognized. The way that Preston used to talk when I was really in trouble. When things were going to get really bad. That was something I'd learned. Men were not most dangerous when they were screaming at the top of their lungs. That's not to say they weren't dangerous then, but they were most dangerous when they spoke softly. Like a cougar, quietly and gracefully stalking before the pounce.

But Swiss was not Preston. I'd come to learn that. Not once had he given me any kind of indication that he was anything like him. And I was not a naïve, young girl who couldn't spot red flags. I had honed my instincts. But that didn't mean that I wasn't still traumatized. That I didn't hold muscle memory.

"Kate." Swiss spoke my name as a demand.

I blinked away my thoughts. His expression had not changed, had not softened. His grip had not loosened even a little.

"What the fuck was that?" he asked when I still didn't speak.

My mouth was dry, and my head throbbed. It was clear he wasn't going to let this go until he got an answer, and I wasn't prepared enough to come up with an alternative that made a little more sense and wasn't massively embarrassing.

"I forgot to shave my legs," I said quietly.

He blinked at me in confusion. "You forgot to shave your legs," he repeated. "And that's why you flinched away from me like I was burning you."

My face flushed with embarrassment. "I, um, I don't know. I guess I overreacted" I gripped the neck of my beer so tightly my knuckles were turning white.

Swiss was still staring at me with intensity and didn't speak for a long time. I was frozen in place.

"Your ex really fucked you up, didn't he?" he asked finally. All hardness was gone from his voice. All danger. What lay there was not pity. No, concern. A simmering, protective anger.

I swallowed, hating that Preston had entered this conversation. Had polluted it. Beyond the fact that I didn't want him here, didn't want him poisoning this, I also didn't want to get too close to the lies I was telling.

Yes, in my heart of hearts, Preston was well and truly my ex. I had severed all ties with him the moment I left our town's limits. There was no way I was ever going to be his wife again, even though, if you wanted to get technical, in the eyes of the law, I was still his wife.

But Swiss and the Sons of Templar didn't seem to concern themselves about the eyes of the law and technicalities. So that was how I was justifying it.

"It doesn't give him power, you know," Swiss tacked on when I didn't reply. "To admit that." He was slowly and lazily stroking my prickly legs, as if to make a point. I focused on the movement to keep me calm.

"It doesn't give him shit," he grumbled. "It means you're wonderfully soft, you love with your whole heart. And there are motherfuckers who will take advantage. Who will see how pure and precious that is and will want to ruin it."

Tears welled up in my eyes.

"I'm not a good man," he continued. "I'm not gonna pretend to be. I've done some terrible fuckin' shit. And I surely will have terrible deeds in my future too. I need to make that clearer to you, but I've been afraid."

It felt like my heart splintered my ribs, it was beating so intently. Not because of what Swiss was confessing to be—I didn't care about that—but because there was real fear, genuine feeling in his voice.

He was still stroking my leg. "Afraid that you'll see me for what I am, the violence inside me, and you'll want to run." He gripped my calf. "Although you've taken my violence with a hunger I've never seen," he said, voice deeper now.

My pussy prickled with desire, despite the subject matter.

"And that's why I think you're strong enough to stomach what I am," Swiss told me, laying a gentle kiss on the corner of my mouth. "But, Kate, despite the violent, dangerous man I am, I will promise one thing. I will not ruin your precious heart. I will protect it with everything I am." His eyes burned into me. "And I'm one wretched motherfucker."

A tear trickled down my face at his declaration.

Then another.

He wiped them away with his thumb.

I opened my mouth to tell him the truth. Not about Preston, I wasn't there yet. But to tell him that my heart was his. That I loved him.

But then a bang vibrated against the closed door. We both jumped, so deep in each other we'd forgotten that other people existed.

"Hurry up!" Cody yelled. "Freya won't shut the fuck up about Kate and tequila shots."

Swiss's eyes turned a little less serious. "Although I'm not done with the conversation, I'm definitely in the mood to get you drunk on tequila."

My toes curled. Though I had partied plenty since I'd unofficially moved in here, I had yet to repeat the tequila shot night.

Now that the promise of tequila and what it would wash away—also what it would give me the courage to do in the bedroom—took over, the truth could wait another day.

Swiss pulled us both up, taking my beer and setting it on the nightstand beside his. He pulled me to him.

"You shave or don't shave whatever part of your body you want," he told me, tangling his hand in my midnight black hair which was quickly growing longer. "Though if you want to shave this, I might have a spirited argument against that," he hummed as he cupped me between my legs, kissing me long and hard.

"Now let's go and get my woman drunk on tequila," he declared.

⌷

It was the day after I'd gotten drunk on tequila. Like the first night, all of my inhibitions had shed, and I'd had fun using the restraints on Swiss. He'd been more than willing.

I was feeding my hangover, and everyone else in the club, with the vodka pasta that had become my signature dish. We were all gathered around the dining table, empty plates in front of us. I was leaning against Swiss's arm.

My phone vibrated, and I jumped up the second I saw Violet's name.

It had been almost a week since I'd heard her voice, and despite all of the wonderful things happening to me and how busy I was, I thought of her every moment.

"Sorry, it's my daughter," I told everyone, snatching the phone and standing up. "She's in Paris. And she's in love with her older university teacher." I gritted my teeth at the way that sounded out loud.

Jagger's nostrils flared. "Need us to fly over there and scare him off?"

I laughed. He didn't.

Surely he wasn't serious... I didn't have time to ponder that because I didn't want to miss Violet.

"Sweetie," I answered the phone, turning from the crowd, my eyes touching Swiss one last time. He was watching me with an expression I couldn't decipher.

"Either that's a ninth grader over in Paris with a boyfriend— in that case we *really* do need to go over there—or she had that fuckin' kid in the ninth grade," Anderson, one of the patched members, said as I walked out of earshot.

"Mom!" she called out.

I stopped in my tracks. My heart stuttered, and my skin went ice cold. "What's wrong?" I demanded. I was already mentally pawning off my remaining jewelry to get the next flight to Paris.

Silence rang out behind me, but I didn't have time to worry about that.

"Oh my god, why do you always think something's wrong?" Violet whined.

My body sagged right against Swiss's chest, who had, at some point, gotten up from his chair and rushed to my side, presumably because he heard the concern in my voice.

"I always think something's wrong because you shout 'Mom!' at me in greeting instead of, I don't know, hello?" I snapped.

"Mom, I'm dramatic. You've known me all my life," she returned.

Swiss was rubbing my upper arms now, despite hearing that there was nothing he needed to hold me up for. As if he sensed I was still not on an even keel, still recovering from that paralyzing worry that something would happen to my girl. It was the undercurrent of every waking moment.

"All of your life, you've lived in my house," I retorted. "All of your life, you haven't been on another continent where a myriad of things could happen to you. Don't you remember *Taken*?"

There was a long sigh from across the phone. "Yes, Mom. I remember *Taken*. I can recite *Taken* word for word after the sheer amount of times you made me watch it."

"What was the 'Mom' for then? If you are not currently being kidnapped by human traffickers?" I demanded, leaning back into Swiss's chest.

He kissed my head, and delightful shivers went down my spine.

It felt incredibly odd to have Swiss so close to me while I was talking to Violet, who knew nothing about the biker I was living with. As far as she knew, I was happily married to her father.

And as far as Swiss knew, I was divorced from her father.

My worlds were colliding, and I didn't like it. As much as I wanted to escape that feeling, I didn't want to leave Swiss either.

"Well, Jacques got us the most amazing little villa in Côte d'Azur," she enthused. "It looks like a castle. It's so beautiful, Mom. And super fancy. Like a *Kardashian* has rented it!"

"Oh my god," I exclaimed in my best Valley Girl accent.

Swiss chuckled from behind me. Luckily Violet was too wrapped up in her excitement to notice the masculine laugh that did not belong to her father.

"Okay, I know it's cliché, elitist and superficial to be impressed by that," she admitted sheepishly, "but he did this for us. Because he's been busy, and he gets time off at the end of November so we will be able to have a proper goodbye."

"Wait," I frowned. "The end of November? That can't be right, you're meant to be back in the US by Thanksgiving."

There was a loaded pause on the other end of the phone.

"Violet," I probed in the 'Mom voice' I rarely had to use with her after potty training.

"Okay, so yes, it would *technically* mean I wouldn't be home for Thanksgiving," she stated quickly. "But I already talked to Daddy, and he said you're going to likely still be in California then anyway and—"

My spine went straight, and I was rigid in Swiss's arms. I didn't have the phone on speaker, and Violet was speaking so quickly that I doubted he would've heard the 'California' part of that, but I was still on guard and needed to get away from him.

But his hands were tight around my body.

My mind was whirling with everything that Violet said.

"You already spoke to your father?" I asked quietly.

She'd already spoken to him, and he'd already said I'd still be gone, which likely meant he still had no idea where I was. It was technically good news, but my insides were combusting at the mere thought of him.

"Mom, I'm sorry. I know it wasn't cool of me to speak to him first, but I know you've got so much on your plate," she sighed. "And it had just come up when he happened to call. He was really understanding and supportive about it, which is... unusual for Daddy," she continued, a smile in her voice.

I was fighting not to throw up.

Her father was supportive because he wanted his daughter away for as long as possible, so he had more time to find and likely punish her mother, and have time for the injuries to heal.

"I know that you were excited for me to come home," Violet murmured apologetically. "And I miss you, Mom, I miss you so, so much. But I promise that I'm going to be home before Christmas. We'll make cookies. Decorate the tree. Watch Christmas movies while drinking hot chocolate."

Tears welled up in my eyes, and the very foundation of my soul felt like it was crumbling to pieces. Not just because it was going to be longer without my daughter—and I'd be spending an important holiday without her for the first time—but because all of our holidays were gone now. We would not be drinking hot chocolate, decorating the tree or making cookies. Because those were all routines we'd established as a family.

Preston included.

And no matter how this turned out, I would never live in that house again. The house I'd raised Violet in. The house I had all of those memories in, not all of them terrible. Some of them wonderful.

"Yeah, honey," I replied, my voice high, thin and full of tears.

Swiss's arms flexed around me.

"Mom," Violet cooed. "Please don't cry. I can come home.

Daddy already changed my flights, but I'm sure when you talk to him next—"

"No, sweetie," I interjected, my voice a tad stronger now. "You should stay. Have your experience at the Kardashian house. Get your proper goodbye with the age-inappropriate boyfriend."

"Not funny, Mom," she muttered.

I smiled weakly. "I know."

"Are you sure you're going to be okay?" she asked with audible concern. "Daddy said he hasn't been able to see you yet because of work. You must be so lonely."

I choked down her words. "Sweetie, please don't worry about me. It's my job to worry about you. I'm fine. I'm great, actually. I just miss you."

"I miss you too, Momma," she said with a hitch in her voice.

"I love you," I whispered.

"I love you more," she replied.

Then she was gone.

And I promptly hung up the phone, turned into Swiss's chest and burst into tears.

━━

"I'd like to meet her," Swiss said while drawing circles on my back.

I was naked and splayed against his torso, several hours after dinner.

After my crying jag that had lasted for about ten minutes. Swiss had held me tight in his arms, rubbed my back and didn't say a word.

Once I was done, I was incredibly embarrassed at my outburst and had wanted to retreat to Swiss's room. But everyone else wouldn't hear of it, and Caroline had hugged me—fighting

Swiss to let go of me—and had poured me a very large glass of wine.

It was then I managed to get myself together, Swiss watching me closely.

After the drinks that we had with dessert. The board games that everyone had played. Bikers played board games.

Bikers also got very passionate about board games, with Swiss nearly stabbing Lucas for 'cheating.'

That was when the game ended, and Swiss and I commenced games of our own.

I was delightfully sore and satisfied.

"Meet who?" I asked sleepily.

"Violet," he replied.

I was instantly awake and trying my best not to tense all of my muscles, something Swiss would've noticed.

My heart dropped. Then it cracked.

I wanted nothing more than for Swiss to meet Violet. For a multitude of reasons. Because I was immensely proud of the person my daughter was. Because I wanted him to see that. Because I wanted him to see that part of me. She was a huge chunk of who I was. She was most of my heart... He was what remained. I wanted Violet to see how I was with him. To see the real version of her mother. When she was happy. When she wasn't terrified, putting on an act.

I wanted to integrate these different versions of myself so I could turn this into something permanent. Violet would be fascinated by club life. The conservative part of me would want to protect her from some of the racier realities, but my daughter was now an adult. In Europe, where she was legally allowed to drink. She was sleeping with a man years older than her. I could not imagine that this life would be a negative influence on her.

If anything, I wanted her to learn from it. See how these men loved their women. See how these women loved their children, loved each other, were unapologetically themselves.

Violet would adore all of them and idolize them immediately.

"I know it's soon," Swiss said. "And that this is probably worlds away from how she grew up..." he trailed off, and I got his meaning.

I'd been quiet for so long, he'd interpreted my silence as me having reservations. He was insinuating that I could possibly think the club wasn't *good enough* for my daughter. The fact that he thought that was horrifying, as was the vulnerability in his voice.

I turned, propping myself up with my elbow so I could look into his eyes. The dim light from the lamp beside the bed illuminated the tenderness in his gaze. I lifted up my other hand to gently cup his jaw. "I would love for Violet to meet you," I said honestly, my words tasting like acid because I knew there was no way in hell he'd ever meet her. Meeting her would expose all of my lies. "I would love for her to see the club, to meet your family. She would adore it." I paused, thinking of my daughter in this atmosphere. "Though she'd likely challenge Hansen on the rule about women not being able to patch in," I added on a smile.

Swiss's eyes lightened. "I would like to see that," he murmured.

"She would like you," I told him, again with more of that honesty that burned my insides.

He smiled. "Of course she would," he said, voice lighter. "I'm fuckin' amazing. Plus, I plan on making her mother a very happy woman."

My grin stayed frozen on my face as my heart splintered, my chest searing with the pain of it all.

Tell him now, something inside me screamed. *Do it. There is time to make him understand. To save this.*

My mouth opened to spill it all out. But I couldn't do it. Not now. Not ever.

"You have made her mother the happiest she has been in her entire life," I said instead. I moved to straddle him, my body delightfully tender.

Swiss caught hold of my hips.

"Now," I pushed his legs apart with my knees. "It's time that I make you very happy," I murmured, kissing my way down his chest.

And then I proceeded to distract him with a blow job. I wasn't proud of it. Not even a little.

But I didn't know what else to do.

There was no saving this. Saving me. All I had left was to savor every moment. Every opportunity to touch him, ride on the back of his bike, sleep next to him. Before I left him behind.

CHAPTER TWELVE

KATE

TWO WEEKS LATER

MACY AND HANSEN were having a pool party.

Or a 'pool warming' as Macy had tried to call it. Hansen had argued that there was no way they were calling it that because it sounded like a bunch of people were "pissing in my fucking pool."

They argued about it.

A lot.

So it was being called a pool warming.

It was still somewhat unnerving to me, to see these women openly challenge their husbands. To throw sass. Unafraid of men society deemed to be dangerous. Deadly. *These* were the kind of men who beat their wives, if the popular narrative was to be believed.

Except they didn't challenge their wives. They barely raised their voices to them. They conceded. They backed down. They shook their heads, smiling, bringing them in for a kiss. Dragging them off to have wild sex. I'd seen it in person with each of the women and their men.

It was a journey, finding my voice with Swiss. Feeling brave enough to speak up, to disagree with him without fear of reproach. But the way I lived, the way I *thought* when I was with Preston, was trial by fire. With Swiss, everything was so primal, so reactive, sometimes I said and did things without even thinking. And he proved, consistently and continually, that he might've been a dangerous man, but I had nothing to fear from him.

"I've put on weight," I exclaimed, staring at myself in the mirror, wearing the bikini I'd bought for the occasion. My boobs were spilling out of the triangles, my stomach no longer had ribs visible and my hips were much wider.

"Yep," Swiss agreed.

I gaped at him. "Now I'm not exactly an expert on how to survive in this outlaw world, but I am aware that is not the right response to give a woman if you want to live to ride another day," I snapped.

"Fuck you're cute," he smiled at me hungrily before pulling me in to kiss my head.

I placed my hands on his chest so I could push back and glare at him. "And fat, apparently."

His expression turned serious. "You're not fuckin' fat," he growled. "You put on weight you needed to gain." His hands ran down the sides of my body. "And not enough of it, in my opinion. As beautiful as you were when I first saw you, you were much too fuckin' skinny."

He toyed with the string that tied the side of my bikini together.

"Not something I ever would've said if you'd stayed at that size," he added as his eyes trailed up to meet mine. "Which, of course, you haven't because that was not a size you were meant to exist at. My guess is that life you lived before all of this was amongst a bunch of other women who were starving themselves for pieces of shit husbands."

My fingers curled with unease at the sudden change in subject.

"You were living a life that didn't fit you, so you had to shrink down in order to make room for yourself. As much as I hate that you ever had to do that, I'm glad you're finding space now. Here. With me. I happen to love your curves."

His palms moved to my ass, grabbing the ample handful that was there now.

"And I'll love it if you grow more of them."

Then his hand skimmed my hips again, diving into the front of my bathing suit.

"Swiss," I breathed. "We have to get there early."

His hand did not stop.

"Seriously," I protested weakly. "I told Macy I would do the appetizers for her. And as much as I like where this is going, I don't want to let her down."

In a few seconds, I was liable to forget all able appetizers, forget who in the heck Macy even was.

Swiss's hand stopped, and he let out a frustrated sigh. "Fine," he grunted. "But I'm fuckin' you in their bathroom the second you're finished, and they've got only themselves to blame."

I smiled up at him as erotic anticipation flooded my system. "How are *they* to blame for us having sex in their bathroom?" I asked playfully.

"It was their choice to get a pool," he returned, shrugging on his cut.

He was wearing jeans and a tank. To a pool party. He'd informed me earlier that he'd change into swim trunks when he got there. Apparently, walking around in swim trunks would "fuck with his street cred."

"It was their choice to throw this pool warming," he continued, turning to look at me. "Therefore, they must've expected you to be walkin' round in that fuckin' swimsuit. And I wouldn't be a man if I didn't fuck my woman while she was wearin' that." He waved at my bikini.

I bit my lip, my cheeks warming.

"Well, far be it for me to argue with that logic," I giggled.

He narrowed his eyes. "You keep bein' cute at the same time you're bein' sexy as fuck, I'll be chaining you to the bed, appetizers be damned."

My belly plunged all the way to my toes, and the breath whooshed out of my lungs.

I was not immune to Swiss when he said things like that. I had not gotten used to the way he spoke. It still affected me.

"We can do that later," I murmured, moving out of his grip to pull a floaty linen dress over my head. It was sheer and finished at my ankles. The red swimsuit I was wearing was clearly defined underneath, and I didn't care. No one else would.

I slipped into some cheap sandals I'd gotten from Target, my toes painted the same red as my bikini. My hair was piled into a messy bun on top of my head, and I wasn't wearing any makeup. I reasoned it would all get washed off in the pool anyway. My cheeks were rosy, and there were a few freckles dusting my nose from the amount of time my bare face saw the sun lately. SPF slathered on it, of course.

"Fuck," Swiss muttered.

I turned to see him staring at me, rubbing the back of his head.

"What?" I asked.

"Well, I'm havin' a dilemma," he said, eyes running over me. "See, that dress is not at all gonna work on the bike. But you look so fuckin' hot in it, I am physically unable to ask you to change."

I couldn't stop the smile that lifted my cheeks. "Well, it might behoove us to drive anyway because I picked up some last-minute supplies for the appetizers, and I don't know how well they'll travel on the bike."

He tilted his head, regarding me with amusement. "Might it 'behoove us', Countess?" he teased.

I rolled my eyes.

"Don't like riding without you pressed up against me," he complained.

I smiled at him. "Well, I'm not overly fond of it either," I dropped a kiss onto his sulking lips. "But I do like this dress, and I got some kick-ass cheeses, so will you make an exception, right? Just this once?" I widened my eyes. "For me?" I even tried to pout.

Swiss shook his head, smiling. "Anything for you, Kate."

His voice wasn't as teasing as it had been before.

There was another layer there, blanketing what he just said.

Something that filled me up and scared the crap out of me at the same time.

I didn't look at the number when the phone rang. I was too distracted by finishing off the appetizers, too busy thinking about Swiss's promises of what we were going to be doing in the bathroom later.

Ordinarily, I'd be worried about how disrespectful doing that in someone else's house would be, but apparently, we wouldn't be the first to do such things. Each of the married men could not keep their hands off their wives, and no one seemed to mind one bit.

Swiss had been giving me looks from the breakfast bar until I'd finally banished him outside because he was distracting me.

He'd grumbled about that then came up to slip his hand into my bikini top, kiss my neck and whisper about the things he planned to do to me before we left.

It had taken me five minutes to get my breathing under control after that.

We had been the first to arrive. Macy was dealing with the kids after asking me about ten times if there was anything she could do then thanking me profusely when I'd assured her I had it.

And beyond thinking about Swiss, I did have it. Their kitchen was beautiful, open plan with plenty of counter space. All of their appliances were top notch, everything I could need was laid out for me, and what wasn't I could find easily. The kitchen was clean but cluttered. Scattered with photos in mismatched frames. There was a dying basil plant by the stove. Recipe books were stacked unevenly in a corner. Everything was lived in. Warm.

Music played from the speakers they had mounted on the walls. The house smelled of lavender and sage. A balmy breeze brushed through the open sliding doors that led out toward the pool area—where Swiss was with Hansen.

My mind wandered happily as I put the finishing touches on the food, my soul light. I'd never felt so... at peace. So happy.

Of course, I missed Violet with an ache that never left my heart, but inside myself, outside my identity as a mom, I was someone else now. Someone I liked.

I was thinking of Violet when I answered my phone.

Only her, Julian, and everyone in the club had this number. Julian had closed the café for the day, deciding we all needed a day off. Everyone from the club was due to arrive in the next few minutes—not that the bikers worked on timelines; people tended to arrive whenever they wanted to—so by process of elimination, it had to be Violet.

"Hey, sweetie," I greeted, tucking the phone into the crook of my shoulder as I wiped my hands on a kitchen towel.

"Kate."

The single word had me literally freezing. I stopped breathing. My heart stopped beating. The ground fell out from under me. There was a low ringing in my ears. My mouth opened. Closed again.

"Do I not deserve a greeting from my wife?" Preston asked.

I found power of my limbs as I snatched the phone, ending the call and blocking the number.

The phone fell to the counter with a clatter. My hands were shaking, my heart roaring. That identity, the one I'd been reveling in just moments ago, slipped through my fingers.

"Kate?" My name was spoken with concern, though it was muffled, as if it was coming through water.

Macy was standing at the breakfast bar, Xander on her hip, frowning at me. "Honey?" she pressed. "Are you okay? You look like you've just seen a ghost."

A ghost.

If only.

I quickly plastered on a fake smile. "No, I um..." I trailed off, trying to find a convincing lie.

"Who was that on the phone?" she asked softly. Knowingly.

Shit. I hadn't realized she'd been there for that long. I wasn't skilled enough at lying to come up with someone else.

"It was my ex." I decided something as close to honesty as

possible would work in my favor.

Her eyes went stormy. "Is he giving you trouble?" Her voice was no longer soft. "Because we can make sure he leaves you alone. If Swiss knew he was calling you—"

"No!" I didn't mean to shout, but the mere thought of Swiss filled me with panic. I took a breath, mindful of Macy's eyes on me. "No," I repeated, much more calmly this time. Which was incredibly hard while on the edge of a complete breakdown.

"It would create drama," I expounded, hoping I sounded convincing. "And I really don't want that. I just want to leave Preston in the past where he belongs, you know?"

None of this was a lie exactly. I did desperately want to leave Preston in my past. If my reaction was anything to go by, I was nowhere near strong enough to see him again. The mere thought of it had me tasting bile and my vision blurring.

Macy came into focus, staring at me intently.

Her face remained pinched, as if she wasn't buying it one bit.

"Are you sure?" she probed. "You can talk to me, you know. About anything. Especially about this asshole ex. I promise I won't tell Swiss."

It was tempting. Exceptionally so, to talk to someone. To get some advice. Some support. As much as the experience with the Sons of Templar and their women had given me a sense of family I'd never experienced, I'd also had to hide a part of myself. A large part of me. I'd never felt more supported, more part of something at the same time as feeling terrifyingly alone.

I ached to gain some perspective. To talk to Macy, who was so strong, so together, who had a life that she'd fought for. She'd shared her past so easily and openly with me, and it was not all hearts and flowers. She was proof that you could make something divine out of rotten beginnings.

But no. She would tell Swiss, Hansen. Not because she

wasn't loyal. The opposite. She would want to help me. She was shrewd and smart enough to know the only way to help me would be to get the men involved. Even if she didn't do that, I would be asking her to participate in my lie. I respected her too much for that.

"I know," I replied, still smiling so hard it hurt. "And I appreciate that. Appreciate you, more than you know. But there is seriously nothing to talk about regarding Preston. I don't want to waste air on him."

Macy still didn't look like she was going to let it go, and I was hanging on by a freaking thread.

As she opened her mouth to say something, Xander tugged on her face so she was now looking at him—a gesture miniature badasses learned early, I guessed. "Mommy, I want to go and swim," he whined.

I admired his patience for waiting so long and was beyond thankful for his timing.

Macy smiled down at him. "Sure, sweetie." She kissed his head before pointing to me. "I'm all for leaving assholes in the past, but I'm also all about getting my girlfriends drunk so they can purge their demons. Fair warning, you look like you've got to purge this motherfucker."

Oh, she had no idea.

I did need to purge Preston from my life. Unfortunately, that involved leaving the family I'd created here. Because there was no way of getting rid of him without dragging them into it, without exposing all the lies I'd told.

The thought was like a punch to the stomach, and it was an effort not to double over at the force of it. This could be the last time I stood in Macy's kitchen.

I'd miss the woman who'd made me a part of her family in a

matter of months, the one who was still staring at me shrewdly. Luckily, she had a small human to contend with.

She looked down at Xander. "Swim time!" she exclaimed in her 'mom voice' before carrying him toward the pool.

I let out the breath I'd been holding as she disappeared, but I didn't get a moment of respite. A moment to process.

Swiss sauntered into the kitchen from outside, having changed into his swim trunks at some point.

They were slung low on his hips, showing off his glistening six pack, and his 'Adonis Belt' looked like it had been carved with a knife.

No, he looked like he had been *sculpted*.

But even Swiss, in swim trunks, with droplets of water running down his abs, was not enough to distract me, to slow my racing heart. I tried my very best to fake my composure, to stare at his abs instead of his face—something I likely would've done with or without Preston's call.

He came up behind me, encircling me in his arms and gently pulling me away from the platter I had finished arranging five minutes ago.

"Remember what I promised to do in the bathroom?" he murmured in my ear.

My heart continued racing, but for a different reason now.

Preston's voice was still an echo in my ear, though it was getting quieter and quieter.

"I vaguely recall," I replied, my voice breathy.

"Vaguely?" he rasped, kissing my neck. "Well, I think I need to make sure there is nothing vague about what happens next. In fact, I need to make sure that the only thing you think about is my cock inside you."

Then he threw me over his shoulder and walked us to the bathroom where he fucked me against the wall.

And there was nothing vague about it.

I didn't entirely forget about Preston's call—that was impossible—but I pushed it to the back of my mind, settling even further into my mindset of denial. Him finding my phone number was problematic—I'd later find out that Violet gave it to him because he'd spun some lie as to why he didn't already have it. And of course, why wouldn't she give her father her mother's number?

What kind of damage could one little phone call do?

Quite a lot, it turned out.

CHAPTER THIRTEEN

KATE

TWO WEEKS LATER

IT WAS MY FAULT, I guessed.

How it all fell apart.

I got too comfortable.

Content in a way I hadn't thought my soul was capable of.

There was a ticking clock somewhere deep inside of me, and I was always mindful of it, knowing that I would have to make serious decisions soon. Very soon. As much as I loved it here, with Swiss, I couldn't abandon my daughter. I needed to see her. My heart wasn't beating right without her, and I was counting down the moments until I got to see her face again.

But I spoke to her often. I knew she was happy, healthy, safe. That was enough for now.

And I had an identity outside of being her mother, outside of being Preston's wife and punching bag.

I was... alive in a way I'd never thought possible.

"You know your pinky is out," a voice teased.

I blinked to my left, to where the voice was coming from.

Swiss was grinning at me, his eyes warm molasses.

My heart skipped at that grin. At the movement of his muscles as he walked toward me. My eyes ran over the exposed skin hungrily, even though it had been pressed against mine less than an hour ago.

"Only you, Countess, would drink beer with your fucking pinky out," he teased, yanking me in to kiss the side of my forehead.

"My pinky wasn't out," I argued.

His eyes danced. "Your pinky was most definitely fuckin' out." He looked to Hansen who was leaning against the bar, close to Macy. "Brother, help me out. She was definitely drinkin' with her pinky out."

Hansen looked at me, the left side of his mouth turning upward to expose his teeth. "Sorry, Kate... There was definitely an upturned picky."

Macy slapped him on the chest. "You're not supposed to agree with Swiss," she snapped.

Hansen looked to his wife. "Sorry, darlin'," he conceded immediately.

I grinned into my beer, leaning against Swiss as I watched the president of one of the most dangerous outlaw motorcycle clubs in the country back down without a fight to his small, fairy princess looking wife.

A sight to see.

"Kate."

The smile froze on my face as the beer slipped from my fingers, smashing on the floor.

Everyone looked to me, smiles gone.

"Baby?" Swiss asked in concern, pulling us back from the glass and liquid quickly spreading on the floor.

But Swiss didn't exist. The man who spoke my name had all of my attention.

I turned my head to see Preston, standing in the middle of the common room.

I had no idea how he got in there. Much later I would find out how he'd found me, how he'd managed to make an appointment at the garage then walked into the clubhouse as if he owned the place.

But that wasn't important now. What was important was that my husband had found me.

He was wearing a cashmere sweater with a shirt underneath, designer jeans and leather sneakers. His skin was tanned, jaw square and clean shaven. Not a hair on his head was out of place.

For a second, I thought I was hallucinating until Swiss turned his head to Preston and said, "Who the fuck are you?" pulling me closer into his body.

"I'm Kate's husband," Preston replied, not even looking at Swiss. His eyes were glued on me.

I was frozen in place, quickly shrinking all the way down to the size I had been before.

"It was a challenge to find you, Kate, I'll give you that," he scowled. He shook his head slowly, his hands were dangling casually at his sides, his posture too relaxed. An act, a careful one. "Though obviously not impossible. But it seems I'm too late."

It was then that his eyes went to Swiss, who was staring daggers at him.

"You left me to take up with this..." his eyes traveled Swiss's body with a sneer and a curled lip, "criminal."

My blood turned hot. It boiled, in fact. Suddenly, I was no longer two feet tall.

Swiss was already stiff with fury, already wearing the dangerous, alpha male battle stance which Preston hadn't noticed because he was much too narcissistic and self-absorbed. Beyond that, he was so insulated from any kind of danger. He truly thought that he wasn't at risk here, that he was the one in control here.

I'd known the man was deluded, but this was something else. You'd have to be detached from reality to not recognize that Swiss was in control of everything right now, that Preston was minutes away from getting his arms ripped off. As much as a part of me wanted to watch that happen, I wasn't going to let Swiss fight my battle. I was more than capable. So I stepped forward, around him because he'd done the alpha male thing and stood in front of me. I'm sure he wasn't happy about that, but I wasn't focusing on him.

"You're either coming to that conclusion because of the color of his skin or the cut on his back, and neither of those options are okay in the slightest," I hissed at Preston. I knew that he liked to be seen by the town as accepting and liberal, but behind closed doors he was nasty and small-minded.

It weighed heavily on me just how long I'd let this man control me. How I'd rotted in his presence, held captive by fear and helplessness.

It was me who left that day. Only me. But it was Swiss, this club, that introduced me to a different part of myself. One that was far from helpless.

Something in me snapped in response to the way he'd looked at Swiss. The way he'd spoken about him.

I leveled my gaze at Preston. "I am not yours," I announced, the words tasting sweet with truth. "In fact, I was never yours. The way you ordered for me at every restaurant was misogynist and not at all charming. I literally had to stifle the urge to stab you with my fork every time you did it." I sucked in a frustrated breath. "If I had a fork right now, it would be protruding from your eyeball."

Preston's face was red and getting redder. Usually, this would be when I stopped speaking. When I tried to apologize, when I tried to appease him. Try to escape a beating. But not now. Not with Swiss behind me.

"You are one of the most selfish people I've ever met, sexually or otherwise. You look so stupid in those fucking glasses, and none of your jokes are funny. I faked every orgasm you ever thought I had."

Not a lie. I'd thought I knew pleasure with Preston. He was all I had to measure it against. But Swiss had shown me that I hadn't even known what my body was capable of feeling.

My eyes never left Preston's. I was aching to call him out for what a coward he was for putting his hands on me, but I knew this room was already a powder keg. I knew that on the surface, these were bad men, but I also knew in their cores, they were good. And they had some really strong opinions on how women should be treated.

As much as I would've loved Preston to get pummeled for once, I couldn't risk it. Wouldn't.

For better or for worse, he was the father of my child. And I couldn't be sure that Swiss wouldn't kill him if he knew the truth.

The prospect of his death did not bother me in the slightest. Until I saw what a hole it would create in my daughter.

So I pressed my mouth into a thin line. "I'm not coming home with you," I informed him. "That place, that fucking museum, was never a home. It was never warm. I was just your trophy. Find someone new for that role."

I knew that if he could've by now, he would've. Although there would've been women lining up to be with him if we had divorced, they were not the same as me. They had families, resources... They would not be whipped into submission as easily as I had. Preston had something truly evil inside of him, and I was the only person who could feed that.

My pain and fear were the only things that could feed that.

But I wasn't afraid anymore.

"I'm done with you," I spat.

Preston stared at me, then at Swiss who was still rigid beside me.

"Our daughter is due to come back in two months," he said evenly. "Our *daughter*. The one you seem to have forgotten about."

The words hit their mark, and I flinched at their impact.

"I have not forgotten about Violet," I bit out. "I would *never* forget about her."

Preston's expression didn't change, but I saw the glint of satisfaction in his eyes. He knew me well enough to know when he'd hit his mark.

"You leave with me now, I'll... forget about your little vacation." His eyes flickered around the room in distaste. "I'll make sure our daughter doesn't find out what a whore her mother is."

A sound came out of Swiss's throat, very close to a growl. It was the first time he'd made any kind of noise since Preston announced himself as my husband.

The sound was feral. Dangerous.

Freaking deadly.

And Preston was not immune to it. I was satisfied to see pure terror flash across his face before he masked it.

"I'll be in the car." His voice didn't betray the fear he couldn't completely hide. His eyes burned into me. "I trust you'll make the right decision. For our daughter."

He turned on his heel and left, his shoes clicking against the floor as he did so.

Both Swiss and I watched as he left the compound.

The silence ringing in the room was deafening.

Someone cleared their throat.

I blinked, realizing it wasn't just the two of us in the room. We had an audience.

All of the people I'd come to love. To respect. Who'd made me feel like I belonged in a way I never had before.

Now they knew who I was.

Who I wasn't.

I couldn't look at their faces, not when my own was hot with shame.

There was only one person in the room who mattered right now anyway. One I wished I didn't have to face, but I needed to. I needed his eyes, his strength. Needed a reminder of who I'd become in just a few short months.

So I took a deep breath and turned to face him.

He was already staring at me. But his brown eyes were hard, as unyielding as stone.

He was mad. Rightly so. I'd lied to him.

But he would understand. I hadn't lied to him about what was most important. About who I truly was. He saw me. He'd be pissed, but he would forgive me.

"Rowan," I said, using his real name, my voice scratchy. He'd told me it, not even a week ago, when he had started sharing more about himself with me. Trusting me more. My skin crawled in discomfort, not just at having an audience, but at the way he was looking at me.

Like I was a stranger.

It hurt, but it was fixable. We were fixable. We were permanent. I just needed to tell him.

"I can—"

"You're married." His voice was off. Something about it was foreign to me and downright terrifying.

His expression was exactly the same. Cold. Detached.

I was suddenly extremely cold, despite the warm temperature of the room.

"It's... complicated," I said, my voice frail. Tiny. He'd never heard my voice like that. Only one man had scared me enough to make my voice that small. And though I knew Swiss was dangerous, deadly, I never, not in a million years, imagined he would scare me enough to awaken that voice. That version of me.

"Are you married? Yes or no?" Swiss spoke through gritted teeth, nostrils flaring, staring at me like I was a stranger.

No, a *traitor.*

My heart felt like it was being squeezed by a vice.

The silence between us was a thousand knives, plunging into my skin.

"Yes." Though barely audible, I somehow found enough strength to force the word past the emotion lodged in my throat.

I was shrinking back into myself, retreating back into a mold that I thought I'd shed, thought I'd left behind.

I didn't retreat, not completely. Not as I stared at him, remembered what he'd made me feel, how he'd awakened me, the life I'd slipped into like it was made for me.

"But it's not—"

"It's not what I think?" he interrupted coldly. "You really gonna spout that tired shit?"

I stepped forward, even though I was terrified, even though his body language told me not to. Even though every instinct I'd honed about volatile men screamed at me to stay put, or better yet, run. But I ignored those instincts, recalling the memories I'd created with him, focusing on the way he had empowered me. How safe he'd made me feel. All the room he'd given me to grow.

"Honey," I started, voice subdued.

"Don't you come near me, or I swear I will not be responsible for my actions," he snarled.

Snarled.

I stopped abruptly, skuttling back, expecting a blow.

One didn't come.

Because Swiss would never lay a hand on me in anger. I knew that. In my soul I knew that. But my instincts weren't there yet. Not with Preston right outside.

Something shifted in Swiss's eyes, something puncturing through whatever ice shield he'd created. Unfortunately, it disappeared quickly, along with my hope.

I felt rather than saw a couple of the men move closer to me, as if preparing to get in the middle of something. As if Swiss would hurt me.

They were scared he was going to lay hands on me.

Swiss was angry. Beyond angry. And he was the most dangerous person in this room, but I knew to my core that he wouldn't lay a finger on me.

He didn't need to in order to destroy me completely.

"I don't want to hear your bullshit." The words were spoken by a man who looked exactly like Swiss, but as if the man I'd come to know was a figment of my imagination. He stared at me with a detachment, a coldness I didn't know he was capable of.

"You're just a bored housewife who was sick of getting fucked selfishly by her rich, douchebag husband. You are not special. You are not unique. You were just an easy fuck." His eyes panned over me in disgust.

Disgust.

Hansen stepped forward, toward Swiss. "Brother, think you need to take a second."

Swiss didn't so much as glance at him.

"Older than I'd like, but you've taken decent care of yourself," he spat at me. "It wasn't a chore. But now I'm done. I need a new piece of ass. Younger, without strings."

My palms were damp with sweat, knees buckling, my body working as hard as it possibly could just to stay upright.

That couldn't be true. He couldn't possibly be saying this. This was a man who could be ruthless, cruel, heartless. He'd told me as much. I'd witnessed as much second hand. But I'd never been afraid of those things. Of him. I'd never thought that he would direct his wrath at me.

I'd been comfortable with him. Felt safe.

This was a man who had lived a lifestyle that I couldn't even dream of. Who knew freedom, true freedom. Power.

My eyes scanned around the room, looking at the shapes of the people I'd come to care greatly about.

I didn't look at their eyes, though. I wasn't brave enough for that.

Family.

They were his family.

Not mine.

These were people who truly loved each other. Fought for each other. Would die for each other.

I hadn't known relationships like that existed. The closest thing I'd had to friends were people who would delight at seeing me brought down. And families. I didn't have any of that.

I didn't belong here.

The cold detachment in Swiss's eyes told me that.

I did not belong here.

My fate awaited me outside, waiting for me in a hundred-thousand-dollar car, listening to pretentious music, likely thinking of all the things he'd do to punish me.

"Whatever you think of me, I love you," I whispered, not strong enough to look into his eyes. "Thank you for giving me this. Giving me... me."

Then I turned on my heel and walked out.

I was gone, girl.

CHAPTER FOURTEEN

KATE

I GOT in the car without word or protest. I didn't say a thing about my car, about my things. Preston wouldn't approve of my new wardrobe anyway. I didn't even mention my wedding and engagement rings at the motel. I didn't utter a word.

Preston didn't speak for thirty minutes after we started driving.

I counted.

Every second for thirty minutes.

I'd expected to be scared. To be absolutely terrified. This was going to be bad. I already knew. Could tell by the energy in the interior of the car, the calmness in the way Preston held himself. I always thought of it as the eye of the storm, that's when I knew things were going to get bad. When he got calm like this. He was almost... meditative. Peaceful even.

Then, of course, he'd beat the shit out of me.

He'd broken my arm once, in one of those episodes. Violet

was a teenager. She had been staying late after school, so I'd been enjoying an afternoon where I had everything done. The house was spotless. There was a casserole in the slow cooker. Laundry was clean and pressed. I had an hour, maybe an hour and a half to lay on the sofa, watch a movie.

Then I'd heard Preston's car in the drive. The second I heard the crunch of his tires, I'd known. I hadn't known what I'd done—it didn't much matter—but I knew I was going to pay.

Preston hadn't spoken for a long time then either.

Until after he was done beating me.

It was apparent my arm was broken the second it happened. The bone was pressed up against the skin, almost protruding out of it. The pain was like nothing I'd ever experienced. I hadn't screamed. Or cried. I knew better than that. We'd both looked, wide-eyed, at the arm I cradled while curled up on the floor. I'd stared at it for some time before passing out. I came to in the emergency room, to Preston stroking my head, murmuring softly about how much he loved me. Soft but loud enough for nurses to hear, I'd guessed.

He'd spoken about how I'd fallen down the stairs, how lucky it was he'd come home from the office early.

I'd gone along with the story. I was well trained.

He'd been sorry. Very sorry. He treated me with kindness, love. He didn't hit me for a year. An entire *year*. It was bliss.

But it didn't last forever.

That wasn't in Preston's nature.

I figured, sitting in the car, driving back to the life I thought I'd escaped, that I likely had another broken bone in my future.

If I was *lucky*.

He wouldn't kill me. I was almost sure of that. It would be too messy. Preston wasn't a criminal mastermind; he didn't know how to cover up a murder. Beyond that, in his own twisted way, he loved me. He loved his daughter. And he knew what my death would do to her.

"You hurt me, Katie," he proclaimed in a level tone, after thirty minutes and thirty-one seconds.

My hands were fisted on top of my thighs. I barely heard him. Barely saw him. I was too busy going over every second of the interaction with Swiss before I left. The way his expression had changed, the way his entire body had changed. Like he'd turned into a different person.

A stranger.

My heart burned in agony at the thought of it.

I wasn't afraid of what Preston was going to do to me. Not even a little. I was too busy being heartbroken. It felt like my bones were splintering. Like my muscles were being ground into hamburger meat.

I'd loved him.

Swiss.

I'd fallen in love with him. The very core of me was his. I loved him because he'd showed me who I was. No, he gave me the strength to discover that for myself.

The reality of what was happening was starting to sink in. Preston was driving us back to New Hampshire. Back to the life I'd been a prisoner for years. The life I'd hated. But the life I'd survived in because I hadn't known anything different.

But I knew differently now.

I was different now.

I would say I was stronger now, but a strong woman wouldn't have gotten into this car. Even after the heartbreak and humiliation at the clubhouse.

A strong woman would've walked away from both men, the one that she loved and the one that had tormented her for years.

A strong woman would've figured it out, would've carved out a new life for herself without either of those men.

I was not her.

So I'd gotten in the car with Preston. I had accepted defeat without a fight. I was thoroughly disgusted with myself.

"Kate."

He spoke sharply now, my name cutting through my thoughts like a serrated knife, tearing at my already frayed consciousness. Panic was slowly setting in. The future yawned ahead of me.

Working on muscle memory, I obeyed the command threaded into my name. The threat.

He was staring at me intently.

We were no longer driving.

In fact, we were parked in the lot of a hotel.

Not a roadside motel. Nothing fancy either because we were still in a remote part of New Mexico. It was the most expensive the area had to offer, to be sure.

How had I not noticed we were parked? That we'd pulled off the highway? Sinking so deep into myself was not a luxury I could afford. Not with Preston. I had to be alert. On guard.

I had to obey. Shrink back into the mold he'd made for me.

Already, the edges cut into my skin, drawing blood.

"You have to understand what I've been going through these past months," he said when he had my attention, his tone no longer as harsh.

"You have to understand what I've had to tell people," he continued. "The lies I've had to tell my parents." He took his hands from the careful ten and two position to swirl his wedding ring. His fury thrummed through my bones, despite his even expression, his tender tone. "The lies I had to tell our daughter," he gritted out.

My eyes slid to his hands which were back on the steering wheel, at ten and two. His knuckles were white.

The mention of Violet turned my stomach. Icy fingers of dread clutched my heart. My own hands were fisted on my thighs as I forced myself not to throw up in the car. Preston would not appreciate me making that kind of mess.

"Everyone has been worried about you," he murmured. His eyes trailed down my body, mouth pursed in distaste. "And they had a right to be. This little...break from reality can be explained, though." He took a long sigh. "It can be fixed." His eyes found mine once more. "You can be fixed. Some diet and exercise, a trip to the salon. Yes, it can be fixed." I wasn't sure whether he was talking to me or himself, going through the list of things that needed to be done in order to turn me back into the Stepford Wife he'd created.

"I can forgive you," he declared. "We will go back to our life. We will have another baby. Everything will go back to how it was."

My nails cut into the insides of my palms. I didn't feel the pain, even though I felt the stickiness of the blood I'd drawn.

My throat swelled up, my lungs burning to the point where I started seeing black dots in my vision.

"Now, I'm tired," he said evenly. "Because I spent hours driving here. Days, actually. Because I've had months of sleepless nights, worrying about you."

His hand landed on my thigh.

My skin burned from his touch, but I didn't react. Couldn't. I was paralyzed by his words.

"But I don't have to worry anymore." He was staring straight ahead. "Because I have you back. And I won't let you leave me again."

It was a threat. A death sentence.

"Now, you're going to wait in the car while I get us a room."

He squeezed my thigh harder.

The grip might've been designed to hurt me, but I couldn't say for sure. I couldn't feel anything.

His hand lingered there in silence for a few seconds more. Or maybe it was minutes. Hours.

Who knew?

The door slammed shut, and I realized that his hand was no longer on my thigh, that he had left me in the car alone.

This was it. My chance. To run. Who knew where. Maybe back to the motel in Garnett where I had my things. I had cash. Not much, but enough. I still had my wedding rings. Preston somehow hadn't noticed they weren't on my fingers. How long had we been driving for? How long would it take me to walk?

It didn't matter. Shouldn't matter. I should've got out of the car and ran. Crawled, if need be.

But I didn't move a muscle. Not for minutes. Hours. Lifetimes. Not until Preston got back in the car and directed us to the hotel room.

He had trained me well.

＝＝

I expected a blow the second the hotel room door closed. I was braced for it. The soft footfalls of his eight-hundred-dollar sneakers against the hotel carpet echoed in my ears, my body taut, tensed. Preston's eyes were intent on me, his expression carefully blank. There was a low ringing in my ears as I watched him move closer.

I could feel the punch already. The crush of his knuckles against the soft flesh of my stomach. Those expensive sneakers kicking my ribs once I was down on the floor. I could see every moment of it.

But no impact came.

Instead, one of his hands settled on my hip, and the other brushed my cheekbone.

I flinched at his touch, disgusted by him, his smooth hands, his expensive cologne.

Preston's eyes darkened at my flinch, and my teeth sank into my lip, readying for the consequences of such a flinch.

But still, no impact came.

"You let another man touch you," he whispered, and his fingers pressed into my hip. "Touch what was mine." His hand moved so his thumb brushed my bottom lip. "But it's okay. I just need to take it back."

There was no longer a hand at my hip. His fingers were undoing my jeans.

"I need to take you back."

I squeezed my eyes shut as he pulled off my clothes.

SWISS

I was drunk.

Or at least I *should've* been drunk considering how much whisky I'd consumed. But the image of her was still sharp in my mind. My sober fucking mind. Her face as she retreated back from me. In fear.

Real fear.

Not fear that was born in that moment, in reaction to the man I'd turned into in the face of her betrayal. No, that fear was older. A conditioned response. Ingrained in her.

Over years.

That fear had been living inside of her for *years*.

And that voice... I could barely fucking hear her. When she spoke, I watched her deflate.

Something drained out of her. Before my very eyes.

No. That wasn't when she'd deflated. It had started the second that asshole walked in the door. I hadn't noticed at first. It wasn't as stark at first because she was standing beside me. Because she believed she was mine. She believed she wasn't going anywhere. That she was safe with me.

She'd been brave. Despite the terror that washed over her. She'd felt strong enough by my side to say that shit. And then, when I showed her that she was alone, she deflated.

My mind spun, thinking of all the little shit that had piled up. Shit that had bothered me but that I hadn't connected the dots on. The way she was surprised, fucking shocked at me doing simple things like thanking her, helping her with the dishes. The way she always apologized for shit that didn't require an apology. The way she spoke about herself. Constantly criticized herself.

Her running down the road in the middle of the night like she was running for her fucking life.

Everything clicked. Everything that should've come together much fucking sooner.

"Fuck!" I roared.

My bottle exploded against the wall.

Hansen barely blinked even though it happened just as he walked into the room, missing his head by inches.

"You liked her, I gather," he commented dryly.

His casual stance sparked more fury in me. "We need to go and get her," I bit out.

He blinked at my tone and the look on my face, then he smirked. He was used to outbursts from me, so he didn't distinguish how this one was different.

He did not see the fire in me, the panic that was acid in my veins.

"Of course, you need to go get her," he agreed. "We placed bets on how long it would take you to get out of your own way and hop on that bike and find her." He jerked his head to Hades. "Somehow this fucker won. A romantic... Who would've thought?"

I stepped forward, clutching the sides of his cut and yanking him toward me. All teasing left his eyes.

Finally, he saw how close to the edge I was.

Now I'd gotten his attention.

And the rest of the brothers in the room, who had seen a lot of shit from me, but they'd never seen me lay hands on a president.

I knew all of them were preparing to take me down. I was well aware of the protocol if I truly lost my shit.

Hades would be the one to do it. I knew that. Had known it since I patched into this charter. Appreciated it. Liked knowing where my exits were if I should need them.

Not that I wanted to die. Fuck no. I enjoyed being alive. Most of the time.

But there was something inside of me I couldn't always control, something looking to burn the world down with me inside of it.

But right now, I had iron clad control over that shit. And I very much needed to be alive.

"You don't get it," I gritted out. "We need to get her, and we need to kill that mother fuckin' husband."

Hansen's eyes darted behind me, and he shook his head, probably telling Hades not to pull me off him just yet. "Okay, brother," he patted my back. "We'll go get her."

I squeezed his cut once more before I let him go.

My chest itched.

"Promise me you won't look at it until... just until I say."

That had confused me. Worried me. The way her voice was so small, hesitant. I'd wrongly thought it was 'cause she didn't like the violence of it. Which was wrong... I'd seen the way she'd come alive holding that knife.

But I'd been too mad with need to think too hard on it. Too hungry to fuck her with her brand on my chest.

Brothers scattered as I damn near sprinted to the closest bathroom, ripping off the bandage I'd worn for the past few days—before then, I hadn't looked. Kate had changed the bandage, cleaned it for me, and I'd kept my promise—to stare at the angry red letters on my chest.

K.C.

Her married name was Edwards.

There was a chance, a small chance, her maiden name started with the same letter as mine.

But I knew that it didn't.

Down to my fucking soul, I knew it didn't.

She'd given herself my name.

That's when the mirror smashed.

It was my fist that did it.

When I walked back into the common room, everyone was standing there. Jagger was on the phone, probably talking to Wire to get location data.

Hansen had been speaking but stopped when I walked in.

"We need to go and get her. Now," I growled.

Hansen's eyes motioned downward. "Want to take care of that first?"

I glanced downward. My left hand was covered in blood. It was dripping on the floor. There was glass embedded in it. "Nope," I said to Hansen. "What I need is to get my woman."

Hansen nodded concisely before looking to Jagger. "We got a trail?"

Jagger's eyes flickered to me before he looked to our president, nodding in response.

"Good," Hansen clapped his hands together. "Let's go."

"I just hope we're not too fuckin' late," I muttered.

KATE

I was slathering moisturizer on my body when Swiss came in. He had an odd look on his face. One that made everything in me spark. Come alive. I kept rubbing my skin which seemed a thousand times more sensitive.

"It's time." His voice was deep and throaty as he took slow, measured steps toward the bed.

He was stalking. Like a predator might.

The sparks inside me burning brighter.

When he made it to the bed, he pulled the knife from his belt.

My stomach dropped delightfully.

It was only when he was in a particular kind of mood that Swiss used the knife on me. The first time he'd drawn my blood with that knife, he'd raised the blade to his lips and licked it off the steel.

Maybe it was fucked-up. All I knew was that I loved it. Loved him... consuming me in that way. Every mark he gave me erased something from my past.

"I need my name on you, Countess," he murmured, the tip of the knife cutting through the fabric of my tank.

I trembled in delight as I watched him.

"I want my real name on you," he amended.

My chest rose and fell rapidly as the torn material split apart, exposing my pebbled nipples.

Swiss ran the dull side of the blade along them.

I gasped in anticipation.

His eyes were on fire. "It's a name I've left behind," he explained. "One that I want on you because it's the one I was born with. One I will die with, even if that's not who I am anymore."

The knife traced down the center of my body, the tip kissing my navel. Fire remained in its wake.

The cotton, boy short panties I was wearing were next.

The steel was cold against my pussy, and my back arched upward.

"This is gonna hurt, Countess," he warned, the tip of the knife drawing circles at the curve of my hip.

His other hand pushed my thighs apart. All the way apart. So I was completely exposed to him. Not that long ago, I would've felt defenseless, vulnerable and ashamed in this position. I would've pushed my legs back together on instinct.

But I spread them farther apart, to further expose myself to Swiss.

His eyes, rapt on the apex of my thighs, flared wider, and he let out a hiss between his teeth.

His eyes found mine once more. "My goal is to make you cum so hard that all that pain will be nothing compared to the pleasure you feel from me eating your cunt."

And then he proceeded to eat my cunt.

He turned out being right. It hurt.

But he was wrong about it being nothing compared to the pleasure that came from my orgasms—which were fucking amazing. Seeing him carve his initials into me—R.C. for Rowan Carter— feeling the pain explode in my hip as he scarred me with his initials, it was some of the most intense pleasure I'd felt in my life.

I was covered in blood by the time he was done—it didn't take long. He was quick and efficient, not to mention surprisingly neat with his script—and it was trickling down between my legs.

Swiss's eyes were alight with something I'd never seen before as he sat up to stare at the two letters he'd carved into my skin.

"We need to get that disinfected and cleaned up." I barely recognized his voice it was so thick, hoarse. Almost animalistic.

"No," I gripped his arm to stop him from standing, my own voice sounding beastly. "You need to fuck me."

His body jerked. "Kate, you're bleeding." It was not a protest. Not for him anyway. He was battling, I could see that clearly. With his need to care for me versus the beast inside of him that didn't care if I hurt. No, the beast inside that wanted me to hurt. That got off on it.

I sat up, sucking in a harsh breath at the pain that came with the movement, then I yanked him down so his body was flush with mine. His hard cock pressed into me through his jeans.

"You like my blood, remember?" I murmured against his mouth.

"Oh, I remember," he growled. His eyes locked onto mine. "When we're done here, you're gonna take this knife…" he brushed the blade against my cheek, still warm with my blood.

"And you're gonna carve your initials onto my chest."

My blood sang at the mere thought.

Then he fucked me, covered in my blood.

We didn't get to his turn that night. But two nights later, I was the one holding the knife.

My hand shook. Not because I was afraid to make him bleed. I was hungry for it. Especially seeing the state he was in, how crazy it was making him to see me on top of him while holding the knife.

No, that's not why my hand shook.

It was because I didn't want to mark him with the last name

I'd been born with. Or the one that had been forced upon me. Neither of those were mine. Not even a little.

I cut the letters K.C. into his skin.

I hadn't let him see it. Had quickly washed and bandaged it, making him promise that he wouldn't look until I explained it to him.

He'd looked at me questioningly, but he'd promised. Because he trusted me.

Because he loved me.

Hands. Different hands tugged my jeans down. Hands that truly hurt me. Hands that broke me apart. They yanked my jeans and panties down.

They brushed over the scab.

The one that, though still healing, was very distinct.

That's when he started hitting me. And he didn't stop. He was killing me, I realized.

I was gone, girl.

SWISS

We found her in a ditch.

A *ditch*.

He'd tossed her there like she was trash.

Like she was *trash*.

She was alive. Barely. If he'd known that, he would've rectified the situation. It was obvious that he'd thought she was dead.

She looked fuckin' dead.

We'd only found her 'cause Wire had managed to hack into the husband's phone, check it against locations. It had been at a hotel for a handful of hours before driving to this road off the highway.

He was still on the move. We were following his exact route.

And I only saw her out of sheer luck. 'Cause I was searching the sides of the road with dread. Because Wire—a patched hacker in the Amber chapter—had been able to find one hospital record for Kate. Four years ago. Broken arm. Nasty fucking break. Required surgery. I remembered running my lips across the faint scar on her arm, her telling me about a break, so breathless that I hadn't heard the edge in her voice. I'd been too far gone to push it. Push for more.

Notes said she fell down the stairs.

Kate was not clumsy. Not even a little. She held herself with grace, poise. I remarked on it many fucking times. And no way could someone get the injuries she got by falling down stairs. In addition to a broken arm, two of her ribs had been cracked. She'd been thrown down the stairs. Or had the shit beat out of her.

The bastard had *broken her fucking bones,* and I'd let her leave with him. That would haunt me for the rest of my life.

That was the moment my gaze found an unnatural shape on the side of the road, when my headlight had illuminated it.

Illuminated her.

I'd all but tossed my bike to the side and skidded down the bank to where she laid.

She was fuckin' naked. Covered in blood. Her hair was matted with it, sticking to the swollen, purple skin of her face.

She didn't even look like herself. I wouldn't have fucking recognized her if not for the heart shaped birthmark on her hip. If not for my initials carved into her other hip. If not for the thing inside me screaming in pain, in fucking fury. The thing that knew she was mine.

My hands were shaking when I touched her. When I pulled her into my arms. She was ice fucking cold.

"I got you, baby," I whispered, kissing her head. "I got you."

I started to rock her slowly.

"You're okay," I told her. "You're okay." I stroked her hair. My hand was wet with her blood.

"You're okay," I said for the third time. It wasn't a statement. It was a prayer.

She didn't make a sound.

Not a fucking sound.

The crunch of the ground underneath boots was the only thing I heard.

"Brother."

The word came through a vortex.

There was a hand on my shoulder. My piece was out of my cut and pointed at my president in one smooth move. My other arm stayed tight around Kate.

Hansen held his hands up in surrender. "We need to move her. Cover her. Get her to a hospital." His eyes stayed on mine, and I saw the silhouettes of my other brothers behind him. "We need to get her fixed up. First, can you let me look at her?"

I gritted my teeth. Every instinct in me was thrumming to protect Kate, shield her, not let another man touch her, fucking look at her. But that was fucking pointless. The damage was already done.

Plus, Hansen had been a combat medic in another life. He was in love with his Old Lady. He was a good man. He would take care of her.

Even knowing all of that, I couldn't let her go.

"You can hold on to her," he said placidly, evenly. "You don't have to let her go. I just need to check her vitals."

With my jaw clenched, I nodded to him, unable to speak. He needed to check her vitals. He needed to see if I was holding a dead woman in my arms. For the second time in my life, I was holding the world in my arms, and it was already fucking gone.

Hansen moved forward slowly but urgently, as if he were trying to deal with a rabid dog. I *was* a rabid dog.

His hands moved carefully, touching her reverently and professionally. His fingers were stained with her blood.

"I've got a pulse," he uttered. "A faint one."

A pulse. A faint pulse. I held on to that. Her heart was barely beating, but it was beating. That meant I still had something to hold on to. One thread to grip on to before I tore this fuckin' world apart.

He looked at me. "She needs a hospital." Although he spoke in a low, even tone, there was a sense of urgency in there that scared the hell out of me. "Can tell she's got broken ribs." His eyes scanned her face. Her ruined face. "Broken nose for sure. Maybe a fractured eye socket." He spoke with a calmness that came from the battlefield.

There were muttered curses from behind him as he listed Kate's injuries that were anything but calm.

"She may be bleeding internally," Hansen continued. "We can't treat her at the club."

Hospital.

It was with only the very worst-case scenarios that we fucked with hospitals. Sarah, the doctor the club trusted, could do almost anything at the club.

Almost.

Hospitals had protocols, paper trails, things that would become inconvenient for us.

Life or death. That's what hospitals were reserved for.

"Well, then we're gettin' her to a fuckin' hospital," I snarled.

Hansen nodded, watching me carefully. I realized I was still pointing my piece at him.

"We've got a Prospect with a van fifteen minutes out," Cody reported, staring at Kate in horror.

All of the brothers were. Except Hades. That motherfucker had nothing on his face. Which was most dangerous.

"Can get an ambulance here in five," Elden grunted, phone at his ear.

"Does she have five minutes?" I asked Hansen, lowering my gun.

We were all on bikes. There was no way to transport her even if she didn't.

Hansen nodded. "Yeah, she'll hold on," he said firmly. "She's strong."

I looked down at her, brushing the hair that was stuck to her face in blood. "Yeah, Countess," I murmured. "You're strong. You can hold on. Hold on for me."

My eyes found Hades. The only person I would trust with the request I was going to make.

"You need to find the husband. Find him. Make him hurt. Don't cut anything off, but make him fuckin' hurt. Make him want to die. Take him back to the club where I can finish him."

Hades nodded, not hesitating to climb back on his bike and roar off.

The husband would die. Slowly. If he died or not, did not depend on whether Kate made it or not.

If *I* died or not depended on whether Kate made it or not.

CHAPTER FIFTEEN

SWISS

"SIR, we can take it from here."

I stared at the man in the white coat who was trying to separate me from Kate.

I'd ridden in the ambulance with her, watching the paramedics work on her.

They'd had to perform CPR about five minutes after they got there.

Hansen had been right.

Kate did have five minutes.

But she wouldn't have had ten. If I'd fucked around for *ten more minutes*, she would've died alone on the side of the road.

They managed to bring her back.

Faint pulse.

That's what I was reciting in my mind.

Faint pulse.

"You aren't takin' her anywhere where my eyes aren't on her," I informed the doctor, holding onto Kate's stretcher with an iron grip.

In my mind's eye, I saw double doors close, the image gritty, faded with age. I saw a man in a white coat stop me as I tried to walk through them. Though they certainly couldn't be the same man, they looked the same to me. Older. White. Went to the country club on Sundays.

Because I'd been brought up to respect and fear such figures, I'd listened that time when he'd told me to wait. That he would take care of things. I'd believed the rich, older, educated man because I'd been conditioned to.

Since then, I didn't respect anyone who wasn't wearing a Son's cut. And in that moment, I didn't fucking fear anything other than Kate going through those doors without me.

The doctor's eyes went sideways, probably looking for security, a burly orderly, whatever the fuck passed as protection here. He looked like the kind of fuck who would offer up the petite nurse beside him instead of face me himself. Then his eyes went behind me, where I assumed all of my brothers were standing. I didn't take notice of anything but Kate.

Faint pulse. Faint pulse.

The doctor swallowed visibly before clearing his throat. "It's against hospital policy, sir."

I sighed, knowing that he was a pussy. A bureaucratic pussy which meant he was gonna waste time. Time that Kate did not have.

So that was when I took my piece out of my cut, still holding onto Kate's stretcher as if it were fused to my palm, and pointed it at the doctor's head.

"I'm not fuckin' around," I informed the sufficiently scared doctor.

The bustle of movement around me told me my brothers had my back against whatever rent-a-cops might've had any ideas.

"This is my woman," I bit out. "And you are obviously one of the last people in town who understand what my patch means. But I'll educate you by telling you that I'm not afraid to use this," I shook the gun, "if you do not get your ass into gear, and fix my woman. And forget all about hospital policy."

The doctor gaped at me for a second, and I idly wondered if I'd be shooting a man today. I would do it in a heartbeat. Without hesitation. I would not regret it. But it would be messy and inconvenient.

Luckily, the doctor didn't have a death wish. "Okay, we need to prep her for the OR," he told the nurses. "Get him a gown." He motioned to me.

I lowered my gun and started moving behind the doors, glancing to Hansen. He nodded to me, takin' his place by the doors. As did the rest of my brothers.

I trusted they would stand guard, make sure no one would come to take me from her side. They were in for a war if they did.

———

Kate went into surgery.

Which meant I did too.

I watched them cut open my woman.

Save her life.

Eventually, she was settled into a room. In intensive care.

At that point, Sarah, the club's unofficial doctor, who worked at this hospital, took over for the doctor who was shit scared of me.

Sarah was not shit scared. Sarah respected the club. Sarah took a lot of fucking risks for us. Because she grew up in Garnett. She'd benefitted directly from the club.

And because she'd been in love with Jagger for a long time.

She wasn't bitter about him and Caroline... She was happy for them. She was a better person than all of us fucking scoundrels.

"How you holding up?" she asked, staring at me while she walked over to Kate.

"Will be better when you tell me that Kate is gonna make a full recovery."

It was the first time I'd spoken in a while. How long had she been in surgery? I couldn't say. A lifetime, at least.

Sarah didn't answer me at first. She reached down to squeeze Kate's hand in a gesture of tenderness that was not unlike her.

Her blue eyes found mine. "She had internal bleeding which we managed to stop." She glanced to the chart in her hands. "Three broken ribs. Collapsed lung. Ruptured spleen. Her eye socket is fractured. And her windpipe is severely bruised."

Every item on the list of Kate's injuries was a bullet through my skin. Through my flesh, my bones. Each one fucking ripped me apart.

My eyes found Kate's neck where the skin was shades of red, purple and black. Where he had strangled her. Where he had tried to take the life from her.

I remembered when those had been my hands. When I couldn't fucking come without teasing death out of women—Kate included. Kate especially. My stomach roiled in disgust.

"I know it sounds like a lot." Sarah spoke gently. "And it is. She's incredibly lucky to be alive. But I can tell you that she is going to heal. It may take some time, but she'll heal."

Sarah was not one to lie to me. I understood that. She might've been kind, but she didn't bullshit.

So I knew she was telling the truth. But looking at Kate, so pale except for the black and purple of the bruises covering her face, the machines she was attached to, the breathing tube down her throat... I found it really fucking hard to believe her.

"When will she wake up?"

I needed to see her eyes. Needed to watch her inhale and exhale under her own power. Nothing else would make me believe. Nothing else would bring me back from the edge. Only Kate could do that.

Sarah sighed. "I can't tell you that. It may be tomorrow. It may be a week from now. She's undergone serious trauma. And her body will do a lot of healing while she's unconscious."

She glanced down to Kate and then back to me. "With her windpipe how it is, she'll need to rest it for at least a week before she even attempts to speak." There was a loaded pause while Sarah's eyes roamed over Kate. "And we have to wait until she wakes up to assess the damage. She should be able to speak fully in time, but I can't make any guarantees."

Her voice. I might never hear her fucking voice again.

Right then, I tried to call it up in my mind. And for the fucking life of me, I couldn't remember what her voice sounded like. I couldn't hear shit above the dull roar in my ears. The pumping of blood through my body. The need to get the fuck out of the room and pull the skin off the man who did this.

But I stayed still. Completely still. I held on to Kate's pale, limp hand. It was my anchor.

"Was she...?" my voice broke. I sucked in a breath. I was stronger than this. And I deserved this fucking information. This was my fault after all. I deserved to feel every ounce of pain that came with these words. "Was she raped?" I asked evenly.

The handful of seconds between my question and Sarah's response were some of the longest and most terrifying of my life.

"No." It took a while for Sarah's words to cross the chasm I found myself in. To descend into the hole of self-hatred I was residing in.

"We don't have any physical injuries to suggest sexual

assault," she expanded.

I didn't sag in relief. Not even a little. No injuries did not mean that he hadn't touched her. That he hadn't raped her.

At some point, Sarah had crossed the room and was squeezing my shoulder. "She's going to be okay. She's strong. A lot of people wouldn't have survived this. But she did. She survived, Swiss." She spoke firmly, as if she sensed that the words needed to be heavy to sink through the layers of panic and blood-lust in my system.

"I'll also do my best to convince my colleague to forget about the gun you didn't point at him," she added, a hint of amusement in her voice.

"Much obliged," I managed to bite out.

"I'll be back to check on her," she promised, giving my shoulder one last squeeze before she walked out.

"She survived."

Yeah, there were machines telling me that she'd survived. There was the beeping of whatever was measuring her heartbeat. She was alive.

But it remained to be seen if she'd truly survived. What he did to her... What I did to her... Abandoning her when she needed me most.

It remained to be seen if I could survive that.

"Cops are here," Hansen remarked.

It had been a while. A day. Maybe more. Maybe less. I didn't fucking know. All I knew was that Kate hadn't opened her eyes. Kate still had a tube down her throat.

I didn't take my eyes off Kate.

Faint pulse. Faint pulse. Faint pulse.

"Figures," I muttered.

"Want to arrest you," he added.

My hand tightened around hers.

"They can certainly try," I grunted.

He chuckled. "Yeah, I told them as much. When Kate wakes up, you'll probably have to go down there, make some kind of statement."

Faint pulse. Faint pulse. Faint pulse.

"Won't be going anywhere until my woman walks out of this place on her own two feet," I said, still not taking my eyes off her.

Hansen sighed loudly. "You pulled a gun on a doctor, brother," he reminded me.

"I'm aware."

"Doctor in question is luckily having some memory issues, thanks to Sarah," he continued. "But there were witnesses in the waiting room who haven't been as open to our... *suggestions* as we would've liked. Even with our connections, the cops still have to go through at least some of the motions. They are definitely takin' it seriously."

My jaw hardened. "And you can tell them I'll happily hop down to the station, do a song and dance for them, when my woman walks her ass out of the hospital and gets off life support."

Faint pulse. Faint pulse. Faint pulse.

"We pay them enough," I added. "They should be doing the song and dance for us."

Another chuckle. Hansen slapped me on the shoulder.

It was a dangerous move.

"Okay, brother," he conceded. "I'll convince them that it's in their best interest to wait."

My eyes ran over the bruises and cuts on Kate's face. "You do that."

His boots thumped against the floor as he walked out.

It was just me and Kate again.

Faint pulse. Faint pulse. Faint pulse.

———

Heels clicked along the floor.

I smelled her perfume, hating it immediately 'cause it drowned out the very faint smell of Kate, gettin' lost amongst all the cleaners and disinfectants in this fuckin' place.

Freya pulled a chair to sit down beside me.

I didn't look at her.

"I can sit with her," she offered. "So you can get something to eat. I know better than to ask an alpha male to go and get some sleep—even though he's been awake for over twenty-four hours—when his woman is..." she trailed off, staring at Kate, probably. Her breath hitched. "When his woman is healing," she finished, her voice stronger, after clearing her throat. "But I happen to have hard evidence that even though they may be able to exist on no sleep, alpha males do need to do things like eat. You know, to sustain life?"

I didn't answer.

The sound of the monitors took up the silence in the room.

Freya sighed and reached over to squeeze my thigh. "Do you think we should call her daughter?"

Now my eyes darted away from Kate to Freya. I tried to read the emotion I saw in her eyes. Fear? But she didn't flinch back. She was married to Hades. This bitch was not one to spook easily.

Almost anyone else probably would've gone running from the room. Old Ladies weren't just anyone, though. They were one of a kind.

Irreplaceable.

"No," I ground out.

Her expression was soft, eyes brimming with tears. "Sweetheart, her mother is on life support. Her father..."

Her father was hopefully being tortured by Freya's husband.

"No," I repeated. I looked back to Kate. "She would not want Violet to see her like this."

Kate had lived through fucking hell for her daughter. She loved her with an intensity that radiated from her. She would want to protect her from seeing her in this condition. Unfortunately, she wasn't able to make that or any other decision right now.

But I could.

I would.

Freya's gaze bore into me, and I knew she was debating over whether to push me on this. It was brave to even consider that. She was doing this 'cause she cared for Kate. Rationally, I knew that.

But there was nothing rational about me right now.

So I prayed she didn't push it.

She squeezed my thigh one last time.

"Okay," she stood up. "I'm going to bring a cheeseburger in here and you're going to eat it. You won't even have to let her go. I'm pretty sure a badass can manage a cheeseburger one handed." There was a heavy silence as she stood there, not leaving. "Kate will be pissed if you faint from hunger when she wakes up. It'll also damage your street cred."

She lingered for a few moments longer before she walked out. Sometime later—exactly two thousand one hundred and thirty-one of Kate's heartbeats—she returned with a cheeseburger.

I ate it one handed, holding on to Kate with the other.

KATE

I had been having a lot of weird dreams.

Swiss was in all of them.

He was eating a cheeseburger in one.

In another, he was murmuring something about a heartbeat.

There might've been something about him dancing or singing. But that couldn't have been right.

Each time, he was close enough to smell. My left hand was encased in his dry, firm grip. I ached to squeeze it, to let him know I was there. But I couldn't reach. I was down too deep, coming in and out. At one time, there was something stuffed down my throat, and I had clawed at it, trying to pull it out.

Swiss was there too. I was reasonably sure he said the word 'fuck' at least five times in two sentences.

I'd wanted to smile at that, but I drifted off again.

This latest time, though, I managed to claw my way out.

There were a lot of things going on. Various machines beeping, which I deduced were attached to me as the hospital bed and room came into focus. I must've somehow survived Preston trying to beat me to death.

And if I'd survived, there was no way I wouldn't be in a hospital. I distinctly remember the sounds of my bones cracking, a warmness and fullness in my stomach that I was pretty sure signified internal bleeding.

I assumed I was on drugs since the pain was just under the surface, urgent and overwhelming.

My throat stung. Burned. Like the pits of hell. Whatever drugs they were pumping into me weren't strong enough to numb that.

Flashes rushed through my mind.

Preston's hands on my neck, his nostrils flaring. Preston's

furious eyes as they took in the letters on my hip, bulging with fury.

With evil.

Pure evil.

Then there was cold. Empty coldness. The hard ground. Arms around me. Swiss murmuring things. His warmth.

Not much else after that.

My eyelids felt like they were made of cement. Sticky. Heavy. Gritty. It took some time to open them. Considerable effort. And I was tired. Exhausted, really. Even though I surmised I'd just woken up from something resembling a coma.

But I fought against that. I used the hand in mine to grip on to as I pulled myself out. When my fingers flexed around it, there was movement.

"Baby?"

The voice was coarse. Full of anguish. Worry. Hope.

I worked harder to lift my eyelids. The room was blurry at first, so I had to squeeze my eyes shut against the harsh light.

"Countess?" Softer this time. Pleading. The hand holding mine lifted, then his lips pressed on my fingers. "Wake up for me, baby."

I held on to that.

Swiss came into view. He was leaning forward, our intertwined hands resting against his mouth as if he were in prayer.

He looked rough. There was stubble on his face. I'd never seen him with facial hair. He was religious about his shaving routine. I recalled teasing him about it. Then he skipped it one morning and left me with rashes on my inner thighs.

His eyes were bloodshot. As if he hadn't slept in years. There was a ruggedness to him, a wildness that even I could recognize while feeling groggy and drugged up. He looked like an exposed nerve. A wild animal.

His clothes were rumpled. Stained with blood. My blood, I deduced. Fortunately, his cut covered most of that.

And he was the most beautiful thing I've ever seen.

I smiled. The gesture stretched skin that felt foreign, numb and tight.

But I did it anyway.

His eyes glistened, and he laid his forehead on our hands for a moment. "Thank fuck," he muttered.

He stood then bent over to lay a kiss on my lips. The gentlest kiss he'd ever given me. As if I were made of glass. He brushed the hair from my face with that same gentleness. His face hovered inches from mine. A tear ran down his cheek.

"Never been so afraid in my life," he whispered, resting his forehead against mine. We stayed like that for a long time.

A gloriously long time.

Until we were interrupted by a very pretty doctor named Sarah. She checked my vitals and informed me that I couldn't speak for another forty-eight hours at least, due to vocal cord injuries.

The burning throat made sense.

Swiss stayed at my side during the checkup. He didn't let go of my hand. I suspected that he hadn't let go of my hand for however long I'd been out. There was dark scruff on his jaw that could almost be called a beard.

I had been meaning to ask about how long he'd been here, if he'd slept, eaten. Or at least gesture for a piece of paper or phone where I could write such questions. But I quickly became very tired and had to fight against my drooping eyelids.

Swiss's thumb rubbed circles on the top of my palm. "Sleep now, Countess," he murmured. "You're safe now. I'm not goin' anywhere."

His promise wrapped around me like a warm blanket.

I forced my lids open and saw a wretched apology swimming in his eyes. There was blame there. A whole bunch of it. For letting me leave in the first place, I guessed.

Preston, I assumed was somewhere in the clubhouse. If he was alive, that was. I didn't waste more than a second thinking about that.

But something else sparked in my mind, and my eyes jerked open despite the fast-approaching oblivion.

My hand squeezed tight against Swiss's, and he sat up in response.

"V—" I managed to get the single letter out before my voice broke completely. As it was, it sounded more like a scratch than a letter.

But Swiss knew what I was talking about immediately.

Who I was talking about.

"She's fine, baby," he reassured me. "She doesn't know you're here."

I sagged in relief.

I couldn't bear the thought of my daughter rushing home from the time of her life to see her mother half dead at the hands of her father.

No. I would not sentence her to that memory. Ignorance, whether it was ethical or not, was going to be my gift to her. For now, at least.

"I've got your phone." He reached into his cut. The screen was smashed, but it was still working. "Been holding her off with texts. Well, I had to get Caroline and Freya to do a lot of the texting for me since I have no fuckin' idea what she's talkin' about half the time." He scrolled through, turning the phone to show me photos in the text thread.

My heart bloomed with warmth, seeing my daughter's smiling face. Her black hair was whipping around her face in the wind. Her eyes seemed to glow purple against the lavender field she was posing in front of. Her shoulders were dusted with freckles I hadn't seen before.

Swiss scrolled slowly, letting me take in my happy, healthy, unharmed girl until I lapsed into darkness.

I woke again in the middle of the night.

The only light in the room was from a lamp in the corner and a sliver coming from the bottom of a closed door.

My eyes went searching for him, expecting to find him sleeping in the large chair he'd claimed at my bedside.

But he wasn't sleeping.

He was wide awake, staring at me. Still clutching my hand.

"I had a little girl," his voice punctured the quiet. I could barely hear it, but the words were thunder in my ears. "She would've been the same age as Violet." His chin dipped, looking down at our clasped hands. "A year and six months older, to be exact."

The monitor measuring my heartbeat beeped faster as the words sunk in.

"I got married young," he explained. "Real young. 'Cause I got my high school girlfriend pregnant. My parents insisted we get married. They were good Christians, you see."

My hand tightened in Swiss's. Or at least it tried to. I wasn't strong enough to squeeze it as hard as I wished I could.

"My dad grew up in the 'hood,' worked really fuckin' hard to make sure I wouldn't. My brother wouldn't. He met my mom, got her pregnant, and they moved to a nice, mostly white neighborhood outside St. Louis."

His voice had a smooth cadence. Even. It might've danced

against my skin if it wasn't for the information he'd provided. The information that had torn through me.

"They wanted more from their kids, ya know?" His eyes held onto mine. "Wanted us to be doctors. Lawyers. Whatever the fuck people become after goin' to some fancy college."

He shrugged. The gesture was almost violent, his hand tight on mine.

"But then I went and got my girlfriend pregnant," he sighed. "My white girlfriend, whose parents weren't exactly thrilled some black kid got their princess pregnant." His eyes were dry, solid. "But they were good people, a little bigoted, which was something I was used to by then. So they accepted it. Accepted me. Begrudgingly."

My heart thrummed. and the monitor continued to beat erratically. My skin ached for the pain in Swiss's voice, hidden expertly, which wouldn't have been detectable if not for how well I knew him. How well I thought I knew him, at least. I'd suspected there was something in his past. A trauma of some kind. But I had never imagined this. I could never have imagined this. There was no happy ending here. If there was, then Swiss wouldn't be sitting here. He'd be in a home with his wife. His child.

"Wedding was small but nice. We moved in with my parents. I wanted to get a job immediately, provide for my family. But my dad wouldn't hear of me droppin' out of school. We butted heads on that." He grinned without humor. "We butted heads a lot."

He didn't continue immediately, so we sat there in silence. I watched him linger in that memory.

My soul was splitting apart. His grief was palpable. Pain a living thing.

"Mary stayed in school too." Her name was stated hoarsely. "For as long as she could, at least. Planned on goin' back when the baby was born... Our moms were gonna take turns with the baby. It was all sorted."

He looked up to the ceiling, as if he was looking for strength to say the rest.

Swiss, the strongest man I'd ever met, was struggling to find what it took to tell me the rest.

He found my eyes once more. "Mary got into a car accident. She was eight months along. I didn't like her driving. We had arguments about it. She won." Another smile. No humor in it either. No joy. Only a regret that made my teeth hurt. A pain that made my bones ache.

"She was dead on arrival to the hospital," he said, voice flat and empty. "They took her in for a c-section. To try to save our daughter." He blinked a few times as if calling up an image. "She was so small," he whispered. "So beautiful. Her head fit in the palm of my hand."

Tears ran down my cheeks.

"I didn't go to either of their funerals," he muttered. "I was gone by then."

My throat burned with all the things I wish I could've been able to say. The things that wouldn't make a difference. Wouldn't change the pain in his voice or heal the open wound inside him that would always bleed.

I was desperate to hold him. But my limbs were lead.

"Anyway, I didn't go to college." He rubbed the back of his neck. "Lot of shit happened between then and now. Shit we'll talk about whenever you want. I just wanted to let you know that I'd never held anything in my arms that mattered like my daughter did. That meant the whole fuckin' world."

His eyes burned into me, and he clutched my hand tighter. "Until you," he whispered. "You're my whole fuckin' world,

Countess. You're my proof that I'm not ruined beyond repair. And if I'd lost you, there would've been nothin' left of me."

I opened my mouth, desperate to speak to him at that moment. The moment after he'd laid his soul bare to me. It did not deserve my silence.

"Don't talk, baby," he instructed, watching my mouth. "I know you. There're probably a million things you want to say. I know them all. So you don't need to say anything. Just keep breathing." His eyes studied the monitors. "Keep that heart beating. That's all I need you to do for me."

I closed my mouth again, knowing that I was not strong enough to speak anyway. Physically or mentally.

Instead, I used every ounce of strength left in me to tug on Swiss's arm.

With devastating slowness, Swiss stood and carefully climbed into the small bed. He tucked me into his shoulder, and I found my home on his chest. The one that had my initials carved into it.

CHAPTER SIXTEEN

I HAD FINALLY BEEN GIVEN the all-clear to slowly start speaking again, though most of my meals were still coming from a straw.

And I was also disconnected from my catheter. That was a win, though the trips to the bathroom were painful, to say the least. I was already being weaned off the heaviest of painkillers, and the agony I was in surprised even me. Although I shouldn't have been surprised considering the extent of my injuries.

Swiss had had a... *spirited* argument with the doctors about my painkillers when I'd winced and collapsed into him the first time I'd tried to stand.

I'd shaken my head rapidly, grating out, "Stop, I'm fine."

But I'd managed to communicate that, despite the pain, I wanted to be off the painkillers. Sure, they numbed things, but they made everything hazy and flat. Made my mind cloudy and unfamiliar. I didn't like it at all. I wanted to be me, or as close to me as I could be. And I needed the pain. For clarity.

Swiss took a while to understand that, and it was hard to write it on a phone with weak fingers, but I managed.

He was the one who helped me to the bathroom, who stood in the shower with me. He would not hear of a nurse—male or female—doing either.

The first time I'd seen my face, it was with him behind me in the mirror. He'd showered and shaved in the bathroom inside my hospital room. He ate in my room. Slept there. He'd vowed at some point that he would walk out with me.

So very Swiss.

My body had jerked when I met my own eyes in the mirror. I barely looked like myself. The eye with the fractured socket had only just been able to open on its own again, since the swelling had gone down. One of my eyes had very little white, just bright, angry red where a blood vessel had burst in my eyeball. But both of them were black and blue. My cheekbone was the same. The split on my lip had healed, so the skin was scabbed.

It was my neck that was by far the worst. Even counting my midsection that was varying shades of purple with a new scar running down my stomach where they'd opened me up to stop the internal bleeding.

My neck was almost black at this point. It didn't look real. It didn't look as if a human could survive whatever had caused the skin to do that. The force it would've taken to create those bruises.

But I had survived.

"You let another man mark you. You'll die with that mark," Preston spat, dribble trailing down his chin.

His glasses had fallen off at some point, and his eyes were cartoon-like, they were so wide.

I clawed at the hands around my neck, trying to thrash. Something cut into my stomach. Something tore through my insides.

Black spots danced in my vision, my lungs burned. I was going to die. And Preston was going to be the last thing I ever saw.

"I fought him," I rasped, holding on to Swiss's espresso gaze so that memory didn't yank me away.

I could only speak a couple of words at a time and hadn't attempted full sentences yet. This was the first one I'd uttered since I woke.

Swiss jerked in the mirror, his hands tightening ever so slightly around my waist. But nowhere near as tight as he was capable of. There was none of that. Each of his touches were purposeful, consistent. Either to show tenderness or to help me stand, pee or walk. He hadn't been afraid to hurt me... before. But now he touched me as if I might break at any moment. Now I was plenty hurt for him, I guessed.

I wondered idly if he would ever touch me that way again. Or if the image of me like this would haunt him. Already, I ached for him to mark me, so that Preston was not the last man who bruised me.

"When it was cl-clear he wa-was..." I cleared my throat and swallowed razor blades. "When it was clear that he was going to kill me, I fought." My words came out slowly and were barely audible, but Swiss hung on every one.

He was shaking. Shaking with rage. With emotion. Hurt. Guilt. I didn't know which. Maybe a combination of all.

"I fought," I repeated. Both for him and for me. "For me," I croaked. I held his gaze even though parts of me were breaking apart. "For you," I managed before my voice gave out.

Swiss was still shaking. His eyes were shimmering with tears I'd never seen in his eyes. "I know." His voice cracked. He laid his lips at the top of my head. "I know," he repeated against my head. "And I'm gonna thank God every day for that."

We stood there for a long time, staring at each other, staring at my bruises, staring into the abyss still lingering, close enough to touch. The one where I didn't fight. The one where I died on the side of the road.

"Let's get you into the shower," Swiss said when he'd stopped shaking.

I nodded once, even that benign gesture sending splinters of pain down to my toes. I bit my lip trying to hide that, but of course, Swiss saw it. He was watching for every hitch in my breath, every pinch of my brow. It was as if he were waiting for something to fall from the sky, just so he could push me out of the way, save me from it.

His fingers worked slowly, getting me undressed.

My body was covered in bruises. It didn't take long to get me naked, and when I was, Swiss shed his clothes quickly. I grasped his cut, my fingers sinking into the leather, soft as butter. It calmed me, that piece of clothing. Something that could've been a part of Swiss for how important it was to him. How integral it was to his identity.

To mine, too, now.

It was heavier than a simple piece of clothing. But despite my injuries, my weakness, it was a weight that I could carry. I hung it carefully on the hook on the back of the bathroom door. It took me a while to cross the small distance, my steps measured, slow, careful. As if I were learning to walk again. I half expected Swiss's hands to steady me; he'd made it clear he wasn't going to let me go anywhere without his help.

But I made this small journey without his help.

When I turned, Swiss was standing naked in the middle of

the bathroom, staring at me. Staring at me in a way that took my breath away.

Literally stole it.

My heart jumped in my throat.

Swiss was staring at me like I'd just hung the moon. Like he was staring at the whole world. With love. So much of it my chest burned.

But pain too. Utter anguish.

My knees barely took me back to him.

The second I stood in front of him, Swiss grabbed on to my hips and fell to his knees.

To. His. Knees.

His forehead rested against my stomach, and his arms went around me. Like I was the only thing tethering him to this earth. Like he had no other choice but sink to his knees in front of me.

My hands found his head, and my eyes closed, finding peace that shouldn't have existed in a moment like that. But that's the closest word I could use to describe it.

Swiss lifted his head slowly, after a minute or so. His lips found the scar on my hip, almost healed now.

His scar. The only mark on my body that belonged to him. The only mark on my body that I had obtained willingly.

Swiss's lips landed on that scar, lingering there.

His head lifted, and his eyes found mine. "Did he touch you?" Every letter of the words he spoke were carved into the air.

I knew what he meant immediately. The words came out of somewhere visceral. Some ancient, feral part of him. They were dripping with pain. Blood.

In that moment, I made the decision, made the promise to myself, that Swiss would never ever know what had set Preston off. That it was his mark on me that started it all. I would not let him carry that. Cut himself to pieces on that serrated knowledge.

It didn't matter that it very well could've been what saved my life, in a way. If that mark had not been there, Preston would've raped me. I wouldn't have fought him, but it would've been rape. And then, something inside me, something integral, would've broken. Smashed into a million pieces. Never to be repaired.

Swiss's mark was the reason Preston almost killed me. But it was also the reason I was still alive. Still me.

I wouldn't be able to get him to understand that, though.

"No, honey," I rasped.

His eyes studied me as if he were searching for a lie I was telling to protect him.

"I swear, he didn't," I croaked.

Swiss's hand slipped between my legs, cupping me gently there before moving to my ass.

The gesture wasn't sexual, though I sucked in a rough breath, and my core prickled with hunger. It was something more intimate.

Swiss got to his feet once more, forehead resting on mine. "Let's get you cleaned up, Countess."

When we got into the shower, I did something I hadn't thought I was capable of doing. Not yet, at least.

I laughed.

Of course, it was a garbled, fractured sound, but it was a laugh nonetheless. Because inside that hospital shower was a red bottle.

Of four-in-one.

And that's how I realized I would heal. Completely. Largely because of the man in the shower with me.

My room was covered in flowers. There were crystals too. For 'healing energy,' according to Macy. There was an essential oil diffuser. I was wearing silk pajamas thanks to Marilyn, Freya's best friend, who had dropped off a huge basket of high-end skincare and nightwear. My nails were painted bright red. That was Freya. There was a large stack of paperbacks—most of which were steamy romances—and magazines from Caroline. *Lord of the Rings* was playing on a loop thanks to Macy. Swiss had muttered about it being 'weird elf bullshit,' but I'd woken from a nap or two with him watching the TV rapt, hand still in mine but eyes glued to the screen. I'd smiled and gone back to sleep.

Julian brought coffee and pastries every morning.

Every single member of the Sons of Templar had come in to wish me well, to glower in that angry, masculine way when seeing my injuries.

I'd never felt so overwhelmed, so cared about, so *loved* in my entire life. I'd never had so many people make an effort for me. Not one person, not one single person looked at me different—apart from the angry, masculine glares at my bruises—or gave any inclination that they were mad at me for my lies. Then again, it was hard to be mad at someone in a hospital bed. But no one treated me differently. Like I was some weak woman to be pitied. Not even a little.

I'd finally spoken to Violet, a quick phone call to prove the 'bronchitis' I'd said I had as an excuse for not being able to speak on the phone. She'd sounded appropriately concerned and had even offered to fly home early to 'take care of me.' I'd quickly squashed that idea, filling with panic at the mere thought of my daughter seeing me like this.

Although I was desperate to see her. To touch her. Smell her. Even more so after what Swiss had told me about his daughter. It was something that hung between us now. Not keeping us apart but gluing us together even tighter. He'd shared a piece that he'd been holding back. That explained many things about who he was.

There was more I needed to say to him. A lot more. But we hadn't had a chance to say all of those kinds of things. Not just because of the constant stream of visitors, but because I could only manage a handful of sentences at a time. And doctors had warned against me trying to push myself, saying I could cause permanent damage to my vocal cords if I did.

Swiss's fist, the one not holding my hand, had been clenched tightly on top of his thigh when he heard that. Fury danced in his eyes and rippled in the air around him.

He'd shielded me from that for the most part, kept it locked down inside of him. But it was so all encompassing, some of it finally slipped out. And I saw the other side to his concern, to his turmoil. The need for revenge. It was a living thing inside of him.

Though we hadn't said a word about Preston, except that moment in the bathroom, I had a feeling that he was still alive.

Swiss had been with me since they found me. Which meant that someone else had gone after Preston. And I knew for a fact that someone had gone after him. No way in hell would Swiss have let him make it back to Carver Springs after what he did. No way anyone in the club would've let that happen. And although I wasn't hip to the inner workings of the club, I was willing to bet a lot on the fact that they wouldn't have handed him to the police.

The police who had taken my 'statement,' which Swiss had given for me since I couldn't speak. The slightly overweight sheriff in his mid-fifties had taken the statement, not blinking at the fact that Swiss was doing it for me.

According to Swiss, I'd been attacked by someone wearing a mask and could not remember anything about it.

The sheriff had nodded once, saying he'd be on the 'lookout' then wished me a speedy recovery.

There was some kind of understanding there that I didn't have the energy to ask about.

So they had Preston somewhere. Keeping him alive until Swiss was comfortable enough to leave my side, presumably to kill him.

As unbelievable as it was, I didn't have the energy to ask about that either. Or even think about. Not yet, at least. I was going to be discharged in a couple of days, thankfully. The hospital room was becoming suffocating. The nurses, the sounds, the smells... All of it was too much. Swiss and everyone connected to the club were the only things keeping me sane.

It was just the two of us now. Freya, Hades and Eva had just left. Hades and Swiss had had a man-huddle in the corner of the room while Freya sat Eva on my bed, talking about the 'coming home' party they were planning for me in the next few days.

Home.

She'd said it as if it were a foregone conclusion. As if I hadn't lied about a thing. As if there was nowhere else for me to go.

And there was nowhere else for me to go. Not now. Not ever. Although I was sure there was a lot to deal with in Carver Springs, especially if Preston was to be killed.

But that was all pushed to the back of my mind. There was something much more pressing. Someone. The someone whose hand had barely left mine since I woke up. Whose hand had been in mine practically the entire time I'd been unconscious. The someone who looked absolutely tortured. *Wretched* over this.

And I couldn't stand it anymore.

There was something playing on the TV. We were both only pretending to watch it. Swiss wasn't able to keep his eyes off me for an extended period of time. They kept darting back to me, as if making sure I was still there. Still alive.

I caught them the next time they made their way in my direction, my hand tightening around his in signal that I had something to say.

Swiss sat up a little straighter in his chair and moved slightly so his body was facing me. He leaned closer, knowing that I wasn't strong enough to project my voice.

"I don't blame you," I declared, my voice sounding weird, garbled, and my ribs stinging from the breath used to expel the words. My throat felt raw, as if I'd swallowed pure acid.

The pain was constant, grating and overwhelming. I'd forgotten what it felt like to not have this pain. Forgotten what my body had felt like before all of this. When it was mine. When it was mine and Swiss's. I ached for him to claim it once more. But I knew from the way he handled me that *that* wasn't going to happen anytime soon.

"Don't try to talk," Swiss murmured, brushing my hair gently from my face. Oh so gently. As if I were a porcelain doll. That had not changed in all of these days. As much as I loved Swiss, his presence, his scent, his hands on me, I was coming to hate that gentle touch. It was saturated in his pain. He was going above and beyond to not hurt me further, but little did he know, that gentle touch hurt more than my injuries.

"No," I argued, bracing against the pain. "I need you to know, I don't blame you." I held his eyes. "I'm mad at you, let's not get that wrong." My voice was scratchy, high, thin. Every word sounded like it was about to break.

He smiled, but it didn't reach his eyes which were full of agony. I gritted my teeth, seeing that.

"I wouldn't expect anything less, baby." His voice was bursting with regret and guilt.

"Mad, we can get over," I coughed, wincing at how shredded my throat felt. "Mad, we can work with. But you blaming yourself for another man hurting me, you thinking I blame you... We can *not* work with that."

Swiss's face turned stormy, despite whatever promise he'd made to himself to stay soft and gentle with me in the wake of my injuries. I was glad about that. I couldn't stand him being soft and gentle. That wasn't him.

"We'll talk about this later," he growled. "When you're healed."

"No," I choked out. "We'll talk about this *now*." I squeezed my eyes shut, taking a breath before I spoke again. "Before this becomes a wound that will not heal." I stared into his eyes, determined. "I do not blame you. There is no blame except for the man who I guess is either chained up in a basement somewhere or in a shallow grave."

His jaw was rigid. "Oh, it's much, much too early for him to feel the cool embrace of death," he grumbled.

Ice crept across my skin.

I couldn't think of the reality of that right now. Couldn't think of my daughter, the one who adored her daddy, losing him, no matter what kind of monster he was.

"Right," I wheezed. "So there is one man responsible for my bruises, my broken bones."

Swiss flinched as I spoke, his eyes running over every inch of me.

"He is responsible," I whispered, the pain exhausting me. My eyelids fluttered. "*He* is responsible," I managed to squeak out before I drifted off to sleep.

I was discharged a few days later.

Well, I was only discharged after Swiss took me home against medical advice.

It was the middle of the night when he did all of this insisting. After I'd jerked awake from a nightmare. I'd been having them every night since I'd woken up and resumed a semi-regular sleep schedule. Swiss was sleeping with me at that point. Each time I'd jerk awake, he'd hold me tighter to him and murmur, "You're safe. I'm here. You made it. I'm not going anywhere. You're not going anywhere."

I wasn't sure whether he was talking to me or himself.

He repeatedly whispered those sentences, kissing my hair, and eventually I'd drift back off.

But not that night.

I knew that I wouldn't go back to sleep. That I couldn't.

"I need to get out of here," I croaked. My voice was still scratchy, still unrecognizable, but able to form more complete sentences without breaking off.

"A couple more days, baby," Swiss muttered, voice tight. My nightmares shook him. To the core. As if he wasn't already shaken up.

He hated the nightmares I had. That he couldn't chase them off.

"No," I demanded as firmly as I could in my gravelly voice. "I can't be here a couple more days. I can't be here for another *moment*." My croaky voice had an edge of hysteria now. I couldn't help it. I felt hysterical. Like my skin might split open if I didn't get out of here.

I expected Swiss to try to argue with me. To go all alpha male on me, insisting I stay here on the doctor's orders.

But Swiss just kissed my head and murmured, "Okay, Countess. Let's get you out of here."

Then he got out of bed and created somewhat of a ruckus.

The ruckus didn't last long. And I was being wheeled out of the hospital room less than an hour later.

When we got to the exit, I pushed out of the chair, with Swiss's hand in mine, and we walked out of the hospital together.

CHAPTER SEVENTEEN

KATE

THE CLUB WAS quiet when we walked in. No partygoers, no one sitting at the bar, nothing. But the second I walked into the common room, I relaxed. My gaze landed on the bar area, memories of my last moments there rushing forward. Of Preston, of Swiss and his cold stare, but I quickly shook those off.

I would not let those scarce moments ruin a place that signified so much for me.

A place that was my home.

Swiss was watching me very carefully, his own tortured gaze on the area where he'd been so cruel.

"Let's go to bed," I whispered. Sure, there was a part of me that wanted to berate him for his cruelty. How fickle he'd been. How cold. How he'd broken my heart in less than a minute.

An angry, bitter part of me ached to throw all of that at him, hurt him for how he'd hurt me.

This was not the time for that. Besides, there was nothing I could say to Swiss that was worse than what he was repeating to himself.

His gaze lingered for a second longer before we walked down the corridor to his room.

With every step, my pain, though ever present, somehow became duller. Lighter. No more sterile hospital smells, no beeping of monitors or far-off conversations from nurses and doctors.

My body relaxed as Swiss closed the door to his room, and I inhaled the scent of him. Of us. The bed was still mussed from when we'd gotten out of it... A week ago? Two? Before everything happened.

My things were still neatly arranged on top of the dresser, a pair of my jeans thrown over the chair in the corner. Everything was how I'd left it.

My eyes found the hooks attached to the bed, pleasant memories swam through me, filling me with warmth and need.

It had been a long time since Swiss touched me without being cautious, with pure hunger, without worrying about hurting me. Fuck, *wanting* to hurt me.

Desire pooled at the bottom of my stomach, looking at those hooks, longing to be attached to them by Swiss. But when I looked at the man in question, it became clear that desire was the last thing on his mind.

"Jesus," Swiss murmured, his eyes moving from the hooks to me. "You let me do those things to you." His expression was haunted.

Fucking wretched.

"You let me *hurt* you," he whispered brokenly. "After years of a man laying his hands on you, I fuckin' hurt you."

The pain in his voice cut across my skin.

"Yes, Swiss, I let you do those things to me," I agreed.

He flinched.

"Listen to me," I squared my shoulders. "I *let* you do those things to me. If you remember correctly, I was the one who initiated that." I tried to make my tone lighter, to coax us back to a time when none of this existed.

It didn't work. Not in the slightest.

A muscle in Swiss's jaw twitched.

"Yes, you did. When you thought that you'd get a fuck. A good time. A fuckin' escape from the shit you'd been living with... Fuck." He ran his hand over his head in distress. "An escape from everything you'd been living with, not another fuckin' version of it."

I raised my brow at him. Or at least I tried to. Such facial expressions weren't possible with my current injuries.

The pain didn't bother me in that moment, though. It was the naked emotion on Swiss's face that did. The guilt. Shame.

Over us. Over what we did.

It cut me somewhere deep. Somewhere vulnerable.

"I chose *you*," I looked at him intently, hoping he saw the truth in my eyes. "Now I don't believe in magic, and I certainly don't think I have any kind of magical abilities, but I do know that there is something about us. Something special. Something magical that has been there since the start. And on some level, I knew what I was going to get from you. You gave me something." I took in a deep breath. "You gave me everything. You saved me, Swiss."

I stepped forward, grasping the sides of his cut to bring him downward, so I could kiss him. Not gently. Hungrily.

Swiss responded immediately. His hands went around my waist and yanked me to him with a roughness that was instinctual. His tongue plundered my mouth, and I moaned in delight.

Then he stopped. Abruptly.

"Fuck, Kate," his hands flew to his hips. "Did I hurt you?" His eyes scanned my body in concern.

"No," I said, my voice hoarse. "You didn't hurt me. That was exactly what I needed." I gripped the back of his neck, though the motion sent pain splintering through my ribs. "You're exactly what I want." My breath hitched. "I need you, Swiss."

I watched him battle. Battle between that darkness inside of him that needed me, too, needed me more than anything. And the other part of him that loved me, wanted to protect me. The part that was responsible for the gentleness, the concern.

"Kate," he warned.

"Please," I moaned. "Please make me feel something other than pain."

His eyes were liquid fire. "Kate." His tone was more guttural this time. "Don't fuckin' do this. I won't be able to control myself."

"Good," I breathed, laying my lips on his. "I don't want you to control yourself." I kissed him again, coaxing a response out of him.

He stayed stock still for a couple more beats before he let out a low growl in the back of his throat, and he kissed me back.

Ferociously.

His hands went around me once more, and his palms found the soft silk of the pajamas I'd worn home from the hospital. His calluses caught on the fabric.

Though he was kissing me with all of the pent-up desire inside of him, he didn't lose control completely. He didn't throw me on the bed like he would've before. No, he walked us there, lips still on mine, hands still tearing at the silk.

Then he placed me, gently, on the bed, head lifting only so he could tear at my shirt. When the buttons went flying, I internally cheered.

He hissed air through his teeth as his eyes found my naked torso. The bruises, angry, black, blue. The surgical cut complete with stitches.

Worry struck me like lightning, panicking that he would stop. That the better side of him would prevail, and he'd tuck me into bed.

Luckily, the worse side of Swiss—the one that I loved—was stronger, and his hands went to the elastic waistband of my pants.

"Lift your hips for me, baby," he murmured.

I did so, not even cringing at the spear of pain that came with the movement.

Swiss let out a guttural sound as he exposed my naked pussy.

"Prettiest cunt in the world right there," he crooned.

My toes curled in response to his tone, at his eyes feasting on the part of me that was aching for him. Desperate for him. On instinct, I spread my legs wider and was rewarded with his sharp intake of breath.

His eyes found mine as he knelt at the side of the bed, slowly bringing my legs over his shoulders. He kissed each of my thighs as he did so.

"As much as I know you want my cock, as much as I want to give it to you, I'm not gonna fuck you," he breathed against the apex of my thighs.

I let out a sound of protest.

His grip intensified ever so slightly on my thighs, and my pussy pulsed in anticipation of the pain.

It didn't come, though. He was still holding back.

"I'm gonna eat you, though. And you're gonna come for me. Hard. You're gonna split apart. You're gonna be a good girl and wait for my cock."

My heartbeat thrummed in my chest as my breaths got shallower with need.

"You gonna be a good girl and wait for my cock, Countess?"

I nodded, unable to speak.

Swiss didn't move. "Do I have to ask again?"

"I'm gonna be a good girl and wait for your cock," I told him, my voice barely audible.

"That's my girl," he whispered.

Then he dove in.

Dove. Right. In.

And he did split me apart.

Took me off the face of the earth. He gave me a respite from both of our troubles. For a while, at least.

━━━

I woke up alone. It couldn't have been that long since I first went to sleep, the darkness outside was still thick and heavy.

It had been a couple of hours at most. And Swiss was gone.

He was gone because we were back at the club, because he knew I was safe here. Because he thought that I would sleep through the night now. He was gone because of my nightmares. Because of the rasp in my voice. The bruises around my throat. The scar on my stomach.

I knew he wouldn't leave me for anything but revenge. To feed the thing inside him that demanded blood, retribution for what had been done to me.

Preston.

They had him, somewhere.

I vaguely remembered the conversation we'd had about it.

Of course, they'd found him. And they weren't going to hand him over to the police. Not after what was done to me.

He was going to die.

My first, primitive instinct to that was glee. Utter freaking joy.

But then reality rushed in.

The father of my child was going to die.

Violet, who loved her dad, thought he hung the moon, was going to lose him. Sally and Frank were going to lose their son. And I would have to construct some kind of narrative. I would have to lie about it. To their faces.

To my daughter's face.

Suddenly, the room was stifling, suffocating. The place that had been my refuge was now a prison.

I pulled back the covers, crossing the room as quickly as I could with my current injuries, intent on fresh air. On relief.

I didn't bump into Swiss on my short journey out to the back patio area of the clubhouse. I hadn't expected to. If he truly was somewhere hurting Preston, there would be no crisp fall breeze. There would be only stale, underground air mixed with the stench of blood. Just the thought of it chilled my exposed arms.

I was wearing only Swiss's tee and nothing else. No shoes. The stone patio was cool against my feet, and I sat down on a step that led out to a grassy area. There was a playground for the kids, a vegetable garden—Macy's idea—and fire drums. Someone—again, likely Macy—had strung fairy lights through the trees, so the area was faintly illuminated. The sun was just starting to kiss the horizon, but it was mostly dark.

Quiet too. There wasn't even the harmony of cicadas that I'd become used to. No birds signaling the incoming morning.

Nothing but the shriek of my thoughts.

I must've been on that step for a while because the sun got progressively brighter.

"Jesus, Countess," a voice sounded from behind me, a mixture of relief and agitation threading through it.

I jumped, even though the voice was familiar. Swiss stomped around to face me, his eyes stormy. He was still wearing the same clothes from earlier. There was a small spec of blood high on his cheekbone.

"You scared me to fuckin' death," he clipped, bending down to pull me up. "And you're chilled to the goddamn bone." He rubbed my arms. "Let's get you inside."

I pulled out of his grip, even though I ached to sink into his warmth.

His eyes flared in surprise and what looked to be irritation.

"Did you kill him?" I asked. My voice would've been flat if not for the uneven tenor caused by my still healing throat.

Swiss's expression cleared. "No," he replied right away. "Not yet. He's got a long way to go before he's lucky enough to die."

My knees started to shake. Not at the casual way Swiss was talking about killing, torture. Not even at the way something inside him burned with satisfaction. With hunger. Not even because the person he was talking about was the man I was married to.

No, all of that didn't surprise or affect me. Although before all of this, Swiss had not shown me this part of himself—not entirely, at least—I knew existed. Knew that violence was a part of him. He'd shown me that the very first night.

My mind was not on Swiss. Not on Preston. Not even on myself.

"You can't kill him," I pled.

Swiss blinked very slowly. Once. Twice. "What?"

"You can't kill him," I repeated.

He stared at me. "You're asking me to let the man who almost killed you live."

I shook at his tone, but he didn't pull it back, didn't gentle his features.

He was too far gone.

"You want me to let the man who tormented you, beat you for *years,* live. The man who bruised you, scarred you, who discarded you in a fuckin' ditch to die... You want me to let him continue to breathe air."

When put that way, it sounded rather crazy. Preston did deserve to suffer. He did deserve to die. I wasn't caught up on the ethics of it all, what version of justice needed to be served. I was caught on one simple fact: my daughter did not deserve to lose her father.

"I want you to let the *father of my child* continue to live, yes." I forced my voice to be even in the face of Swiss's fury.

"You don't get to ask that," he shook his head, stepping forward. Although I knew he wasn't aware that he was doing it, his goal was to intimidate me with his size.

A fury of my own awakened. "Don't I?" I snapped, going toe-to-toe with him. "When *I'm* the one he tormented for years. Who he beat for years. Who he controlled. *I'm* the one who lived through that. Suffered through that. *Me.*" I pointed to my own chest as I glared at him. "And I had one light through all of that. One gift. That was my daughter. My whole freaking world. I would go to war for her. I would die for her. I would do anything and everything in my power to ensure that she doesn't have to feel a moment of pain. So I will suffer through knowing that Preston is breathing, even though he may not deserve to, because my daughter does not deserve to suffer."

I was shouting now.

Almost screaming.

My lungs burned in pain from the force of it, and my head throbbed with my anger, but I wasn't going to back down. Not on this.

Swiss was examining me coldly. In a way I fucking hated. Like he had the day Preston arrived.

He stepped back, pacing the patio like a violet animal before he turned to face me once more. "I get what you're saying," he said softly. "I don't want to hurt your daughter. Or you. But I'm not gonna let him walk out of here. Not after what he did."

His words were set in stone. As if they were law.

Swiss was used to his menace getting him places. Used to his ruthlessness resulting in him getting what he wanted through fear and violence.

So here I was again, with another man, one completely different than my husband in every way, but one who still planned to take away my power.

If I let him.

"If you do that, I'm gone," I hissed, arms folded in front of me.

He blinked, jerking as if I'd hit him.

I was too far gone to feel anything but satisfaction at landing that blow. "I swear to God, if you take my choice away from me, take my control away from me and do this, I'll leave. You'll never see me again." Although the thought of that filled me with dread and panic, I meant every word.

I was just learning what my boundaries were, my limits. Because I was just learning about who the hell I was. But when it came to protecting my child, I knew my limits. I knew I didn't have any fricking limits. I would die for her, kill for her, hurt every day of my life if that meant I got to save her from an ounce of pain.

I also knew that as much as I trusted Swiss, I wasn't going to let him make decisions for me. Especially when those decisions pertained to killing my husband.

His expression had changed. It was no longer cold. It was hot. Hot with fury. He stepped forward, the air seeming to shimmer around him. My heart thundered in my chest, but I stood my ground.

"You are not threatening to leave me, Countess," he purred with violence.

I jutted my chin up. "You are not using your size and general badassery to intimidate me just over a *week* after I was beaten within an inch of my life," I snapped back.

Swiss flinched and stepped back, already looking apologetic. But I wasn't having that. I was too pissed. And hurt. And confused. I hadn't forgotten how quickly he'd abandoned me for Preston. I couldn't blame him for what happened to me—how was he to know that my husband was an abusive piece of shit? — but I could blame him for not fighting for me. For being cruel to me, cold to me, the moment he found out I was married, without giving me a moment to explain.

But I couldn't call him out on that now. Not when he was punishing himself so completely. It was written all over his face. The guilt he felt.

My eyes burned with unshed tears, from the pain caused by what I was expressing coupled with the pain coming from the injuries all over my body. "You have a choice," I said, my voice sounding stronger than I felt. "You feed your vengeance and you get only death. You don't get me." I paused for a handful of heart-beats, letting my words sink in.

"Or you respect my wishes. You save my daughter from a life-time of hurt. You get life. A life with me." I faltered for a second, wondering if that was too presumptuous. Before all of this, he'd spoken easily and freely about his future. One he made clear included me. But then things had changed. He'd changed. On a dime. "If that's what you want," I added on a whisper. I didn't let the look on Swiss's face penetrate once I uttered that.

Instead, I turned on my heel and left.

Swiss and I weren't speaking.

He hadn't come back to bed after our argument. As much as I was mad at him, I missed him terribly. Sleep was impossible, but there wouldn't be much of it anyway since the sun had risen at some point during our argument.

So I showered, on my own for the first time in what felt like forever. Even before Preston's arrival, almost every single shower I'd taken was with Swiss.

I was under the spray of the water for a long time. Both because it took me longer to do basic things now and because I was doing my 'full shower' routine. Double hair wash, mask, exfoliating. I'd attempted shaving, but bending down was impossible as was lifting my arms above my head.

The shower pressure, the scents of all of my favorite products and the familiarity of the shower stall with its erotic memories did little to salve my frayed nerves and frantic heart.

By the time I dressed in a long, loose maxi dress—the easiest thing to wear yet still took me triple the time to get on—and pulled my hair into a low, sleek bun, Swiss had still not returned.

The club had woken up by the time I slipped my feet into some slides. Laughter and female voices coaxed me out of the room. I felt nervous, entering the common room without Swiss, despite having done it a number of times... before.

But now I was wearing my bruises and my truth.

Xander was running around the living area with Hulk Hands. I grinned at him as he shot past.

"Hi, Kate!" he yelled, not pausing.

His little brother chased after him in a Spiderman outfit. "Hi, Kate!" he parroted.

Macy looked up from her embrace with Hansen.

"You ruined the surprise!" she pouted, detaching from her husband.

He lifted his chin in greeting.

Macy stomped over to me in order to kiss me on the cheek before she resumed scolding me.

"You were supposed to be at the hospital still," she snipped, eyes raking over me. "You also look very cute," she added. "Which works for what I have planned."

I looked at her quizzically. "You have something planned?"

She nodded before turning her attention behind us. "Honey?"

Hansen, who had been in a man-huddle with Cody and Elden—there had been a lot of those lately. I tried not to be a narcissist and think they were about me. This was an outlaw motorcycle club... They had a lot of things on their plate.

"Yeah, babe?" he replied, instantly looking up.

"Would you be a dear, and go and fetch Kate and I two coffees from Oliver's?" she asked sweetly as her eyes found mine. "Are you hungry?"

My stomach growled, my throat still throbbing but finally able to handle swallowing real food.

I nodded. "But I can just make—"

"And two of those almond croissants he has that I'd almost sell Xander for!" she called out to him, not listening to me.

I pursed my lips. Those croissants were amazing.

"Babe," Hansen whined, staring at her. "I'm a busy man. I'm the president of this fuckin' club, I can't drop everything to go on a fuckin' *coffee run* for you."

Macy linked her arm with mine. "If you could take them to the place, Kate's surprise place, that would be great," she added while walking us out. "Love you!"

A manly chuckle followed in our wake.

Because I wasn't brave enough or strong enough, I didn't fight Macy. Plus, I really wanted a croissant.

I tried not to think of Swiss as we walked out.

I failed.

CHAPTER EIGHTEEN

KATE

"ARE you going to tell me where we're going?" I asked as Macy drove out of town.

She glanced over at me. "No," she replied happily.

I pursed my lips. We were taking the desert road, out toward where Freya lived. Her house was at the very end of a quiet road with her closest neighbors miles away. The lifestyle I'd been coveting.

"Swiss wasn't with you," she remarked, her eyes on the road.

"He wasn't," I agreed. Just the mention of him had my chest burning, panic building low in my stomach.

I'd given him an ultimatum. One I'd meant. One I intended to follow through on. But what if he didn't care? What if he killed Preston anyway?

"He's pretty much been surgically attached to your hip since..." Macy trailed off.

"Since my husband beat me half to death?" I offered.

She sucked in a breath. "Yeah," she nodded, her voice not as carefree as it had been moments ago. "And men, especially badass alpha male bikers, tend to keep up with that surgically attached at the hip thing long after the healing is done." She looked at me over the top of her sunglasses. "And your healing is nowhere near done. So where the fuck is he?"

Her gentle, high voice had a hardness to it now. An anger. On my behalf.

It was still odd, even after how much she'd proved herself to be kind, loving and genuine, to feel comfortable around Macy. To feel comfortable in this friendship without waiting for the other shoe to drop. I wondered if I would always feel like this in my relationships, never able to fully settle, to relax, always holding just a little back.

"We had a... disagreement." My eyes shifted to the desert that was passing us by. There was still a large amount of houses down this stretch of road, but the farther we got out, the larger the space in between them was.

"A disagreement?" Macy repeated. "And what did you disagree about that caused an alpha male to abandon all of his senses—however misguided—which are to forgo all earthly delights such as food and sleep in order to be ready to protect you lest a piano fall from the sky?"

Despite the entire situation, I smiled at her question. Although each of the Sons of Templar men were remarkably different in almost every way, they did share a lot of important qualities. One being the over-the-top protectiveness that Macy was obviously an expert in.

"We disagreed about whether or not he should kill my husband," I told Macy.

I supposed I could've hedged a little. But I knew when to pick my battles. Well, technically I didn't—I didn't fight back for a decade and a half—but Macy was not someone to let something like this go.

And I was dying to talk to someone about it.

I braced myself on the dashboard, wincing from the pain when Macy slammed on the brakes of the car.

"Jeepers," I muttered, gaping at her. "Did that warrant stopping in the middle of the street?"

She raised a brow. "Yes, I think that did. Plus..." she jerked her head to the right. "We're here."

I looked to my right where, off the road a bit, was a small but adorable Spanish style ranch. The front garden was an explosion of colors, and there was no uniformity or symmetry to it. I absolutely loved it.

Behind the house there was nothing but sprawling desert, save for a collection of houses which were nothing but specs in the distance.

I was unsure about what this house had to do with anything. Maybe some friend of Macy's lived here.

"You don't want Preston dead?" Macy asked with interest but without judgment.

I turned to look at her. She'd pushed her oversized aviators to the top of her head.

It was somewhat surreal, talking about whether my boyfriend? Old Man? Was going to kill my husband with a beautiful, free spirited, fashionable woman who had become one of my best friends. One of the only true friends I'd ever had in my life.

I sighed. "I would like him dead... I think." I screwed up my nose. "Don't get me wrong, I've fantasized about him dying more than once over the years, but I've never really been in a situation where it was plausible that he'd actually die. I don't know if I'm that bloodthirsty."

I took a pause to rest. This much conversation was hard on my throat which was still burning. My head throbbed, and it hurt to breathe. I gazed out into the desert, remembering hands around my throat. The million times I'd been told I was stupid, fat, ugly, worthless. Those times, rare but not infrequent, when I'd laid awake in bed, Preston sleeping beside me, and I'd imagined going into the bathroom and taking a whole bottle of painkillers.

"Yes, I am that bloodthirsty," I nodded.

Macy smiled. A smile that was also a little bloodthirsty and didn't mesh with her hippy, ethereal image.

"But," I raised my hand, "I have a child. A daughter. One it's my job to protect." I focused my gaze back on Macy who was listening intently. "And letting my..." I struggled to find a title for Preston to say out loud. "And letting Swiss kill him, no matter what I want, would be failing at my job of being a mother."

Macy tapped her lips. "Fuck," she muttered. "As much as I would love to see that fucker hung from his entrails, I tend to agree with you."

I blinked at the visual, and at the fact the sweet, fantasy-obsessed Macy was talking about hanging up Preston from his entrails.

Before the conversation could continue, honking of horns sounded from behind us. Macy glanced in her rearview mirror.

Her lips stretched wide. "They're here!" she clapped her hands. "We'll continue this later."

"Swiss will come around, though," she informed me while pulling into the driveway. "Of course, he has to throw the alpha male tantrum, which pales in comparison to any tantrum we could throw, and looks a little more like something my three-year-old would have." She put the car in park in front of the colorful, chaotic garden. "But my three-year-old does not have a semi-automatic weapon...yet." She reached over to squeeze my hand. "He knows you're right. Even though it goes against every instinct he has. His most important one right now is to keep you safe. And he doesn't know how to do that after he's already failed."

"He didn't fail," I argued.

Her hand squeezed mine. "I know, sweetie. You know that. All of us womenfolk know that. But we could hire someone to write it in the sky or tattoo it on our foreheads, and it still wouldn't sink in for him," she shrugged. "He will carry it with him. But it will get better. Trust me."

And despite all of my traumas and fears, I did trust her.

A gentle tap on the window made me jump.

Freya was standing there, the bottle of champagne in her hand the source of the tapping.

"We can't wait in here all day!" she called through the window.

"Time for your surprise!" Macy exclaimed, jumping out of the car.

I followed suit, albeit a little slower than her.

Caroline was standing next to Freya, a large bouquet of flowers in her arms. She was in jeans that fit her like a second skin, a simple white tee and bright red lipstick. Freya was wearing a tiny skirt, knee-high boots and a long sleeved, cropped tank. Her blonde hair was piled on top of her head.

"Well, what do you think?" Macy asked, linking her arm with mine.

"What do I think about what?" I questioned slowly.

"Your new house," Macy replied as if it were obvious.

I stopped in my tracks.

"Excuse m-me?" I stammered.

"Hansen and I invested in this place a little bit ago," she waved a hand around. "Short term rental type thing. It's been great, but I've been searching for an excuse to stop dealing with picky tenants who do weird shit. Don't worry, we've had it deep cleaned. Twice."

"And saged," Freya chimed in.

Macy nodded. "And saged. We were just about to put it up for rent, then..."

"My husband beat me half to death?" I offered.

Macy winced ever so slightly. "Yeah, that. Well, we actually had been considering this before that happened. Just in the interim, while Swiss found the perfect house."

I stared at her, my body freezing. "What did you just say?"

"Shit, that was meant to be a surprise, and not mine," Macy clasped a hand to her mouth.

"Macy, what are you talking about?" I asked, more urgently this time.

She sighed, looking to Freya and Caroline for help, both who held up their hands and did a good job of checking out the garden.

"Swiss had been looking to buy a house. For the two of you. But he's really fucking picky, and I kept trying to tell him he couldn't intimidate people into selling their home. Obviously, he disagreed," she rolled her eyes. "It was a *thing*."

My heartbeat was so loud, I wondered if I'd heard her correctly. "He was buying us a house?"

Macy nodded slowly. "If we want to get technical, he was trying to coerce a really nice couple into selling their home, but same difference."

I opened my mouth then quickly shut it again.

There was nothing to say to such a thing.

Swiss was planning on buying us a house.

"Should I open this?" Freya raised the bottle of champagne in the air.

"Yes," Macy and Caroline said at the same time.

I had not regained the ability to speak.

That was when the rumble of motorcycles drowned out even the rapid beating of my heart.

All four of us looked in the direction of the highway, which was taken up by a... gaggle? Of Harley's.

My stomach swirled, looking for a familiar figure and a familiar bike. When they got closer, it became clear that Swiss was not with them.

I tried to hide my disappointment, tears prickling the backs of my eyes. I didn't do well at that if Caroline reaching for my hand was anything to go by.

She held it until the men parked and dismounted their bikes.

Hansen had coffee and croissants. I had no idea how they traveled on the bike. But they did.

Hades and Jagger were with him, obviously knowing their women were there because these men had some kind of badass, alpha male, sixth sense. Or they tracked their wives phones, which considering everything they'd been through, made sense.

I silently urged myself to ignore the disappointment and sadness I felt at Swiss's absence.

This moment felt pivotal, big, important. And he surely knew about it because Swiss made it his business to know everything about me.

Yet he still wasn't here.

"What do you think?" Hansen nodded to the house while handing me a coffee.

"I don't know what to say," I replied honestly.

"Well, we need to show her the inside," Hansen said to Macy.

"I'm aware, honey," she replied, taking a sip of her coffee. "I was waiting for caffeine."

On wooden legs, I followed our little group into the small but adorable house.

The pathway to the house was bordered by lavender that brushed the natural stones we were walking on. Two rockers sat on the porch with hanging baskets of flowers along the overhang. The garden sprawled to the left of the house with greenery, large trees and a porch swing nestled underneath them.

We walked right into an open and airy living room. The floor was gleaming wood and mismatched rugs covered it. There were windows all along the house, natural light streaming in. A deep amethyst sofa was a bright jewel of color amongst the whites and earth tones. Candles were arranged on the vintage wood coffee table, and a TV was along the wall on an entertainment unit that had cluttered bookshelves on either side.

To the right was a compact but lovely kitchen. Two wicker barstools sat in front of a breakfast bar. Succulents were littered across the windowsill above the sink.

A circular dining table sat in front of more windows and double doors that led out to another sprawling garden. This one with a stone patio and wicker furniture, a hammock strung between two trees.

At the back of the house was the bedroom. A white, wrought iron bed faced double doors that boasted a breathtaking view of the desert, somehow perfectly placed to avoid the surrounding houses, making it seem like we were in the middle of nowhere.

There were two worn, comfortable armchairs at the end of the bed, pointing toward the doors. I imagined myself sitting there with my morning coffee or evening wine.

The smell of jasmine filtered through the open windows.

The bathroom was tiled with mosaic and had a large claw-foot tub as well as a tiled shower and large vanity.

There was a smaller bedroom on the other side of the house,

with an adorable twin bed, vintage dresser and its own small bathroom. "For Violet," Macy had said offhandedly. I'd jerked at the mention of my daughter here, in this life.

But I didn't have time to focus on that.

Macy took me through, chattering the entire time about the work they'd done, the complaints that Hansen had about the tub and how he'd eaten his words once it was put in.

There was certainly more information which I missed because I was taking in the house. Macy didn't seem to mind that I hadn't said a word during the 'tour.'

We ended up back in the kitchen, sipping coffee and nibbling on our pastries. I did so mindlessly, unable to process what was happening.

Conversations were going on around me, conversations that no one required my input for. Luckily.

"So we'll set a day to go shopping for some touches to make it yours," Macy's words jerked me out of my reverie.

"I'll be coming," Freya chirped. "My house needs a refresh too."

Hades raised a brow but didn't say anything. He didn't speak often in groups, just did his badass, hot guy glowering thing. Except, of course, when he was looking at his wife. Then it changed into a badass, hot guy melty look.

"And me," Caroline added.

"Babe, our house is done," Jagger groaned, obviously not content to just glower.

She scowled at him. "It is nowhere near done. I need an ottoman for my office and some more planters for the garden. And I need shoes."

Jagger's lips twitched. "Managed to slip that in there, didn't you?"

She smiled back sweetly.

"Let us know if there's anything you want us to haul out. Can get a coupla' prospects to do it," Hansen offered. He was leaning against the breakfast bar.

Macy's eyes narrowed at him. "What would she want to haul out?"

"Babe," he pointed, "right over there is a purple couch."

"I know," she scoffed, hands on her hips. "It's vintage. It took me months to find."

"It took you months to find an old purple couch?" Hansen clarified.

Macy's expression was stormy. "It is not old, it's *vintage*."

Hansen's eyes twinkled in the face of his wife's fury. "Vintage is a fancy word for old."

When it looked like Macy's head was about to explode, I decided it was time for me to step in. "I love the couch," I interjected.

"See," Macy beamed in triumph. "She loves the couch."

"She values her life," Hansen corrected.

Macy's toothy smile quickly morphed into a scowl. "Don't you have badass biker things to do? Because that, my dear, is your area of expertise, and you don't see me advising on the best ways to disembowel someone or how to radiate masculinity. Stick to your strengths."

Hansen was full on laughing now, as was practically everyone else in the audience.

He stepped forward, bringing Macy in for a kiss that definitely did not need an audience. I burned with envy for a second, wishing that Swiss was here to verbally spar with me, smile at me, kiss me.

"We do have shit to do, as it happens." He stepped back from his wife then nodded to his brothers who had also been making out with their women.

I felt like the odd one out, which I was.

"Let us know if you need anything, darlin'," Hansen said to me.

"We can move the couch under the cover of darkness," Jagger stage whispered.

Macy pointed to the door. "Out!"

The badass bikers conceded to her order.

I smiled at the easy and natural interaction between each of the couples. I'd never seen anything like it. And I couldn't get used to it, seeing people truly, genuinely in love.

"So?" Macy asked once the men left. "Do you like it?"

"Like it?" I repeated, looking around. "*Like* is not a word that works in this scenario. I'm speechless."

She smiled softly. "That's kind of what I was going for. We were going to have a big party here for a surprise, but then you got out early... I think this works better, though, honestly."

I agreed. There was no way I would've been able to handle all of this with more people present. I was finding it hard to stand as it was.

"I can't, I can't accept this," I stuttered, looking around the room, staring at the double doors that looked out onto the patio. The cloudless sky stretched on forever. Or at least to the mountains in the distance.

"Of course you can," Macy replied. "Because I'm forcing you to accept it."

I stared at her. "I'll pay you rent. I insist on that." I thought of the jewelry that might still be in the motel room I'd completely forgotten about. If it wasn't, I was totally broke. Well, I had some cash I'd saved from the café. It was a decent amount since Swiss had never let me pay for anything, but it wasn't enough to pay rent indefinitely.

If Swiss did respect my wishes, I'd be looking at a long

divorce where I most likely wouldn't see a dime for a while. If I saw anything.

I'd signed a prenup. I hadn't thought anything of it, sixteen and pregnant.

And my injuries meant I wouldn't be working at the café for a while.

Macy waved her hand at me. "You cook me dinner when you're better, we're square."

I shook my head. "No, I cannot pay rent by cooking you dinner."

She returned the brow raise. "Uh, have you tried your beef Wellington? You could buy *a lot* with that. You could buy *our* house."

I stared at Macy, then Caroline and Freya. Three women who hadn't hesitated to welcome me into the fold, who'd stepped up when I needed them. Three incredibly strong, badass women who didn't seem to be afraid of anything.

"Do you think differently of me?" It took a lot of strength to push out the words, my voice low, full of shame.

Macy blinked.

Caroline stopped arranging flowers on the breakfast bar to turn her eyes to me. "What do you mean?"

"Now that you know about who I am. Who I truly am."

Caroline kept watching me intently but didn't say anything, didn't ask another follow up question. She had a way about her that seemed to communicate she was comfortable in that silence. That she was happy to bathe in it for as long as it took me to be uncomfortable and blurt out more words.

A journalistic trait, I assumed. A really fricking good one.

"Your job had you working in warzones," I addressed Caroline. "You were one of the only women reporters in a dangerous, high stress job. One most men wouldn't be able to handle. Yet you handled it. All while mourning the man you'd thought you lost."

My eyes moved to Macy. "You have a past that breaks my heart. One that could've easily turned you into a bitter, angry person. Instead, you created a family. You are the head of that family."

Now it was Freya's turn. "The world tried to break you in the worst of ways. Many times. Yet you found a family. Created a home. A fricking empire, all on your own."

"You are three of the strongest women I've ever met in my life. Three of the strongest *people*," I corrected.

The women were staring at me intently.

"Yet I couldn't do something as simple as leave the man who was beating me," I whispered.

Caroline was the first to respond. Probably due to her previous job, she was used to processing things quickly, coming up with a response, a follow up.

"Honey, leaving a man who is beating you is the furthest thing from simple." Her voice was firm. Sure. "And it has absolutely nothing to do with strength."

"Living through that for the amount of time you did, being able to be kind, trusting, loving, to bring up your daughter... *That* takes strength," Freya added, her eyes shimmering.

"And though I did a great job of making it look differently, I did not handle being over there in the middle of warzones well," Caroline shared. "I survived it, sure. But I broke down in my hotel room countless times after interviewing women who were beaten, raped, who walked miles carrying a dead child. Seeing what humans do to one another," she shivered. "I still have nightmares about it. But that's how we know we're human. That we carry around our wounds, that they define us. They can either make us softer or harder." Her gaze gentled. "Please don't measure yourself up against what you see in us right now. It's taken us years to get to the places you see. It's taken finding our men, for me the second time," she grinned. "And it's taken a fight. For this life. We've fought. Just like you. And you're finally coming out the other side."

"As for the ridiculous concept that we think differently, somehow less of you," Macy interjected, "That is impossible. If anything, we think more of you, knowing what you survived. You're family to us. And as with your stubborn man, this thing is for life. And we aren't going to let you talk down to yourself. To blame yourself. To downplay the strength it took to stand right here," she pointed to the ground. "One more thing... You're gonna take the help we're offering. It doesn't come with strings, requirements. It comes because we adore you, and we want to help you rise up."

"It's selfish, really," Freya giggled. "We're trying to build our girl gang, and you're the perfect addition. We don't want you going anywhere."

My throat was burning, my eyes were misty and my heart heavy in a way that felt restorative.

"I'm not going anywhere," I croaked out, my voice thick. But certain.

I was sure, for the first time in my life, beyond any reasonable doubt, that right there was where I was meant to be.

SWISS

It was the first time I'd been back at the club alone since we'd found Kate. After she gave me that ultimatum, I'd had to escape. I'd rode for hours. Fucking *hours*.

Up and down the interstate. Then I'd parked outside the house I had managed to convince the owners to sell to me.

For an above market price.

Money didn't mean shit to me, I had plenty of it. Years I'd been with the club, different charters, doing various, mostly illegal, shit. And mostly illegal shit paid pretty fucking well. Lifestyle I lived wasn't exactly lavish. All I needed was my bike, handful of shit to wear and not much else. I paid my taxes like any good, law-abiding citizen. But that tax was on whatever meager salary I'd earned from whatever legitimate business the charter I was running with owned.

Currently, I was a mechanic.

A mechanic without rent, without utilities, any of that shit.

So in short, I had a lot of money. Enough to pay cash for the house, the six acres of land around it, and have plenty left over.

Enough to take care of Kate.

Take care of Violet, if need be. Her college or whatever the fuck. That was when I'd been planning on killing Preston. Sure, he probably had a fuckload in the bank, and Violet was taken care of, but I wanted to cover my bases. Anything Kate needed or wanted.

Which was all I fucking needed.

I'd stared at the house for a long time.

Big. Kind of quirky, Spanish inspired with trees bordering the long driveway. Huge pool 'cause it was my goal to see Kate in as many swimsuits as possible. Greenhouse. Garden.

And the kitchen... Fuckin' huge. An island, gas range, fancy fridge. All the shit Kate had practically drooled over that first night at the club. The night she made pasta while wearing my tee.

The night I fell in love with her.

I imagined her cooking for us in that kitchen. Then I imagined fucking her on that counter. And on pretty much every other surface in the house. And in the large bedroom that had a view of the mountains, the desert and nothing else.

I imagined a life outside of the one I'd lived for years. A home. Something I also hadn't had in years. Something I hadn't had since I held my dead daughter in my arms.

I might've sat there all day except there was church.

You didn't miss church unless you were missing a limb, and even then, you were expected to cauterize it and get your ass in the chair.

Of course, I hadn't been recently 'cause I was with Kate. And no one expected my ass in that seat at a time like that. Especially since, for once, things were fucking quiet at the club. Gun shipments were going smoothly. New business ventures were cruising along. No new, bloodthirsty enemies to speak of. All of the shit we talked about at church was mostly logistical. Who did what runs. Who was guarding the warehouse, assembling guns, overlooking distribution. Who wanted to do protection detail or the more sinister contracts that came in. Hades and I mostly handled killing for hire. We didn't make a habit of doing it, that wasn't what the club was about. But we collected favors. And it was always handy, having evidence that a powerful figure paid to have someone tortured or killed.

"Macy took Kate out to the house this morning," Hansen commented as we walked in.

His tone was even, unjudgmental, but it was also pointed. Also acknowledging that I wasn't there. Wasn't with my woman when she discovered her new home.

Hers.

Something spasmed in my chest. Burned like a thousand sons of bitches. I tried to imagine Kate's face as she took in the small house. With flowers and all kinds of other shit that bitches like.

Eclectic. Cozy. Warm. Safe. Enough shit to make it feel homey but also enough space to fill with whatever she wanted.

No one had ever given her that before. And I wasn't there to see the look on her face. I wasn't there with her.

Yet another fucking way I'd failed.

"I was busy," I grunted.

Hansen squinted at me, probably thinking I'd been up to my elbows in Preston's blood during the occasion.

I fucking wished.

The room was getting' fuller with brothers, so I found my spot beside Hades. He lifted his chin in greeting.

The air was heavy in the room, all faces were grave. I had claimed Kate as my Old Lady, and when someone hurt our women, they hurt us. Add to that, my brothers had come to like Kate. It was impossible not to. She was kind, soft, fucking funny. She cared genuinely and deeply about everyone, took time to talk to everyone, get to know them. She cooked some badass food, the kind of food you could taste the love in. The kind of food most of us hadn't even known existed. So them seeing what was done to her had hit everyone hard.

We'd all seen some dark shit. Done even darker shit. Our stomachs were strong when it came to death and violence.

But when it came to hurting women? No. Each of the men at this table who had a woman had gone through shit to get them. Hades's Old Lady, Freya, had the shit beaten out of her in a parking lot then was fuckin' kidnapped by her ex's father. While she was pregnant. Then she'd almost died giving birth to their kid.

Fucker was intense by nature, but when it came to Freya and his kid, he was something else. Same with Hansen and Jagger.

"She doesn't want me to kill him," I announced as soon as everyone had sat down. My fists were clenched on the table, and I was barely able to sit still due to the rage coursing through my body.

Hansen blinked at my announcement. Surprise flashed on the faces of my brothers. Each of them had considered Preston's death a forgone conclusion. You laid hands on what was ours, you died. It was that simple. The manner of death related directly to just how bad things were.

Kate looking how she did, almost fucking dying, they had all known the manner of death would be long and ugly. And I knew each of them was happy with that.

"She hasn't got the stomach for it?" Jagger guessed.

I shook my head. "She doesn't want to do that to her kid." Even though I was majorly pissed at her, I couldn't help but feel proud of what she was doing for her daughter. I saw in her eyes the hatred she had for that man. What he'd taken from her. She was not plagued by the morality of killing. I had a hunch she'd slit his throat in a heartbeat if it wasn't for her daughter.

It would haunt her. Him walking this earth. I knew her, understood her well enough now to get that. But she'd live with it for her daughter.

And as much as I didn't want Kate's kid to hurt, I couldn't watch my woman go through that. I couldn't just let him go.

"Kill him anyway," Hades put in, his face blank. "Kid will be better off without him."

"I don't disagree," I responded through gritted teeth. "But she said she'll leave if I end him." I looked to my president. "And she means it."

"Fuck," he muttered in understanding. Somethin' moved in his eyes, something like an empathetic fear. Each of the men here who had Old Ladies loved them fiercely, would walk to the ends of the earth for them. Breakups were not a thing. It was death or nothing. Of course, we wouldn't hold a woman against her will. If she wanted to leave her man she could, but it would irrevocably ruin them.

In my gut, I knew I'd never breathe easily again if Kate walked away from me. I didn't think I had a chance at happiness, at anything but fucking and killing, until her.

"Yeah," I cracked my knuckles, really needing to kill something.

"Okay," Hansen replied. "We need to get Wire from the Amber chapter on the phone. Get him to dig up any and all dirt we have on this fucker. Without a doubt, there is shit he doesn't want coming out. Then we get Kate the best divorce lawyer in the country. Get them to draft up a very generous settlement with stipulations that he can't be within the same fuckin' state as her. He doesn't leave this compound until he's signed it."

That's why he was president. Because he could think rationally, even with shit swirling.

He'd already managed to gather a boatload of info on the fuck. We'd figured out how he'd even found Kate here. He had enough contacts to get a track on her phone, then he'd hired some P.I. to tail her for a couple of days, found out she was at the club. Then he'd managed to book in at the garage side of the club, making his way in the front fucking door of the clubhouse 'cause the prospect who was supposed to be on watch was texting his fuckin' girlfriend.

Safe to say he wasn't a prospect or a resident of this town anymore.

Hansen looked at me. "Is he whole?"

I thought of the man in the basement, tied up, beaten, bleeding. "Save a few fingernails and teeth, yeah."

Hansen nodded once. "We'll get enough collateral to make sure he keeps his mouth shut about his stay with us." He looked around the room. "We got anything else pressing?"

"Got a weapons run in a week," Colby said.

The rest of the table began speaking of other things, both legitimate and not. Club was diverse in times like these. Money was better than ever, and no one had been locked up in years.

Things were going well for the Sons of Templar.

But my mind was not on that shit.

My mind was on Kate.

And how the fuck I was gonna keep her and survive, knowing her piece of shit husband still walked the earth.

CHAPTER NINETEEN

KATE

THE HOUSE WAS quiet for the first time in hours.

My house.

I still couldn't quite fathom that. I was still waiting for someone to come along and rip it all away from me.

My veins were swimming with nerves and unease, even though I was in a beautiful, peaceful place. Cicadas and birds sang in tandem as the sun crept toward the horizon. The breeze made the curtains dance in toward me.

I was sitting on one of the comfortable chairs at the end of the bed, drinking a cup of chamomile tea.

There had been plenty of wine with all of the women today. They'd taken me back to Swiss's room at the club, helped me pack up, then they took me to the motel room to gather the meager amount of belongings I'd left there. My wedding rings were still in their hiding place. I'd put them in my purse without looking at them for too long. My purse seemed much heavier with those inside them. I had a strong urge to hurl them out of the car window as we drove, desperate to be rid of anything connected to Preston, but I knew that wasn't wise. Money was never something I'd had to worry about before. Now I had to be smart, plan for my future.

Caroline, Freya and Macy had hung out for a while, keeping me company when it was clear I was going to be alone. There was still no word from Swiss, and his absence was the elephant in the room.

Luckily, my phone rang, and it was Violet. The women took their leave, each blowing kisses at me as I greeted my daughter.

She was packing to leave for her trip with Jacques, who was apparently still in the picture. She sounded happy, ecstatically so, then she made a passing comment about not being able to get her father on the phone.

My throat had ached, and my heart spasmed as I croaked out some lie about him being busy, barely able to push the words off my tongue.

She hadn't picked up on my panic and mentioned that I still sounded bad, chastising me for not taking better care of myself. Then she'd gone on a tirade about all of the natural remedies I should be using and how antibiotics were likely making me sicker.

I barely made it through the conversation and considered myself lucky my daughter went a thousand miles a minute when she was happy or enthusiastic, therefore too caught up to notice the change in her mother.

We'd hung up after promises from her to let me know when she got to the chateau and to call me on Thanksgiving. She finally hung up after telling me how excited she was to see me in a month.

A month.

I'd see my precious daughter in a month. The part of me that had been missing. The ache in my heart would be healed with her presence.

My bruises would be healed by then.

But that's all that would've healed.

Her father may or may not be dead by then. If he wasn't already. I'd have to craft a lie as to how it happened if he was. Even if he wasn't, there was a swamp of reality to wade through.

That had caused me to spiral, hence the chamomile tea. Which did precisely nothing to quell my panic. I'd lit some incense Macy had placed on the dresser in the bedroom.

Although it smelled wonderful, that hadn't done much either.

Nor had the long bath I'd taken in the claw-foot tub. At any other time, I would've been able to enjoy the luxurious bath products, the candles, the speaker that I hooked up to my phone to play spa sounds.

At any other time, it might've been bliss.

Even with my bruises, my injuries, my looming reality.

I just needed one thing to give me calm.

One man.

The one I hadn't heard from or seen all day.

The one that might've chosen death and revenge over me.

My mind wandered to what he'd told me. About what he'd lost. It had lingered between us, that knowledge. It was a new ache inside of me. A profound sadness that he had to know such visceral pain. A kind of pain that time could not or would not heal. A kind of pain that had helped shape him into the man he was today, like water eroding a rock. The kind of man who needed pain, blood, violence and death to live. It helped me understand that. Even without this devastating knowledge, I would've accepted the darkest parts of him.

But knowing his trauma was a gift. A horrible one. But a gift nonetheless.

If he returned to me—fuck, I hope he'd return to me—I'd have to give him a horrible gift too. Something that I'd buried so deep inside of me that I'd have to rip the skin off my fingers in order to retrieve it. It was something I needed to purge.

The sound of a motorcycle jerked me out of my thoughts, and my pulse spiked from nerves and excitement. I all but ran to the front door. Well, tried to run. I could barely manage a brisk walk.

So he'd already made it in the front door by the time I reached the living room.

I stopped in my tracks.

He wasn't covered in blood. That was a start.

But he was shimmering with a menacing energy that had my hair standing up on end.

He closed the door behind him, eyes bouncing around the room.

I held my breath as he walked toward me. I ached for him to cross the distance, to pull me into his arms. But he stopped short, putting a purposeful distance between us.

His gaze explored my entire body, it skimmed over every one of my visible injuries as pain contorted his face. He was torturing himself with the sight of me. But there seemed to be an edge of relief too. Like he was a man who had been holding his breath for a long time and could finally inhale and exhale comfortably.

Or at least, that's how I felt. Like I'd only been halfway breathing this entire time without him. It was the longest we'd been apart since I woke up in the hospital.

We stood there staring at each other for a long time, the room darkening quickly. Candles I'd lit dimly illuminated the room, and the light from the kitchen helped further.

"I'm ready to be mad at you now," I told him, my voice scratchy but understandable.

He stared at me and didn't say anything.

My heart thrummed.

"It's hard," I whispered. "Because I can see the regret and turmoil on your face. I can feel it in the air. I can barely breathe through it."

As if to prove it, I took a ragged breath, and it singed my lungs.

"It would be big of me to let it go, forget about it," I continued. "I could pretend to forget about it, at least. It would make things much less complicated. Might make them hurt less too. But eventually, it will come out from somewhere. It will rot inside of me. Inside of us. And I can't let that happen. I can't bury my feelings for the temporary comfort of anyone. To temporarily protect anyone." My eyes watered as I spoke. As I stared at the pain on Swiss's face.

"So I'm mad at you," I whispered. "I'm terribly mad at you. For turning so cold to me. For dropping me like I was dirt. For letting me leave with him. Not because he hurt me. I do not blame you for what he did to me. I know I've said it before, but it bears repeating because I see you're still intent on carrying what's not yours to carry."

"You're my woman," Swiss growled. "And you got hurt. He almost beat you to death 'cause I let you walk away with him. It *is* mine to carry, Kate."

I flinched at his voice. His words. The conviction in them.

"I showed you a specific part of me before all of this," he continued. "I didn't hide who I was. What the club was. But I wasn't in a rush to peel back the curtain entirely. I was enjoying the honeymoon phase, I guess. I wanted to put my best foot forward." He ran his hand over his head. "Fuck, I wanted to trap you. I wanted you to fall in love with me, to be too far gone by the time you saw the ugly parts of me. In too deep to leave. I'm not the good guy, Kate. I'm fucked-up. From the shit I've done. Shit that's happened to me. It's crippled me in ways that aren't obvious until you get too close. Most people who see that side of me are not long for this world."

Swiss's face remained an expressionless mask. Whether deliberate, to intimidate me, or in order for him to get through telling me this, I wasn't sure.

"When I feel hurt, betrayed, vulnerable, I turn into the person I am for the club," he explained in a softer tone. "The killer. The man who doesn't feel remorse for causing pain. For ending lives. For doing any number of fucked-up things. The man who *likes* that shit." His eyes scrutinized me, waiting, inspecting, dissecting.

He was looking for disgust, I guessed. A sign that he was pushing me away.

I gave no such sign. Because I wasn't disgusted with him. Wasn't going anywhere. I tried to communicate that with my face, even if I was still mad at him.

"Not trying to escape the way I treated you," he shook his head. "'Cause that shit is inexcusable. All I'm doing is making sure that you don't take any of this on. That you don't somehow warp my reaction into you not being good enough. Aren't worth fighting for. 'Cause you are. You're too fucking good for me. And I knew it. Knew it since the moment I laid eyes on you. But I went after you anyway."

The cicadas sang louder, yet not enough to drown out the quick thumping of my heart.

"I've been patched in the club for almost as long as you were married."

I pursed my lips, or at least tried to, pain spearing through my mouth as I attempted the gesture. Though that pain was dulled by my fury toward Swiss. Instead of the lip pursing, I narrowed my eyes, but even that hurt.

"After I lost them, the club was what saved me," he continued. "Turned me into someone completely fucking different, of course. Someone my family doesn't recognize or understand." He paused, staring out the doors to the fast-approaching twilight. "I see them once a year, maybe. Christmas. Or my mom's birthday. Out of guilt more than anything else. I just make it harder for them, when they see what I've become."

Seeing the pain etched in his expression, seeping off him, it was pure torture to stand in front of him without touching him. Without comforting him. The anger that I'd been so sure I wanted to hold on to slipped through my fingers.

"Almost two decades. I turned into someone dark, ugly, twisted. But that was my version of healing. I got myself a family. A fucked-up one to be sure, but I had one I truly belonged in. For that same amount of time, you had nothing. No one but a man who beat you." His voice cracked then, with fury or some other emotion, I wasn't sure.

But fury factored in there somewhere because his hands were fisted at his sides.

"You had no one but your daughter," he bit out, eyes piercing me with their intensity. "You had one cherished thing. One thing that truly mattered. You lived for. You fought for. And because you fought, because you lived, I have you."

Tears blurred my vision.

"I have you because of that girl," he ground out. "Because of what a fuckin' amazing mother you are. I have you because of that fire you have inside you that would do anything to protect her. And I threatened that by doing something that comes natural to me."

He took a gun out of his cut and laid it very purposefully on the console table behind the couch, next to some crystals.

My heart thundered.

"I had planned on using this," he nodded to the gun. "And this," he took the knife from his belt. It gleamed against the light. He placed it next to the gun.

My eyes left the weapons and went to him. He'd been watching me the entire time.

"I was going to end his life with those," he murmured. "It was going to be slow. Messy. It was going to be fucking spectacular."

I bristled at his tone, but something in me responded positively too. I liked it. The passion in his voice, talking about torturing and killing Preston.

"I was blind. Blind with my love for you. With the guilt over what I let happen to you. Rage. Fuckin' fear. Terror that for the second time in my life, I'd lose everything. And that's why I was prepared to kill him. Despite what it would do to Violet and, in turn, to you." He took a breath. A visible, deep breath. "I'm filled with shame over that, Kate."

The words were coming from a visceral place. They were being torn from him. That's why he'd been gone for so long, because he'd been looking for those words. The strength to face me.

"Not gonna say it's not hard," he continued. "One of the hardest things in my life, not killin' him. Letting him walk out..." He didn't finish the sentence, visibly shuddering.

Shuddering at the thought of Preston walking away from this.

"But that's my shit," he patted his chest. "Years of it. And it isn't right. And I'm not gonna let it cost me my second chance."

My shoulders sagged.

He wasn't going to kill Preston. He wasn't going to break my daughter's heart. There was some relief there. A lot. One problem, a sizeable one, had been solved.

"He's not leavin' until he gives you a divorce," Swiss informed me in a much firmer, much more recognizable tone. The 'I'm an alpha male, and I'm going to take care of everything' tone.

I blinked.

"And a healthy fuckin' settlement," Swiss's lips tilted up just a tad. "There's no number that can pay you back for what you've been through, but I'll make sure we drain him dry. Make sure you get what you deserve... Which is everything."

This was probably my moment to ask how exactly Swiss and the club were going to manage getting me a divorce. How they were going to make it so Preston would go back to Carver Springs without pressing charges for what I was guessing was felony assault and kidnapping.

Then again, I wasn't going to press charges for felony attempted murder, so the threat of that would likely keep him quiet.

This was all really fricking complicated. Surely there would be lawyers, statements, meetings. Yes, this was definitely the time for me to ask questions.

But I didn't.

Whatever I said or asked wasn't going to make a difference. Swiss wanted to take care of me. Wanted to atone for what he considered his sin of letting me go. This was his way of doing it. Of helping him sleep at night. And I was coming to understand that the club and the men in it didn't stop once they were on one of these crusades.

So instead of asking questions, I said something else entirely.

"My stepfather raped me when I was thirteen."

He stopped breathing.

Or at least that's what it seemed like. Like he had suddenly turned to stone.

"He... groomed me first. I think that's what they call it these days," I continued before I lost my nerve.

Oh, how I ached to look away. To lower my eyes in shame. But I held fast. Held on to Swiss.

"He made me trust him," I spoke quickly. My voice still was raspy, and I was thankful it wasn't familiar. So I could pretend it wasn't really me saying all of this. "He made me think I was safe with him. I didn't want to have sex with him. He was old and overweight, and he was my stepfather. But I didn't want to... *disappoint* him." I shook my head in distaste. Not in myself, but in a grown man who'd manipulated a girl into thinking she was doing something to make him proud.

"I didn't even fight him. I just laid there and cried." I squeezed my eyes shut for a second, guarding against the memories, the pain. "He whispered things in my ear. About me being a good girl. About it being our secret. About how good I was making him feel."

The memories came flooding in, so I steeled myself against them by opening my eyes again and holding Swiss's gaze, not letting his expression penetrate.

"And I just cried," I croaked. "I knew what sex was. Knew what rape was. But I couldn't bring myself to tell anyone. Because I didn't fight. And rape is when you fight. When you scream. When you do anything you can to make sure that doesn't happen to you. I didn't do any of that. And..." I gasped, covered in shame and the filth of the memories.

Swiss was still as a statue, his hands still fisted at his sides, his eyes never letting go of mine. But something was fuming inside of him. His nostrils were flaring, his breathing rapid and shallow.

"And I still *liked* him," I whispered. "That sounds insane, I know." I rolled my eyes hearing it out loud. "But my mother was a cold and cruel woman. She was a former beauty queen. One with big dreams about getting out of the small town she grew up in. She was going to live in New York. She was going to be famous," I scoffed. "But then she got pregnant with me, and her Catholic parents forced her to marry the man who did that to her. My dirtbag father."

It was speaking of my mother that made me break, not Hal. Made me succumb to those memories I'd pushed back for almost twenty years.

Her entire bedroom was a shrine to the life I took from her. I still remembered it vividly. The crown sitting in a glass case on her vanity. She polished it daily, even though I was pretty sure it was plastic. Framed news clippings. There were only two of those, but she showed me them weekly to remind me of what she could've been if it wasn't for me.

Perfume bottles littered the vanity, her cheap satin robe, the high heeled 'slippers' with the pom poms on them that she'd screamed at me for trying on once.

"My father—I don't remember," I said, realizing I'd been silent for a long time, thinking about my mother.

Swiss hadn't moved. Hadn't spoken. Hadn't breathed, it seemed.

He was waiting, for more. Because unfortunately, there was more.

And I'd done it now, made the decision to give him every-thing. Absolutely everything. So there were no secrets, no lies. Nothing to hide behind. So there was a solid foundation for us to start over. I wanted him to really know me. Know me in a way that no one else did. And in order for that to happen, I had to give him pieces of myself no one knew existed. Pieces that had never seen the light of day.

"She divorced him. My father," I cleared my throat. "And her parents disowned her. Which meant they no longer helped her out with me or financially. Which meant she had to get a job."

I folded my arms across my chest, suddenly cold, the weather turning outside. My bones protested at standing for so long, but the hurt was good. Something to focus on.

I took a deep breath and continued. "She quickly discovered that she hated working, yet the only way to stop working while keeping the roof over our heads, food in the cupboards and perfume on her vanity, was to find a man willing to take on a widow with a child who wasn't his. Our town was small, so there weren't many of those, and even less of those men were decent, but she made do."

I licked my lips. "Hal was the third. And he was the only one I liked. The only one who was kind to me. So I didn't say anything. Because I didn't want him to *leave*."

My cheeks flamed in shame, but I had to keep going.

"I didn't want to be stuck with my mother. She would've found a way to blame me for him leaving. Found a way to punish me. And then she would've just found another one. And I couldn't be sure he'd be nice. Kind. I couldn't risk him being like number one."

I shuddered, thinking about the first of my stepfathers. The memories were blurry, muffled with the effort my brain was taking to repress them, but the fear I remembered. It was stark. Curled in a corner as glass rained down on my head.

The fury radiating off Swiss was red hot, but I ignored it.

I had to finish, and I was far from done.

"I dreaded the nights Hal would come to my room," I rubbed my palms up and down my arms. "I'd tried pretending to be asleep, but he just... did it anyway. The only saving grace was that he didn't take long. Three minutes and fifteen seconds, give or take. Three minutes and fifteen seconds. I told myself I could handle that. Anyone could handle anything for three minutes and fifteen seconds."

Sometimes, I realized in horror—something I hadn't put together until this very moment—I had repeated that mantra when Preston was on top of me, kissing me, apologizing for the fresh bruises on my body.

I shook off that realization, unable to hold the weight of that right now.

"Eventually, I told myself it wasn't that bad," my voice cracked. "That I must've *liked* it. If I didn't, I would've screamed, despite my cruel mother. But I didn't. Luckily, he died of a heart attack on my sixteenth birthday. But I cried when he died too. Real tears. I loved him. And I hated him."

I laughed without humor. Swiss's lips were a grim line.

The cicadas still sang outside, unaware of what was going on in this small house. Outside, the world kept turning, even though it felt like Swiss and I were the last people in the universe.

"I met Preston three weeks after my stepfather died."

I considered that statement, rolling on my heels and steeling myself against my body aches.

"Three weeks," I repeated, shaking my head as I realized how little respite I'd had between evil men. "I was a mess. Grieving over the loss. Relieved that he'd never touch me again. Scared of being alone with my mother. She was bearable because she was grieving. That meant sleeping until two in the afternoon and walking around the house humming showtunes with her sunglasses on. She thought a big payday was coming. Insurance," I scoffed, thinking of my mother.

She had not shed one tear.

Well, apart from at the funeral, obviously. She'd howled. Sobbed. Lifted the lace veil she wore over her face to blow her nose loudly with a silk handkerchief one of his business partners had given her.

My mother knew how to play her part well.

Once we were behind closed doors, after everyone left, Mom was cheerful. She was nice to me.

Nice.

She told me about the new house she was going to buy. The car, the clothes. All for her, of course.

For a short period of time, my mother forgot that I was the complication that ruined her life and had anchored her to our small town. Her mind was on the riches that she was sure were coming.

Me? I wasn't so sure. Hal had worked at an insurance agency. One of the three in town. He made decent money—not up to my mother's standards, something she told him often. But enough so she didn't have to work. Mom was sure that working at an insurance agency, he would surely have some big-ticket life insurance policy.

Maybe he did. But I also knew he did not live a healthy lifestyle. He was a smoker who loved fast food. Although I wasn't exactly worldly. I'd left our town exactly three times, once on a field trip to Washington DC, another time to the funeral of a great aunt I'd never heard of, and lastly on a trip to Roswell with one of Mom's boyfriends who was obsessed with aliens.

No, I wasn't worldly at sixteen. But I liked to read. Research. Mom always told me how stupid I was, so I'd made it my mission to learn as much as I could about anything and everything. I got straight A's. Mom used my report cards as ashtrays.

But I knew that an insurance agency wasn't likely to give mid-level employees huge policies. And even less likely to pay out if they could find an excuse not to.

I also knew that the money would be a good thing. Sure, I'd

likely never see any of it, and certainly none would be going to a college fund. But I was getting scholarships anyway.

All I needed was for it to be enough to distract my mom for two more years. Two more years, then I could move across the country and never ever come back. Two more years of her being so preoccupied with the money that she'd forget I existed.

Yes, that would've been a good thing. A great thing.

I might not have been a worldly teenager, but I knew great things did not happen to us.

So the money was not going to come.

I was grieving, I was relieved, I was trying to come to terms with the feelings left on my skin after being assaulted. And I was terrified.

Preston was the quarterback.

One of the most popular boys in my grade.

His father owned the bank in town.

Owned it.

His family was rich. Super rich. In a way I couldn't even comprehend.

It had been established that my family was not. My mother didn't exactly have the reputation of being trash, but she'd been through three husbands. That kind of thing wasn't looked kindly upon.

I wasn't popular at school, but I wasn't bullied either. I had friends I sat with at lunch, nothing more than that, though. I didn't get close to people. Didn't trust them. Especially after what started happening with my stepfather.

I was pretty, though. I knew that. Knew on some level that was why my mother hated me so much. As much as she tried to fight it, her looks were fading, and I was just growing into mine.

Boys had asked me out before, but I'd always said no, uncomfortable in my own skin, at the idea of my stepfather finding out.

But he was dead.

And Preston noticed me.

It was as simple as that. One day he walked up to me at lunch, told me I was pretty, asked me out.

"He was charming, even then." I found my way back to Swiss, who hadn't moved but was watching me intently, hanging on my every word.

"I didn't know if he saw how vulnerable I was then," I shrugged, thinking back on it. "I don't think he was that calculated. Maybe he was. Maybe at sixteen, he saw exactly what I was and how easily he could control me. All I saw was the boy everyone loved, noticing me, making me feel like I mattered. Making me feel suddenly so very far away from the girl I used to be. That was huge."

I remembered it clearly. Despite the trauma I'd gone through, my emotional wounds, I was still a teenage girl. And the most popular boy in school noticing you can conquer all your demons... for a while, at least.

"I was desperate to redefine my sexuality. To replace what had happened with something consensual, something... normal."

I rolled my eyes. I definitely did get normal—a teenage boy who had no idea what he was doing, no consideration about my pleasure. But he said he'd loved me after it was done.

I had felt dirty. Odd. Uncomfortable. But I'd focused on Preston's blue eyes, his sandy blond hair falling across his face.

"I got pregnant two months into dating," I exhaled loudly. "We were using the pull-out method, so it shouldn't have been that surprising. But to me it was. I loved him in a way a teenager could love the first boy that made her feel like she mattered. But I wasn't delusional. I wanted a *life*. I wanted out of that town. Away from my mother. So I was devastated."

The words were sour in my mouth, thinking of Violet. My

perfect, beautiful, kindhearted daughter. The light in my life that I loved with everything I was.

But at that time, it was the truth.

"Preston was not. He was happy. Happy," I laughed mirthlessly. "At sixteen, happy to be a father with a girl he'd been dating two freaking months." I shook my head. "Then again, he was a man. He didn't have to give birth. Drop out of school. Be labeled as a slut or trash or whatever was going to be said. And he was rich."

I thought about the smile that had lit up his face when I told him, sobbing. And the way his eyes had darkened when I mentioned going to Planned Parenthood. It was a glimmer, a glimpse of what was to come in the future. Of course, I didn't know it then. And it had passed quickly.

"His parents liked me. They weren't snobs. Didn't look down on me. They were kind. They loved each other. Loved their son. Welcomed me immediately. And when we told them together, they were upset, of course. It was not their plan for their son. But they also started planning. Immediately. Told us it would all be okay. That we would be married."

I remembered sitting in their impossibly nice living room, drinking a soda, listening to Preston's mom talk about a dress with a forgiving shape and his father discussing the country club for the reception.

It was all so incredibly surreal. No one had asked me whether I *wanted* to marry Preston. No one had asked me anything. They just set about planning the rest of my life.

I should've been thankful, I was being given the golden ticket, after all. An in with the wealthiest family in town.

It hit me, the parallels between Swiss and I. How we'd started out in somewhat similar positions and both of our lives had hurtled out of control.

"My mom kicked me out when we told her," I frowned. "Called me a slut and a disgrace. I think she might've actually hit me if Preston hadn't stepped in."

That was when I really fell in love with him. A deeper kind of love than teenage infatuation. He had stepped in front of me, stared down my mother and promised her that she'd pay if she laid a hand on me.

He was tall, over six foot. And muscled. Even at sixteen, he towered over my mother. He was a threat to her.

"We walked out of that house, and I never saw her again. She never met her granddaughter. Which I'm thankful for."

Violet asked about my mother often when she was smaller. I told her the truth when she was old enough to understand. I didn't keep secrets from her. Except about the monster her father truly was.

Violet knew that her grandmother lived in the same town as her and that she 'wasn't a nice lady.' She accepted that the way a little girl did, with a no-nonsense nod before going back to playing with her dolls.

Her real grandmother—Preston's mom—was enough for her. More than enough.

"We got married two months later," I whispered. "And I was happy. Until all my dreams for myself disappeared. I dropped out of school when I started to show. Everyone thought it was for the best."

I hadn't questioned them. Hadn't voiced my desires to stay. It wasn't seemly. Me being visibly pregnant and attending school.

Appearances mattered. Sally and Preston had plenty of things to keep me busy. We cooked. Went shopping. Decorated the nursery. I didn't see Preston a whole lot. He had training, games, schoolwork. He was still living the same life.

But when I did see him, he was loving, doting, affectionate. He'd talk to my belly, make all kinds of promises.

"We lived with his parents the first three years of Violet's life," I spoke softly, as if that would make this story more palatable. As if my lowered voice might melt the ice statue Swiss had turned into. "Enough time for Preston to finish school, to get used to working at the bank, get situated."

I sighed.

"That was the best time of my life, those three years," I told him with a quiver to my voice. "Violet was a special baby. Quiet. Inquisitive. Soulful. She adored everyone. And her grandparents adored her right back. They were very hands on, ready to help me with anything and everything."

My arms went around my body, as if I were trying to hold myself together. Which I was. Whatever remained of myself, I guessed.

"But Preston was an adult, working," I explained. "He didn't want to be living with his parents anymore. So he let his father give us the down payment on a house down the street. I was excited, even though I was so sad to leave. We'd have our own home. One that I would be the lady of, that I would fill with the same warmth and love as Preston's parents."

Sally had, of course, helped me decorate the entire thing. Her eye was excellent, and I trusted her taste. Plus, I hadn't really developed one of my own.

"I didn't have many friends. Everyone I'd known from high school was in college. But I had Violet, and I didn't mind. I viewed our life as perfect. We were talking about another child. I thought I was miles away from the life my mother had."

I squeezed my eyes shut.

"He hit me for the first time after he'd come home late from work," I pushed the words out on little more than a whisper. "I'd made roast duck. I was mad because it was my first time making something fancy, and I'd spent all day on it. I told him that. And he just punched me square in the face. He left me on the floor and went to bed."

The tile was cool against my body, and my face was stinging with pain. I didn't even cry. It felt like my body was not my own. Like I was living out a story, a movie, a scene out of something that couldn't be my life.

Eventually, Preston came back.

"Come to bed," he demanded.

I'd stayed on the floor.

My body tensed as he walked toward me. I flinched away from his hands. But he'd lifted me up and carried me to bed.

The next morning, I'd woken up late. Preston had Violet in front of the TV. He brought me coffee.

His hair was wet from the shower, he was dressed for work. I'd watched him approach carefully. This was my husband. The man I'd been married to for four years. The boy who'd stood up to my mother. He was my safe place.

And in that moment, he was a stranger.

He leaned in to brush the hair from my face, and I stiffened.

"Not too bad," he murmured, inspecting the area where I suspected there would be a nasty bruise. "You should be able to cover the worst of it with makeup," he told me, straightening. "Just so Violet doesn't notice. I'll tell my parents you both have the flu. You won't leave for a few days, until you can cover it properly."

I'd blinked at him as he spoke, unable to compute his even tone, as if we were discussing an upcoming barbeque.

It filled me with anger. Fury.

"You need to move out," I blurted suddenly.

Preston's face cleared. Completely. It turned horrifyingly blank.

"Excuse me?" he asked.

I sat up in bed, wincing at the pain in my face. It felt tight and hot. "You need to move out," I repeated, stronger this time. "If you do, I won't press charges."

Preston's features transformed into the patronizing expression he wore with waiters. It was something I'd never realized I hated until this moment.

How he looked down on almost everyone.

Including me.

"You won't press charges," he informed me jovially. He seemed amused.

That only fed my anger. "You hit me," I gritted out. "That is a crime. One that you could go to jail for."

Now he laughed. Laughed in my face.

"No, sweetheart, it's not," he proclaimed once he was done. "My father plays golf with the chief. They go way back. Most of the force have mortgages with our bank. They know what would happen if they convicted an Edwards." His eyes tracked over me. "Not that anyone would take you seriously anyway. Not with who your mother is."

His tone sickened me. He'd never talked to me that way. Spoken to me like he truly thought I was trash.

"I'll leave," I choked out, realizing what he was saying was true. "I'll take Violet."

His eyes blazed with anger. "How will you leave?" he scoffed. "Both of the cars are in my name. Same with all of our bank accounts. You don't have a fucking cent to your name."

I blinked at the truth. He was right. Everything was in Preston's name. It had made sense at the time. I'd trusted Preston to take care of it all. I had my car, I had the card in my purse that I used to buy whatever I wanted for the house, for Violet.

But none of it was mine.

The reality of that fact was suffocating.

Preston smiled cruelly.

My stomach curdled in repulsion.

"Yeah, you get it, babe," he sneered. "You don't have a high school education. No credit score. No family. Nowhere to go." I held my breath as he leaned down to brush my cheek. "I do love you, babe. And I intend on keeping you as my wife for as long as I see fit. Our marriage will be a happy one."

He stepped back and adjusted his tie. "You just need to learn how to stay in line." He winked at his reflection. "You need to get up. Violet needs to be dressed. And you need to clean up from last night. I'll be home early. I have a sick wife to look after." He leaned in to kiss me on the cheek before he walked out.

I heard him kissing Vi goodbye, and then the door closed.

My breath caught as I realized I wasn't in that house. That I was standing in the middle of a lovely, Spanish inspired cottage in New Mexico with the man I loved in front of me, damn near shaking from fury.

I'd been talking for a long time. It took a long time to split yourself apart, separate all the ugly pieces and shine light on them, didn't it?

But I'd expected Swiss to interject at some point. Maybe to jump in and save me so I didn't have to keep going. But he hadn't spoken. Not a peep. Not to save me from this.

"It was easy for him," I whispered. "Exceptionally so. I barely put up a fight. I had nowhere to go, no one to turn to. And I had a nice life. What could I complain about? He didn't hit me often. Often enough that I walked on eggshells around him. Never anywhere visible after that first day. And he never, ever touched Violet. If he had even shown an inkling of that violence toward my daughter, I would've gone. I would've fought to the death for her."

I meant that too. Every word. For the first couple of years, I'd watched him like a hawk. Watched for the change in his eyes if Violet started crying about something, accidently spilled something. But there was no sign of his temper. He would soothe her, clean up whatever mess and be patient with his princess.

"He was a wonderful father," I said, looking down at my feet. I felt ashamed, saying anything good about Preston in front of him. "A wonderful husband, to the rest of the world. To the public, we seemed perfect." I shook my head. "It was easy. So fucking *easy* for him to break me down. Trap me. I didn't try to leave once. Not once. Didn't make plans. Didn't fight back. No. I submitted to him 100 percent. I gave in. Without any kind of fight."

Once, only once, I thought about leaving.

Violet was twelve. She wasn't showing any signs of growing into a teenager. She loved cuddles with her parents, adored horses and still slept with her stuffed animals. She was perfect and impossibly pure. She was my whole world.

I had a few broken ribs. Not diagnosed by a doctor, but I'd come to know my body. And by then, I'd learned to hide the pain well.

Staring at my daughter doing her homework at the kitchen table, her dark brows knitted into a frown as she worked on a math problem, I envisioned her growing up. Her getting her first boyfriend, falling in love. Then I thought of a man putting his hands on her. And her staying because she might've somehow known that her mother stayed, even though Preston was meticulous about making sure she never saw that side of him.

I thought of my baby being trapped like I was.

And that rage from that first morning after awoke in me once more.

For my daughter.

Her dark head suddenly snapped up. "Daddy!" she cried, running toward Preston.

I hadn't heard him come in.

He took Violet into his arms, but his cold eyes were fixed on me.

"Vi Vi, you doing your homework?" he asked in a voice that didn't match the look he'd given me, nodding to the table.

"Yes!" she replied. "And I'm almost done. I haven't even needed Mom's help."

He ruffled her hair. "Of course, you haven't. You don't need it. Why don't you go finish so we can have whatever delicious dinner your lovely mother has made for us."

He smiled at me, and I smiled back, my heart in my throat.

Violet ran to do as her father said. The man in question walked over to me, pulling me in close and kissing me on the cheek.

I didn't stiffen at his touch. I'd learned not to do that. To respond negatively to it. Some part of me even relaxed into it. Some part of me still loved him. Because when he was loving, it felt right. Warm. Safe. And I'd imagined that everything he'd done was just a nightmare. A phase. Whatever. I imagined that we had a perfect life ahead of us.

Then he'd get angry. I'd do something wrong. And our perfect life shattered.

"Isn't she a doll?" he murmured into my hair.

I ran my palms up and down his back, my instincts picking up on his energy. The safest thing to do was to act like everything was normal. "Absolutely. She's the most perfect thing on this planet," I told him, meaning every word.

Violet had gotten the best from both of us. My midnight black hair, my delicate features. Her father's eyes. His height. The confidence in which she moved was incredible to see in a young girl. She lived in her skin in a way even I didn't.

"She is," he agreed, rubbing his hand along my bare arm. "And if you ever tried to take her from me, I'd kill you. You know that right?"

Everything in me froze.

He'd said it low, much too low for twelve-year-old ears. He'd kept the smile on his face, kept moving his hand.

My heart thundered, watching Violet who was utterly oblivious.

I believed him. That my husband, the man I slept next to, the man I still let make love to me, the one who nursed my daughter back to health when she had the flu, who coached her soccer team, who braided her hair... I believed that man would kill me.

I didn't realize I was crying until Swiss's thumbs brushed my cheeks, wiping the tears away.

I hadn't seen him move, hadn't seen him cross the distance between us. I'd been that caught up. That deep in my memories.

"I need you to understand," I sobbed, clutching at his cut. It was the only thing holding me up right now. "How I got trapped. How it happened. Why I stayed for so long." I hiccupped. "Why I left." I blinked the tears from my eyes so I could focus on Swiss. "Why you are so important to me. Why you're everything to me."

Swiss pressed his forehead against mine. It wasn't until then that I saw his eyes were wet too. "Don't have the words, Countess," he rasped, voice thick and broken. "Don't have any words for you after all of that." His hand gripped the back of my neck. Hard but not too hard. He was still being gentle. "What I will say is that you're fuckin' everything to me too. And I'm gonna spend my life tryin' to make sure you get the happiness you deserve."

He kissed me gently, closemouthed and quick.

Then he lifted me into his arms and took me into the bedroom.

I was out before my head hit the pillow.

SWISS

I watched Kate sleep for a long time after I took her clothes off, cataloging every inch of her skin, making note of what was healing quickest, what was takin' longer. Every time my eyes touched a mark on her skin, I saw red.

She didn't so much as move as I took off her clothes, put her under the covers. Not even when I moved the chair at the end of the bed so I could sit beside her.

No, she was out. Understandably. Purging all that shit, secrets she'd kept her entire adult life. That must've been like running a fucking marathon.

She shared it with me, even though it hurt her. Fuck, it took every ounce of energy and life from her. I watched it happen. She did that for me. For us.

It was something I couldn't wrap my head around. A weight on my chest that kept me up the entire night, watching her, making sure her own chest rose and fell. I'd imagined the ways I would've killed the fuck who did that to her if he hadn't been lucky enough to die from a heart attack. The fuck who had raped her.

Stole her innocence.

Her first experience of sex was forced. By a man she trusted, one who took something from her. Something I could never get back. Something I could never fix. And I didn't even get the satisfaction of torturing and killing him.

The mother... If she was still alive, I'd deal with her.

Kate had gone from that house straight to a life with someone who made her feel worthless. Who belittled and terrified her. Another motherfucker who had abused her.

My blood was pumping hot through my body as I stared at Kate. It blew my mind. I had no idea how she'd survived all of that and still became the person she was. Soft. Loving. Magnificent.

It would torture me for the rest of my life, what she'd been through. What I couldn't change. It's what kept me up all fucking night, staring at her, stewing in my rage.

It was just before dawn when I rose from that chair. I'd been battling with the decision I'd finally made. Had tried to convince myself to peel off my clothes and get into bed with her like my instincts were screaming at me to do. But I had other instincts. Ones that were louder, hungry, and more powerful.

Those instincts had me brushing the hair from her head, laying a kiss there and leaving the house.

I'd come to know a lot about Kate's body, attuned myself to it, out of survival more than anything. I'd watched her while she was unconscious for days. Fucking *days*. With a tube down her throat. Watching as her bruises bloomed. Hearing how her voice changed after someone tried to strangle the life from her.

I knew Kate. Every inch of her. So I was mostly certain that I had a handful more hours before she woke up. Which was the only reason why I left in the first place. If I had an inkling that her sleep was thin, that she was apt to wake up from one of those horrific fucking nightmares, I wouldn't have gone.

But she was out.

So I'd climbed on my bike and rode here, creeping through the silent halls of the club before heading down to the bowels. Where we took people who made it personal. Who needed to die a specific way.

The room smelled of piss and shit.

This fuck soiled himself the first fucking day down here. 'Cause he was that much of a coward. The ones who laid hands on women always were.

He'd cried, begged, of course. They all did. I'd gotten tired of that and gagged him, kept it that way. Hades had fed him enough food and water to keep him alive 'cause I couldn't stomach giving this piece of shit anything that would prolong his life.

There were muffled cries against the gag as I walked into the room.

I ignored them and yanked over a metal stool to face him in the chair he was tied to.

"I've heard a little story about you." I struggled to keep my voice even. "About your past." I clenched my fists on top of my thighs. "With my woman."

I gritted the last word out, unable to lock my shit down, thinking of Kate telling that story.

The story that fucking tore my insides apart. I'd had to stand still, stock fucking still, the entire time, even though I'd been desperate to go to her. To touch her. Comfort her. But I couldn't. 'Cause if I had moved during the time she had been telling me about the stepfather who fucking raped her, about the husband who beat her, there would've been no comfort. I would've torn the room apart. Then I would've come here and put a bullet in his brain. No matter what promises I'd made. I would've done it. Would've ruined Kate and I if I'd moved.

So I'd stayed as still as a statue while my woman bared herself to me. Second to holding my daughter, to finding Kate on the side of the road, it was the hardest moment of my fucking life.

"Years of her life you stole," I said quietly. "Fuckin' years. That she had to live under your rule." My eyes met his. His were wide with fear. At least one of them was. The other was swollen shut. He had a fractured eye socket. That's what I'd been going for. Recreating every single one of Kate's injuries, but with a little more flair, of course.

He'd be lucky if he regained full sight in that eye.

Lucky.

That's what the fucker was.

Lucky that Kate loved her daughter. That Kate was a good mother. Lucky that I loved Kate more than I needed vengeance.

"I had been planning to take years of yours," I cracked my neck. "I was looking forward to it. Fuck was I looking forward to it."

For a moment, my resolve wavered. My hand twitched, instinctually going for the knife at my belt so I could start carving him apart. But that knife was sitting on a table in the house my woman slept in. Along with my piece. I'd left them there on purpose 'cause I fuckin' knew I couldn't trust myself.

Sure, I could still kill him with my bare hands, and I fucking itched to.

But I stayed on that stool, my eyes on him.

"Unfortunately, you're gonna walk outta here."

The fuck sagged in relief, and ferocity lanced through me.

"Let's get this straight, you fuck," I spat. "Your life is not gonna go well after this. It's not gonna look anything like it did before. You will never see Kate again."

My heart fibrillated at the thought of him laying eyes on her. Him touching her.

"You will give her a divorce," I grated out. "You will give her fuckin' everything. You won't say a word about our time together, or I swear to fuck that I will tear you apart with my bare hands, and I'll enjoy it."

A part of me hoped he'd try something. Prayed that I'd be given a valid reason to end him. One that I could take to Kate as being outside of my control.

"We will be watchin' you," I stared into his good eye, his eyelashes fluttering faster the longer I glared. "For as long as you draw breath on this earth, we will have eyes on you. I will make it my personal crusade that you eat shit until the day you fuckin' die. I will ruin everything you have until you live in a fuckin' wasteland."

I grinned at him.

"Kate, my woman, the one I'm gonna spend the rest of my life with, has requested that I not kill you."

His body jerked.

"Yeah, I was shocked too," I agreed. "But she wants you dead, know that. You're alive now 'cause of your daughter. That's the only reason. And again, you say fuckin' anything to your daughter about Kate, your dick is the first thing I cut off."

My fingertips buzzed with the thought.

"I'm here 'cause I wanted to look you in the eye when I tell you I'm taking everything you had. Everything you threw away 'cause you're rotten... to your fuckin' core."

I stood, staring down at him. I spat in his face.

"I'll do that on your grave one day too," I promised, then I turned on my heel and walked out.

That was the first of two very fucking difficult things I had to do that day, and the sun was only just coming up.

CHAPTER TWENTY

KATE

IT WAS the smell of coffee that woke me. And the distinct scent that could only come from Swiss. Leathery. Musky. A hint of vanilla.

I smiled before my eyes even opened, the sheets like butter around my body. The warmth of the sun streamed through the windows, illuminating my eyelids.

My body hurt a little less every day. But my mind was the biggest difference. I felt... changed. Lighter. Not only was I waking up in a place that was mine, I was waking up with Swiss, with all of my secrets laid out, nothing rotting inside me anymore. Sure, there was still a long road to go, but I felt equipped for the journey now.

"Mornin', Countess," Swiss's gruff voice greeted.

My smile widened, and my eyes opened to Swiss, sitting on the side of the bed, staring at me.

He was fully dressed, which made sense since two coffee cups from Oliver's were sitting on the nightstand.

"How long was I out?" I asked, my voice a scratchy wisp. My throat was much better but was worse in the mornings and nights, like when trying to shake the last of a nasty cold.

Swiss leaned forward to brush the hair from my face. "A little over thirteen hours."

I leaned into his touch "That long?"

"You needed every minute of it."

I thought on that. On everything that had happened the past few weeks, the conversations had.

Yeah, I really did need it.

And I was waking up a new woman. Sure, I had a lot of the same bruises, but they would fade.

I was lighter, infinitely so. My slate felt clean.

I was in my house. My house. A place where I could hang that painting from the antique store. Swiss was right here, there was coffee.

All was right in the world.

My body melted as I took him in, the light shining, illuminating the rough stubble on his square jaw, those eyes, the cords of his neck.

Desire grew in my body as I lifted my hands to his cut, grasping it so I could pull him down to me.

"Speaking of things I need..." I murmured suggestively.

Swiss's eyes did not melt into the familiar look of hunger I'd expected. No. They darkened, his jaw going tight, his face closing off into something cold, distant.

He leaned back, and I immediately wanted to crawl into myself, to hide under the sting of the rejection. My neck turned hot, and I wanted to sink into the floor. I didn't do that, though.

Swiss stepped back from the bed and walked toward the window. "That's not a good idea, Kate," he said tightly.

I climbed out of bed quickly, all of the melty feelings I'd been having nowhere to be seen. I was far too vulnerable lying in bed.

Though standing wasn't much better since I was wearing a tank and panties, no bra. I itched to find something to wear, but the small walk-in closet was all the way across the room, and I didn't trust myself to make that journey.

So instead, I lingered by the nightstand, taking a big sip of coffee before placing it down, watching Swiss pace by the window.

My hand crept self-consciously up my neck. I was much better than I had been before. Doing things like smiling, speaking and eating didn't cause excruciating pain. Breathing wasn't like inhaling broken glass. I was walking around almost without limping. All in all, I was doing well. Hence my need for a little distraction, for Swiss's hands on my body. For the blissful nirvana of our bodies joining, the disconnection from reality that I knew that always brought.

It might not have been entirely sane or healthy that I was eager—or more accurately, desperate—to have him inside me, to have him hurt me, but I didn't much care at that moment.

I just wanted him.

It did not occur to me that he might not want me. I looked far from my best. The bruises covering my face weren't black and blue anymore, they were shades of green and purple. The rings around my neck were still angry. Yeah, I wasn't exactly desirable.

"I know this look isn't exactly... sexy," I waved at my face, my voice smaller than I liked.

Swiss's gaze ignited, and he stopped pacing, crossing the distance between us in two long strides before he lifted his hand up to caress my cheek gently. Much too gently.

"You shut that shit up right now," he commanded, voice husky. "I see those gears turning, thinkin' about me not wantin' you, thinkin' it has somethin' to do with last night. About me lookin' at you differently or some shit."

My body jerked. That had been exactly what I was thinking. That he thought I was somehow dirty or wrong after what I'd told him. Which logically was insane, but considering how raw and unhealed all of that trauma was, it made sense to me.

Swiss frowned at me. "This is not about that," he stated firmly. "If last night changed anything, it made me want you more, which I didn't think was possible." He cupped my cheek slightly harder, and I leaned into his hand, my body singing for him.

But I knew him, I knew his body. I knew the way he tensed before pulling me to him, the fire in his eyes when he was seconds away from making me scream. No, there was none of that now. There was a... distance. A restraint that I hadn't seen from him. The cords in his neck were hard ridges, his body tensed, coiled.

"I want you, baby." He shook his head as if he were trying to shake something off. "Fuck do I want you." His thumb brushed against my swollen lip. "But everything that's happened to you, everything you've shared with me..."

He shook his head again, but this time it was clear that his thoughts were not on sex. His eyes were warm, dark bourbon. "I want you in every way a man could want a woman. I want you on the back of my bike. Want you in my bed. Want you to wear my ring, wear my name inked on your skin, want scars from your nails on my back." Though his eyes were soft, the words were rough, raspy, and the most beautiful words I'd ever heard in my life.

My stomach bloomed with warmth, settling in my bones like sunshine.

"But that's what *I* want," he added, slapping his sternum. "Me. And I'm selfish. I'm bad. I haven't done an honorable thing in a very fuckin' long time. Even now, in the middle of doin' the only honorable thing I'll do in my life, I'm second guessin' myself. I'm fightin' my instincts to tear off those panties, plant my dick inside you and make you scream."

My fingertips tingled, and my breathing quickened. Yeah, I really wanted that too. Like, a lot. The panties in question were soaking wet.

Swiss was not immune to my reaction. Fire danced in his eyes, and his body turned even more rigid.

"But," he gritted the word out with violence. "Kate, you make even the most wretched of men do honorable things if it means they get to keep you." He bent closer, his forehead resting against mine. "And I intend to keep you."

His proclamation was a balm, penetrating my skin. My hip, the one with his initials carved into it, throbbed.

"But," he said again. "Your whole life, you've had to live on someone else's terms. You've had a man take things from you 'cause he wanted to keep you. He wanted to mold you into something you weren't."

Fury radiated off him as he spoke about Preston. He was a presence between us because he was still living. Because I'd forced Swiss to let him live.

"But I want *you*," I whispered.

"And you have me," he slid his knuckles across my jaw. "For a long time, you've got me. For the rest of time, if I've got anything to do with it. Which means we've got time. To take it slow. Be friends."

I stared at him, my mouth dropping in shock. Of all the things Swiss could've said, I never would've guessed that. Not in a million freaking years.

"Friends?" I echoed, my voice dry and scratchy.

He nodded once, frowning, obviously not happy with this decision, but it had been decided nonetheless.

"You want to be *friends*?" I clarified, because it was all too strange.

Another nod. Slightly more violent than the last.

I stepped back from him, unable to have his hands on me at that moment. "You've been inside me." I folded my arms in front of me. "You've been *everywhere* inside me. You've seen and tasted every inch of me. I've done the same to you."

He flinched, telling me that he was not immune to my words.

"You expect us to be *friends* after that?" I asked in disbelief. "For how long?"

Swiss's jaw was tight, eyes were solid. Resolute. "For as long as you need. To let you get on your own two feet. To know your own mind."

Fury bloomed within me. "You don't think I know my own mind?"

His hands were fists at his sides. This was hard for him. This was hurting him. But in that moment, I didn't give a crap.

"I think you deserve to get to know yourself without a man gettin' in the way," he said softly.

I put my hand on my hip. "So you think the best way for me to do that is to have another man make decisions about my life?"

Swiss gritted his teeth, clearly pissed. That made two of us.

"Friends," I shook my head, nearly hissing. "For an indefinite amount of time, whenever *you've* decided I know my own mind." Fury was palpable in my tone.

Swiss said nothing, just stood there, taut with his stiff jaw.

"From what I've come to know of you, you're a man with a healthy sexual appetite," I continued, my mind moving. "And for what I've come to know of myself... you know, what little a lowly woman could know about herself," I added the jab because I was pissed. "I've learned that I love to fuck. That I have a very healthy sexual appetite. So what are we to do while we're friends? Fuck other people?"

Swiss's glare turned dangerous, deadly. "Any other man touches you, he's fuckin' dead."

I tilted my head, regarding him. "And what about women who touch you? I'm sure the same doesn't go for them? I'm sure the rules are different for you."

The mere thought of Swiss with another woman made my stomach lurch, and my nails sank into the insides of my palms as I clenched my fists.

Swiss regarded me as he stepped forward so his scent enveloped me, so his cut brushed my body but our skin didn't touch.

"You really think I'm gonna touch another woman after knowin' your body?" He spoke quietly, intensity coating every syllable. "You really think I even *see* other women?"

My heart thundered in my chest.

"Make no mistake, this is gonna be torture for me. My cock fuckin' aches for your cunt, Kate. My hands are itchin' with the need to touch you. I need to taste you more than I need to breathe. I'm gonna jack off thinkin' about what you taste like, the way your back arches when I make you come."

My knees quivered, and I was impressed with my ability to stay standing. My pussy pulsated with need.

I leaned forward, leaned into him. We were like magnets. There was no way he could deny this. Me. Us.

But Swiss stepped back moments before our lips touched.

My desire turned to dust.

"You're really doing this?" I groused, wishing my voice was much bigger. Angrier.

Swiss's eyes blazed. "I'm doin' this for us," he gritted out.

I let out a bitter laugh. "Oh, for us, are you? You're so fucking noble, making decisions for the both of us."

"Kate—"

"Get out."

Swiss stilled. "What?"

I pointed to the door. "You heard me. Get out. If you hadn't noticed, this is *my* house, and I think I still get to make some decisions here. And I need you to get the fuck out." There it was, the strength I wanted in my voice. The sharpness. I didn't recognize the authority in my tone, but I liked it.

Instead of the glare or the iron jaw I expected from Swiss, I got something else entirely.

A grin.

From ear to ear.

"There it is," he murmured. "There's your temper. There's your claws." His eyes went down my body slowly.

Despite my mood, they left fire in their wake.

"Hot as fuck, Countess." His voice was thick with desire.

My toes curled, and it was an effort to keep the scowl on my face.

"I'll leave," he said. "But I'm comin' back," he promised. And on that, he picked up his coffee cup, his cut brushing my hard nipple as he did so.

"Be thinkin' 'bout those tits, that cunt when I make myself come in the shower," he whispered in my ear.

Then he turned on his heel and left.

THREE WEEKS LATER

I had come to discover that I loved the sounds my house made in the middle of the night.

My house.

It felt insane to even think such a thing.

Okay, it wasn't technically *mine* since it was owned by Macy and Hansen, but I was paying rent here. Or I was going to be once I figured out how to slip the money into her purse.

But I picked out the comforter. Rugs. There were framed pictures of Violet scattered around the house. Violet, who was coming home in just over a week. She'd had her weekend with Jacques that was *ah-mazing* and was making preparations to come home.

I'd half expected that she'd announce she was engaged to him. That thought, among other things, kept me up at night. She was still ignorant as to what exactly was going on with her parents. I needed to tell her. I knew I needed to tell her. But I had to garner the strength.

Preston and I were divorced.

Just like that.

Well, not *just* like that if you considered everything that had happened. But I didn't have a hand in anything. I just signed the papers prepared for me. Papers that originally said I had ownership over the house, the stocks and bonds that Preston held and a bunch of other assets.

I'd donated it all, except a sum that I'd calculated I'd need and for Violet's college fund.

Everyone had thought I was crazy for refusing the donating and assets. Everyone had tried to talk me out of it.

I'd held firm, something that was new to me but that I'd enjoyed. I'd lived a life of excess and been miserable. Been damn near suicidal. I did not want money to keep me in a lifestyle to which I had been accustomed.

Just the thought of that lifestyle made me sick.

Instead, I liquified all of his investments and donated all of the cash to various domestic violence charities, to women's shelters, to paying legal fees for women trying to divorce abusive husbands.

The house was trickier, though.

I certainly didn't want my name on a house that had been a prison for years. Macy suggested I sell it, take the money. I'd considered that, but for better or for worse, Violet grew up in that house. She had wonderful memories there. She deserved the option to go home there, if she wished.

I nurtured a hope that she would want to come home, here, to New Mexico. Of course, she had to go back to school. She was going to Brown. *Brown.* I was exceptionally proud of her. But it was just so far.

I itched to be close to her. Close enough to drive and take her out for dinner, go shopping. But this was my home now. And my precious girl was turning into a woman.

Planes existed. I could and would visit her whenever I wanted.

I'd make it work.

Somehow.

Although the logistics of Violet's homecoming had been on my mind for some time now, it was not what kept me up.

It was the couch.

The purple couch that Hansen had teased Macy about. The purple couch that I just happened to love.

It was a couch that currently had a six-foot, hulking biker sleeping on it. The biker who had been sleeping on it ever since I moved in here. Ever since he decided we were going to take it slow.

That we were going to be fucking *friends.*

He still slept in this house every night. He was still with me every free moment he had. If I went anywhere with him, it was on the back of his bike. My body pressed against his, the Harley vibrating between my legs... It was pure torture. From the pained look on his face every time we got off, it wasn't just torture for me.

Yeah, he was going near mad with need too. But he'd held fast in this *friends* bullshit. And I was too stubborn, too hurt, too freaking confused to try and seduce him, argue against this.

Well, until that very moment.

Three weeks.

Three fricking weeks.

My body had almost completely healed. There were still some stubborn bruises, a thin, red scar on my stomach that would hopefully fade, still some aches and pains, but I was back to normal.

I was even back at the café, although Swiss had tried to argue against me going back too soon. I'd argued back, passionately. He'd had a weird look in his eyes, one that made my thighs clench and my stomach dip. His face had lingered close to mine. I'd held my breath, near salivating with need. Then he'd muttered about, "Going on a ride," and left.

Turned around and left.

I'd been pissed off. And horny. So I'd used the vibrator that Freya got me as a gift after I'd spent a night ranting about Swiss and the bullshit 'friends' arrangement.

It was the first time I'd used it because before that, I'd held out. I was uncomfortable about orgasming without Swiss. About using a vibrator in the first place. I wasn't in tune with my body like that.

But I'd gotten mad enough to get in tune.

And it was great. Really freaking great. It had nothing on what Swiss and I had, but it was different. It was erotic because I was the one in control. It wasn't about a man. Wasn't about someone else's pleasure. It was something deeply personal and intimate.

Swiss had come back an hour later, took one look at me, and let out a low growl in the back of his throat. "You're trying to fuckin' kill me," he ground out. Then he left again. For two more hours.

Needless to say, he knew me well enough to know what I looked like after I'd come.

That was two days ago.

And we'd barely seen each other in that time. Swiss was creating distance.

And I was over it.

I was pissed off.

I was lonely in a bed that he was supposed to be in.

I was horny.

Sure, I could've used the amazing little device in the night-stand, but I didn't want to. I shouldn't need to. There was a six-foot something biker on my sofa who I knew could make me tremble in need, who could make me leave this freaking world. And he wasn't doing that because of some stupid idea he had in his head.

So I was done.

"Screw this," I said to my bedroom ceiling, throwing off my covers and stomping toward the living room.

Summer had come back with a vengeance, one last hurrah before fall gripped us. The nights were hot, and I liked to sleep with the windows open, so I was wearing as little as possible. And because I was hoping that Swiss would catch a glimpse of the short silk nightie and reconsider this whole 'friends' deal.

The TV was a low hum, and the lamp in the corner illuminated Swiss on the couch.

He was shirtless. And he was not asleep.

His eyes went to me immediately, flicking up and down my body, focusing on where the lace was sheer enough to see my hard nipples.

His low hiss echoed through the room. I felt it in my pussy.

"You were right that day," I said, going to stand in front of him, my hand on my hip. I didn't miss the way it bunched the silk over the curve of my ass, nor did I miss Swiss's eyes traveling to that location.

My body thrummed with need, but I had shit to say. "I have had men making decisions for me for almost two decades. Before Preston, was a stepfather who stole precious, priceless, irreplaceable things from me."

I could feel Swiss's anger as I mentioned Hal. We hadn't spoken about him since that night, just like we hadn't spoken about his daughter and wife, but all three still lingered like ghosts.

"And before him was a mother who hated me for being born," I continued, nowhere near done. "I have not lived a life without pain, without being controlled in one way or another, without walking on eggshells."

I watched Swiss as he got up from the sofa. I fought the urge to drool at his sculpted torso, the jeans he wore that did not hide his need for me.

I held up my hand. "You're not going to say anything or touch me..." My eyes skated downward. "Yet," I finished before my eyes roamed back up to meet his stare.

"I appreciate what you wanted to do, what you were giving me when you took a step back. What you were trying to give me." I stepped forward, and his entire body stiffened.

I ignored that.

My fingertips ran down the naked skin of his chest. "I understand that you were trying to be the good guy."

Swiss's breathing was rapid, his body shaking as I toyed with the waistband of his jeans.

He wasn't wearing anything underneath them. Swiss was a commando guy.

"But you're not the good guy," I licked my lips as I looked up at him. "I knew that the moment I laid eyes on you. And I wasn't looking for the good guy. I don't *want* the good guy. I know my own mind, and I'm not having anyone, even you, tell me I don't. So I know what I want. I want you."

"Thank fuck," he growled so loudly my bones seemed to vibrate. Before I knew it, I was up in his arms, my legs wrapping around his waist on instinct more than anything else. "I was about to lose my fuckin' mind," he bit out as his hard cock pressed against my lace panties.

He was walking us in the direction of the bedroom. Our mouths were millimeters apart.

"*You* were about to lose your mind?" I teased. "What are you talking about? I thought you wanted to be friends."

Swiss stopped in his tracks. "No way in fuck did I want to be friends with you, Countess," he ground out. "I've tasted your pussy. I've fucked your ass. I've watched my cum drip out of you."

My body jerked at his words, my nipples hard, and my limbs already tightening in preparation for climax.

"Make no mistake, I want to be your best friend," he added. "But one who fucks you senseless on any given day of the week."

I blinked through the fog of my desire. "What have the last three weeks been about, then?"

Swiss grinned wickedly, showing gleaming, white teeth. "It's been about that," he hissed. "That fire inside of you. Those claws. The fuckin' wildcat I know is inside you that can take control. It's been about you findin' your voice and usin' it to get what you want." He started walking again. "And I'll admit, you had me worried for a minute there, that it wasn't me you wanted. Us. But thank fuck you used it tonight, Countess. I wasn't gonna be able to function much longer."

He leaned in to kiss me, and although it was hard, although it felt downright insane, I pulled back.

Swiss let out a warning sound in the back of his throat, jostling me so his cock rubbed against the most sensitive part of me.

I let out a low moan but narrowed my eyes. "Are you telling me that this has been some kind of fucking... *test?*"

Swiss shook his head. "Not a test, Countess. Furthest thing from it. Just wanted you to discover yourself. Didn't want you to be afraid of standin' up to me. Wanted you to know that you steer this ship."

He threw me on the bed.

Though I itched to fight him more, he was illuminated by the jade lamp on my nightstand. His chest appeared to be carved from marble, even more defined than the last time I saw it, if that were possible. Black hair teased the open buttons of his jeans, where his hard cock was straining against the fabric.

"And I swear to fuck, I near ripped this house apart when I came home and saw you used this without me." The drawer of my nightstand rattled as he opened and closed it.

My eyes widened as they took in the vibrator he was gripping.

"Yeah, baby," he murmured. "You used this without me, you naughty little slut."

My blood pumped at his words, they lit me on fire.

"I'd be mad at you for that," he inspected the pink vibrator, then his eyes found mine, "if it wasn't so fuckin' hot."

Yeah, him holding a bright pink vibrator, shirtless, was somehow really, *really* fucking hot.

"Was it the first time you'd used one of these?" he asked.

I nodded slowly, my mouth too dry to speak.

Swiss let out a low hiss. "Drives me mad I wasn't there to see that." His eyes ran over me hungrily, but there was something softer too, more reverent. "But I think it was somethin' you needed to do alone."

My vision blurred for a moment, reacting to the feeling in his tone, the knowing.

"Spread your legs," he commanded, his tone familiar. Darker now.

My body obeyed automatically as my heart beat furiously.

Swiss's eyes flared as he stared in between my legs, my panties still on.

A low buzz was the only sound in the room as he turned on the vibrator. Instead of moving toward me, he surprised me by turning and grasping the chair at the end of the bed, lifting it and positioning it right beside the bed.

He sat in the chair, legs splayed.

"Show me," he demanded, his voice hoarse. The hand holding the vibrator was outstretched. "Show me how you made yourself come."

My hand was shaking when I took the vibrator from him. My entire body was crying out for release already, but a small part of me was shy, fearful of doing something like this—something I'd just learned to do—with an audience.

Even when that audience was Swiss, a man I trusted with my life.

Especially when that audience was Swiss.

His attention was intent on me, so he instantly clocked my hesitation.

"Kate."

My name was a command.

My thighs quivered as my eyes found his.

"Show me how fuckin' powerful you are."

The words caressed my sensitive skin, they brushed away any and all insecurities, they forced my focus on the moment. On him. On how long it had been since his eyes had been on me that way. Since his mouth had been on me. Since he'd been inside me.

Without fully realizing—thinking about that, about him—I had moved the vibrator in between my legs, my back arching as I placed it exactly where I needed it.

"Don't you dare fuckin' come yet," Swiss growled.

As if he'd seen that I was seconds away from exploding. My body was so primed that I'd been ready to explode the second I placed the vibrator on my clit. And now he was telling me to hold it all together. To stop myself from releasing all of the pent-up energy that had been simmering inside of me.

As if he could command such a thing.

But my body obeyed, my hand lifting the vibrator off the most sensitive area, hovering it around, prolonging that sacred and maddening stretch of time on the edge of climax.

I squeezed my eyes closed, wrestling with myself. With my hunger.

"Open your fuckin' eyes, Countess."

My eyes snapped back open.

Swiss had his hands around his cock, not pumping furiously as his tone might've suggested but stroking slowly. His eyes were glued to me.

My legs splayed open wider, and my free hand found the comforter, clenching it in my fist. Seeing Swiss touch himself like that while staring at me like that... There were no words.

"I can't..." I couldn't get the rest of the words out, my body was using every ounce of its energy to hold on to the side of the cliff, waiting for approval from Swiss.

"You waitin' for my permission to come, Kate?"

I nodded furiously, unable to speak.

"You don't need it," he bit out. "You're powerful. You're in charge here. I want you to choose the moment."

I bit my lip in frustration for a moment before I seized control. Before I found, in my foggy, half wild mind, what I actually wanted.

The vibrator landed on the bed, and Swiss's eyes flared in surprise.

"I want to come with you inside me," I pled, my voice a thin rattle.

Swiss didn't hesitate. The second I uttered the words, his hands were underneath my back, positioning me in the perfect position for him to plunge into me.

I cried out, seeing stars as I came the second he seated himself fully inside of me. Swiss must've felt me clenching around him, he knew my body well enough to understand that I was coming apart. But he did not pause. Did not stop thrusting.

He didn't give me a second to catch my breath, to find my bearings as his cock sent me over the edge once more.

"Look into my fuckin' eyes, Kate," Swiss panted.

I hadn't even realized I'd squeezed my eyes shut. They burst open, Swiss's face inches from mine.

"I love you." His voice was unexpectedly soft.

The world stopped turning. My heart stopped beating.

I'd known that, of course. That he loved me. It was never a question.

But he'd never said the three words out loud. Not with the permanence that settled over me now. Not when he was deep inside of me.

"I love you too," I returned without hesitation.

His eyes flared. "I'm never letting you go," he grunted. "And as soon as we can make it happen, we're gettin' married."

I blinked at him, trying to battle against the aftershocks in my body, the sex haze I was in to process what he'd just said. "Is that a proposal?" I breathed.

"Nope," he clipped out the word. "You love me. You're my fuckin' world. Your scar is on me, mine on yours. Want you to be mine in every way possible. So we're getting married. You can try to fight me on it." His eyes were so intense, further enhancing the passion behind his words. "I welcome it. But it's gonna happen. And I know you want it too."

Without waiting for my argument, or for my agreement, he started moving once more. Fucking me into oblivion.

"I'm mad at you, you know," I told Swiss when I was able to regain my breath.

It had surely been hours. It felt like it.

Swiss and I were naked, damp with exertion, tangled up in each other, both breathing heavily.

We were on the floor.

I was not exactly sure when we made it there, but there had been one part of the night when Swiss ordered me to bend over one of the chairs.

And things had gone horizontal from there.

I was tucked into his shoulder, staring at the ceiling, trying to regain my sense of balance even though I was lying on the floor.

My entire center of gravity had shifted. Something pivotal had changed inside me. Maybe inside both of us.

Sure, we'd had sex before. Many times before. But this was

something other than that. It was a claiming. Not just by him but by me too.

It was the first time we had come together knowing every single piece of each other. It was the first time I'd had full ownership over my body. Over myself.

"You sure did a good job of communicatin' that," Swiss replied dryly.

Despite myself, I laughed. "Okay, well, I *should* be mad at you," I amended.

His arms tightened around me. "You abandoned everything you *should* be the moment you decided to proposition me at a club party."

My body tensed at the memory, the one that felt like it happened a lifetime ago. It still gave me butterflies thinking about it.

"I guess I did," I snuggled deeper into him.

We lapsed into comfortable silence, for a time, at least. I wasn't mad at him, not really. For a moment, maybe I had been. For forcing the separation between us just because he wanted me to be pissed enough to take charge. But then he didn't really separate us. He had been with me, every single night. He had been right there with me, waiting.

"You didn't..." I tried to find the right words. "When you... you didn't—"

"When I came, I didn't put my hands around your neck, strangling you until you almost passed out?" he offered.

I swallowed. "Yeah," I whispered.

During the many, many times Swiss and I had had sex, it had always ended with his hands around my neck, squeezing until I saw stars, until my lungs burned. It was a kink of his, connected and born out of trauma, no doubt. But surprisingly, it had become a kink of mine too.

He stroked my arm. "Baby, I saw you lyin' in a hospital bed with a tube down your throat, with your neck black from the evidence of that piece of shit tryin' to end you."

My skin prickled, his words corrupting what had been a perfect moment. But it wasn't his words that were responsible, it was Preston's actions. They had tarnished everything, changed everything. But somehow not entirely for the worst. Swiss and I were lying here together after the best sex I'd ever had in my life.

In the house that my friends had given me.

Given me.

I was alive, breathing. I was divorced.

Yeah, things were not bad. Objectively, things were wonderful.

Still I needed to pick at things, it seemed. I needed to open the wound.

"I'm fucked-up, babe," Swiss dragged a hand down his face. "That's not gonna change. Even someone like you cannot change that. So I imagine I'll still need a fair bit of kink when I fuck you... Though if what we just did was vanilla, I'm content with that." He continued stroking my arm.

"That was certainly not vanilla," I replied.

He chuckled. It was low and throaty and warm.

"I know that seeing me like... *that* did something to you," I whispered. "Changed something. But I also need you to know that even after that, especially after that, I want you to mark me. I don't want you to be afraid of hurting me." I bit my lip, moving to position myself so my elbow was on his chest, propping me up to look him in the eye. "I need you to hurt me," I confessed. "Your marks on my body are ones I'll wear with pride. Because if you haven't noticed, I'm a little fucked-up too." I smiled softly.

Swiss did not smile back.

"I'm sure I'll get to the point where I enjoy that again," he reached up to brush the hair from my face. "Where seein' you writhe in pain and pleasure makes my cock explode."

I shivered in expectation and excitement. I was hungry for that, for a different kind of pain. But maybe I was being a little hasty, wanting that from him when I was barely healed.

"Besides that, it's my job, the one I take really fuckin' seriously, to give you what you need." He rubbed his thumb along my bottom lip.

His hand ghosted downward, to my neck, which had returned to its regular coloring.

"But I will never put my hands around here again," he vowed, eyes displaying the conviction in his words. "I've needed to taste death when I come. A woman's death. 'Cause of my past. 'Cause I like to torture myself." His eyes shimmered. "But, Kate, I didn't just taste your death. I had to swallow it whole. Now it's inside of me. And the only thing I need when I'm fuckin' you is to know you're alive." He laid his palm on my chest. "To feel the life inside of you."

My heart thundered underneath his hand. I swallowed roughly. "Did you mean it?" I asked in a meek voice.

"Everything I say I mean to you, Kate," Swiss replied soberly. "But what in particular are you talkin' about?"

I drew circles on his chest, tracing over the raised skin of my mark.

"About marriage," I said. "Ours."

Swiss stilled. I glanced back up at him.

"Fuck yes, I meant it," he murmured, taking my hand to lift it to his lips.

"I understand if you need some time," he hedged. "Considerin' you've been someone else's wife since you were a teenager."

His voice changed at the brief mention of Preston. Preston, who had seemingly been released from wherever they had been keeping him. Preston, who I hadn't seen hide nor hair of since he was strangling me to death.

I assumed he'd made it back to our former home, and I wondered idly how he'd explained the injuries he no doubt left with. How he'd explained my absence.

But I didn't wonder about that for long. He wasn't my problem anymore.

I did have a pang in my heart thinking about his parents, who were the closest thing I had to a mother and father. Who I likely would never see again. Who very likely hated me because of whatever lies Preston no doubt spun about me in order to come out the hero in the story.

But I didn't want a hero.

I certainly didn't want to learn what my life would be without the villain who saved me from the man everyone thought was a hero.

"I don't need time," I declared suddenly. "I want to be your wife."

He jerked. Literally jerked with emotion. Emotion so visceral it hit his body. Made impact.

"Thank fuck," he murmured. "I've been waitin' all my life for you, and although I would've survived waitin' a little longer to marry you, I would've been an ornery bastard to everyone else. Someone would've definitely gotten stabbed."

"Well, we can't have that," I grinned.

We were silent for a while, bathing in the happiness that was infusing the air.

"What do you want for a wedding?" Swiss asked eventually. "I imagine no one asked you that the first time around."

I let out a chuckle. "No, they did not."

I didn't choose the location. The date. The guest list. Or even my dress. Everything was planned around the child growing inside me and the image that Preston's parents wanted to portray.

It hadn't bothered me much, people making decisions for me about the 'most important day in my life'.

It hadn't felt like that to me.I wasn't one of those girls who dreamed of her wedding day. Who imagined the dress, the flowers, the groom.

I'd had enough weddings, grooms and marriages to last me a lifetime. My mother had ensured that. In fact, my dream had been to never get married. To never define my identity based on a man. Never have a man responsible for my security, for my happiness.

And look how that turned out.

"I don't mind what the wedding is," I answered honestly. "I want you there. The club. Violet, hopefully..." I trailed off, struck with worry about what my daughter would say to the news that I was not only divorced from her father but marrying an outlaw biker she'd never met.

My first instinct was to protect her from that at all costs. And in order to do that, I would either have to lie to her about the wedding, about Swiss, or I would have to delay it indefinitely.

Neither of those options were plausible. Neither were options I could live with.

I'd protected my daughter from enough, lied to her enough. I was no longer willing to sacrifice my happiness in order to do that. That was not a decision she would respect. That's not the woman I wanted to be.

I hoped, prayed, that my wonderful little girl would be understanding. Would forgive me. I had to trust in that.

I blinked at Swiss who was watching me carefully, as if he were witnessing the wheels turning in my mind.

"The marriage," I whispered. "That's what's most important to me."

Swiss smiled then lifted himself up in order to lay a soft kiss on my lips. His eyes turned serious. "What about kids? Do you want more?"

I hadn't been expecting that question nor the grave tone in which it was spoken. Neither of those things should've surprised me, though. It was a completely rational and necessary thing to talk about before committing to someone.

But I didn't think of Swiss as a particularly rational person, or someone to tick off all of the necessary boxes needed before marrying someone.

Though it made sense.

He'd lost his wife and daughter.

He'd lost his child. Something I could not fathom. Something that you never recovered from.

That pain had stayed with him, so it made sense that he might not ever want another child. Might never want to know that pain again.

Beyond that, neither of us were particularly young. A child was hard work. Was years of hard work. All-encompassing but rewarding hard work. Swiss lived a particular lifestyle. He liked freedom, liked partying, staying up late, doing what he wanted.

I liked that too. I'd just discovered that. And for the first time in my life, I could make choices for myself.

My daughter was grown and out of the house. Of course I never stopped being her mother, but I'd entered a different season of motherhood. Did I want to start all over again?

With Swiss.

With a baby with his eyes, with his smile, seeing him hold that baby in his arms. Seeing him as a father.

"I don't know," I said honestly after processing for a while.

"Maybe. I want everything life has to offer with you. And I know that a child deserves to have you as a father."

Swiss's expression was carefully blank. He didn't speak for a long time. "I don't know if I can do it," he confessed hoarsely. "If I can face that fear."

There was incredible, heartbreaking vulnerability in his voice.

I reached up to stroke his face. "Well, if you can't, if you don't want to, you don't have to. I want you. That's all I want. Everything else is just gravy."

A ghost of a smile twitched the corner of his lip. "Just gravy, huh?"

I smiled, nodding. "You're all I'll ever need."

His smile flattened. "You too, Countess."

Eventually, we found our way back to bed. But even in Swiss's arms, I didn't find sleep for a long time. We had had sex unprotected. Not something new for us. When he learned I was on birth control, Swiss had been adamant about taking me 'raw.' I wasn't one to protest that.

But I'd been in the hospital in intensive care. Then I'd been recovering from those wounds in a new home. Then I'd been pissed at Swiss. I hadn't exactly prioritized getting my birth control prescription filled.

And we'd just had sex. A lot of it. In what could be described as my 'fertile window.'

In the wake of everything we had just gone through, the choice very well could've been taken away from us.

That thought kept me awake for a long time.

CHAPTER TWENTY-ONE

KATE

"SO I GUESS I'm kind of... engaged?" I announced as we sat down. It was a statement of fact but also kind of a question.

We were at my house.

I was hosting girls' night for the first time ever.

Well, it was *kind of* girls' night. The men, our men, had agreed to go to the bar in town for a 'spell,' but Hades had stared at Freya in an odd way and told her 'she was getting an hour, no more no less.'

Even Macy, who was well versed in alpha male stares and intense utterings, had raised a brow at this.

But then we'd gotten distracted at the various ways in which our men said goodbye. Swiss, for his part, had yanked me into a kiss that made everyone else fade away, and when he'd let me go, everyone had been whistling and cheering.

It seemed our goodbye had gotten X-rated for even this group.

Swiss had grinned widely and kissed the side of my head. I'd shrank into his side and gotten very red.

"Oh my fucking god!" Macy screamed.

She slammed her glass down on the table so she could come and give me a hug. Then she grabbed my left hand, yanking it up to inspect my naked finger. She rolled her eyes. "The asshole didn't get you a diamond," she scoffed. "They always do things backward."

I grinned at her as she released my hand. "I don't need a diamond. I've had plenty of those," I waved her away. "I just need the life I know we can have together."

Macy's eyes sparkled, and she squeezed my hand. "That's beautiful, babe," she murmured. "And you are going to have an amazing life, I know that."

"Seconded," Caroline called out from her spot in the armchair I'd just bought at my new favorite antique shop.

Swiss had complained about all the trips, but he'd been rather hard to drag out of there on our latest trip and had added a handful of items to our cart. It had warmed my heart, to see him picking things out and putting them in our home. Putting pieces of him here.

We no longer stayed at the club. His room was cleared out of all of his belongings, which was a good happenstance since a new member had just patched in.

Blade... Yeah, that was his name. He was a man of few words, and of course, ridiculously attractive, if you liked that 'he might kill you or fuck you' kind of vibe.

I only had eyes for Swiss.

"A toast!" Macy declared, holding her freshly poured glass up in the air. "To all of us getting the lives we deserve, and giving them to the men who deserve them too." She waggled her brows. "And to never having to fake an orgasm."

I let out a chuckle and raised my glass as did Freya and Caroline.

The cool liquid slipped down my throat, warming me from the inside out. I was sitting here enjoying wine with three women I trusted implicitly. I was able to—and encouraged to—get as drunk as I wanted if I so wished. I could say anything I wanted to these women about my relationship, about Swiss, and it would go no farther than this room.

Oh, how much had changed in less than a year.

"Freya," Macy barked. "You know it's bad luck not to drink on a toast."

I looked to where Freya was sitting beside me, holding on to an untouched flute of champagne.

Her lower lip was clamped between her teeth. "Well, if we're announcing things," she mumbled, chin practically pinned to her chest. "I'm pregnant." She raised her eyes.

"Oh my god, you so are," Macy rolled her eyes in a warm way. "I can't believe I hadn't noticed, you're glowing."

Freya rolled her eyes. "If I'm glowing, it's sweat from all the throwing up I've been doing," she countered.

Caroline narrowed her brows. "Are you not happy about this?" she asked, leaning forward, catching the edge in her tone.

You can take the journalist out of the warzone, but she'll never stop being a journalist, it seemed.

"I am happy," Freya answered, her expression not matching her words as she placed the wine glass on the side table. "Or at least I *was* happy," she corrected. "Until I told Hades."

I pursed my lips. Although Hades was an intimidating—okay, downright scary—dude, he did not hide his love for Freya or his daughter. He adored them. With a love that radiated badass intensity but a purity too.

"He's hung up on last time," she explained to me.

"When she almost died," Macy expanded.

"It was bad," Caroline added, voice grim. "Hades was... on another level, even for him."

"And he's scared something is going to happen to you?" I surmised.

Freya nodded.

"Everyone thinks men are most intense and dangerous when they're angry, but those people haven't ever seen a badass, alpha male scared," Macy said. "Scared for the life of the only woman that they have ever or will ever love."

I sipped my wine. Yeah, I had seen that firsthand.

"He'll come around," I reassured Freya.

Her eyes glistened. "I hope so," she said in a small voice. "He doesn't have any choice, anyway," she continued, sounding stronger.

"He will come around," Macy repeated my sentiment but more firmly. "Sure, he'll be a homicidal bastard for the next eight months or so, but that won't be unlike the time before you met him." She winked at Freya.

Macy lifted her glass once more. "To marriage and babies."

We clinked our glasses. "To marriage and babies," I murmured, thinking about my own alpha male and what his reaction would be if I gave him this kind of news in about two weeks.

Would he come around?

He would have to, I guessed.

And so would I.

The men arrived home, and everyone had congratulated Hades who, unsurprisingly, did not smile or have much reaction to the well wishes. He only had eyes for his wife. Understandable, given what Freya had said.

Then the men had been banished outside to the grill area to cook dinner. Hades only went when Freya stood to whisper something in his ear, and then he leaned to kiss her hard and fast before stalking off.

"Do you ever wish that they moved away from the things that could get them killed or incarcerated?" I asked the women while watching Swiss.

The way he moved was mystifying, enchanting, hypnotizing. It was fluid, strong, purposeful.

Infinitely arousing.

As if he sensed me, his eyes traversed toward our little group, focusing on me.

My body jolted with the electric current of our eye contact.

All of the women quieted at my question.

"Do you mean do we think about the club going in a more legitimate direction?" Macy clarified. "Like the Amber charter?"

The Amber charter was in California, and from what I'd gathered, close with the New Mexico Sons. Macy, Freya and Caroline talked about women like Gwen, Amy and Mia, along with many others with fondness. There was going to be a big trip out that way in a couple of months.

I was incredibly curious to meet all of the people I'd heard so much about, and to see if the hot guy thing was unique to New Mexico—something in the desert air—or if patching into the Sons indeed required muscles, a smoldering glare, a strong jawline and an intensity that brought women to their knees.

I was also incredibly curious because the Amber charter was unique in that they were not outlaws in the traditional sense of the word. I was sure they didn't live their lives to the letter of the law, but I'd also gleaned that the club operated entirely above board.

This club did not. I'd asked Swiss about the realities of club life, about what he did with his days, how the club made its money. He hadn't skirted around the truth, not even a little bit.

The club ran guns.

It was a nationwide thing, I'd come to find out, and it was a huge portion of their income. Along with the local strip club they owned, and the garage. There were other, smaller 'rackets' but apparently none as lucrative as the guns.

I didn't know how to feel about that. About the men I'd come to admire and respect contributing to a gun violence problem that was very real in our country. But then again, I couldn't sit too high on any morality horse, considering the men on Wall Street and in office were committing terrible crimes on a daily basis were celebrated by society for doing so.

Life was very rarely black and white.

"Yeah, like the Amber charter," I agreed.

Macy sucked her teeth. "Sure, maybe I think about it from time to time. Only because I worry about my Old Man, because I don't ever, ever want to live through what happened on Christmas."

She shuddered as shadows passed her eyes.

Christmas. When the club had lost almost all of its members aside from Jagger and Hansen. A massacre.

Just thinking about these people I considered family being brutally killed had my throat closing up. Just thinking about something happening to Swiss had my vision blurring and my limbs going numb.

"But I don't dwell on it," Macy continued. "I can't. This is who they are." She nodded outside. "The club is part of them. Of who they are at their cores. It has saved their lives." Her gaze roamed over to Caroline.

I knew Jagger had come back from the Army all kinds of screwed up, and instead of going home to Caroline, his high school sweetheart, he'd let her—and his entire family—think he was dead because he couldn't face who he'd become. Caroline, in turn, had gone to warzones all over the globe, reporting on foreign bloodshed, looking for a connection to the man she'd thought she lost.

Through an act of dizzying fate, Caroline had decided to do an investigative piece on the Sons of Templar, intending to expose the reality of club life, and instead, she had found Jagger.

Macy's gaze zeroed in on me. "Without this club, working the exact way it's working, these men wouldn't be here. We wouldn't have found them. And though I worry about my husband every day, it's not the specifics of club life that keep me up at night. It's a car crash on the way to the grocery store. It's some fucking illness or brain aneurysm."

Caroline tilted her head. "Do *you* wish that the club were different?" she asked without judgment.

I didn't answer straight away, didn't offer a response that I thought would make them like me more, accept me, or keep me safe. I didn't lapse into old routines, which was important. Thinking for myself was important.

My eyes strayed back over to Swiss who had already been staring at me intently. For however long.

"No," I answered honestly. "No, I don't."

For better or for worse, the outlaw life was what I chose. And I wouldn't change a thing about it.

Because the outlaw life was what saved Swiss. That was all that mattered.

Everyone left relatively early, considering everyone in attendance had small children at home, and Freya had a husband who was making it his life's mission to make sure she survived her pregnancy.

They all said their goodbyes, proper goodbyes since I wouldn't be seeing them for a while. I'd hugged each of the women tightly, realizing just how much I'd miss each and every one of them.

Swiss had cleaned up. He'd ordered me to stay on the sofa and finish my wine. It felt foreign, slightly uncomfortable and nice. Or it would've been nice had I not had something to do. Something I'd been putting off for far too long.

Swiss's body rounded the sofa and stood in front of me.

"It's time," I told him, staring at the phone sitting in the middle of the coffee table.

Swiss didn't ask what it was time for, nor did he say anything at all. He just sat down beside me and caught hold of my hand. It seemed he wasn't going to offer me privacy to do this alone.

Which I was incredibly thankful for.

I did not want to do this alone.

In fact, I did not want to do this at all.

But Violet was arriving back in four days.

Four freaking days.

A large part of me was counting down the seconds until I saw my daughter again. I missed her so much it hurt.

But then came the reality. Somehow, through some kind of badass communication system, it had been 'settled' that I was picking Violet up from Manchester-Boston airport and staying in a suite with her in the city for three days. Violet didn't know about the suite. Nor did she know it was me coming to pick her up.

She was expecting me and her father followed by a drive back to Carver Springs, to her home. I could not spring all of this news on her at the airport after a long international flight and a tearful goodbye with the boy she was convinced was her soulmate. Then again, she'd been rather quiet on the subject of Jacques the last time I spoke to her, so I'd wondered if he was history.

I kind of hoped for that. Even though it was a horrible thing for a mother to think. A good mother would want her daughter to be happy. To find that happiness wherever it came. But I wasn't exactly a good mother. Not with everything I'd kept from her, everything I was piling onto her. So I was secretly wishing that the older French man was not going to keep my daughter halfway across the world from me.

I was secretly wishing that my almost nineteen-year-old daughter was not going to define her young adulthood around a man. I wanted her to discover herself, explore the world, go to college, do all of the things that I couldn't do.

Of course, Violet was much too strong-willed to live a life that someone else wanted for her. That was one of the things I loved most about her.

It was that strong will I was worried about. If she decided that I was the villain of this scenario—without the truth I wasn't willing to give her—then it would be a battle to get her to forgive me.

And as much as I wanted to tell her this news in person, I needed to give her some time to process. Some distance if she decided she hated me.

I was already full of guilt and self-hatred.

Swiss was also coming because he was not letting me go anywhere without him. I should've argued on that one. Violet was going to have enough to handle without introducing her to my biker fiancé on top of it all.

But I didn't argue about that. I couldn't. I'd traveled across the country absolutely and utterly alone, much weaker than I was now. I knew that technically, I was very capable of doing it now that I was much stronger and surer of myself. I just didn't want to.

And selfishly, I did want Violet to meet Swiss. Even if the timing was supremely fucked-up.

I picked up the phone, dialing then putting it on speakerphone.

Violet answered after a handful of rings. "Yes, Mom, I have my passport in my purse, and yes, I have double checked that my departure time is a.m. not p.m.," she said by way of greeting.

I smiled despite my sense of impending doom. "Good to hear, darling."

"I'm not going to oversleep, I promise." She spoke fast, and I imagined her packing her bag—stuffing things into a suitcase, not carefully folding. I wondered if Jacques was there, lying on a bed, smoking a cigarette and drinking espresso. I hated Jacques, having never met him, having no basis to form that opinion, just on instinct.

"I don't think you're going to oversleep," I lied. She would totally oversleep. And she'd call me, frantic in a cab to the airport, asking if we could rebook her flight if she missed it.

Not that she made a habit of doing such things—this was the first time my daughter was getting herself to an international flight in a foreign country—I just knew my daughter.

"I'm calling to... um, talk to you about something else, hon," I said, gaze flickering to Swiss. His hand found my thigh and squeezed.

"Oh my god, do you have cancer?" she exclaimed. "I knew

353

your voice was not bronchitis. Okay, so you need to stop eating any and all processed foods right this instant. And apricot seeds. They have been proven to be more effective than the poison drug companies peddle," she ranted, working her way up to hysteria. I knew if I let her keep going she would be booking me into some alternative medicine retreat somewhere I couldn't eat Oreos.

"No, I do not have cancer," I interrupted quickly. "Your father and I are divorced, and I'm living in New Mexico with a man I've fallen in love with and plan on marrying."

Swiss raised his brow at everything I'd blurted out in one sentence. We'd spoken about how this conversation might go. Or rather, I'd paced the bedroom, while he laid in bed naked, and muttered my 'script' under my breath.

That was not part of my script.

My script took about twenty-seven minutes. I'd timed it.

It was careful, thoughtful and eased Violet into the truth.

What I'd just blabbered was not careful or thoughtful. It certainly did not ease Violet into the truth.

There was dead silence on the other end of the phone.

Dead silence.

Never in her life had my daughter been struck speechless. She had a response for anything. She was the best on her debate team, she sparred with strangers who had years on her. She was sharp, brave, and a little argumentative.

But... nothing.

Shit.

"Okay, honey, I hadn't exactly planned on saying that all at once," I said, leaning into Swiss. "I was going to ease you into it. And I understand this is hard to hear on the other side of the world, especially since when you left you had no idea anything was happening, and now you're coming home to a whole new normal."

More silence.

I took a breath, needing to throw up. "Your father and I obviously love you very much," I said, Swiss's hand flexing on my thigh at the mention of her father. "Nothing will ever change that. Your home will always be your home. You can spend your holidays with whomever you wish, wherever you wish, and you have a room here..." I looked down the hallway, where I very much hoped my daughter might be sleeping sometime soon.

If she ever spoke to me again.

"I understand if you're mad at me," I pressed on, still hearing nothing on the other end of the phone. "You are entitled to feel however you—"

"Are you happy?" she interrupted, and for the first time in recorded memory, her voice was unexpressive.

I blinked. Of all the things I'd expected, that question was not one of them.

I looked at Swiss once more, his jaw hard with worry. He knew that this was haunting me, that I was losing sleep over it, therefore he was losing sleep over it. He didn't even know Violet, but he cared about her. Because she was something to me. Everything to me. A part of me.

"Yes, sweetie," I whispered, not taking my eyes off Swiss. "I'm the happiest I've ever been in my life. Except, of course, the day you were put into my arms."

A knife sank into my belly with those words, with the precious memory of that day. Seeing her beautiful, wide, inquisitive eyes blinking up at me, her little fist tightening around one of my fingers.

Swiss didn't get that. He didn't get any of that.

And a part of me, a large part, wanted to give him that. Wanted to give myself that as an adult that was sure of herself, not as a child terrified and unaware of the horrors to come.

"You've been sounding different," Violet said, still in that flat tone that stilled my heart. "For months, I knew something was going on, knew that you were different."

I fought to swallow down the lump that had somehow lodged itself in my throat.

"Sweetie..." I began.

"I've got to go," she stated coldly.

I flinched as if I'd been hit. It felt as if a bus had slammed into me.

"Violet—"

"I'll see you at the airport. You're still going to be there, right?" There was a frailty to her voice that I hadn't heard in years. No, that I'd never heard. It was wounded, unsure.

I hated myself.

"Of course, I'll—"

"I love you, Mom."

"I love you too, honey..."

But I was already speaking to dead air.

I stared at the phone for a long time.

Swiss squeezed the back of my neck. "She'll come around," he told me with confidence.

I kept staring at the phone. "Yeah," I replied weakly, without any confidence.

I spent the rest of the night hoping, praying that I had not lost my daughter.

CHAPTER TWENTY-TWO

KATE

I HAD NOT HEARD from Violet in two days. I'd called her constantly, but each time it went straight to voicemail. She was screening my calls, which was understandable.

I'd sent her a couple of texts, telling her I loved her and that I would always be there for her, but other than that, I refrained. I barely restrained the urge to buy a ticket to Paris to see her.

Two days. Two more days and I would see her face. And if it was contorted with anger or hatred, I didn't care. I just needed to see her.

Swiss was doing a wonderful job at keeping me calm, distracted, at eating the small feast I had cooked the past two days. I cooked when I was nervous, so the fridge was bursting with food.

Hence Macy arriving to pick up the majority of things I'd cooked that would go to waste otherwise.

Swiss and I were leaving tomorrow. We'd have one night in

the suite together to get our bearings. Despite all of my nerves and anxiety, I was almost excited to be traveling with Swiss. To see him outside of this environment, yes, but also to have a whole bunch of new experiences with him.

He was packing. A duffel. With some tees, jeans and one other pair of shoes.

Despite having to rebuild my entire closet with limited resources, I had accumulated a lot of stuff. More recently I had accumulated stuff because Macy, Caroline and Freya took me shopping when my portion of the divorce settlement landed in my brand-new bank account.

My bank account. Under my name.

I was reasonably sure that divorce settlements weren't meant to be paid out that quickly or a divorce itself was not usually settled in a matter of days. Then again, most divorces were not sped along by bikers threatening to torture and murder the man who was giving up the majority of his assets.

Maybe the Sons of Templar should add that to their repertoire.

I made a note to mention that to Swiss as I ran toward the front door. Unlike Swiss, I did not just have a duffel. I had a suit-case. A rather large one. Mostly because I was uneasy about what I would wear to the airport to see Violet, so I needed a lot of options.

Her entire life, she'd seen me in expensive, perfectly tailored clothing curated by her father. Designer blouses, sheathe dresses, heels. Hair styled just so, makeup light but purposeful. She'd never seen me in jeans.

My daughter had never seen me wearing them. Such thoughts hit me every now and then, the little realities of the life I'd lived that had escaped me when I was doing the big things like running away and falling in love with a biker.

I suspected it would take years for all of those things to stop hitting me at random points in the day. But they were no longer puncturing my skin in the same way.

So my thoughts were on outfits when I opened the door. What best would communicate to my daughter the person I was now without making her mother look like a stranger?

I supposed I probably already looked like a stranger. My hair was jet black and longer, worn in wild, bouncy curls. My makeup was heavier, sultrier. My face rounder because I was... rounder. I'd gained back the curves I'd lost while in the hospital since Swiss had made it his mission to get me looking 'healthy.' Every pound I gained was a new part of me for him to worship.

I certainly wasn't fat, I was the size that my body was designed to be. But compared to how malnourished and small I was before... Yeah, the change was profound. I realized I'd tried to teach my daughter to love her body all her life when the example I'd been setting for her was the complete opposite. She'd only ever seen me half starved.

"Why are you ringing the doorbell?" I asked as I opened the door. "I know you want to make sure you don't walk in on anything, but—"

I stopped short when I took in who was standing on my doorstep.

"Violet," I gaped at my daughter.

Shock ran through my system as I drank her in. My little girl. Who I'd been picturing, missing and thinking about constantly.

She was as beautiful as ever but different somehow. In a way I could recognize yet not put my finger on.

She looked positively chic—which wasn't something unusual, but it definitely had a French influence. The slouchy pants she was wearing clinched in at her tiny waist, stopping at her ankles

showing off an anklet that I hadn't seen before, and Chanel ballet
flats that used to be mine.

The white linen shirt she was wearing was crinkled, likely
from all the traveling she had been doing, and showed off her
generous chest, which too had a scant amount of new freckles.

The diamond necklace her father had given her as a going
away present was around her neck, and the moonstone earrings
I'd given her for her eighteenth birthday were at her ears.

Her hair was pulled into a loose braid at the back of her neck,
accentuating the slim curve of her neck, her delicate features and
the faint red gloss on her lips. Her high cheekbones were slightly
rosy, and a scant amount of freckles were stark against her ivory
skin. Her dark lashes framed the eyes that were her namesake,
and those eyes were wide, taking me in as I was her.

I suddenly realized what I looked like. I was wearing worn,
ripped jeans, leather flip flops and a bright pink tank that had
'Sons of Templar MC' in white, scrawling script. Macy had it
made.

My hair was piled into a messy bun on top of my head, and I
wasn't wearing any makeup.

So much for easing my daughter into my new identity. My
true identity.

Even that reality could not stop me from working on instinct.
"Oh my god," I screamed, pulling her into my arms.

I'd forgotten about the fact that my daughter could very well
hate me and held her tightly. She did not stiffen in my embrace,
nor did she try to struggle out of it. She hugged me back with the
same fervor that I was hugging her. Slowly and magically, the last
piece of me slotted back into the vacant space that had never
filled despite all of the evolving I'd done.

Being Violet's mother was the one part of my identity that I
was proud of, that was pure and right amongst everything else.

We hugged for a long time, neither of us feeling the urge to cut the embrace short. I had months to catch up on.

"I was leaving to fly to see you at the airport tomorrow!" I exclaimed, still holding her tightly. She smelled of pear and freesia, the perfume I'd gotten her for her fifteenth birthday. The perfume she'd worn every day since then.

That calmed me somehow. With everything that had changed so drastically, so pivotally in these past months, at least my daughter smelled how she normally did. How I remembered her.

Though I didn't actually want to, I wanted to hold on to her forever, I let her go but held on to her arms so I could look at her, try to find that thing about her that seemed different. Then again, there were a lot of things about her that were different, not just the freckles or the style. She'd been in love. Traveled on her own. Experienced an entirely new culture. Had her world rocked by her mother two days ago.

Jesus, *everything* about her was likely to be different.

"Come inside." I yanked her into the living room.

"How did you get here?" I demanded, my mind racing, thinking of my child rebooking all of the flights her father's travel agent had organized. She would've had to take connections, she would've had to get herself a ride out here in the desert—we were almost forty minutes away from the closest airport. My eyes fixed on the red Jeep in the driveway beside my brand-new Mini Cooper. Swiss had bought it for me. Without asking. And I loved it. Adored it.

Violet had rented a car. I was pretty sure you couldn't rent one until you were twenty-five, but then again, I'd never had to rent a car. I wouldn't know how to rent a car. Yet Violet had. The Violet I knew could not do all of that.

"How did you even know where I was?" I added, my stomach

curdling with the thought she might've got the information from her father. It sickened me to think of what other information she might've gotten. He'd retreated to lick his wounds without a fight, but I didn't think Preston was done. He was too petty for that. He'd want to hurt me somehow... And turning our daughter against me was the surest way to do that.

Violet pulled back her shoulders. "I tracked your phone," she said matter-of-factly.

I blinked at her, processing the information. My body relaxed ever so slightly at hearing that Preston wasn't involved. "You can do that?"

She rolled her eyes. "Mom, it's seriously *so easy* to track people down nowadays, if you know what you're doing. Plus, I've got a friend who knows how to circumvent certain security firewalls."

I knew all too well how someone could be tracked with a phone number. I had a hospital stay to prove it. Something I wouldn't tell Violet, though.

She looked around the house for the first time. "After everything you told me, I couldn't fathom staying in Paris. I needed to see where you moved to. How everything has changed so much."

Her voice was more reserved now, full of emotion.

It was a spear to my heart.

"Sweetie," I whispered.

Violet looked at me. "I like it," she murmured. "This place. This town. I like it a lot. There's... something about it. It's special."

My heart thrummed. "Yes, it is."

Violet moved to throw her purse on the sofa. "How did you end up in New Mexico, of all places?" she asked, not the first question I expected but as complicated as all of the questions would be from here on out.

I sighed. "Um, it's a long story, honey. Can I make you something to eat first? I know it was a long flight with terrible food. I can whip up cacio e pepe or roast a chicken?" I offered hopefully.

"Mom," she said, the word full of everything that lay between us. A warning. I was not going to be able to distract her with food. "I didn't come all the way here for roast chicken, we'll get to that later," she said with a weak smile.

I tried my best to smile back.

"I just need to know why," she said in a voice that was somehow grownup and childlike at the same time. "I need to know what happened."

I pursed my lips together, my throat burning and my hand involuntarily going up to my neck, to where my injuries had long healed.

"It's just me!" a voice called through the open door, saving me from having to answer Violet. "I brought more outfit options because I figured you might need them, and I also brought stuff to make margaritas because I want you to try on the outfits and, oh—"

Macy stopped short, her arms full of bags of clothes and indeed, the ingredients needed for margaritas. Her eyes focused on Violet who was staring at her. Who was gaping at her.

Violet didn't have much of a relationship with my 'friends' before because she never truly interacted with them beyond what was expected to be polite at parties. My friends did not stop by unannounced with clothes and margaritas.

My friends did not look like Macy in a white sundress and tan cowboy boots.

And my friends did not smile at Violet in delight like Macy was doing with a warmness that could be felt from across the room.

"Oh my god, Violet's here!" she squealed, depositing the bags on the sofa. She pulled a stunned Violet into her arms for a hug.

"You're absolutely gorgeous," she gushed once she let her go. "Which isn't surprising, since your mother is a stone-cold hottie, and you two could be fucking *sisters!*"

She was still yelling, speaking rapidly and with a familiarity that was likely confusing the crap out of Violet.

"Did you know she was coming?" Macy directed the question to me.

I shook my head, keeping my eyes on my daughter.

Macy clapped her hands in glee. "I'm so happy you're here!" she was back to Violet now. "I know your mom was so excited to pick you up from the airport, but that's two whole days away, and then you wouldn't have been able to meet your mom's kick ass girlfriends." She winked, rummaging in her purse for her phone. "Who I am about to text to get the makings of all sorts of snacks so we can have a welcome home party for Violet." She narrowed her eyes at my daughter. "I'm assuming you just got off a horribly long flight yet somehow look amazing. Ah, the sorcery of youth," she sighed. "If you're terribly jetlagged, we can postpone to tomorrow?"

Violet was still processing all that was Macy, but she was smiling because it was impossible not to. "Um, no, I'm not actually that bad," she replied before she looked to me. "And I would love to meet Mom's girlfriends." Her nose crinkled. "And her fiancé."

Unease raised the hairs at the back of my neck. There was no hostility in Violet's tone, but there was a placid curiosity that was perched on the edge of it.

"Oh, don't worry. Swiss isn't ever away from your mother for long," Macy waved one hand while she typed quickly with the other. Her eyes darted to me. "Am I terrible for hijacking your first night with your daughter?" she asked sincerely. "Because if you want it just the two of you, I can text my husband to physically restrain Swiss in some kind of dungeon to stop him from coming home to you and cancel the party." Her eyes twinkled with humor. "Though even if it was some serious dungeon, I'd give you two hours max before Swiss escapes."

Although she was joking about the dungeon thing—at least I was pretty sure she was joking—I knew she was dead serious about tonight. Knew that she truly wanted my honest answer and that she would not be offended if I told her I just wanted to be with my daughter. I didn't feel obligated to go along with her for the sake of politeness or to avoid potential conflict. That's not how it worked in our little circle. And though it had taken me a long time to get there, I was just now comfortable being wholly honest.

A part of me selfishly did want tonight with Violet. But I also wasn't ready to answer the questions I knew she wasn't going to let go of. A gaggle of women and bikers would serve as a nice buffer.

Beyond that, I was eager for Violet to see the life I had quickly created here. To feel the love in it. The authenticity. I knew it would help her understand everything and how I'd changed so quickly.

"As long as you're okay with it, honey?" I asked Violet. "We can just stay in, you and me, if a lot of new people sounds like too much?"

Violet shook her head without hesitating. "No. I really would love to meet everyone in Mom's life."

"Awesome!" Macy exclaimed.

"I would love a shower, though." Violet looked around the house. "And I need to get my bags inside. Is there somewhere for me?" Her voice was petered out at the end, sounding more vulnerable and unsure.

"Honey, of course there is somewhere for you," I said reassuringly, reaching out to squeeze her hand. "No matter what happens, there is always somewhere for you."

Violet smiled sadly. It was much too mature a smile for someone that young. It was melancholy I was responsible for. And she didn't even know the full truth.

"As for the bags, don't you touch them. The men can do the heavy lifting when they arrive. Now I am a feminist," Macy clarified, "but I just don't believe we should be carrying anything that a man can carry for us." She winked at Violet.

"Sweetie, why don't you use my shower?" I offered. "It's got all the toiletries you like, and you can wear anything out of my closet you want."

Violet arched a brow, eyes tracking up and down my body. "Normally I would not take you up on that offer, but seeing this new look, I am very interested to see what is in that closet," she teased.

I rolled my eyes.

"Love her already," Macy giggled. "I knew I would." She leaned down to gather the bags from the sofa. "I'm going to start the margs, you show Violet her room," she ordered, turning and walking toward the kitchen.

I did just that, first showing Violet where she'd be sleeping and then taking her into my bedroom.

No, *our* bedroom.

I couldn't possibly forget about Swiss and him living here, but I didn't grasp how jarring it might be for Violet to go into a whole new bedroom with the things of a man who was not her father scattered around the room.

Okay, the things were not exactly scattered. I might've changed in a lot of ways, but my penchant for neatness remained.

But Swiss's cologne was mingled with my perfume on the dresser, and some of the rings he wore were sitting in a small bowl, again mixed up with some of my jewelry.

A pair of his jeans were draped over one of the armchairs, the book he was reading was on 'his' side of the bed—closest to the door, as any man's side should've been, I'd learned.

At our old home, Preston and I had separate dressers. Closets. Our things never touched, never mingled with a familiarity, a casualness like this. A way that suggested I put my earrings on while Swiss brushed my body with his as he sprayed his after-shave. It communicated a closeness that Preston and I'd never had.

I watched Violet take all of this in, her expression unreadable.

"He's a biker, this man?" Violet surmised.

"He is." I was surprised she was able to come to that conclusion.

"I can't imagine how confused you are right now," I said gently.

She stared at me in a penetrative way that was utterly foreign, a way my daughter had never looked at me before. Like she was seeing me as something else than just her mother. Like she was realizing I was also a human being. A separate person with needs, with dreams.

"I'm not," she shrugged. "Seriously," she added, seeing my raised brow. Violet looked around the room once more. "I've never heard you happy, Mom," she whispered, emotion leeching into her tone.

Tears instantaneously filled my eyes.

"I didn't realize it until right now," she continued, voice full of tears of her own. "Until I saw a house that you belong in, fit into more than you ever did ours. You always moved like a..." she scrunched up her nose, deep in thought. "A guest," she said finally. "Like nothing was yours. Like you were afraid to spill, to break something. I didn't see it before because—"

"Because it wasn't your job to see that, sweetheart," I interrupted softly, cupping her cheek. "It was my job to make sure you didn't see that."

Violet was still frowning. "I'm not sure I agree, Momma," she argued just as softly. "But I want to understand. I want us to talk about what really happened with Daddy." She sighed. "But first, I would really, really like to have margaritas with your friends. And I'd like to see the man who created this," she waved her hand down my body. Then she scrunched her nose up. "No, that's not right. The man who gave you the opportunity to grow into this."

I was dumbfounded by the complexity of what my daughter understood, things that I'd been so sure I'd hidden. Things that I'd been sure were much too adult for my child to comprehend.

But there it was, the truth that she was no longer a child.

I smiled. "We can do that, although you will be limited on the margaritas. Macy has a very strong pour." I thought back to a blurry night only a couple of weeks ago when I'd had four of those margaritas, then Swiss and I had had sex on the patio.

Then I blinked my daughter back into focus, chastising myself for thinking about sex in her presence.

My daughter rolled her eyes. "Mom, you know I was in Europe where the drinking age is eighteen, and it's safe to say I've developed a tolerance."

I felt comfort in the familiar dynamic, in seeing the eye roll, hearing the sarcastic tone.

"We'll see," I muttered, deciding now was not the time to argue with my daughter about alcohol consumption, even though she might've technically been right.

"Towels are in the bathroom. Let me know if you need anything else." I leaned forward to kiss her head. "I'm so glad you're here, honey."

Violet's eyes shone. "Me too, Mom," she said sincerely.

My walk back toward the kitchen was somehow lighter. Though there was a crapload of shit to wade through, my daughter did not hate me. My daughter was... dare I say, *happy* for me? My daughter was a well-rounded, sensible young adult who was compassionate and caring.

Yeah, the walk was lighter. But I was still dragging a very heavy anvil of truth. One that I was wrestling with.

"Figured you'd need this." Macy handed me a freshly made margarita with a salted rim.

I took it thankfully. "Yeah, I really fucking do."

"*Fucking*," Macy repeated, sipping her own. "It must be intense then."

Although I cursed now, I did it mostly in the confines of the bedroom with Swiss, when we were naked. Or when I sliced into my finger cooking dinner. I enjoyed the act of it, it felt rebellious. Yet I was still somehow hesitant, too, still acting a part that no longer belonged to me.

Macy knew me. Noticed things, just like the rest of the women did. They noticed things and didn't pretend they didn't see them, didn't use those perceived weaknesses as footholds for manipulation. No, they cared. They changed our interactions accordingly.

I glanced to the hall where I could still hear the water running and Violet singing in the background. She had a beautiful voice, and I'd loved the idea of her becoming a singer. But, of course, that hadn't lined up with her father's expectations. Anything in the arts was considered 'crude.'

Satisfied that she wouldn't hear, I sank onto one of the stools at the breakfast bar.

"She wants to know more," I told Macy. "About why her father and I broke up."

"And you think telling her that he's a piece of shit who beat you for years and almost killed you might cause a boatload of trauma?" Macy guessed.

I grinned weakly, taking another long sip. "Bingo," I muttered.

Macy didn't say anything, didn't press me, she just waited as I processed.

"I don't know what to do," I whispered.

Macy sat watching me, her eyes filled with sympathy but not pity. She had an energy about her that put me at ease, even with all the thoughts swirling around my head. There was a... calmness to her.

"He's a vile man," I continued after I took another large sip. "Evil, to his core. Of that I am certain. But he is her father. He's her hero. He is the man she is going to model all of her relationships after. And he's always treated her well." My mind wandered to the singular time Preston had even come close to losing it with Violet.

He had some important client over. Someone from out of town. Someone who was a big fish in a pond much larger than the one Preston swam in.

I'd been a mess all week, trying to plan the menu, clean the house, design a table setting and make sure I had the right flowers, candles and outfit for the occasion. I knew that my punishment would be unlike anything else if I screwed something up. I had been walking on eggshells all week, terrified, anxious, barely sleeping. All the while, I had tried to make sure Violet didn't notice the change in the atmosphere.

She wasn't a child anymore. She was observant enough to see things that she'd been blind to before.

She was almost fifteen. She was growing into a lovely young woman already, not showing signs of that awkward transition between childhood and becoming a young adult. No gangly limbs or acne. Her midnight hair billowed down her back, her nose was high and delicate, lips full and faintly pink. Her eyes were blue but not like mine. They were almost lavender. They had been since she was born.

I feared that beauty. What it might invite. What kind of boys it might attract. The ones with the square jaws and good families like her father. The ones with monsters beneath all of those masculine lines and good breeding.

But she was not timid and naïve like her mother. No, she already knew her own mind. She was obsessed with philosophy, feminism, civil rights. She was almost a fully formed adult.

She already challenged her father on some of his more misogy-nistic ideals—all of them—and I'd had my fists clenched under the table as she did so, taut, ready to jump between them if need be.

But Preston had never shown an inch of irritation that his daughter believed in women's rights when he so obviously didn't. He was charmed by her independent spirit.

Except the night at the dinner table when his guest had complimented my cooking and complimented Preston on finding a woman who 'knew her place.'

Me, I'd smiled tightly and looked down at my plate with a meekness Preston expected.

My daughter did no such thing. "A woman who knows her place is a woman who knows her voice," she offered sweetly. "A woman who knows her place is a woman who knows it's wherever a man says it's not. I think we're all liberated enough to under-stand that men who try to confine women to certain roles and rooms within the household are terrified of the power women will have if they are allowed to reach their full potential." She reached over to take a dainty sip of her iced tea. Not rushing, no... Taking her time as everyone at the table watched her. It was a power move most adults wouldn't be able to pull off.

She put her tea down. "And most of those men are deeply insecure and inferior to women in every way," she finished, smiling sweetly.

The short but loaded silence after she spoke was a cacophony in my ears. That was until Preston plastered on a fake smile and made some joke. He forced the conversation forward, but the mood in the room definitely shifted.

I'd moved food around on my plate, my hand shaking. Violet had eaten without a care in the world, wearing a self-satisfied smirk.

By the end of the meal, it became clear that the business associate was sufficiently shamed by a teenage girl, therefore, he wasn't likely to ever deal with Preston again. Despite his attempts to get him to stay for a cigar and a drink, the man left.

And Preston turned on Violet the second the front door closed.

"Do you have any idea how important that man was?" he asked in a low tone, walking into the dining room where Violet was eating her chocolate cake without a care in the world.

I was sitting beside her pretending to drink tea with a slice of my own in front of me. I wouldn't eat it, obviously. But I didn't want to imprint any unhealthy eating habits on my daughter, so I would always pretend to eat dessert.

Violet looked up at her father and rolled her eyes. "Do you have any idea how much of a gross misogynist he was?" she countered.

Preston stared at her. "It is not your place to try and challenge grown men at the dinner table," he told her with an edge to his voice.

An edge that my daughter did not recognize. Because she did

not have to recognize it.

I did.

"What? I'm supposed to be seen and not heard?" she asked sweetly. "Come on, Daddy. As much as you've got that in Mom, you're not going to get it in me."

The barb wasn't intended to hit me, but it drew blood none-theless. I hated that my daughter saw me that way, wished for things to be different, for me to give my little girl a strong female role model.

But things were not different.

"Yes," Preston agreed. "Your mother knows how to act with company. And you will learn too."

Violet narrowed her eyes and pushed up from her chair. "No, Daddy, I will not," she snapped. "I have a voice, and I intend to use it to call out assholes. Which, if I may, includes you right now."

I blinked rapidly, and even Preston looked shocked for a moment. Our daughter might have been strong-willed, but she never cursed. Never challenged her father or spoke to him that way.

Preston's shock didn't last for long. He took a step toward Violet with a look on his face that I recognized all too well.

I had scrambled out of my chair before he could make it near her. Violet had not retreated. She would not retreat. She had never learned that she had to retreat. She had nothing to be afraid of because her father had never given her reason to be afraid. Until now.

I placed my hand on Preston's chest, putting myself between them. "Honey," I murmured, looking up at him. "It's been a long night. How about we go to bed, and Violet can too? Everything will look better in the morning."

It was a plea. My heart was thundering in my chest in

response to Preston's harsh, cruel gaze. I was already looking around the room for weapons to use if he decided to snap. The silver candlesticks we got from his parents as a wedding present... They would work.

His temper hung in the air, and I watched it, praying it wouldn't snap, but also ready to bludgeon him to death if need be. If he tried to lay a hand on my daughter.

But the moment passed. The promise of violence was no longer focused on my daughter. Instead, it landed on me.

"Yes," he nodded slowly. "Let's go to bed."

There was a promise there. One I understood. Punishment for stepping in, for getting in his way.

I sighed in relief.

And the next morning, as I gingerly poured coffee at the breakfast table, nursing bruised ribs, I considered what I would do if Preston did do something to Violet.

I'd kill him.

But it didn't come to that. Violet stumbled into the kitchen, half clutched by sleep, and gave her father a hug, apologized. He kissed her head and apologized too. And he never looked at Violet that way again.

But the fact remained that he had. The potential lingered. And it kept me awake for months afterward.

I blinked my way back into the present.

"If she finds out the truth about her father, she'll hate him," I told Macy. "She'll hate me a little too... if I'm lucky."

I considered the look my daughter would give me if I told her that I'd let her father beat me for years.

"She'll lose whatever respect she has for me," I choked out the words on a whisper. "For staying with him. She will resent me for my weakness. And for destroying the image she has of her father. She will have to reevaluate everything she's ever known. Her entire identity, which has been built around the parents she thought she had." I took another, longer sip of my margarita. Though it was strong, it wasn't bringing forth the numbness I sought.

My hand shook.

I couldn't stop it. The magnitude of this decision was a devastating earthquake, splitting apart the very foundation of my life.

"If I don't tell her, then I-I am lying to m-my only child," I stuttered. "I'd also be endangering her with her ignorance. Because even though he loves our daughter, his love is warped, twisted and ugly. That there is a chance he could harm her. Even use her to get to me. However small that chance is, I will never be able to live with myself if she is hurt because of me."

I stared at Macy, looking for judgment where there wasn't any. There was only empathy, kindness, unwavering support.

The very act of being able to say this out loud was somehow therapeutic, so it no longer ran in circles around my mind. I hadn't said any of this to Swiss. I knew if he heard the turmoil this was causing me, he'd kill Preston. He wouldn't be able to stop himself, despite all the promises he'd made. He wouldn't be able to watch me suffer this way.

"Granted I'm a little newer to the role, but being a mother is an identity that I thought I was ready for, thought I was born for," Macy finally said after waiting to make sure I had nothing else to say. "But nothing prepares you for the reality of it. Even though every fucking person tries to tell you how hard it is. I never got it. Because it isn't hard. No, that's not the right word. It changes your very existence. Your purpose. The whole goal you have in life is to protect these humans who you love more than you realize you ever could." She smiled, her eyes filling with happy tears. With love.

I understood that love. The deepness of it.

"They come from your body," she continued. "They grow within you. They get life from you. And then they leave you, and they're so fucking vulnerable, outside in the world. In an ugly world that is designed to hurt them."

Her eyes went faraway before they refocused on me.

"But, babe, *you* grew her inside of you. *You* brought her into this world. You fed her, protected her, nurtured her. You nursed her hurts, *you* did all of that."

She reached over to squeeze my hand. "That means that no one else, not even me, can tell you what decisions to make when it comes to your child. No one can tell you what the best decision is. No one can shame you once you make that decision. You earned the right to make that decision. Since the second she took root inside you, you have earned that right, Momma."

I stared at Macy, dumbfounded by all the knowledge she'd just laid on me. The respect. The support. All of it bundled me up and gave me the clarity. Told me exactly what I needed to do.

Before I could do something embarrassing like burst into a sobbing fit, the thunder of a motorcycle drowned out my thoughts. My first, carnal reaction was excitement. That giddy kind of excitement that I'd been sure only teenagers felt before their first time, before they realized that romance and sex were constructs created by Hollywood and Hallmark.

But it was not a construct.

Hollywood and Hallmark could not create that feeling. Could not replicate it and regurgitate it to the masses.

The next feeling was nerves. At Violet and Swiss meeting.

"What if she doesn't like him?" I asked Macy, panicky as I realized the shower was no longer running.

I'd been so lost in the conversation, I hadn't noticed when it turned off. I really, really hoped she hadn't overheard anything.

But then the hair dryer turned on from the bedroom, and I sagged in relief.

"She's going to like him," Macy said confidently as the front door opened.

"Honey, I'm home," Swiss called out as he walked in the door, a sexy smile on his face.

That smile fell the moment his eyes landed on me and Macy sitting at the breakfast bar. Swiss was on me in a handful of long strides. "What?" he demanded. "Who do I need to kill?" His hands framed my face, his expression telling me that he was totally serious. "Has that fuck done somethin' stupid? 'Cause I know the promise I made, but if—"

"Baby," I interrupted gently. "It's nothing like that. Violet's here."

It took a second for the murderous glare to leave Swiss's face. "She's here?" he repeated.

I nodded once, smiling despite the cocktail of emotions racing through me.

"Fuck, do I look okay?" he asked self-consciously, looking down at the grey Henley and black jeans he was wearing.

He had on motorcycle boots and his cut, of course.

I couldn't help but giggle at his concern about what he wore while meeting my daughter. "Yes, babe, you look great," I told him honestly, reaching around his neck and laying a soft kiss on his lips.

Swiss's hands went around my waist, and I melted into his embrace, my entire body calming from his presence, his scent, his warmth.

Macy cleared her throat loudly. We both looked at her, and she jerked her head in the direction of the hallway.

Where Violet was standing, dressed in a pair of my jeans and a silk cami that looked much better on her than it did on me.

And she was staring at me. And Swiss. In an embrace.

Her face was blank.

I quickly stepped out of Swiss's arms. Or tried to. His hand curled into mine, squeezing once before letting me go.

"Honey," I said sounding breathy, nerves eating up the single word. "This is Swiss."

Violet regarded him shrewdly, purposefully looking him up and down. It might've amused me at any other moment to see Swiss move rather uncomfortably from foot to foot, something I'd never seen before.

But I was too busy freaking out, hoping that Violet wouldn't hate him on sight, wouldn't wrongly think that this man had somehow stolen me away from her father.

"You have a motorcycle?" she asked, zeroing in on his cut.

I wasn't too sure of how much my daughter knew about outlaw motorcycle clubs... probably more than I did at the beginning. She was also a lot more open-minded than me and probably even romanticized such things.

Swiss nodded in response to Violet's question.

"You've taken my mother riding on it?" I bit back a smile as she continued her interrogation.

Swiss nodded again. "I have," he spoke for the first time, his voice was raspy and low.

Violet stared for a few moments, her gaze penetrative and unreadable.

Swiss shifted on his feet under my daughter's gaze.

"And you make my mom laugh." Her comment told me that she had been watching us longer than I'd thought.

Swiss smiled. "I do my best."

Violet folded her arms. "Will you take me for a ride on your motorcycle?"

"Absolutely not," I exclaimed at the same time Swiss said,

"Fuck yeah."

Violet's blank expression turned into a bright grin.

"Okay, you've got my tentative approval," she decided.

I swear, I saw Swiss sag in relief.

"Thank fuck," Macy announced. "Now margaritas!"

And, as if on cue, the clamor of more bikes sounded.

It seemed my daughter was being dropped into the deep end of my new life.

CHAPTER TWENTY-THREE

KATE

IT WAS safe to say the night was a success. Violet had damn near lost her shit when Caroline arrived. Well, on the surface, she was very cool, calm and collected, but I noticed the smalls signs that she was 'fangirling,' as she would put it.

Likewise with Freya, who I had realized long ago had a very popular YouTube that Violet adored.

Both had reactions similar to Macy, both hugging Violet tightly, speaking to her as if they'd known her for years, complimenting her on her beauty, her style, her sense of adventure.

Violet settled into the group like she was born into it. I watched her carefully throughout the night, interacting with everyone, smiling and laughing easily, contributing to conversation with confidence and joy. She lit up, and everyone else around her did the same. It was impossible not to.

It brought tears to my eyes and a smile to my face. I'd never seen Violet like this. Snatches, sure, when she was with her girlfriends, or when it was just me and her. But never in large crowds. Never at whatever party or event she was required to attend. Violet was strong-willed for sure, never one to act based on other people's expectations. Or so I'd thought.

How blind I'd been was painfully clear, seeing Violet come alive around people who didn't burden her with expectations. She'd acted a certain way because despite her strong beliefs, she loved her father. Wanted him to be proud of her.

And in doing so, she'd shrunk herself. Not in the exact same way I had, but in a way that made my belly ache. In a way that solidified my decision to tell her the truth.

The night didn't last as long as it normally would've, presumably because everyone sensed there was a conversation that needed to be had between me and my daughter. And because everyone had children to get home to. Because Hades was apparently 'done' with Freya being on her feet and flitting around the party in six-inch heels with her small baby bump visible under the tight dress she wore.

We all said goodbyes with promises to meet at Oliver's for brunch. All the women hugged Violet warmly, and after she got over the shock of such easy and natural affection from adults, she hugged them back.

Then it was time.

Swiss was cleaning up the kitchen, and Violet was walking around the room, looking at framed photos I'd placed everywhere. Freya was big on taking photos, so even before Preston's arrival, there were a bunch of us all together, of candid ones she'd taken of Swiss and I at various parties.

He'd been the one to put the first picture up. It was at the pool party, the infamous one when Preston had called me. In the photo, I was in my bikini, his arms were around me, about to lift us both into the pool. I was laughing, his eyes were on me, serious and loving.

It was my favorite photo of us, evidence that he knew how to make me smile, laugh, hours after the phone call that had shaken me to my core.

I wondered what was going through Violet's mind. She was used to curated, posed, professional photos in matching frames, placed purposefully throughout the house. Not ones like this. Not ones where her mother was laughing in a bikini in the arms of another man. She was witnessing a whole other life I'd lived in the short time she'd been gone. I couldn't imagine how jarring that must be.

She was moving slowly, and I could see the exhaustion in her body. She'd flown halfway across the world, driven almost an hour on unfamiliar roads, and then waded into my brand new life.

As much as I wanted her to be able to drift off to sleep without this knowledge, I knew her too well to think that she'd go off to bed without answers.

Swiss knew what I was going to do since I'd pulled him aside earlier in the night to quickly explain my intentions. Unsurprisingly, he'd supported me. Unsurprisingly, his eyes had gone dark with rage at yet more carnage that Preston had unleashed. More pain.

I knew he wasn't going to go anywhere, let me out of eyesight as I told my daughter news that would change her life.

He gave us privacy, but he remained nearby. In case I needed him.

I loved him immensely for that, but this was something I needed to do without his help.

The walk from the kitchen to the sofa was one of the longest and hardest in my life.

"Normally, I'm not one to slam tequila shots with my underage daughter." I laid two shots on coasters on the coffee table.

Violet turned from the bookshelves to look at me. Her eyes went to Swiss in the kitchen then back. She was still a little wary around him, understandably, but he was winning her over. It was impossible not to. He hadn't schooled his affection with me, hadn't toned it down for the sake of my daughter. The entire night, he'd absently laid kisses on the side of my head, took dishes from my hands when I'd tried to clean up, pulled me onto his lap when I walked by. Violet had seen all of this, and I'd watched her scrunch her nose in confusion, trying to process it. She had not witnessed easy and genuine affection like that before, because I'd never experienced it until Swiss.

I patted the cushion for Violet to sit.

"What I'm about to tell you isn't going to go down smooth, so I want to give you this to soften the edges." I chewed my lips. "If that's even possible."

"You're scaring me, Mom," Violet said gravely.

My insides shredded. "I know, baby, and I hate it," I whispered.

I lifted the shot glasses, handing her one. She took it, and we both stared at each other for a tick before downing them.

The burn was the only thing on my mind for a split second, and it was a welcome respite. But it didn't last for long.

"Okay, sweetie, I'm gonna tell you something." I took in a deep breath while placing the shot glass back on the coffee table. "And it's something I've wrestled with. Something I've doubted whether I should burden you with the truth of. And ultimately something I feel you deserve to know." I tucked a strand of her hair behind her ear. "If you weren't such an adult, so shrewd, worldly and thoughtful, I could maybe get away with some half-truths. But you, my darling, are not someone to be satisfied with those. So I'm going to give it to you. The gruesome truth. Are you ready?"

Violet stared at me, really exploring my face, gauging my expression and the severity I guessed was painted on it.

She took a deep, visible breath. Bracing herself. "I'm ready."

"You're going to have a lot of questions," I sighed. "And this is not something that I will be able to give you in one sitting or be able to explain away. It's taken me months to even digest this myself, and I suspect it'll take a lot longer to accept and fully process everything. I hate that it will do the same to you."

Tears prickled the backs of my eyes, but I fought them. With what I had to tell my daughter, I couldn't be a weak, sobbing mess. My only saving grace was that I was stronger now. A different person. One I felt comfortable with my daughter looking up to.

"You know I met your father when I was young," I began. "Younger than you."

She nodded, very aware that her mother had been a teenager when she gave birth to her. When I was her age, I was married. I was about to move into my first home with my husband. I had an almost three-year-old.

"And you know that I had a... difficult upbringing," I swallowed thickly.

Violet nodded again. She did not and would never know the specifics of what my childhood was like. I was giving her enough harsh truths tonight.

"I didn't know much love or kindness," I explained. "So when I met your father, your grandparents, they were the only true family I'd ever had. And I didn't have anything or anyone else but you and them." I reached over to squeeze her hand. "And you, baby, were and still are my entire world. All I've ever wanted was to give you the life I never had."

I sucked in a deep breath.

"So when your father hit me for the first time, when it became clear that if I left him, I wouldn't have anything... that I wouldn't have you, I stayed. I stayed because I was young, I was your age. Because I didn't know what else to do. Didn't have anywhere else to go."

There they were. The words, the knowledge. It was out there. I couldn't take it back.

I watched my daughter's face contort with shock and pain as my words sank in.

"Daddy... *hit you?*" she choked out.

It felt like someone was squeezing my lungs when I heard the pain in her voice. "He did, honey," I managed to reply evenly.

"And it wasn't just once." My throat burned as I took a deep breath, hating that I wasn't done, hating that there was more. "And it wasn't every day either. He wasn't constantly cruel or evil. He was loving, kind and caring a lot of the time. He was the daddy you knew for a good portion of our marriage. Until he wasn't."

I wished for another tequila shot. I wished for Swiss's hand in mine. Instead, I focused on the soft clang of dishes in the kitchen, signifying his presence. Signifying that that life, that version of me, and most importantly, Preston, was in my past.

"When you left, something... changed inside of me," I explained. "I started driving, and didn't stop until I got here." I smiled. "You said it yourself, there's something about this place that pulled me here. Urged me to stay." I looked over to Swiss in the kitchen, catching his eyes. He was watching me carefully, with concern.

Violet's gaze flickered that way, too, looking between the two of us.

I rubbed my sweaty palms down my legs, preparing to tell the truth that I wasn't sure I was going to utter until that very moment. "Your father found me here, darling, because he is a powerful man with a lot of resources. He found me here and he..."

My voice broke, whatever semblance of strength I was holding on to crumbling.

I squeezed my eyes shut, opening them when I felt a small hand squeeze mine. Violet was holding my hand, tears filling her eyes.

"You didn't have bronchitis," she guessed slowly.

I shook my head.

"Daddy did *that* t-to y-you?" she stuttered. I watched her conjure up images in her mind. My daughter had a wonderful imagination, so she was likely trying to match the way I sounded to a violence that she'd never seen first-hand. A violence that had never touched her life... until now.

I nodded. "He did. And it was Swiss who... saved my life." I decided not to tell her that Swiss had found me naked and half dead in a ditch on the side of the road.

She didn't need *that* horrific of a truth.

But it was important to me that she understood Swiss's part in this. That Swiss, despite appearances, was not the violent man who could hurt me. He was the kind, gentle and loving—and yes, kind of violent—man that saved me. In many ways.

Her eyes slid to Swiss, and they stayed there for a long time before making it back to me. I guessed she was deciding who to address, what questions to ask.

"Why didn't you leave?" she asked after a long silence. It wasn't an accusation. Not quite. "The first time."

She studied my face as if trying to make sense of me imploding her whole childhood and everything she knew in a matter of seconds. "Why didn't you take me and leave?" Closer now to an accusation.

I smiled sadly at her. "Oh, my darling girl. I hope with my entire heart that you never have to know how such a simple question can be so complicated. I wish with everything I am that you will never ask yourself a question like that."

I regarded my beautiful young woman with her furrowed brows, with her clear skin, the stubborn tilt of her chin.

"No, my sweet, you will never ask yourself that question," I decided. "You're not like me. You're so much stronger. You know yourself so much better. And despite what your father did to me, he gave you the resources to make sure you'll never be in the position that I was when he first hit me. He gave you the ability to get an education so that you feel confident. A home where you feel loved, where you were celebrated, nurtured. Despite who he was to me, he made it so you'll never be vulnerable like I was. And I will make sure you are never isolated like I was."

I sighed, my eyes filling with tears at the mere prospect of my daughter being put in the position that I was.

I'd kill him. Plain and simple. I'd gladly do the time for murdering the man who dared lay hands on my daughter.

"He is still your father," I added, taking note of the shadows in my daughter's eyes. The shadows that had not been there moments ago. "He was still at your softball games, your debates, at your father-daughter dance. I am not telling you this to make you hate him. I do not want you to choose sides in this." I sighed under the weight I was putting on my daughter. "But you're an adult. I could not hide this from you even though I was sorely tempted." I stroked her face. "I told you without any kind of agenda. He is your father, and he loves you. Despite everything else."

She stared at me, blinking rapidly as she absorbed the information. I gave her a moment. Then another. I was demolishing her world, after all. I was bracing for any and all reactions.

My Violet was everything I hadn't been. Strong. Passionate. Stubborn. Unafraid to speak her mind, to go toe-to-toe with whoever she thought was in the wrong.

I'd been lucky with her, though. In a lot of ways, I'd grown up with her, having her so young. She never gave me the crap a lot of teenage girls gave their mothers. She did not test me or Preston with boyfriends who were bad for her; she did not break curfew or skip school. There were no screaming matches or slamming of doors in our house.

Sure, there was some attitude, some disagreements, but my daughter was gifted. She didn't win state debate for nothing. She had a way about her, an elegance when she argued. An intelligence. She never lost her cool, raised her voice, and often, you didn't even know she'd won the argument until hours later. Even Preston wasn't immune to her. Something he'd always found endearing, despite his hatred for me even hinting that I disagreed with him.

I was afraid, deathly so, that this news would cause my beautiful girl to explode. That I'd get the screaming, the silence, the 'I hate you' that many mothers had to weather.

I deserved it all. So I braced myself. I was ready for any and all reactions.

Or so I thought.

"Daddy beat you for almost my entire life, and you expect me to... forgive him?" she asked slowly, a wrinkle forming between her eyes. "You expect me to continue to speak to him, to spend holidays with him, to be in the same room as him?"

It was my turn to blink rapidly at her. "I don't expect anything from you, Violet," I said gently. "Whatever you wish to do, whatever relationship you want with your father, it's yours to have."

She stood, obviously unable to take this in while seated. I stood, too, in case she tried to do something like run from the room.

"Relationship?" she repeated. She began pacing. "You think I want a *relationship* with him now?" Her voice had risen, her cheeks reddening with emotion.

"Honey, you don't have to make any decisions—"

"No," she interrupted. "You're right. Dad was at all my games. Only because he knew that's what everyone expected him to do. What made him look the part. He was at my father-daughter dance even though I didn't want to go in the first place, but he forced me because some big shot finance guy had a daughter going to my school."

My breath hitched, unable to fathom that Violet had managed to see those things when she was so young. Unable to fathom that I'd been blind to how much my daughter had seen, and hating myself for not noticing.

Her eyes found Swiss who was now standing behind me, apparently no longer able to watch from afar.

"You're not going to let him hurt her again, are you?" she asked, though it was more of a demand.

"No, darlin'," he promised. His hands were tight around my hips. My knees felt like they were made of rubber, so I was grateful he was there.

Violet nodded purposefully after measuring Swiss's response. "He's dead to me," she declared, emanating an iciness I'd never thought her capable of.

I flinched at the tone.

"Violet, you—"

"No, Mom," she held up a hand, halting me. "I understand what you're trying to do. I respect it even though I don't fully understand why you'd defend him after what he did to you." She stood still, staring at a blank space on the wall for a moment before pulling her shoulders back. "But no. I don't want a relationship with *a father who almost killed my mother*."

She exhaled deeply after she said those words aloud, the reality of them truly sinking in.

I decided there was too much space between us and approached her. No, I didn't just approach, I rushed toward my daughter and caught her right at the moment she broke down. I found I had more than enough strength to hold on to her as she grieved for the father that she'd loved. The father she'd never have again.

―――

I brushed the hair from my sleeping daughter's face, watching her sleep for a few more minutes before I quietly left the room, shutting the door behind me.

She had cried herself into unconsciousness, laying on the sofa with her head in my lap.

Swiss had sat on the armchair, watchful, protective, a calming presence. He was pissed. Seeing my daughter in pain. It affected him. Visibly.

I knew he was likely thinking of all the ways he would like to torture and kill Preston.

But he didn't do that.

Instead, when Violet fell asleep, he lifted her into his arms and carried her to the bedroom.

I followed him, fighting tears. Then he'd left me to put her under the covers myself with a kiss on the side of my head.

He was waiting for me in our bedroom, two mugs of tea on the table between the armchairs.

Instead of choosing the one beside him, I crawled onto his lap, desperate for the closeness.

His arms circled around me without hesitation.

"Very hard not to get on my bike, drive to New Hampshire and put a bullet in that fuck's brain," he murmured into my hair.

Ah, how correct I'd been.

"It's very hard not to do it myself," I whispered into the leather of his cut.

"But my place is here," Swiss decided. "With the two girls he was stupid enough to fuck with. The two girls he will never fuck with again."

"Do you think she's going to be okay?" I asked in a defeated voice, positioning myself so I could look into Swiss's eyes.

He gently gripped my face as we stared intently at one another. "Countess, not only is she the spittin' image of you, she has your strength. She's gonna be great. It'll take a while, I'm sure. But she has you. Has us. Has a whole new family who's got her back. For good."

Tears filled my eyes at that realization. And then it was my turn to break down in tears. Swiss eventually carried me to bed too.

ONE WEEK LATER

SWISS

Violet was like her mother.

An exact replica. With the same midnight black hair, the same face shape, the same spirit. She had taken the news of who her father was—*what* he was—in stride. She hadn't hesitated to cut him off, to stand by her mother. Everything she knew about the man who raised her was a lie, yet she didn't fall apart, throw a tantrum like some spoiled rich girl. No, she was more worried about her mother. It was clear she adored her.

In the week she'd been here, I'd been fucking floored at seeing Kate in a different role. Seeing the way they interacted. How they laughed easily, treated each other with kindness and respect. Their bond was forged by them growing up together. It was something special. Fucking precious. I could not believe how that piece of shit could've had that in his home and tried to poison it the way he did. Pure fucking evil. That's what he was.

Violet had called him and said something to that effect. Then she'd blocked his number. We had people watching him, making sure he didn't find his balls, didn't risk his life to mend things with his daughter.

But he was too much of a coward for that.

Fucking piece of shit.

Violet was wary around me, I knew that. Appreciated that. Had appreciated it a fuck of a lot more when she found me cleaning the grill while Kate was inside making some fancy dessert.

I'd known she was there watching me for a while. I didn't acknowledge her presence, knowing that she needed to make the first move, that she wouldn't have come out here unless she had something to say.

"Do you love my mother?" she finally asked.

Straight to the point. No bullshit. I respected it. I met her eyes. They were unusual, bright, almost purple. She was as pretty as her mother, but those eyes were something else. Boys would go wild over her. Even the thought of it had me squeezing the shit out of the scrubber I was using. I felt protective over her, and I barely fucking knew her.

But I knew what she meant to Kate.

That was enough.

"Yes," I answered simply.

"Good," Violet nodded once, not smiling. "My mother deserves someone who loves her. Who will do anything for her." She eyed me shrewdly, her gaze skated to my cut. "Who will protect her."

"Darlin', you don't have to worry about that. I'm gonna protect your mom. Not gonna let any harm come to her."

Her eyes narrowed as she regarded me, as if she were weighing my words. The gaze was much too mature for a girl her age, who'd grown up as sheltered as she had. Maybe she saw more than Kate gave her credit for.

"I know," she said finally. "I also know that if you hurt her, you'll have me to answer to."

A threat coming from an eighteen-year-old girl should've been laughable to someone like me. But somehow she delivered it with strength and promise that made me take her seriously. Made me respect the fuck out of her.

"I'm not gonna let another man hurt her, including myself, for as long as I live," I promised.

She nodded again. "Good."

Freya, Hades and Eva arrived not long after, and Violet and

Kate promptly got distracted by having a baby and another woman in the mix.

Hades and I congregated by the grill, beers in hand while Violet chased Eva around the yard, and Freya and Kate sat in the wicker chairs, drinking and chatting.

It felt fucking suburban, something that I was sure would've been the death of me before Kate.

"Who the fuck would've thought this would be us?" I scoffed, vocalizing my thoughts.

Hades didn't answer. His penetrative gaze was focused on his wife, his child. He was probably juggling a lot of serious shit. Like sitting in a hospital, not knowing if his woman would live. I understood that. Hurt for him. Fuck, did I know that pain. But unfortunately, there was nothing either of us could do about that.

I focused on Kate. Her head was thrown back, laughing at something Violet said. As if she hadn't a care in the world. As if she had known no difficulty or pain.

I'd seen men grit their teeth and fight through gunshot wounds, tortured men who didn't scream as I peeled their skin off, but that, Kate's unbridled happiness, her ability to laugh after everything she'd been through... that was the strongest thing I'd ever seen.

"I'll do it," Hades's words punctured my thoughts.

I turned to him, seeing that he was staring at Kate. "Do what?"

"Kill him," he answered, lifting his beer.

I knew he wasn't joking 'cause the motherfucker didn't joke. I also knew who he was talking about. He was watching my woman and her daughter laugh in the sunshine like they didn't know what waited for them in the shadows. It was impossible not to want to avenge them. To make sure there was no one on this earth who was a threat to them. It wasn't in our nature to do nothing.

"Brother, I promised her I wouldn't do it," I gritted out. That promise still sat heavy on my shoulders, jerking me awake at night.

"You won't," Hades said, still looking at them.

I chuckled without humor. "Yeah, the distinction of who pulls the trigger won't fly with Kate. Her husband ends up dead, she'll know it was the Sons."

"I can make it look natural," Hades offered.

He could. He was an expert in killing, like all of us were. Anyone could pull a trigger, draw blood. But there was an art to it that few men possessed, enabling them to make a death slow, painful or quick and painless.

"I'm sure you can," I replied, tempted to take him up on the offer. "But Kate is smart. I know Macy's got her into crystals and shit, but I doubt even she thinks karma works that fast."

"If she knew what this was doing to you..."

"She knows," I grunted. "But what this is doin' to me don't mean shit compared to what this is doin' to her. She wants him dead. Even though she's not bloodthirsty by nature. Even though she saves strays. Even though she's got the softest, kindest heart I've ever known." I reached down into the cooler for another beer. "She would wear his blood if she could," I continued, staring at Kate. "But she will live in agony forever if it means saving her daughter from even an inch of pain." I let the cool liquid slip down my throat. "Plus, I've come to the decision that letting him live without his money, without them," I nodded toward my girls, "that's the worst punishment. A fate worse than death."

CHAPTER TWENTY-FOUR

KATE

"I WAS THINKING," Violet said as she dressed the salad.

"I've heard it's dangerous when women do that," Swiss taunted from where he was setting the table.

He was not one to sit on the sofa with a beer while we prepared dinner. No, he was involved, helping by refilling drinks, chopping vegetables, pretty much doing anything and everything he could to contribute.

Violet had noticed it during her time here with us. We'd settled into somewhat of a routine. I say 'somewhat' because there wasn't really such a thing as routine in my life now. Not with impromptu dinners at Macy's or Freya's or Caroline's or my place. Or club parties. Dinners at the two restaurants in town that served great food. Visits from other charters which required an 'all hands on deck' situation.

So yeah, there was no Meatloaf Monday or anything like that in the biker world.

Which I adored. I loved that I never knew how a day might end. Maybe a quiet dinner out or getting tipsy in the desert with women who had become my family.

But we did get nights, a good amount of them, just the three of us. I cooked because I enjoyed it, not because I was required too. Violet sat on the breakfast bar, chatting to Swiss and me while sipping wine. She'd acquired quite a taste for it in Paris and had argued about how ridiculous a drinking age was when you could 'enlist in the Army but not buy a beer,' and I was inclined to agree with her. I also wasn't going to disapprove of my adult daughter having a glass of wine or two at dinner.

Those dinners were special. Precious. They had an energy about them, a magic about them that gave me the impression that we would never have quite a time like this again. I was looking forward to the future, looking forward to Violet growing into herself even further and achieving great things.

But I also knew that that would mean seeing less of her, her having a separate life outside of me.

So I was savoring every moment we shared.

Violet poked her tongue out at Swiss at his joke, and he grinned back at her. The two of them had developed an easy relationship, a friendship even.

"I was talking to Colby, and he said there is an extra room at the club."

I stopped dicing, and my mouth opened, but Swiss beat me to it.

"When the fuck were you talking to Colby?" Swiss barked.

I pursed my lips, hiding my smile. Swiss was not just her friend, he was also the protective, alpha male who would go to battle for my daughter without hesitating.

Violet had a grin of her own that she was not hiding. My daughter, it seemed, was not intimidated by the dangerous badass routine. That had become clear at the club gatherings she attended where she'd routinely challenged anyone in a cut about the 'anti-feminist bullshit of a woman not being able to patch in,' and the only people who were able to form a coherent response were the men who were married, madly in love with their wives and saw Violet as more of a daughter figure.

The unattached men were usually too busy drooling at Violet to form an argument. Swiss, of course, had threatened death and dismemberment to anyone who tried anything with her, and no one was brave enough to go up against him.

Violet found this endlessly entertaining and had now moved on from challenging these men to flirting with them relentlessly, much to Swiss's horror. I was more amused by it all, somehow comforted by the idea that my daughter could end up with a biker who respected and worshipped the ground she walked on. Not some French asshole who she had not said a peep about since she arrived back.

Actually, I did not want Violet to end up with anyone yet. She was too young.

"Oh, calm down, Swiss. I was *talking* to him, not engaging in oral sex." She paused, looking up at the ceiling. "Then again, there's no talking then either. Someone always has their mouth full."

I had wrongly chosen that moment to take a sip of my wine and almost choked on it when she said that.

Swiss's cheeks flushed ever so slightly. It was almost a blush. A fucking blush. A blush like a father might have while talking to his daughter about oral sex.

Violet never would've spoken about oral sex with her father. She was too busy playing the role of the perfect little angel. One I hadn't noticed she was playing until recently. Until she started being her unapologetic self in New Mexico, where she felt comfortable to do that, where there were no expectations of her.

I supposed it wasn't just that, she had just spent over six months in Europe. Falling in love. Traveling. Acquiring a taste for wine. She'd changed, as you were supposed to at that age.

"And sex is an appropriate topic since it pertains to why I'm going to be moving into that room at the clubhouse."

Where I'd been delightfully amused at my daughter's adult and slightly vulgar sense of humor moments ago, now I was concerned at my little girl talking about moving into an outlaw biker clubhouse.

This time I beat Swiss to it. "Absolutely not." I scoffed, turning down the burner so I could focus wholly on my daughter.

She rolled her eyes. "Mom, don't worry. I'm not doing it because I have any other intentions other than not to hear my mother and soon-to-be stepfather banging it out."

Now it was my turn to blush. Swiss, the asshole, had found his sense of humor once more and was smiling into his beer.

"Excuse me?" I asked in a small voice.

"Oh, come on, Mom, we're all adults here. And I can see how devastatingly in love you are. How happy you are." Her face turned serious for a split second. "I love that. More than love that. I also understand that what comes with this kind of love is sex that travels through some decently thick walls. I'm not about to ask my mother to stop having that wonderful sex, but I'm going to draw some boundary lines."

I gasped.

Swiss was full on laughing now.

"Stop," I snapped at him. "This isn't funny."

Swiss's eyes twinkled as he crossed the distance between us, bringing me in so he could kiss my head then tuck me into his chest. "Oh, Countess, I disagree. This is fuckin' hilarious."

I scowled at him. "You're not actually okay with the idea of Violet moving into the clubhouse?" I asked in shock.

"Wouldn't say I'm 'okay' with it," he pondered. "But not hip on the alternative either."

I figured the alternative was us not having sex at all, and to be honest, that was not something I was hip with either.

"On top of that, my brothers know the long and painful death that awaits them if they try anything."

Violet laughed.

I did not because I knew he wasn't joking.

"And it'll only be for a few days, a week at most."

I frowned up at him. "Violet doesn't leave for school for another two weeks," I reminded him. I looked at my daughter. "Right, honey? You haven't decided to go early, have you?"

I tried to sound like I'd be totally okay with that, but I definitely failed. I was internally panicking at not only my daughter leaving early but not having her under the same roof as me for the remaining time I had with her. But the *alternative*...

Although I would've liked to think we could control ourselves —in the interest of my daughter, for goodness' sakes—I knew that we couldn't.

Violet's shoulders dropped, her eyes softening at the edges. "No, Mom, I'm not leaving earlier. I love it here."

Too caught up in the moment, I looked back up at Swiss. "Well, then do you know something I don't?"

"I know that Violet's room is gonna be at the other end of the house. Our new house."

I stared at him. "Our new house?" I parotted.

He nodded, a seed of a smile on his face. "As much as I love this place, and I fuckin' do, I think we need somethin' a little bigger... somethin' ours. Place with a kitchen you can spread out in." He motioned to the small, orderly area I was using for prep.

Though I made it work and loved it more than the all-white kitchen with endless space in my last house, I would've liked some more room.

"There were a few last-minute details I had to hammer down, but this weekend is move-in day." His eyes cut to Violet and they shared a look.

A *knowing* look. A look that I was not privy to, so my eyes darted between them accusingly.

"What was that about?" I demanded.

"Well, Swiss wanted to show me before he signed all the papers," Violet shrugged with a smile. "He wanted to make sure you'd like it, and he wanted to make sure I liked it, since he wants it to be my home too." They shared another look. This time it was not knowing. It was more intimate.

It was a look that made me want to burst into tears.

Violet blinked away the emotion in her eyes that I knew came from having a father who would not have asked her opinion on such things. A father who wouldn't have cared whether his wife or daughter liked it, who'd have expected them to accept it.

"And I like it," she exclaimed brightly. "Love it, in fact. And he's right... There's like an entire house between our bedrooms. Plenty of space and sound insulation." She waggled her brows.

I wanted to sink into the ground.

"So it'll only be a few days," she continued. "And I'll be on my best behavior. I promise not to become a prospect, although I did convince Hansen to let me if I change my mind."

I grinned again. "I bet you did," I muttered then I looked up at Swiss. "She'll be okay there?"

"She will," he grunted. "Safest place for her."

Thinking on it, forgetting about the parties with strippers and copious amounts of booze, I had to agree with him. The biker clubhouse had been the safest place for me... my entire life. Until this house.

"Do I get to see the home you've bought for us without consulting me?" I asked snippily. Or at least, I tried to be snippy. The concept of my fiancé buying a house without my input was something Preston had and did do. But this was different.

This was Swiss.

And I trusted him utterly and completely. If I was honest with myself, I did not want to go through the rigmarole of open houses, inspections, figuring out if I liked a place... Because my home was in this kitchen. Not the walls, the roof or the floor. But the two people I was with.

Everything else was extra.

"Nope," he replied happily, his eyes twinkling as he regarded me. "Gonna fight me on that, Countess?"

Desire assaulted me in a way it shouldn't with my daughter in the vicinity. Yeah, maybe it was a good thing she was moving to the club. "No," I answered quickly. "No, I'm not."

So that's how it was decided. My almost nineteen-year-old— her birthday was that weekend, yet she'd somehow convinced me not to throw her a party—would be moving in with outlaw bikers before heading off to college.

And I would be moving into a new house. The one my biker fiancé had picked out for us.

━━━

"I was thinking about something," I said, trailing shapes on Swiss's pec.

It was late. Very late.

We'd packed Violet's things into her rental car—well, Swiss had packed her things. He wouldn't dream of us lifting anything heavier than a purse—then followed her on the motorcycle to the club. I'd settled her into one of the vacant rooms, promising to bring some proper sheets and a comforter the next day.

She, unsurprisingly, had rolled her eyes at that. Though she'd grown up with nice things, she was not spoiled or a snob, something I was delighted to discover. I mean, I'd known that, but I'd never seen her outside the manicured, curated life we'd created for her. And she was thriving in this one already.

Swiss had been in the common room, threatening death and dismemberment to each of his brothers if they tried anything with Violet.

We'd stayed for a drink, and I'd watched Violet interact easily with everyone, playing pool with Colby, Lucas and Elden. She was not self-conscious or intimidated by any of the men, even Elden who was pretty darn intimidating. Although I was hesitant about leaving her there, I knew in my gut that she'd be just fine.

Once Swiss was satisfied that everyone was sufficiently threatened, we said goodbye to Violet—it was much harder than I'd expected considering we were only ten minutes away—and rode back to the house.

Swiss then demonstrated just how much he'd been holding back while Violet had been staying with us.

My wrists burned from the cuffs he'd just taken off, my body thrumming with satisfaction and exertion.

It was a very good thing that Violet was miles away. That the closest house was miles away.

"You're thinking about somethin'," Swiss prompted after I'd been silent for a while.

"Yeah, I've been, uh... thinking about it for a while." I was suddenly very nervous. Swiss and I did not have secrets. Not anymore. This wasn't a secret... exactly. It was a dream. One that I hadn't told anyone about. One that had steadily grown with my confidence, my feeling of safety, security. With the knowledge that we were making a life together.

Swiss adjusted us so I was facing at him. He'd obviously heard my voice catch, understood that this was serious. And he wasn't about to let us have a serious conversation without eye contact.

"Continue," he ordered once my irises were locked with his.

"Well, you know I got an, um, modest sum from the divorce settlement," I cleared my throat.

He nodded. He knew that because he—or someone in the club—had been the one to set the terms of my divorce settlement.

The sum wasn't exactly modest, but considering the amount I'd donated, it was less than a quarter of Preston's money, not counting Violet's college fund, of course.

It was a specific amount of money, for a specific goal.

"There's a building for sale in town that I've been looking at," I told him, thinking of the old, romantic structure with mosaic windows and a view of the desert. It was right at the end of Main Street, before the wilderness began to take back over.

"It's been for sale for a while," I added.

"Know the one," Swiss squinted, looking like he was calling it up in his mind. "Overpriced, that's why it's not sellin'."

I nodded in agreement. "It is. Which is why they'll likely take an all-cash offer well under asking rather than stay on the market for longer."

Swiss quirked a brow. "You really have been givin' this some thought."

"I've never had the opportunity to think about life outside of being a wife and mother," my face warmed. "And although I love the thought of being your wife, I cannot wait to be something in addition to that for the first time in my life."

Swiss's face had softened. "You can be anything you wanna

be," he murmured. "And I'll support it. Do everything in my power to make it happen."

I smiled. "I know you will," I whispered. "And what I will probably need is for you to do some heavy lifting, to make sure contractors don't rip me off, and to taste test my menu."

His eyes danced. "Menu?"

"Yeah," I replied. "I've always wanted to have my own restaurant. Somewhere that feels comfortable and upmarket but not in a snobby way. Where I can cook whatever I want, whatever's in season." I sighed. "I know I don't know anything about running a business, and—"

"I think it's a great fuckin' idea," Swiss interrupted before I could talk down on myself further. "You're an excellent fuckin' cook. Seems to be a crime not to share that. Though I'm not adverse to committing a crime or two." He winked. "We'll put in an offer tomorrow."

I stared at him. "What?"

"This is your dream, right?"

I nodded.

"Well, then it's my job to do everything in my power to make it happen," he said simply.

And he was dead serious.

<hr>

The very next morning, bright and early, Swiss walked into the real estate office with our offer.

Well under asking.

All cash.

The contract was drawn up by the end of the day.

The restaurant was in my name.

Mine.

It had all transpired within twenty-four hours of me mentioning what I wanted. Obviously, there had to be a party to celebrate. Violet jumped around in glee then rushed off to open her computer, designing the space for me. She spent the rest of the night staring at it, deep in thought.

Eventually, she'd closed it and murmured something about doing more work 'back at the club,' kissed my cheek absently, hugged Swiss and left.

Both of us had been shocked.

Her and Swiss were friends by this point. It was clear that Violet liked him, but she had yet to develop an easy affection with him like she had with me. Which made sense... That kind of thing didn't happen overnight.

But a half zombie, her mind elsewhere, she'd hugged him with real affection.

It had warmed my heart and made me think of something that hadn't been far from my mind.

I was not pregnant.

My period had come right on time, and I'd found myself feeling disappointed. It made absolutely no sense since this was a huge time in my life full of change and transition, and throwing a newborn baby into the mix would not have been wise.

Yet I was still disappointed.

And I could've sworn Swiss was too. Or it could've been wishful thinking.

"We haven't been using protection," I commented while we were in the kitchen. After we'd cleaned up from the party, Swiss had fucked me on the kitchen counter.

I'd just cleaned myself up, and had decided we needed chocolate chip cookies. Swiss had not argued. So I was in Swiss's tee, mixing up the batter.

He was in sweats and nothing else.

"Well aware of that, Countess," Swiss murmured, his hand going underneath the tee to cup my bare pussy.

I licked my lips, knees wobbling ever so slightly. "And I'm not on birth control," I continued, voice smaller.

"Noticed that too, Kate," Swiss retorted, more gently this time.

I tilted my head to look up at him. I shouldn't have been surprised, really. He noticed everything about me and about my routine.

"And you've still been..."

"Coming inside you?" he finished for me.

Nodding, I felt my cheeks heat. The blush made absolutely no sense since he'd literally just fucked me on the counter I was making cookies on, but I blushed nonetheless.

"Still scares the shit out of me," he admitted gravely. "Still somethin' I'm gonna wrestle with. And when you get pregnant, I'll probably be as fuckin' crazy as Hades is."

Swiss took the wooden spoon from my hands, lifting it to lick it before he put it in the bowl so he could yank me flush with his body.

He kissed me, and it tasted like cookie dough. "But seein' you with Violet," he murmured against my mouth. "Seein' you as a mother." He kissed me again, deeper this time. "Didn't think you could be any sexier. And the thought of you growing my child." His hand moved to my semi-flat stomach. The one that was doing cartwheels.

"Yeah, I think those things chase away some of the darkest shit my mind has to offer," he rasped, eyes locked with mine. "If you wanna have a baby, that is. Wanna make it clear that any path you wanna take, I'm down with. Only thing that's important to me is you being on the back of my bike for the rest of my life."

My body bloomed with warmth and pure happiness.

"I want that with you," I spoke without thinking. "I want a family with you."

I barely got the words out before Swiss kissed me.

It was safe to say no cookies were baked that night. There were babies to be made.

CHAPTER TWENTY-FIVE

KATE

"THIS IS RUINING MY MAKEUP," I grumbled as Swiss guided me out of the car. He was guiding me because I was blindfolded which had been the case since he'd put me in the car.

It was Violet's birthday.

Nineteen.

She'd slept over and we'd restrained ourselves for one night, though it was harder than it should've been. We had chocolate chip pancakes for breakfast, and Swiss brought coffees from Oliver's. The day we signed the contract on the space, I'd told Julian I had to hand in my notice. He had been pissed off to be losing his barista but also incredibly happy for me. Because he was that kind of guy. Because I'd found myself surrounded with people who only wanted the best for me.

Swiss had also bought Violet a gift that I did not know about but that he'd obviously gotten some female's opinion on because it was kickass and just the right size. A leather jacket. Buttery, expensive leather. Similar to one he'd given me a long time ago, one I wore whenever we were on the bike.

"You're part of my family now," he'd said as he presented it to her. "Gotta look the part."

She'd loved the jacket. Absolutely loved it. In fact, she'd shoved it on top of her PJs and demanded Swiss take her on a ride. Not one to refuse the birthday girl, he did, and she'd come back with bright eyes and a beaming smile. I'd been worried about that smile because I recognized it. It was someone falling in love with the thrill of being on the back of someone's bike.

I tried my best to push those thoughts aside.

I'd bought her a necklace—a simple gold chain with a floating solitaire garnet pendant in the middle—since she'd donated the diamond one her father got her. Along with everything else he'd ever given her. We'd also organized movers to go into our old house, gather up all of Violet's things and have them brought to New Mexico.

She was still going back to school, and I missed her already, but I felt great comfort in knowing that all of her things would be with me.

In our new home.

The one that we were apparently driving to. The one I apparently needed to be blindfolded for. I'd played along, only because it was one of Violet's birthday demands.

"It's Violet who's the one who should be getting a surprise," I whined.

"Trust me, Mom, I've had enough surprises to last a lifetime," Violet commented dryly.

I smiled for her benefit more than anything. My girl had taken all of the news about Preston in stride, and despite her breakdown on that first night, she had not shed a tear. She had refused to talk about her father, committed to her notion that he was dead to her.

I worried about that. About everything that she was burying. But I couldn't force it out of her. She would talk to me when she was ready.

As it was, she had thrown herself headfirst into club life, into helping Julian at the café, babysitting for Caroline, Freya or Macy. Going to the gun range with Colby—the two of them had formed quite a friendship that amused me yet pissed off Swiss. She had told me one night that she was not attracted to him in the slightest because he was 'too young.' That had not put my mind at ease since he was at least five years older than her, but I had to trust that the older men in the club who she likely had her eyes on were much more mature, therefore smart enough to stay well away from my teenage daughter.

The smell of lavender wafted through the air, then I was lifted into Swiss's arms. I let out a little squeal at the unexpected movement.

"What are you doing?" I demanded.

"Tradition," he grunted.

"Tradition?" I scowled. "That does not give me any of the information that I need."

"Calm down, Countess," Swiss replied with amusement.

He shifted my weight so one of his hands could reach back to remove my blindfold. "Gotta carry you over the threshold," he explained, nodding to the front door.

It was not the front door I was focusing on, though. Well, my gaze went there for a second, but then it went everywhere else. To the entryway of my new home. The entryway that was covered in flowers. And candles. There was soft music playing from somewhere in the house.

And then, when I looked for Swiss, he was down on one knee.

Holding a ring.

A simple but stunning solitaire garnet. It could've been a sister to the one around Violet's neck.

It was absolutely perfect.

My eyes instantly filled with tears.

"Know we're already technically engaged." His voice was thick with emotion. "I also know that you know I'm not one to stick to tradition normally. But I'm gonna make an exception for you."

Swiss took the ring and slid it onto the fourth finger of my left hand before laying a kiss on my palm. "I also know that you didn't want a big wedding. That the most important thing to you is family." His eyes navigated to Violet who was watching with a radiant smile on her face. "So I enlisted the help of your daughter and a few others to give you a wedding and a home."

I struggled to keep my breathing under control.

A wedding.

Today. Swiss had organized a proposal, a new home and a wedding. With my daughter.

"What do you say, Countess?" he asked. "Wanna get hitched today?"

Instead of speaking, I did a little hiccup sob thing.

Swiss looked to Violet. "That sound like a yes?"

She nodded rapidly. "A total yes."

Swiss stood, pulling me into his arms and kissing me lightly. "I'll let you go and get ready," he said against my lips. "I've got to go and make myself pretty for my wife."

He laid a kiss on my nose before sauntering off.

As if he hadn't just rocked my world.

I didn't even have time to process what was happening because Macy, Freya and Caroline appeared, and they, along with Violet, spirited me away to 'get ready.'

For my wedding day.

The house that Swiss had bought for us was perfect.

Beyond perfect.

It was exactly what I'd been imagining, sitting on Freya's patio that night months ago. It was on six acres. Not a house to be seen in any direction. A sprawling garden that was wild, colorful and perfect. A large pool, the water glimmering off the sunlight, visible from our bedroom.

Or should I say, our wing.

The room itself was huge with a private patio, views to die for and a gigantic closet and bathroom.

The only thing hanging in that closet had been my wedding dress.

The wedding dress that I didn't pick but somehow fit me to a T. That was somehow utterly perfect for me. It was simple, such a pale pink it was almost white. The neck was high but dipped way down low in the back. It molded over my new curves, complimenting every one of them before trailing down delicately to the floor.

Beaded strappy sandals were designer. "I know about the trauma you have connected to designer shoes, but don't let your asshole husband take away the artistry that is Jimmy Choo," Freya had begged.

I'd relented on that one because they were beautiful.

Marilyn—Freya's friend who had firmly become my friend too—had done my hair and makeup. The rest of the women had fed me food and wine, dressed in simple dresses of varying colors but similar styles.

Violet's dress was light purple, to match her eyes, and criss-crossed in the front, slipping over her slight body and making her truly look like the woman she was.

At some point, the women had realized that I needed some alone time with my daughter and had given me hugs, kisses and hand squeezes, Freya shoving a wildflower bouquet in my hands before she left.

Then it was just me and Violet, standing in the middle of my new closet. On my wedding day.

"You look so incredible, Momma," she whispered, pinning up a rogue strand of my hair. It was in wild curls with two braids pulled back off my face. No veil. It definitely wasn't a veil kind of wedding.

"Honey, it's your birthday," I argued softly, tears in my eyes.

"I know," she replied, her own eyes glassy. "And the absolute best gift I could ever get is my mom truly being happy. In a home she deserves. With a love she deserves."

Tears ran down my face at my daughter's wisdom, at her maturity.

"Don't," she snapped. "You'll ruin your makeup."

A sound that was half laugh, half sob escaped me.

"Are you sure you're okay with this?" My voice was barely a whisper as I wiped a single tear from my daughter's eye. "This is a lot for you to have to deal with."

Violet frowned. "My mother truly happy for the first time in her life is not a lot to deal with, I promise."

I tried to measure her response, tried to look for holes, the shadows that had been flickering behind her eyes since she'd arrived.

I saw none.

"Now," she held out her arm, "are you going to let me walk you down the aisle or what?"

I stared at her for a second longer before saying anything. "Yes," I whispered. "There's no one else in the world I want by my side."

Then I took her arm, letting her walk us out to the garden.

The garden that was filled with lilies, lavender and bikers.

My biker stood at the end of a short, makeshift aisle. Hades and Jagger stood beside him. Freya, Caroline and Macy were on my side, grinning from ear to ear. Hansen was officiating.

It was, quite simply, the most perfect wedding I'd ever seen. If I'd tried to plan it, I wouldn't have been able to create such an uncomplicated, beautiful wedding.

Violet walked us toward Swiss, stopping to give him a large hug when we made it.

"Take care of my mom," she told him when she released him.

Swiss's eyes were shimmering. "I will," he promised.

She smiled, leaning in to kiss my cheek before taking her spot beside Macy.

"You ready for this, Countess?" Swiss murmured, yanking me in close, forgoing the traditional stance.

I smiled up at him. "Yeah, I'm ready."

And just like that, in the home that Swiss had bought for us— the home that was fairy-tale perfect—we got married.

It would be the home we grew old in.

I knew that in my every fiber.

And, five weeks after our wedding, it was the home that we created our son in.

Life was good.

I was not gone, girl. I was home. Forever.

EPILOGUE

TWO YEARS LATER

KATE

PRESTON DIED on the same day I gave birth to our son.

Seriously.

He hung himself in his closet.

He was there for days before the police found him. Only because the gardener called them.

Not because anyone missed him.

There was no one left in his life to miss him.

His parents had disowned him.

Not something I'd ever expected them to do in a million years. He was their only son. Their golden boy. I believed that they never knew about the abuse, never saw the signs because they were blinded by a parents' love. But I also figured that love would blind them from the truth. Would warp it in a way to make them be able to live with what their son was.

I expected them to hate me. I expected to mourn the loss of the only parents I'd ever had.

But one day, not long after our wedding day, I had a visitor.

Violet was working at the café. Apparently Julian had 'vetted' her and was impressed enough with her skills to let her work the coffee machine. Violet had never had a job in her life—something I'd gently fought with Preston about, but he wouldn't dream of his daughter working—and I thought the romance of it might wear off quickly once the reality of the long days set in. But it didn't. Violet loved working. She came home with bright eyes and messy hair, wired from it all.

Swiss was also out. On a run. I missed him already, even though he'd only been gone one night.

Having the house to myself was a treat too, though. Because it was mine. Because I was still puttering away with the garden, moving things here and there as we settled. I was also going through the graphics Violet made for the restaurant which were shockingly. She had true talent.

So my mind was on about a million things when I opened the door, expecting a UPS guy delivering one of the many online purchases I'd made.

But no.

It was Sally.

In a Chanel suit, clutching her purse and staring at me with tears in her eyes the second I opened the door. Those same eyes widened as she took in my sweatpants and tank, my messy hair and bare face.

In the time she'd known me, my mother-in-law had never seen me without an 'appropriate' outfit on and hair and makeup done.

Though I supposed she wasn't my mother-in-law anymore.

I waited. For her eyes to sharpen with judgment. With malice. But instead, they softened, still filled with tears.

"Honey, you look beautiful," she cried, pulling me into her arms.

I relaxed into the embrace, both out of shock and on instinct. I melted into the familiar smell of Chanel, her slight, delicate frame.

She didn't release me for a long time, and once she did, I finally found my words. "How did you know I was here?"

"Violet," she cleared her throat and daintily wiped her eyes. "She sent me a letter."

I shook my head. Violet still believed in letters.

"Of course, she did," I muttered. I folded my arms, leaning against the doorjamb. "What di—" I sighed. "What did the letter say?"

I wasn't surprised that my daughter had tried to bring her grandmother here. She adored both of her grandparents, so I knew she wouldn't be able to cut them off. But she'd also always be firmly on my side, and she had been ruminating on that enough to send a letter, telling her grandmother where to find me.

"Everything," Sally choked out. "She told me everything."

I sucked in a breath. "Well, I guess you'd better come in for some tea."

"Vodka would be better, darling," Sally corrected, making her way inside.

So that's how my ex-mother-in-law and I ended up sitting in my kitchen, sipping vodka at one in the afternoon. She'd been silent as I got the glasses, the ice, while I poured them. I'd stolen a few glances at her as she wandered around, taking in the space.

It was nothing like the home she helped me decorate.

The walls were covered with mismatched frames, candid photos in each one. The sofa boasted multiple pillows that didn't match. The counters were cluttered to communicate the home was lived in. Everything was clean, tidy, of course, but it was warm, casual, bursting with both mine and Swiss's personalities.

I pushed a glass over to her, wary of what was to come. Violet had told her everything. And that had pushed her to come here. But to what end, I didn't know.

Sally took the glass and raised it to me, face melancholy. "To your nuptials," she murmured, nodding to my left hand.

I glanced down at the ring I was going to wear for the rest of my life.

"Sally—" I began, unable to find the words.

"Violet said you're happy," she cut in. "And seeing you, here in this lovely home, one that feels like a home, I tend to agree with her. I also feel as if I've never seen you happy. So we're toasting to that, to your happiness."

Unable to argue with her, I raised my glass, taking a long sip.

Sally did the same.

The silence between us was thick. I didn't say anything. She came here with a purpose, so I let her steer the ship.

"Will you forgive me?" Her voice shook as she set down her glass.

"Forgive you?" I questioned. "For what?"

"For not seeing," she replied, voice breaking. "For not noticing what he was doing to you for years. For raising a son who could do *that*."

I blinked at her. I hadn't known what to expect from Sally. She was not a cruel person. Did not have a mean bone in her body. She had never treated me with anything but kindness. But she was also a mother. I understood she needed her son to be the hero. No one wanted to believe their child was a monster.

"I don't blame you, either of you," I told her honestly. "I could never blame you. I love both you and Frank."

"We love you too, honey," she replied through tears. "Which is why we are here. Why we will never speak to Preston again."

"But... he's your son," I gasped, unable to process what that meant. That she was saying that.

"He is," she looked down in shame. "In nothing but name now, though. I will have nothing to do with him. His father will have nothing to do with him." She reached over to squeeze my hand. "*You* are my daughter, darling. If not by name or blood, in every other way. You and Violet are everything to me. To both of us." She looked around the house. "I know you've got a new family now, a new life, but we'd love to find a way to fit into it... if you'll have us?"

"Of course, I'll have you," I said without hesitation, pulling her into my arms.

We both cried for a long time.

She stayed with us for a couple of days, meeting Swiss and the rest of the club. I knew the biker lifestyle made her figuratively clutch her pearls on instinct, but she did not pass judgment. Not even a little. She made an effort to get to know Swiss, to speak to everyone. Shit, she even had a beer... something I'd never seen her drink.

And, on Christmas, her and Frank were at our table. Along with Swiss's parents, who I'd gently urged him to invite. They were not as at ease as my former in-laws, who had somehow taken to my new lifestyle, after the sticker shock wore off.

They kept looking at their son like he was a stranger—which I guessed he was to them. They mostly kept to themselves but made an effort to speak to me and Violet. I knew that this was not the life they'd wanted for their son, but I also prayed they'd accept him. Especially now that he was happy. It was not something that would happen overnight.

But they were family.

We were all a family.

And that's what mattered.

That's what Preston had lost, in addition to his money, his position at the bank and all of his friends.

He obviously wasn't strong enough to face the reality of that. Wasn't brave enough to try to change into a good person—something I didn't think was possible.

So he hung himself.

It might've been sad.

If he wasn't such a piece of shit.

It was sad watching my daughter battle with the emotions that came with the news. She tried to be tough, acting like she didn't care. I could tell that she was trying to protect me from her pain. She was trying to protect herself from it by hating him. I had tried to reach out to her, to give her the space to feel grief and sorrow, but I'd just given birth to a baby boy who demanded a lot of my attention. I was sleep deprived, hormonal and trying to battle with the satisfaction I felt in knowing that Preston was dead.

Not that Swiss didn't help. Heck, I was lucky to change a diaper. So I did have time, time I utilized trying to help my daughter. But she'd put up a wall. Hiding behind that wall with smiles, with snuggles with her new brother. With cleaning the house, with working at Julian's, with school and travel.

So I had to trust in her. Had to trust she'd come to me when she needed me. Or Swiss. Or Macy, Freya, Caroline. Any of the people who had adopted her into the family without hesitation. The family that Violet adored and fit into effortlessly. The people who would have her back no matter what.

I opened 'Violet's', my restaurant, when I was three months pregnant, working right up to my due date. It was safe to say that Swiss was a hot fucking mess that entire time. It was also safe to say we had a lot of heated arguments about me working in a restaurant kitchen while pregnant.

I was trying very hard to be sensitive to his past, to his trauma. But I also couldn't lie in bed with my feet up for months. I couldn't let someone else cook at my restaurant. Not until I trained them and felt fully confident in their skills.

I guessed I was like Julian that way.

It was a constant source of tension between us, and I didn't drive myself anywhere after six months. Swiss sat at the bar, nursing the same beer, glowering at everyone each night.

And, if he felt like it was too late, he shut the place down.

He shut my fucking restaurant down.

Even though I'd yelled at him about scaring off patrons, his presence actually had the opposite effect.

Word got out about the ultra-hot biker sitting at the bar, and we did even more business, which in turn had us operating later, which in turn had him shutting the bar down. A vicious cycle I found endlessly amusing.

Swiss did not.

Nor did he find it amusing when I didn't tell him my water broke until my contractions were seven minutes apart.

Yeah, there had been a lot of yelling on the fast but careful drive to the hospital. Fortunately, I'd benefitted from the experiences of the Old Ladies who came before me and who had forewarned me that men could get hysterical and dramatic over labor.

Declan Carter was born without incident, with ten fingers and ten toes.

His father held him for hours, just staring at him, just holding his tiny hand. During the first week of his life, Declan barely slept or existed anywhere but his father's arms.

And it filled my heart.

Swiss, as I had imagined, was a wonderful father. He was gentle, patient and adoring. He barely let me lift a finger and took over all of the house and parenting duties.

I'd selfishly feared a change in our relationship with the arrival of a baby. Yes, things changed, but for the better. We worked as a team. We communicated. We injected even more love into our house.

And his sexual appetite for me had not dulled.

Not even a little.

He damn near ripped my clothes to shreds exactly six weeks after I gave birth.

Six weeks. To the *hour*.

Declan was with Hansen and Macy for the entire day. And that was only because we were both so in love with him we could not be away from him for longer than that. And luckily, he'd sleep-trained like a dream and slept through anything because we didn't stop after he came home.

For a while, for a long time, I lived with bated breath. Expecting. Waiting. For that other shoe to drop. I braced myself. For impact. For it all to crumble.

Swiss noticed that. Not a shock since he noticed everything about me. But he didn't push, didn't acknowledge it. He just proved to me, every day, that the other shoe wasn't going to drop. There would be no impact. No crumbling.

Sure, there were speed bumps with the club. Dangers lurking in every corner, a new police chief promising not to be as amiable as the last. There were things to be concerned about. But nothing to scare me. Not truly.

Things were going well. Beyond well.

Except there had been a series of murders in and around the area. Murders of young women who were not at all connected to the club.

Naturally, all of the men were on high alert, even more protective than normal, which was pretty fucking protective.

Not that I minded.

It meant I got to see more of my husband.

Whenever I worked late at the restaurant, he was there. Normally, he was there anyway, but when he wasn't, there was a prospect to drive behind me. Now there were no prospects, just my husband. And he made a habit of fucking me in the kitchen after everyone had gone home.

So I didn't hate it.

Declan was growing like a freaking weed. He was just like his father, full of mischief and energy and already a little badass. It was his first birthday, so we'd planned a party. Anything, large or small, was reason for a party.

Which I loved.

I adored that our garden was full of bikers and their children, jumping in and out of the pool. That laughter, music, and children's voices filtered through the desert.

I didn't expect anything unusual when I walked into my kitchen. At first, I thought I was hallucinating.

But I was not.

Elden and my daughter were in my kitchen, too close to one another for it to be anything casual.

Intensely, intimately close to one another. They weren't making out or anything. But by that point, I was an expert in the romantic body language of the alpha male biker variety.

He had his palm flat on the wall beside her. His body was not touching hers, but his cut was brushing against the white sundress she was wearing. His mouth was inches from hers.

The second I walked in, his Spidey-senses went off, and he took two very large steps backward.

Violet's cheeks were flushed red, and her chest was rising and falling visibly. Her wide eyes found me.

I looked to Elden who was the picture of badass, cold calculation.

"Tell me I did not just see what I think I saw," I said slowly.

"Mom—"

I held my finger up to silence Violet, all of my focus on Elden. Despite me being a part of the club for over two years now, he was the one who still remained a mystery, distant, aloof and cold. I'd even forged a connection with *Hades*, for goodness' sakes. But not this tall, bearded man who was *my age* and kept mostly to himself.

"You know, if I tell my husband what I just saw... things are not going to go well. I'm going to get blood on my floor," I said to him. "And I don't want to have to mop it up. I've got a toddler... I have enough to worry about, you know?"

"Mom—" Violet tried again.

I held my finger up once more.

"I'm going to forget I saw all of this." I waved my hand between my daughter and the biker who was at the least fifteen years her senior. "Because I don't want my husband killing his brother today. And also because I don't want to have to mop up blood. Then again, Swiss isn't exactly one to force household duties on me, so he'd probably mop it up," I mused.

Elden was still silent.

I narrowed my eyes at him.

"And I know I'm married to kind of a depraved badass who has somewhat of a reputation, but when it comes to her," I pointed my finger at Violet, "I can get pretty fucking depraved, buddy. So just remember that."

I turned my attention to Violet, who was standing there looking sufficiently horrified. "We are going to speak in my closet," I pointed in that direction. "Now." Violet looked to Elden then back at me before stalking in the direction of the closet.

"You are going to go outside and share a beer with your brother," I informed Elden in a stern tone. "The one who considers Violet a daughter. The one who would do anything to protect her." I leaned closer to him, pinning him with my stare. "The one who trusted his brothers to protect her too. To not lay a hand on her."

Before he could say any kind of badass declaration that would turn this into a whole other thing, I walked in the direction of my daughter.

Violet was pacing in the closet by the time I got there.

"You need to explain," I said, closing the door. "Right now."

She stopped pacing. Her eyes were red, cheeks still flushed. "I love him, Mom."

I shook my head. There was a lot of things I expected her to say, but that wasn't one of them. Violet had been on somewhat of a wild kick lately. I hadn't been hard on her on account of her losing her father after finding out he abused her mother her entire life. Growing into an adult was hard enough without that bullshit.

I'd been caught up with opening the restaurant, with being pregnant, with a baby, with Swiss, with my new life, but never, not once had Violet not been on my mind. I thought about her constantly. I had long talks with Swiss about her. We were both quietly worried about her. I knew that he likely had her under some kind of surveillance connected to the club. Something Violet would've been furious about if she knew but something I was happy about. It gave me comfort.

But I never, never thought she was having a relationship with one of the men in the club. Let alone one who was old enough to be her father. One who gave me the chills.

And, apparently, my daughter was not finished shocking the shit out of me.

"And I'm pregnant," she choked out.

There it was.

Proof that although I may have gotten my happily ever after, my daughter was just beginning her story.

ACKNOWLEDGMENTS

This book poured out of me. That might've been the norm for me when I first started writing the Sons of Templar, when I had dozens of stories inside of me, when I was young enough to function off two hours of sleep ... but not so much now.

Lately, my stories have taken longer. Have taken everything from me. But this one was different. This story gave me something. It was such a delight to be back with the Sons. To start a new chapter with them. I hope you loved this chapter as much as the rest.

No woman is an island. I'm a peninsula, at the very least. Writing requires me to close some roads, but without people coming to visit, showing me love and support, I wouldn't be able to do this author thing.

Taylor. My husband. My best friend. My whole world. Every day with you is an adventure. You are always my inspiration. My rock. I couldn't write a story like ours. I am so thankful we found our happy ever after.

Mum. You're the one who told me I could do anything.

Who never batted an eyelash as I told you about my 'outlandish' dreams. You always answer the phone, whether I'm calling to cry or to get your opinion on a pair of shoes. Thank you for always being there.

Dad. You can't read this, but you'll always be on my list. You taught me how to shoot, ski and to leave my manners on the side of the court. I miss you.

Annette. Thank you for being there for me always. For helping me constantly. For supporting me. To the moon.

Jessica Gadziala. I'd be lost without you. You inspire me daily. Your work ethic, your talent, your kindness.

Amo Jones. My ride or die. I adore you.

Michelle Clay. You are a truly special soul. I'm so so glad this journey brought us together.

Kim. You not only made this book beautiful, you've been a valuable friend and human being. I'm so so lucky I found you. You're never getting rid of me.

Cat. The covers you create are utter art. You are such a beautiful human being and I adore you.

And last but not least, **you. The reader**. Without you, I wouldn't be here. I'm so grateful for your time, your support. Thank you for making my dreams come true.

ABOUT THE AUTHOR

ANNE MALCOM has been an avid reader since before she can remember, her mother responsible for her love of reading. It started with magical journeys into the world of Hogwarts and Middle Earth, then as she grew up her reading tastes grew with her. Her love of reading doesn't discriminate, she reads across many genres. She can't get enough romance, especially when some possessive alpha males throw their weight around.

One day, in a reading slump, Cade and Gwen's story came to her and started taking up space in her head until she put their story into words. Now that she has started, it doesn't look like she's going to stop anytime soon, with many more characters demanding their story be told as well.

Raised in small town New Zealand, Anne had a truly special childhood, growing up in one of the most beautiful countries in the world. She has backpacked across Europe, ridden camels in the Sahara and eaten her way through Italy, loving every moment.

Now, she's living her own happy ever after in the USA with her brilliant husband and their two dogs.

Want to get in touch with Anne? She loves to hear from her readers.

You can email her: annemalcomauthor@hotmail.com
Or join her reader group on Facebook.

ALSO BY ANNE MALCOM

GREENSTONE SECURITY

Still Waters

Shield

The Problem With Peace

Chaos Remains

Resonance of Stars

THE VEIN CHRONICLES

Fatal Harmony

Deathless

Faults in Fate

Eternity's Awakening

Buried Destiny

RETIRED SINNERS

Splinters of You

THE KLUTCH DUET

Lies That Sinners Tell

Truths That Saints Believe

STANDALONES

Birds of Paradise

Doyenne

Midnight Sommelier

Hush - co-written

What Grows Dies Here